One Flight Up

ALSO BY SUSAN FALES-HILL

*Always Wear Joy*

# One Flight Up

## A NOVEL

## SUSAN FALES-HILL

**ATRIA** BOOKS

NEW YORK   LONDON   TORONTO   SYDNEY

**ATRIA** BOOKS

A Division of Simon & Schuster, Inc.
1230 Avenue of the Americas
New York, NY 10020

First Atria Books hardcover edition July 2010

**ATRIA** BOOKS and colophon are trademarks of Simon & Schuster, Inc.

For information about special discounts for bulk purchases,
please contact Simon & Schuster Special Sales at
1-866-506-1949 or business@simonandschuster.com.

The Simon & Schuster Speakers Bureau can bring authors to
your live event. For more information or to book an event contact the
Simon & Schuster Speakers Bureau at 1-866-248-3049 or
visit our website at www.simonspeakers.com.

*Designed by Kyoko Watanabe*

Manufactured in the United States of America

10   9   8   7   6   5   4   3   2   1

Library of Congress Cataloging-in-Publication Data
Fales-Hill, Susan.
    One flight  up : a novel / by Susan Fales-Hill.—1st Atria Books hardcover ed.
        p.   cm.
    I.  Title.
    PS3606.A4275053   2010
813'.6—dc22                                                          2009035070

ISBN 978-1-4391-2490-1
ISBN 978-1-4391-4978-2 (ebook)

*To Aunt Diahann, Aunt Eartha, Aunt Carmen,*
*Aunt Lena, Aunt Adèle,and the other Premice/Charliers*
*women, most especially, my mother, Josephine, for*
*teaching me that each woman must write her own rules,*
*and that blondes don't necessarily have more fun*

*To the magnificent men who have graced my life*

To err is human, but it feels divine.

—MAE WEST

We've only tasted the wine,
We're gonna drain the cup dry.

—CY COLEMAN AND CAROLYN LEIGH,
FROM "THE BEST IS YET TO COME"

# One Flight Up

# chapter one

At the wise old age of thirty-seven, India Chumley, Esquire, wholeheartedly believed that women should manage their personal lives using logic and reason as their guides. Yet as she looked across the gleaming expanse of her desk at her favorite pro bono client, a majestic, careworn blonde in the autumn of her years, she was reminded that few women could compel their hearts to follow a mission statement, let alone a five-year plan. It never ceased to mystify and sadden India that women could command armies and run Fortune 500s, yet in their personal lives, the best and brightest of them were as hapless and lacking in willpower as Eve herself, who threw Paradise away for a Red Delicious. Hoping to help her "sisters," India had opted to become a divorce lawyer.

India's eyes traveled from her client to the lone family photograph on her desk: a three-quarter-length portrait of an elderly African-American woman in judges' robes, her paternal grandmother, the Honorable Lydia Chumley. Nana Chumley embodied all the qualities this client lacked: discipline, sound judgment, and moderation. It was India's sworn ambition to follow Nana's example and serve as a credit to people of color and to womankind itself.

India was all too aware that for a woman, the smallest misstep in her personal life could lead down the slippery slope to perdition. The wrong man could turn a potential Supreme Court justice into the permanent resident of a psych ward. Experience had taught her that women should avoid the mean, the financially sloppy, and, most of all, the devastatingly seductive who turn out to be as emotionally reliable as quicksand. India herself had almost fallen prey to the latter category of cad but saved herself just in time. Six years later, she no longer dated snakes; she accessorized with them. She had a brilliant career, her dignity, and a closet full of reptile purses—the spoils of her victory over herself. Most important, though she was still single, she had no regrets.

India's eyes wandered over the slightly sagging folds of her client's ivory flesh, propped up by cheekbones as pronounced and perfectly symmetrical as if a sculptor had chiseled them in marble. Elizabeth had sacrificed her beauty and a considerable portion of her sanity trying to steady a marriage harder to navigate than the North Sea during a perfect storm. India placed a café au lait hand on her client's pale arm and gave a tender squeeze.

"You must make a decision," she nudged gently, her large brown eyes conveying compassion.

"I've got it!" Elizabeth exclaimed at last in a nicotine-tempered British purr. "It's cruel and unusual treatment!"

"It's called 'cruelty.' And you used those grounds in the summons we sent him last year. And the one we sent him the year before," India patiently reminded her.

"Then we know it's effective. Besides, he'll never remember," Elizabeth argued.

"He's a writer. They remember."

"Well, I can't bear 'irreconcilable differences.' That's just stating the obvious. Of course, they're irreconcilable. That's what gives our marriage its zest," Elizabeth declared with a dramatic toss of her arm.

"How about 'abandonment'? We've never used it. It's fresh," India proposed.

"No, no, it sounds so pathetic. Like he's never coming back. Like I'm some sort of foundling. I shall turn sixty in a few months, you know."

"You turned sixty four years ago," India pointedly reminded her.

"Must you be a slave to the facts? It's because you're such a stickler for the rules that your life lacks poetry," Elizabeth snapped.

"Thank you for the pep talk," India answered, pained. Elizabeth's hazel eyes revealed that she had instantly regretted her outburst. India chose not to give vent to her own frustrations by reminding this particular client that poetry and passion were of little use when the bills came due.

"Very well, 'abandonment' it is," Elizabeth conceded.

"I'll have the papers drawn up today. We can deliver them tomorrow."

"Bless you, Counselor."

"Is there anything else I can do for you or will that be all, Mom?" India asked.

"That's all, my angel. Say hello to that divine Julien for me. Now *that* is a man worth keeping."

India studied her mother's dramatic, aging face. They shared undeniably identical bone structure. India's face with its Madame X defiant beak of a nose was a dark carbon copy of Elizabeth's. But India always swore to herself that all resemblances ended at the physical. She did not think it wildly ambitious to hope that when she had a child of her own, she would not be spending quality time with her dictating an annual divorce summons. As was her custom, her mother sat perched on the brink of a mental breakdown. It had been India's lifelong mission to keep her from falling.

"We'll have Richard served after his poetry class on Monday. That's at Apsley Hall, on One hundred and fourteenth Street?" India confirmed.

"No, it's at McGregor, Mc—something, at the University of Edinburgh," Elizabeth corrected her.

"In Scotland?" India asked, flabbergasted.

"Didn't I mention that your stepfather's doing a guest professorship there? I'll phone your assistant with his address. Now it's off to rehearsal with me. Don't forget, we open in twelve weeks. I want to panic Richard enough to get him home in time for my first entrance."

And with that, India's mother draped a bloodred cashmere shawl over her right shoulder and flounced out the door.

"This too shall not pass," India said to herself, resigned to the absurdity of the ritual. She slid open the shallow top drawer of her desk. Pushing aside an impeccable stack of pink index cards, she uncovered a fading color photograph of an ebony-skinned man smiling broadly as he tossed a mocha-hued eighteen-month-old aloft. The toddler's beatific smile matched her father's as she flew through the air, secure in the knowledge that he would never let her drop.

India had no memories of her father. He died in a car crash six months after the snapshot was taken. And having no actual memories, she invested in him all the perfections of an ideal. On days like today, she stopped to imagine the life she might have known had he lived. Her mother's tales of their blissful time together confirmed the canonization. Over Elizabeth's nightly bottle of Bordeaux, her face would glow with the memory of his kindness and his steadfastness, qualities her second husband, India's stepfather, lacked. What would her mother have become with the tender ministrations of a man of character instead of the Punch and Judy of her life with Richard Blythe, award-winning poet, alcoholic, and inveterate cheater? She might actually have behaved like a normal parent instead of rattling about the world like a wine-soaked caricature of herself. The arrant waste of gifts, of time, of life itself all made India want to smash the empty Steuben candy dish before her. She slammed the drawer shut, putting an end to the maudlin train of thought and to the temptation to destroy good glassware. Over the years, her mother's outbursts had cost them an entire collection of Waterford crystal, another family pattern India aimed to break.

Her phone rang and the name "Adams, Abigail" flashed across the identity bar. India eagerly picked up, relieved to hear from her best friend. *You can't pick your family,* she mused, *but mercifully, you do pick your friends.* And she'd picked well.

"Thank God, it's you," she said into the receiver.

"Bad morning?" Abby asked in her trademark sunny tone.

"It's that time of year for Mom and Richard." India sighed.

"The divorce thing? Don't they usually do that around Thanksgiving?" Abby asked.

"They're off to an early start this time," India explained.

"You're such a good daughter." Abby was in a position to know. They had met in kindergarten and shared the special kinship of women who had undergone all of the important rites of passage, from braces and training bras to tax planning and contemplating tummy tucks, together. India looked forward to going through menopause and the geriatric years with Abby. She was the kindest person India knew and the only person, other than her Nana Chumley, who understood everything about her life and her family.

"So I'm calling to confirm for the ballet luncheon. Eleven-thirty at the New York State Theater?" Abby inquired.

"Yes. They do the discussion and mini-performance first, and then they'll serve us a really bad and meager meal because every woman in the room is on the overpriced wardrobe diet and needs to keep squeezing into her size-two Chanel."

"My kind of afternoon!" Abby cheered. "Except for the bad food. Is it frowned upon to bring a snack?" she joked. India laughed, the first release she'd had all morning.

"Esme's meeting us there," she said, mentioning the third member of their triumvirate.

"She'll be late," Abby deadpanned. This had been the story of their lives.

"Let me get some work in before we play hooky," Abby continued.

"I'm going to do the same. See you soon," India said, hanging up.

Fully restored to sanity, she grabbed the *Diamond v. Diamond* file, tugged at the hem of her waist-cinching bouclé jacket, and strode down the wainscoted halls of Hallingby and Hallingby.

# chapter two

Within the steely confines of an International Style glass tower, the firm had created an ersatz nineteenth-century gentlemen's office, a bastion of Anglo-Saxon tradition complete with hunting prints in shades of forest green, yellow, and "riding to hounds" red. The setting appealed to India's longing for normalcy, bred during her formative years at the Sibley School for Girls, a private institution that, since 1897, had prepared young ladies ages five to seventeen for prominent careers or marriage to prominent men. It was there that she met Abby. When India attended the academy in the 1970s, hers was one of the only families "in the arts." This was the phrase genteel officials at the school used to explain to the very proper and very perturbed parents of India's towheaded classmates why a white, British woman and her Welsh husband had a half-black child. Today, the parents would assume that India's mother and stepfather had brought her back, along with other quaint and decorative knickknacks, from a safari in Africa. But back in the 1970s, multiracialism had not yet become all the rage in advertising, politics, and adoptions.

Though India would not have traded her mixed heritage for the world, she'd often wished for regular parents who took her on skiing and camping holidays or to Disneyland, rather than on tours of the pub stools of England while her mother performed "the big three" of Greek tragic heroines: Iphigenia, Antigone, and Medea. India was quite certain she was the only child in the Western Hemisphere whose parent dressed her as Mother Courage for Halloween. Walking the endless corridors of Hallingby and Hallingby reminded India of visiting her Sibley classmates, daughters of investment bankers and respectable corporate lawyers, in their immense floor-through apartments on Park and Fifth. Only she was no longer that "strange wooly-headed child" whose parents lived on—horror of horrors—the West Side. She was the mistress of her realm, a well-respected partner at the firm, with long brown hair blown out straight as a pin. She marched to conference room A, the room reserved for the eight- and nine-figure divorce settlements. She had snagged her first big deal since transferring to the New York office from Los Angeles a few months before. India took a deep self-satisfied breath.

She instantly deflated at the sight of Eddie O'Donnell, a junior partner at the firm and an embittered graduate of "safety schools." He had the squat build and perpetually pouting expression of an English bulldog. Whenever he spotted her, his nose wrinkled as if something smelly had crossed his path. India steeled herself for the first unpleasant exchange of the day with the freckle-faced redneck. India had dealt with malcontents like him before, men who saw her as the embodiment of a left-wing liberal conspiracy to rob working-class Caucasians of their rightful place on the ladder of upward mobility. It had been she who had taken Eddie's place at Harvard Law School, though his LSAT scores were reputed to have been in the range of mediocrity. The way Eddie saw it, India had hijacked his clerkship with an appellate court judge, and she stood between him and full partnership at Hallingby and Hallingby. The veins in Eddie's nonexistent neck pulsed with the fury of the white man scorned, a fury exacerbated by the election of the country's first black president. India had no doubt that Eddie perceived Obama as the ultimate "affirmative action baby."

"How's it going? Hear the Diamond case is almost settled," he growled resentfully.

"Pretty much," India said, trying to keep the exchange brief.

"Congratulations," he managed through gritted teeth. "I've got a big one on the line myself," he boasted, desperate to best her. She knew exactly which case he referred to, but she refused to give him the opportunity to beat his chest.

"Great," she said breezily as she moved away, leaving him stewing in his frustration. With a smile, India slipped into the conference room.

"Sorry I'm a few minutes late," she said to her client, Lucinda Diamond, a porcelain doll of a brunette with alabaster skin brought to a high polish by the dermatologist and Botox queen of the 10021 set. Her face glowed with the agelessness of a seven-figure lifestyle. Not a crease dented her thirty-eight-year-old forehead. As India contemplated her client's utterly unfurrowed brow, she thought perhaps she too had reached the age of surrender to the milder forms of cosmetic surgery, but she just couldn't bring herself to it. She liked to laugh too much.

"We did it," India announced to Lucinda triumphantly. "We brought them to their knees."

"I can't thank you enough," Lucinda gushed. "Now maybe I can move on with my life."

"You'll have a lot to move on with. If I were you, I would take myself to dinner at La Grenouille and order a case of Château d'Yquem. Actually, that's a lie. First, I'd go to Saks and buy myself a new handbag."

Suddenly, Lucinda twitched, sparrowlike in her tufted leather seat as Manni Sobel, her husband's attorney, burst in followed by her soon-to-be ex-husband, Irving Diamond, who, with his shrunken physique, could have easily been mistaken for a garden gnome. Mr. Diamond had spent the better part of his twenties and thirties amassing a fortune large enough to compensate for all that he lacked in height and charm. Manni, by contrast, had the swarthy, exotic good looks of a native Israeli, though he hailed from Hackensack, New Jersey.

"Let's get to it," Manni demanded, slamming his briefcase on the table and smacking his ubiquitous gum. He tossed back a thick lock of jet black hair and winked at India who, much to her irritation, had always found her brash former law school classmate temptingly attractive. Watching his biceps ripple beneath his fitted charcoal gray suit coat, she didn't wonder at the fact that she nearly slept with him back in their student days.

"Chumley, I can't believe you're still not married."

"I can't believe you still are. But Mr. and Mrs. Diamond didn't come here to watch us reminisce about our days as legal eaglets, Manni."

"No, they didn't," Manni said as he swept back a forelock of his silken hair. India studied his hands. They were compact and powerful as Marlon Brando's in *A Streetcar Named Desire*. She remembered the feeling of Manni's fingers kneading her neck, as every muscle went limp under the pressure. He had gripped her shoulders as he lay on top of her that afternoon in a cubicle at Langdell Library. Their bodies had writhed in unison as he pressed his bulge against her fully clothed but eager pelvis. His hands had traveled down the length of her spine. He had slid her skirt over her hips and began to remove her panties. She had grabbed his hands to stop him.

"Chumley!" Manni's voice called.

India snapped out of her reverie as abruptly as she had ended the near-intercourse twelve years before. Only in this instance, Manni, the man she almost had sex with on a tabletop, wasn't glaring at her with frustrated desire. He glared with impatience.

"Where were you?" he asked.

"Thinking about another set of briefs," she responded, secretly amused at her own double entendre.

A flicker passed over Manni's coal black eyes. India had the discomfiting sense he'd read her backward-looking thoughts, particularly as he continued to stare at her with a lascivious smirk. She turned away, pulling the shade on the fantasy and his sexual energy. It was India's curse in life to have the morals of a Carmelite nun and the libido of a raving sexaholic. Unsuitable men always lit her fire. She feared that if she allowed herself, her life would degenerate into an endless pursuit of the perfect orgasm. And so she kept her urges and her emotions always in check.

"I have the final decree, so if Mr. Diamond would like to take a few minutes to read it to make sure it reflects the terms we agreed upon, we'll be done," India declared.

"We'd like to sign that, India. Really, we would. There's just one small problem," Manni demurred. India sat up taller, like a gazelle sensing a predator in the bush.

"What would that be?" she inquired, feigning calm while her index finger furiously tapped away at her pen.

"When we agreed to these very generous terms, we didn't have these." Manni snapped his briefcase, the top flew open, and with a devilish grin, he handed India a large manila envelope. India uncoiled the string from the circular closure. She smiled with false reassurance at Mrs. Diamond.

She reached into the envelope and was perturbed to feel photographs. Her heart stopped. She instantly flashed a poker player's smile and slowly withdrew the eight-by-tens.

"Enjoy," Manni commented with a smirk.

India perused the first image: Mrs. Diamond in regulation Upper East Side casual dress: chinos, a quilted jacket, and Tod's driving loafers leaning in to kiss a stud muffin in sweats, as something out of frame tugged at his muscular arm.

India flipped to image two: Mrs. Diamond with her arms around said stud muffin's neck as five dogs strained on leashes he held in his right hand.

Image three: Mrs. Diamond's hands firmly grasping the stud muffin's bionic buttocks.

India's heart sank as she played for time, like her mother used to on stage when she forgot a line. How could Mrs. Diamond have done something so harebrained? How could India have bought her "butter wouldn't melt in my mouth" routine? She knew it from college and at Sibley; it was always the innocent-looking ones, the girls in the flowered Laura Ashley dresses with headbands soldered to their shoulder-length bobs who ended up in the victory position with half the lacrosse team.

She decided upon her ploy: plausible deniability.

"These photos, while highly entertaining, prove absolutely nothing. My client was a bit exuberant in her gratitude toward a man who appears to be her dog walker. There's no crime in a hug," India said, tossing the pictures back at Manni.

"A hug? She's kneading that ass like it's bread dough. But don't worry. There's more." Manni proffered the next weapon in his arsenal. "An American Express bill. Item number eleven. On August 20 your client, Mrs. Diamond, takes a room at the St. Regis Hotel."

"The air-conditioning was being repaired at the house. It was stifling. I mean, who sleeps without air-conditioning in August? I had to spend the night somewhere else," Lucinda hastened to explain.

"And you did. With Mr. Buns of Steel. The room service waiter's sworn affidavit." Manni tossed five typed pages on the table.

"No! Antonio came to walk Demi-Tasse, my teacup poodle," Lucinda protested.

"Who was in East Hampton with your children," Manni countered.

"No! She was with me! And we were alone!"

India raised an eyebrow at Mrs. Diamond like a vicious school marm calling for silence. In such moments she was reminded of the important uses of a Botox-free brow.

"So, ladies, our former offer is off the table," Manni concluded. India willed herself not to smack him. She should have known he would not settle without a fight.

"You can't do that. Even if these photographs prove what you claim, which is very questionable, adultery has no bearing on divorce settlements in the state of New York," she objected.

"But proof of her unfitness as a mother does on custody," Manni proffered yet another photograph, this one of Mrs. Diamond dancing on a tabletop in her brassiere and a miniskirt while the young stud and other men looked on adoringly. India maintained her aplomb while the "creek" rose around her.

"He doesn't want the children! He spends ten minutes a week with them. This is a game!" Mrs. Diamond moaned.

"My client does not want to see his children raised by a drunk," Manni answered solemnly.

"Oh, give it a rest, Reverend Manni," India scoffed.

"The ball's in your court. Come back to us with some solutions or we go before the judge, and with the statements of eyewitness to Mrs. Diamond's little Victoria's Secret runway show, it could get ugly. Hate to see the children have to find out about 'Mommy the booze hound.'"

"This isn't low, Manni, it's subterranean," India said reproachfully.

"Sticks and stones may break my bones, but polysyllables will never hurt me," Manni retorted. His brashness excited her, in spite of her disgust. It was a good thing, yet a shame, that she didn't go all the way on that table in the library. He was probably phenomenal.

"I never figured you for a tramp, Lu," Mr. Diamond said, breaking his silence at last.

"That's uncalled for, Mr. Diamond, especially given your own extracurricular activities," India declared calmly.

"What's a guy to do when his wife has about as much sexual technique as an ice maker?"

"Well, I might have done better if I had something to work with, Tom Thumb!" Lucinda hissed, her porcelain doll face now contorted and crimson. Her sudden burst of rage startled even India. Mr. Diamond lunged for his maddening soon-to-be ex.

"You bitch!" he spat as Manni grabbed him by the arm.

"That's it. Round over. Chumley, call me." And with that, Manni dragged his seething pint-sized client out of the room.

Lucinda collapsed into her chair, despondent. India locked the door after them and turned to face her trembling sparrow of a client.

"Obviously this is a ploy to get you to reduce your settlement. How could you have kept this from me?" she asked.

"I didn't think it was relevant. It didn't start until after Irving moved out."

"But you were still married. What were you thinking?"

"If you saw Antonio, you'd understand. His lips are like pillows. His hands, they're so big and powerful. And his . . . My girlfriends always talked about what it was like to be with someone really . . . endowed, but oh my God, I never knew. And he can last for hours."

India studied the photograph and in her heart agreed. This man could have inspired lust in a frozen fish. Nonetheless, she wished her client had a better ratio of sense to desire.

"Do you realize that you are about to lose fifty million dollars over an orgasm?" she reproached.

"It's not just one. I finally know what those magazines mean when they talk about 'multiple.'"

"Let's see how many multiple orgasms Mr. Dog Walker wants to give you when you have no assets."

"He doesn't like me for my money."

"I'm sorry. I didn't mean to imply." But of course India did. She could have strangled Mrs. Diamond, but instead she turned to her.

"Lucinda, if you want economic independence, and to continue in the lifestyle to which you are now addicted, I urge you to cease all contact with the dog walker. This is a time to keep your eyes on the prize. Once you have your settlement, you can have sex with Antonio in Macy's window. But until then, you are the vestal virgin of 765 Park Avenue; you worship at the shrine of our Lady of the Crossed Legs. Have I made myself clear?"

"Yes," Lucinda mumbled through tears, "but it's going to be hard."

"It would be a lot harder to live in a five-floor walk-up in the outer boroughs and hock your Hermès Birkins on eBay for rent money."

Lucinda shuddered at the thought.

"You have three children to raise. To fight this custody issue, you may have to go to rehab," India said gently.

"No! I'm never drunk. It was only that one time."

"One time caught on camera. And recorded in affidavits. We have to beat them to the punch or he's going to make life difficult."

"I'm not going to rehab. You have to share a room," Lucinda said as if describing the worst of all human fates. India knew to press no further. She did not want to push this fragile Park Avenue princess to the brink of despair.

"Think about it," India urged rising from her seat. Lucinda nodded quietly, nearly tearing up at the thought of a motel-like cubicle at the Betty Ford clinic. India escorted her to the elevator, past the august hunting prints in silence.

"We'll get him in the end," she offered conciliatorily as they reached the elevator bank.

"Antonio?" Lucinda looked up, hopeful.

"Your husband," India answered, doing her best not to betray her frustration at Lucinda's slavish mention of Mr. Orgasm's name.

As the elevator doors slid shut on Mrs. Diamond, India started counting to ten and taking deep "cleansing breaths." After the third, she reminded herself there was a far more sinful and satisfying way to de-stress. She raced back to her office, shut the door, and flung open the bottom right desk drawer. She rifled through mounds of discarded chocolate wrappings: green and gold bags from Teuscher, tiny bronze cardboard boxes from Godiva, even a brown Hershey wrapper—a relic of a moment of true desperation. At the bottom of the pile she struck gold: a half-eaten Lindt Cresta bar, wafers of milk chocolate with delectable flecks of crunchy caramel. She ripped the tinfoil and bit off a full two-inch block.

Her assistant, Una, popped her head in and tensely announced, "Ms. Armstrong is here." India instantly slammed the drawer shut and bolted to her feet.

Constance Armstrong, senior partner of Hallingby and Hallingby since 1984, stood in the doorway. India struggled to swallow the unwieldy chunk of chocolate as her boss entered. Constance Armstrong had graduated from Sibley at the top of her class at sixteen, Wellesley

College Phi Beta Kappa at nineteen, and Harvard Law School summa cum laude at twenty-two. Over the course of her forty-two-year career she had won every award the legal profession had to offer and run the New York Marathon twice. She had raised three children with the good graces never to have a soccer match, a bout of flu, or a nervous breakdown that interfered with the forward march of their mother's career.

*You would never catch her pigging out on chocolate in the middle of the afternoon to steady her nerves,* India reflected with shame. She seemed not to have any nerves at all, though she rattled everyone else's. India could not imagine Constance Armstrong having an inappropriate thought, emotion, or desire. In her perfectly accomplished, perfectly coiffed presence India felt like the child of a schleppy god.

"Ms. Chumley, how are you?" Constance asked cordially. India forced down the last of the Cresta bar, then responded, hoping her mouth wasn't covered in praline cream.

"Very well, thank you, Ms. Armstrong."

"I know your docket is full, but there's a case I need you to take on."

"Of course, it would be my pleasure." India grabbed a fresh yellow pad from her top right drawer, preparing to take notes.

"It's the Winston case. Are you familiar with Mr. Winston's story?"

"The husband of Paula Winston, the founder of Zakan, the company that makes stationery out of elephant dung?" India asked.

"Precisely. Isn't it unbelievable that one can build a fortune by transforming excrement into thank-you notes? I need you to represent Mr. Winston."

"But he's O'Donnell's client," India reminded Constance.

"Was. I'm giving the case to you."

"But O'Donnell brought him in."

"That was good of him. Now you're going to make sure Mr. Winston wins."

"Perhaps O'Donnell and I could work together." India couldn't even believe she'd made the suggestion, but by her code of ethics even Satan didn't deserve to have his cases stolen, particularly the plum ones.

"You don't seem to understand. O'Donnell is completely useless in this instance. Mrs. Winston has retained José Feldman," Constance explained.

At the mention of Jose's name, India's interest was piqued. José Feldman was a legend among divorce lawyers. Trailer parks were referred to as "Feldman-villes" because José had reduced so many wealthy men to Winnebago dwellers. "We get ninety percent, they get ten, it's a win-win," was his motto.

"I've never gone up against Feldman," India admitted, titillated by the opportunity to work against the best.

"We need someone like you, with finesse and sangfroid. O'Donnell was stoked right into the corner. Mr. Winston expressed his concerns to me. If O'Donnell stays on, they'll end up at trial and Mr. Winston will lose everything, his rightful portion of the fortune he helped her build, the children he loves—" With the mention of the children, Constance knew she was hitting India's Achilles' heel.

"Is he seeking custody?" India asked, hooked.

"Yes. And you know how infrequently they grant it to the father. A woman has to be a prostitute addicted to crack cocaine to lose her children. And unfortunately for our client, Mrs. Winston is neither. She's merely heartless and self-centered. If they go before a judge . . ." She trailed off, giving India the opportunity to envision the Winston cherubs' misery at the hands of an unloving mother. India's heart led her to sign on and save them from such a fate. Still, her conscience recoiled at the thought of poaching a colleague's client.

"I just don't feel right. It goes against the rule—"

"Ms. Chumley, this is not a croquet match on the lawn of the Meadow Club. This is divorce. We haven't time for fine sentiments and Marquis of Queensbury rules. In law as in love, there is always a winner and always a loser. Our job is to make sure we're with the winners. Sometimes personal feelings have to be sacrificed for the greater good. O'Donnell is a big boy. He will get over it."

"Can you at least credit him for the fees, since he did bring the case in?"

"Are you campaigning for sainthood, Ms. Chumley? I must alert the Vatican." Constance frequently intimidated with sarcasm. India looked her in the eye and stood her ground.

"I just want to be fair," she answered calmly. Constance raised an eyebrow scornfully.

"Not that you aren't," India amended, kicking herself for the gaffe. "I just don't want to see O'Donnell penalized. He does have a family."

"We'll see what we can do," Constance declared as she exited. India knew exactly what that meant: we'll toss him a scrap of gristle. Though she couldn't bear O'Donnell, she would have hated to be the cause of his suffering. She was tempted to run after Constance and refuse to take the case. Then she thought of the children, three of them. In the end, they did count more than O'Donnell's ego and wallet. Still, she wished she wouldn't have had to build their sanity at the expense of someone else's career. She grabbed her purse. She'd earned her afternoon at the ballet.

# chapter three

India's taxi drove up the ramp and came to a stop in front of Lincoln Center. She paid the driver and raced past the shooting fountain and across the plaza to the Koch Theater where the annual Boxed Lunch with Ballerinas benefit always took place. This was one of a slew of events designed to allow New York's wealthiest women to support a worthy cause while putting their best outfits forward. As India entered through the glass doors, the gong sounded, indicating that the program was about to begin. Perfumed herds of women in knobby tweed suits clattered up the marble staircases, creating a stiletto stampede. India joined their noisily clicking throng. Once they swarmed into the opera house, with its hundred-foot ceilings, the red velvet carpeting silenced their heels. India felt the intense peace that came over her whenever she entered a theater or auditorium, sanctuaries for her since childhood.

She scanned the crowd. A few rows ahead she spotted a woman with skin the color of cinnamon, a standout because people of color were as rare a sight at the Ballet Lunch as blacks in Baroque paintings. The woman looked vaguely familiar. A sizeable diamond sparkled on her ring finger as she ran a hand over the nape of her neck.

But before India could scrutinize her further, a voice called out in a stage whisper, "India! Over here." India turned to see Abby Rosenfeld Adams flashing her trademark thousand-watt smile. It was the same unabashedly open and joyous smile Abby had beamed across the cavernous marble front hall of Sibley on their first day of school thirty-two years before. There they had stood: blond, blue-eyed Abby, next to mocha latte India, the only two frizzy-headed ethnics in a sea of girls with tresses as smooth as corn silk. Now, as then, India knew upon seeing her friend that even in a room full of strangers she was safe.

"Traitor!" Abby taunted, pointing to India's blown-out locks.

"Don't worry, pour water on me and I'm back to being a Chia Pet," India reassured her as she sat down next to Abby.

"I may try that at lunch."

"Watch it. It took two hours and cost seventy-five dollars to iron all traces of ethnicity out of these strands. Touch them and you'll draw back a nub. What have I missed?"

"Nothing, just the moderator, Cece Gall, and her litany of accomplishments. Snore. She should have just said, 'You all know me from *60 Minutes,*'" Abby indicated a sharp-featured fifty-nine-year-old woman on stage whose hair had been sprayed to stock stillness. "You know, my dad dated her back in his twenties. The family would have preferred her to Mom. Her parents weren't Lower East Side communists. And apparently she was doing just as much back then to single-handedly destroy the ozone layer with her hairdos."

"And now," the enemy of the environment announced from the stage, "two of Gotham Ballet's leading dancers, Marcelo Guerrera and Misty Milestone, will perform some selections from *Carmen.*" The heavily female audience let out a collective "ohhh" of delight.

"Yes, aren't we pleased? This piece, choreographed by Roland Petit just after World War II, is rarely performed here in New York. You all know the story: Carmen the temptress seduces Don Jose, the honorable soldier betrothed to an innocent woman. After convincing him to leave his fiancée and come away with her, Carmen heartlessly abandons him for a bullfighter and tragedy ensues, reminding us all that infidelity doesn't pay. We'll see three pas de deux and end with the death scene."

"I saw this in Paris ten years ago," India whispered to Abby excitedly. "It's amazing."

"Thanks for inviting me," Abby said. "It's a great excuse to leave the gallery for the afternoon!"

The strains of "Love Is a Rebellious Bird" began to play as the long-limbed ballerina kindled the seduction of her beautifully built swain. As she teasingly approached him, he hoisted her in the air as though she weighed no more than a swallow.

India loved the ballet's use of the mastery of the human body to express unbridled emotions. She favored big-story ballets: tales that dwelled on impossible love and ended in death or irretrievable loss. From the safety of a red velvet seat, she could live the grand passions without suffering the consequences. And of course, she loved to see men with sculpted V-shaped torsos and powerful thighs display their wares in tights. It was pornography masquerading as high culture, a perfect combination.

"Oh, no, not *Carmen!*" a voice uttered loudly and was greeted with urgent "shhhh!"'s and dirty looks. India and Abby knew their friend Esme had made her entrance at last, just in time for the last five minutes of the program, the death scene. The scent of Esme's perfume, a heady vanilla-laden concoction, preceded her as she unabashedly climbed over the seated spectators. She wriggled her rounded bottom into the seat beside India and fished a hot pink lip gloss out of her handbag. She rubbed the sponge-tipped applicator back and forth across her heart-shaped mouth, turning a mundane act into an erotic invitation that would have made any heterosexual man go weak at the knees. With her lush mane of shining black hair, flawless chiseled nose, wide-set eyes, and high cheekbones, she had the beauty of an MGM screen goddess of yesteryear. The effect was heightened by the fact that she carried her good looks with the nonchalance of a woman who woke up drop-dead gorgeous. India marveled at the fact that after two children and with each passing year, Esme just became a riper version of the traffic-stopping teenager she had known at Sibley.

"I hate this opera," Esme whispered, her English still tinged with the inflections of her native Colombia. She poked out a pulpy lower lip in mock petulance.

"Why does the cheating woman always have to die? It's so unfair, she's just bored and trying to have some fun. Besides, she's not even married to him," Esme complained to India.

India pressed her finger to her lips, a signal Esme had never fully grasped or accepted since their days in the library. The headmistress had once given her a day's worth of detention for refusing to lower her voice when shushed by the librarian. She subsequently took her revenge by sneaking the headmistress's son, a lanky innocent who worshiped her, into the stacks for regular make-out sessions. Abby had served as a reluctant human screen to their activities. True to form, Esme somehow managed never to get caught. At graduation, she'd barreled up to the headmistress and announced, "I taught your son everything he knows about sex in your precious library. That will teach you to try to shut me up," then flounced away, waving her diploma. Like many a bored heiress, Esme got her thrills from defying authority and shocking the stodgy.

"Qué? We're not in church!" Esme said in a stage whisper to India.

The dancer playing Don José advanced toward Carmen and stabbed her with a knife. She crumpled gracefully to the ground as the women in the audience let out mournful sighs.

"Is it true they pad their peepees, or is all that his?" Esme asked. Abby and India suppressed their laughter. The music reached crescendo, as Carmen breathed her last and collapsed into Don Jose's arms.

"Ultimately, that's where passion leaves you," India couldn't help whispering to Abby, "dead, broke, or both."

"Would you brighten up? I married the love of my life and I'm alive and solvent."

India nodded, but she didn't take much comfort in Abby's reassurance. At twenty-one, she'd thought Abby far too young to get married.

Besides, she'd never trusted Abby's husband, Nathaniel Adams, the scion of a once grand but since impoverished Mayflower clan. Still, in spite of India's misgivings, Abby's marriage had lasted sixteen years and produced three wonderful children. That was more than India could claim. At thirty-seven, she was the mother of a large brood of handbags. *Ah well, at least I haven't chosen the wrong man and spawned yet another dysfunctional family,* she thought.

She watched the dancers take their bows and found herself wishing life could be as beautiful and error free as the ballet.

Cece Gall, the emcee, rose to her feet once again. "Wasn't that exquisite?" she gushed. The audience applauded wildly. "Well, that concludes the performance portion of the program. Ladies, if you'll repair upstairs, lunch is served! Thank you for being here and supporting Gotham Ballet."

"Great, basta with culture, on with the pasta! I'm starving!" Esme declared as the house lights went up and the audience rose. She led India and Abby through the crowd and, with the intensity of a heat-seeking missile, found their table.

"Try not to insult anyone," India warned her. "This event is being chaired by one of my clients. Half the women in here are her friends."

"So are you afraid that your firm is going to fire you because I put one or two or ten uptight bitches in their place? Just pretend you don't know me," Esme retorted.

"Spoken like a trust-fund baby," Abby chided.

"Trust fund? Please. My father set it up so I barely have enough to keep myself in Dolce. He wanted me to be dependent on my husband. But that's finished. Little Esme and Julio are plenty old enough. I'm going back to work."

"Good for you!" India cheered, genuinely pleased that her dilettantish friend was putting her intelligence to use.

"If I have to sing 'The Wheels on the Bus Go Round and Round' one more time, I'm going to grab a rifle and shoot the first woman I see in a Lilly Pulitzer dress," Esme said.

"Let's get you some wine, now," Abby said, pouring an ample amount into Esme's glass. "And try not to think about Greenwich head banshees today."

A group of seven women in Chanel or "wish it were a Chanel" arrived. They introduced themselves with stiff grins and anemic handshakes, then drew an invisible but inviolable Maginot Line at the table. India had grown used to such snubs since her return to New York. In certain circles, if people didn't know you or of you, they would not expend the effort to discover if you were a worthwhile human being.

"This isn't wine, it's bidet water. *Feh!*" Esme shrieked. "Waiter! Yes, you." A handsome fortysomething with the carriage and build of the Marlboro Man approached the table.

"Is there something you need, Miss?" he inquired solicitously.

"Yes," Esme answered. "Some real food. How's a woman supposed to survive on this? Chicken and lettuce. What do they think we are, rabbits?"

The waiter blushed and laughed. "Would you like to try the vegetarian meal?" he offered.

"Are you trying to kill me, guapo? We'll be farting all night. Don't they have something else back there? A steak? Some chips? Come on, you can find something for me." She looked up at him with her almond-shaped eyes, letting her jacket slide open to reveal a glimpse of her ample bosom cradled in a black lace demi-bra. Esme had always been able to inspire any man to climb whatever Mount Everest she set before him. The waiter was no exception. India and Abby watched in amazement as he scuttled off, neglecting all his other tables to satisfy Esme's whim.

"Nice ass, nice hands, and nice hair, not to mention big feet. We know what that means—he's got a big salami, not a cocktail weenie," Esme commented. Overhearing, the women on the other side of the table cast disapproving glances as they whispered to each other.

"What? Is there even one of you who wouldn't sleep with him if you could do it and not get caught?" Esme challenged. Appalled, the women turned away and continued their own conversation.

"Is your goal to make us complete pariahs?" India asked teasingly.

"They're not future clients. Those witches are gonna cling to their husbands until the bitter end rather than face the shame of divorce. Trust me, I know the type. It's my entire neighborhood."

"Well, well, well, India Chumley, Miss Thing herself. In the flesh." India turned to see the attractive black woman from the auditorium. It took her a moment to reconcile this chicly dressed professional with the judgmental voice she remembered all too well: it was Monique Dawkins, the former scholarship student at Sibley and her childhood tormentor.

"Hi, Monique," India said diffidently.

"It's actually Dr. Dawkins-Dubois now. I'm an ob-gyn at Mount Hebron Hospital." As Monique uttered the words, she scrutinized India. The latter envisioned her at eight on the basketball court at Sibley, mocking her with cries of "White girl! Oreo!" as she had tried and failed to shoot a basket. Neither India's mother nor her stepfather had understood the first thing about American sports. Her weekends with them had been spent watching them lob insults at each other, not tossing a ball in the backyard.

"You finally put a straightening comb through all that hair. I almost didn't recognize you, Miss Thing," Monique continued good-naturedly, though the comment irked India. Because they had attended different colleges and followed different careers, their paths had not crossed in the twenty years since they'd graduated from Sibley. India had not missed Monique's daily jabs.

"My mother never even heard of a straightening comb. What was a tragic mulatto to do?" India deadpanned.

"I remember you," Esme said to Monique. "You were funny and very smart. I'm Esme Sarmiento. Well, Sarmiento-Talbot for now. And you remember Abby Rosenfeld."

"Abby and I see each other from time to time at Sibley alumni mixers," Monique explained.

"The ones you two refuse to attend," Abby said pointedly to Esme and India. The latter vaguely remembered Abby referencing Monique on one or two occasions. Knowing India's unfond memories of Monique, Abby purposely avoided going into much detail about her.

"And when are you going to transfer your daughter to Sibley?" Monique chided Abby.

"Never. I like schools where the diversity count isn't achieved with an eye dropper," Abby laughed.

"Hey, it's about getting an education. Like we did. Your daughter has the rest of her life to meet colored folks and Chinese people. I see y'all are still the three musketeers," Monique commented.

"The Misfits of Sibley," India assented, invoking the moniker she, Abby, and Esme had adopted in the eighth grade to celebrate their status as outsiders among Sibley's budding bitch-utantes.

"When were you ever a misfit? All those rich girls loved you."

"If they did, they had a strange way of showing it," India answered, stunned by Monique's perception of her as an "it" girl. India remembered nothing so much as being stared at daily by Sibley's overwhelming population of Upper East Side Aryan princesses who would whisper to each other while pointing at her, then ask benighted questions about her hair. "Did you put your finger in the socket this morning?" they'd taunt when she wore it loose. "How do you get it all to stay down, with Crisco?" they'd ask when it was pulled back in a bun. Once she'd hit puberty and the brothers of classmates showered her with attention, she had suddenly found herself barred from more than one sprawling Park Avenue abode. Anglo mother notwithstanding, she had been an undesirable mongrel to most of the Sibley girls and their parents, someone whose genes should never be allowed to enter their "pool" and, heaven and the Social Register forbid, mix with theirs. She couldn't have felt more like an alien if she'd had antennae. But she'd never shared any of these experiences with Monique. It was hard to engage in heart-to-hearts with someone who was usually trying to shove her down a flight of stairs. And, then as now, India had hid her pain beneath a mask of imperturbable calm and the armor of sartorial perfection.

It occurred to India as she stood amiably chatting with the scholarship duckling turned haute bourgeois swan, that perhaps her loony mother had been correct all along. Monique's animus might indeed have come from intimidation, envy, and loneliness even deeper than hers.

"What are you doing here?" Monique asked. "I thought you moved to LA."

"I relocated a couple of months ago. How did you know I lived there?"

"Abby told me when I saw her at the Sibley reunion. And my husband went to college with you. Wayne Dubois."

India racked her brain but could not remember Wayne. She decided to pretend she did to keep this newborn peace with her erstwhile nemesis, rather than confirm Monique's childhood view of her as a hopelessly assimilated "imitation white girl."

"Oh yeah, Wayne," she vamped.

"You don't remember him, do you?" Monique called her bluff.

"Monique, I was pretty much an incognegro in college," India confessed, using the common term for black students at Ivy League schools who shunned the "black table," the corner of the dining hall where students of color congregated for every meal to prove their ethnic allegiance.

"Incog or not, the brothers all wanted to know you. According to Wayne," Monique commented.

"Every guy wants to know her," Abby added.

"So how long have you been married?" India asked Monique, in an attempt to deflect attention from herself.

"Ten years. Two kids. Girls, both at Sibley."

"How could you send your girls to that gulag?" Esme asked, disgusted. "Didn't you suffer enough? Nobody would come to your birthday parties because you lived in the Bronx or something."

"Brooklyn, Bed-Stuy," Monique corrected flatly.

Embarrassed, India and Abby looked at each other, remembering how every year nearly the entire class would suddenly develop a terrible cold or have a family reunion little Priscilla "simply couldn't miss." Eventually, Monique had stopped inviting.

"At least Abby, India, and Bitsey Samuelson came. Anyway, that was then. Nobody skips my babies' birthday parties. Last year we took over the Wollman skating rink."

India surmised that Monique's erect carriage came from her intense satisfaction at having triumphed over her circumstances. She couldn't help but share her pride. She had run those stuck-up witches off their feet.

Cece Gall stood at the microphone in the middle of the room. India rolled her eyes, knowing all fun conversation would have to cease so that the well-intentioned organizers of the event could coax even more money out of the stylish crowd.

"Ladies and few gentlemen, if I may have your attention. It's time to meet our hardworking cochairs and hold our raffle. If you haven't bought your tickets, there's still time!" Cece said in a saccharine gung-ho tone.

"Oh, shoot me," Esme said. "I came to spend the afternoon in the city, not relive my life in Greenwich. Can we get out of here and get something decent to eat?"

"I'm game," Abby said. "I'm not going back to the gallery this afternoon. The client who was coming to see our Lichtenstein canceled. Do you mind, India?"

"No. The ballet was what I came here for. This is the painful part."

"Are you coming, Monique?" Esme queried.

"I'm not on call and I paid for my own ticket, so I can definitely jet," Monique answered, surprised and delighted to have been asked. She looked to India, as if for final approval. India would have preferred an afternoon alone with Esme and Abby, but, seeing Monique practically beseech her, she chastised herself for being so selfish. She could let bygones be bygones, at least for one afternoon.

As the cochairs were introduced, Abby, Esme, India, and Monique left the table and made their way to the staircase.

"Oops! I have to go to the ladies' room. I'll meet you downstairs," Esme instructed. It did not escape India's notice that the restrooms were at the back of the grand tier, right near the waiter station.

# chapter four

"What do I have to do to get a margarita around here, set myself on fire?" Esme yelled at a passing waitress in a midnight-blue miniskirt. India blanched, mortified. The four women sat at a table by the window on the thirty-fifth floor of the Mandarin Oriental Hotel, looking down at the Columbus Circle roundabout with its tiered fountain. Esme had recommended the elegant lounge because of its beautiful views, comfortable white leather chairs, and guaranteed-to-get-you-smashed cocktails.

"Esme, come on," India chided, embarrassed at her friend's display of rudeness. "If my Nana Chumley heard you, she'd slap you."

"She should slap the waitress," Esme gestured toward the statue outside. "Columbus sailed to America in less time than it's taken that super bimbo to bring us our second round of drinks."

"Actually, it's our fourth," Abby corrected her. The assortment of empty wineglasses and tumblers attested to the accuracy of Abby's count.

"And being rude and abusive won't help," India looked around to make certain the other patrons hadn't taken notice of their table. Fortunately, the place was not yet crowded.

"Abuse is the only thing they understand. I hate waitresses. They're just putas in uniform sucking up to the businessmen. Like airline stewardesses who are just the slut waitresses of the air. Look at that girl.

If she puts her blimpies any closer to that man's face she'll asphyxiate him."

"Tell us how you really feel," Monique offered with an amused grin.

"She's being tame today," Abby explained to Monique.

"Monique, I tell it like it is. You want hypocrisy, go next door," Esme asserted, grabbing a handful of macadamia nuts from the bowl on the table.

"I want more of these ginger prawns," Abby said.

"Ugh! It's like eating a rubber penis. We need more fried dumplings," Esme rebutted.

"I don't understand how you keep that fierce body when you eat like that, Esme," marveled Monique.

"I have a lot of sex," Esme explained matter-of-factly.

"You're married and you can say that?" Monique asked with astonishment and more than a hint of envy, India noted. She surmised that, unlike Abby, Monique had not chosen her husband in a burst of youthful passion. She could not for the life of her remember Wayne Dubois, her erstwhile classmate. Though she hadn't "hung black" at college, she had known all the handsome black men. This memory lapse could mean only one thing: Wayne had a face for radio. Much as India believed in subjugating one's heart to one's head, she had to admit it sometimes led to rather dismal choices.

"Hey, I'm married and I can say I have a lot of sex," Abby protested. Then she considered her ample posterior and hips. "It's just not working as well for me," she added. India inwardly seconded that motion. It certainly was not working for Abby to live with a selfish, insecure man with a flinty temper. While being a good friend meant speaking up, being a kind one meant holding one's tongue, so India took another sip of her Merlot.

"I didn't say sex with my husband," Esme pointed out. Monique looked down, embarrassed but laughed anyway and clinked glasses with Esme. Abby shot Esme a disapproving look. This reaction surprised India. Abby had always taken Esme's outrageous comments in stride. India hoped Esme was merely indulging in her favorite pastime of shocking the bourgeoisie, and not revealing the truth about her marriage. Esme's stop at the waiter station before leaving the ballet suggested unsettlingly to India that perhaps her brash words had of late become bad deeds. India would be the last to know. Esme had always preferred to confess her transgressions to the more forgiving Abby.

"Qué?" Esme shot back, exasperated. "I don't need a dueña."

"No, just a chastity belt," Abby commented.

"You take care of your marriage, I'll take care of mine. My husband's not complaining," Esme shot back.

"Blessed are the ignorant," Abby quipped. Esme contemplated retaliation but decided to forgo victory in this round. She turned to India, who was doing her best not to reveal her dismay at what she suspected about Esme's behavior.

"What kind of food does Julien serve at his restaurant?" Esme asked, mentioning India's boyfriend.

"French-Asian fusion," India answered, welcoming a change of subject. She spent her days around unhappily married people. She did not wish to discover that all her friends were living miserably ever after.

"Oh, not more mongrel cuisine. When will chefs learn: mixing only works for people and dogs?"

"Who's Julien?" Monique asked.

"India's fiancé," Esme answered. "When am I meeting him, anyway? I've waited long enough. It's inspection time."

"He's not my fiancé," India corrected, shifting uncomfortably in her seat. She had just convinced Julien to cease his weekly proposals. She didn't need her friends to foist matrimony upon her. She believed in the sanctity of the marriage vows, that it is "a holy estate, not to be entered into lightly, but reverently, advisedly, and in the fear of God," or, failing that, in the fear of divorce.

"Just because you're engaged doesn't mean you have to go through with it. I broke off five engagements before marrying Tim. It's just a 'for now' promise. You moved here to be with him, you might as well say 'I'm yours—for now,'" Esme advised with a dismissive wave of her hand.

India forgave her friend's nonchalance while not sharing it. She had already broken off one engagement in her life. It was not an experience she wished to repeat.

"I did not move here to be with him. I moved here to be back in civilization; in a place where reading the morning paper doesn't qualify you as a major intellectual. And to be with my good friends. And my firm made me a big offer that happened to coincide with meeting him," India insisted.

"Where's he from? What does he do?" Monique asked.

"Let's just say he's a French restaurateur who puts the *h* in 'hottie,'" Abby answered.

Esme added, "From what I've heard, he's the ideal man: an only child with dead parents. No outlaws. Don't look that gift from God in the mouth. I'm stuck with Tim's mother and sister: the witches they forgot to burn at Salem."

"Actually, they drowned most of those women, and it's 'gift horse,'" India corrected.

"Be honest, are you hesitating because he's white?" Abby challenged. India looked at her best friend in total disbelief.

"That is the dumbest question you've asked me in thirty-two years of friendship, Abby Rosenfeld Adams. How can I object to half of what I am?" India protested.

"I'm sorry, but I can't see what other objection there could be."

"Well, not to sound snobbish, but for one thing he's not very bookish. He didn't even go to college."

"Oh, yes, if you can't discuss Proust, what fun is there?" Esme asked sarcastically.

"You are all a bunch of hypocrites. Every single one of your husbands graduated from an Ivy League school. And I can't help it; I'm an egghead. Discussing law or the classics is my idea of foreplay," India rebutted.

"Okay, don't spread that around," Monique warned.

"After a few years of marriage, you worry less about conversation and more about fornication," Esme pointed out. Monique held up a hand to bear witness. India chose not to probe and instead to address the matter at hand.

"Abby, I am a rainbow coalition dater. I just want someone who can accept me and all parts of my background," she explained.

"So you moved back here to shack up with white boy?" Monique asked.

"I said no. And can we please not refer to him as 'white boy'? What is wrong with you monoracial girls this afternoon?"

"You're lying to yourself. You did so move here to be with him," Abby corrected.

"No, I did not. In fact, I've just rented my own little place on 'Dancer's Row,' on Seventy-fifth Street between Amsterdam and Columbus."

"You didn't tell me," Abby commented, startled.

"I just signed the lease yesterday."

"So you're moving out of his place?" Monique asked, taking a large sip of her Bellini.

"Of course not. He doesn't even know about this apartment."

Esme and Monique looked at each other and erupted into simultaneous guffaws.

"What?" India asked, baffled by their amusement.

"You live with a man who has no idea you're renting a separate place?" Monique repeated.

"Can you spell l-o-v-e-r?" Esme teased, as she and Monique high-fived.

India shook her head vigorously. She'd seen enough cheating in her life not to try her hand at it.

"If it doesn't work out between Julien and me, I'm not spending six weeks on his couch while I look for another place," she explained.

"Ever the romantic," Abby quipped.

"Hey, you learn to take precautions when you grew up in a house where hurling plates at each other was the preferred way to say 'I love you.'"

"I just don't understand why you didn't marry Keith Wentworth," Monique said bluntly.

A hush fell over the table as India, suddenly pale, froze at the mention of her former fiancé. Though she had not moved back to New York to be with Julien, she had certainly taken a job in LA six years before to get away from Keith Wentworth, the most beautiful, brilliant man she'd ever known. No man before or since had given her as much pleasure or caused her as much pain. Abby and Esme glanced anxiously at her, but she stoically maintained a poker face.

"Did I say something wrong?" Monique ventured, noting the standstill to which she had brought the conversation. Once again, Esme and Abby looked to India to gauge her reaction. Their gentleness and obvious compassion helped to calm her. It was so comforting to be back among the women who knew her whole story and understood. In their presence, she felt protected, just as she had at Sibley.

"How did you know about Keith?" India asked Monique quietly.

"Who didn't know? It was the talk of the CNN," Monique answered.

"It was announced on the news? When? How did I miss that?" Abby wondered aloud.

"The Colored News Network, the bourgie grapevine," Monique corrected. "Plus Wayne is friends with Keith."

"How does he know Keith?" Abby pursued. Monique rolled her eyes.

"Through the bourgie social circuit," she said as if stating the obvious. "Most of the fabulous black people in this town know each other. And Wayne did the IPO when Keith's family spun off their processed-food business. He lives two blocks from here in that gorgeous new building, 15 Central Park West. In that place, seven million gets you the broom closet," she added.

"How is he doing?" India couldn't help but ask, taking a sip of her Merlot to wash down her emotions.

"He runs the biggest black-owned family business in America, didn't lose a dime in the economic downturn, and he looks like he just stepped off the cover of *GQ*. How do you think he's doing? A couple of weeks ago, he and Wayne played ball, so he stopped by the house all sweaty in his shorts and a T-shirt. You want to talk about body? Girl, I don't know how you passed that up."

"She had a really good reason," Abby asserted.

"I'm listening," Monique challenged.

India's mind resurfaced a memory she'd done her best to obliterate. She saw herself standing in the foyer of the Harvard Club, watching the fiancé she adored neck wildly with another woman: a blowsy, peroxide blonde, a poster girl for floozies. Unable to wrest herself from the spot, she had stood there for a full five minutes until at last Keith took the woman's hand and led her to the elevators. India had not laid eyes on him since the doors slid shut, and she'd called off the wedding. She didn't so much relive the moment as replay it in her mind's eye, and yet it was etched in her heart as the worst betrayal in a far from perfect life. For two years after the breakup, she'd refused to have so much as a cappuccino with a man. Eventually, her libido had gotten the better of her, and she had begun to date again, usually choosing the completely unsuitable (i.e., pea-brained personal trainers or bloodless neurotics) so as not to become attached. In the six years since she'd broken up with Keith, Julien was the first real "contender" for her heart.

As she looked up, she saw Abby, Esme, and Monique staring at her, waiting to hear what she would say. India decided to give an edited account of events.

"He cheated on me. Eight weeks before our wedding," she stated with equanimity.

"Is that all?" Monique deadpanned.

"All? Did you hear what I said?" India cried, then sat back, realizing she'd lost her cool and shown too much of her emotional hand. After all, though Monique had been charming all afternoon, she had turned India's school days into the Stations of the Cross.

"India, men lose their minds right before they get married. Half of them sleep with the stripper at the bachelor party. You can't give up Prince Charming Noir over that," Monique insisted.

"So you'd tolerate Wayne cheating on you?" India countered.

"Hell, no. But my Wayne is not Keith Wentworth. That man has it all. With a package that good, I could forgive."

"Well, then you're a more Christian woman than I am. I haven't spoken to Keith since. And I know I made the right decision." India downed the rest of her Merlot.

"I agree. He was too controlling for India," Abby concurred.

"Hey, control me, baby," Monique chanted.

"Oh please! That would never work. You're a successful doctor. Keith couldn't deal with that. He wasn't letting India be herself. He wanted her to speak less in public, dress less provocatively, wear her hair straight all the time," Abby added.

"Looks like she's doing that now. Why not have a five-carat, emerald-cut diamond and the prettiest man this side of Denzel Washington to go with all that dark, pressed, and lovely?"

"She wouldn't be happy," Abby answered.

"Who's happy in marriage? If you can't be happy, you might as well be fabulous. And I just don't want to see him go to a white girl. No offense, ladies." Monique drained her glass.

"If Tim cheated on me, I'd shoot him—after I chopped off his *cojones*," Esme offered, popping a black olive into her mouth.

"Interesting coming from you, Carmen," Abby quipped.

"Don't hate me because I'm beautiful and I'm not a prisoner of my marriage."

"My marriage is not a prison," Abby said.

"No comment. Check, please. Girls, this is on me. But I have to run." Esme jumped up and grabbed her calfskin envelope purse.

"Where's the fire?" Abby asked.

Esme motioned to the elevator bank, thirty yards away. In front of the elevators, the Actor/Model/Waiter from the ballet, now in jeans and a bomber jacket, paced nervously, scanning the room with a look of some desperation.

"The waiter finally brought me my steak. Hasta la vista."

With that, she threw down a wad of bills and strolled toward her awaiting paramour, hips swaying from side to side with the confidence of a woman with a PhD in giving orgasms. The Actor/Model/Waiter's face lit up at the sight of her, they stepped into an elevator and were gone.

Now India needed no longer suspect; she knew. With her usual delicacy, Abby had never told her. She remembered Esme's wedding and her husband Tim's loving toast. Under the scornful stares of Esme's haughty father, her long-suffering and heavily sedated mother, and their friends, austere representatives of New York and Cartagena society, this reserved all-American boy had risen to his feet and unabashedly declared that when he'd met Esme, he'd found his life's purpose: to love, cherish, and never seek to tame her. Abby and India had squeezed each other's hands under the table, thrilled that Esme had chosen an intelligent, caring man who would allow her to blossom and bask in the light of his warmth. Even flippant Esme had dissolved into tears at her new husband's words when he had described her as "the source of all hope in my life." India had believed in that moment that Esme had broken her family's cycle of accomplished heiresses marrying unfaithful heirs, and withering into luxuriously furnished misery and prescription-drug addiction. India never would have suspected on that auspicious wedding day ten years ago that Esme herself would become the cheater, running off for afternoon trysts with men she barely knew. The discovery depressed her utterly.

"She's bold," Monique said with admiration.

"She's nuts," Abby said under her breath.

"Is she just gonna rent a room? That's an expensive afternoon," Monique commented.

"Her father keeps a corporate apartment here," Abby answered in a tone that India recognized as meaning "Let this be the end of the discussion."

"I really should get back to the office and my life's work: helping women who picked the wrong men get the right divorce settlements," India said with false cheer, getting up.

"Here's my number. Keep in touch. I'd love to meet your new man. And Wayne would love to see you, even though you don't remember him," Monique offered sincerely, proffering her business card. India took it and gave Monique hers, more as a courtesy than out of any real intention of keeping in touch.

"And just so you know, I deal in high-risk pregnancies. I'll be glad to help you when you get around to it," Monique added with a wink. India smiled halfheartedly in response. This may have been Monique's attempt at humor, but India needed no more reminders from well-intentioned and not so well-intentioned people that if she didn't get a move on, she would soon be a candidate for a tabloid headline: "Sixty-year-old Lawyer Gives Birth to Healthy Twins and Lives."

Abby and India hugged.

"Home to homework for me," the former announced.

Once in the street, Monique dashed to the nearby subway station. India bid Abby farewell and started walking in the direction of her office on Park Avenue, but then did an about-face. Within moments she found herself standing in front of the neo–Emery Roth grandeur of 15 Central Park West. The building's limestone twin towers soared majestically toward a translucent sapphire sky. Every square inch of the imposing structure bespoke power, comfort, and wealth. She looked at the brightly lit picture windows in the dusk. *Which floor does he live on and with whom?* she wondered. *He isn't married. Monique had confirmed that. Why hasn't he wed? Is he a commitment-phobe or did her abrupt departure hurt him that much? What would have happened if she had taken just one of his calls or answered one of the half dozen letters he sent her after she left?* India stopped herself in midthought.

She could not allow herself to indulge in such speculation. In the distance, she saw someone she thought she knew. How embarrassing it would have been to be caught standing there, pining. She had wallowed in unproductive emotions long enough. She turned on her heels and walked in the direction of her office as fast as her crocodile pumps would take her.

# *chapter five*

While it was good to escape with the girls, Abby always loved coming home to face the divine chaos of her existence. Today, however, Abby couldn't understand the mild dread she felt as she stepped into the foyer of the Gothic revival apartment on Sixty-seventh Street that she and Nathaniel had occupied for fourteen of their sixteen years of marriage. It wasn't her son Benjamin's windbreaker carelessly tossed to the ground, or the jumble of rubber-soled children's shoes piled against the wall, or even the prospect of hours of homework. Perhaps it was spending an afternoon forgetting that she had four people and a dog to care for and answer to. While she pitied India's empty, lonely workaholic existence, only recently improved by the arrival of Julien, sometimes she envied India's empty, lonely workaholic existence. She longed for the tranquility that came with the accomplishment of finite tasks: helping a client, finishing a book, or even reading the Sunday *Times* from start to finish. Solitude often seemed a desirable alternative to the joyous but exhausting Sisyphean drill that was the lot of a wife and mother, even one with a nanny, a housekeeper, and a decent portfolio. Only time would tell if she had struck the correct balance between work and child-rearing, or whether, while her family's art gallery was thriving thanks to her efforts, her three little darlings would grow into rehab hoppers or, worse, the kinds of monsters on twenty-four-hour news channels: pale, disaffected youths who drove BMWs, wore excessive amounts of black eyeliner, and, utterly without warning, took up automatic weapons against their neighbors one bright day. It hadn't happened yet on the Upper West Side, but she didn't exclude the possibility.

"Daddy! Stop!" The screeches of her eight-year-old daughter Rachel roused her from her self-pitying "slough of despond." She crossed her double-height-ceiling living room into her white and yellow kitchen. There she found Nathaniel turning up the salsa music and dancing tauntingly as a tomato-sauce-splattered Rachel aimed at him with a plastic mustard container. She shook her head at the scene: it was classic Nathaniel. Like a madcap professor, he would go to any lengths to make his children laugh or teach them a new concept. In their house, every day was a "journey to adventures in knowledge." Whereas many couples argued over discipline and methods of child rearing, Abby and he were in total agreement: childhood should be utterly free and nothing short of magical.

"Come and get me, come and get me," Nathaniel dared the eight-year-old as she stalked him around the center island. He tossed back his straight blond locks as the youngest, Noah, cheered.

"Get him, Rachel, get Daddy."

"What is going on here?" Abby exclaimed, slamming her cell phone on the counter next to Nathaniel's and placing her hand on her hip in mock disapproval.

"Hi, Mom! We're having a fight!" Rachel answered, not looking at her.

"I'd say hello, but I'm being hunted," Nathaniel added, not breaking his gaze with his daughter.

"Want to join our team?" Noah asked, flashing a grin that revealed a neat row of pearl white baby teeth.

Benjamin, the eldest at eleven, briefly looked up from his Game Boy and uttered a perfunctory "Hi, Mom." A carbon copy of his father's haute WASP look, his genes had bypassed Abby's entirely, and landed squarely on Nathaniel's ancestral turf: Plymouth Rock.

"At least someone appreciates me. Thanks, Benjamin. So I thought you were making dinner, my love?"

"We were, but then we started talking about Jackson Pollock and here we are," Nathaniel explained.

"We went to the Museum of Modern Art today with the class," Rachel elaborated, still in stealth mode.

"I wanted to demonstrate how Pollock did his paintings," Nathaniel continued.

"He demonstrated on my face with the pasta sauce," Rachel added as she zeroed in on her father with the mustard container and squirted him right on the jaw.

"You got me! Game over!" Nathaniel cried. Rachel raised her arms in triumph, tossing her mane of blond corkscrew curls, and did a victory strut, followed by a chanting Noah.

"We win! We win!" Nathaniel high-fived his daughter. Abby grabbed a paper towel from the dispenser and crossed to wipe her husband's face. Before she could, he swept her into a hug and kissed her passionately on the lips. In spite of his incipient bald patch and the weaknesses of character, large and small, that had been revealed to her over the course of two decades together, every time he took her in his arms, Abby's heart was still in her throat. He hadn't been her first lover, but he was and would remain the best and most mesmerizing. From their first night together on a squeaky single bed in her college dorm room, he'd killed all desire and thoughts of other men. She still hungered for him as powerfully as she had the first time she saw him playing Frisbee on the quad. Even now, part of her couldn't believe that the greatest heartthrob of the Brown University campus had picked her, pursued her with all his might, and married her as soon as he could. She'd assumed at the time that he liked leggy Anglo-Saxon beauties with flat bottoms and symmetrical features, the sorts of girls who without a milligram of makeup looked as though they'd just stepped out of a Ralph Lauren ad. To her shock, he began flirting with her in a semiotics class. She'd never thought her grasp of French Deconstructionist theory would make her a man magnet, but in his case it had. And once she learned that beneath his bold, confident exterior he was a wounded little boy still reeling from his alcoholic father's physical and psychic blows, she vowed she'd never leave him. Life with him was essentially good, she reasoned, in spite of his temper. Her upbringing in an unabashedly loving family had given her the fortitude to deal with his emotional turbulence. Her steadfastness would heal him, eventually, she told herself.

"Where you been? I've been looking for you. You steppin' out on me?" Nathaniel teased with the swagger of a man who knew full well he was the undisputed master of his wife's G spot.

"You knew I was out with the girls today."

"All day?" he said, pointing to his rubber Swatch. "Did you have fun?"

"Yes, but it was a little depressing."

"Three hot chicks out on the town. Doesn't strike me as Prozac worthy."

"Actually it was four. I was Jimmy Carter, the idealist, among the 'marital real-politicians.'"

"'Nuff said. Your garden-variety bitchfest. Want to hear my news?"

"Daddy's going to be famous," Rachel squealed.

Abby's face brightened as she sensed what was coming: finally a break in Nathaniel's career which, after a promising start, had seemed for the last ten years permanently stalled in neutral.

"The Azarian Gallery wants to show my work."

Abby stood motionless and stunned. Nathaniel stared at her waiting for a response. Within moments, his shoulders rounded in a pose of childlike dejection.

"Don't you have anything to say?" he tossed out, masking his hurt in a tone of surliness.

"It's wonderful," Abby sputtered. "Azarian . . ." Abby absorbed the word. "The main gallery and not the annex?" she asked with genuine amazement.

"What's that supposed to mean?" Nathaniel challenged. Abby knew at once she'd pushed the wrong button.

"Nothing. It's just that Azarian is, well, this is really big," she explained, anxious to restore the situation and keep him from erupting.

Nathaniel's coloring went from pale to crimson as his fury mounted. His lower lip trembled.

"You don't think I'm good enough for my own show, do you?" He seethed. Benjamin looked up from his Game Boy, Noah and Rachel retreated to the corners of the room.

"I never said that," Abby insisted with the rote calmness of a woman who managed such outbursts with frequency.

"It's what you meant. You don't believe that one of the best galleries in New York wants to show my work?" he challenged.

"Nathaniel, come on," Abby pleaded, placing a hand on his arm. He ripped it away, turning his back on her. Benjamin started toward her protectively. Abby gave her eldest a reassuring wink and with a wave of her hand, indicated to him he should stay put.

"I always knew you would make it," Abby said soothingly to Nathaniel. "I'm your biggest fan. Your Constanza, Bernini." Nathaniel's shoulders relaxed and he smirked in spite of himself at Abby's mention of their youthful pet names for each other. He turned to look at her and tenderly brushed back the frizz crowning her head.

"Rome," he said softly.

"Rome," Abby repeated, as she did so she could picture the two of them at eighteen, bathing in the Bernini fountain at dawn because the dirt cheap *pensione* where they were staying had no running water. Nathaniel wrapped his arms around his wife. Rachel and Noah exchanged glances of relief and left their corners to cluster around them, circling them with their spindly arms. Only Benjamin stood aloof, leaning against the counter with a mistrustful scowl.

"I know it's beneath your sense of cool, but could you join the celebration?" Abby asked the adolescent. He reluctantly detached his lanky body from its post and went to stand beside her, limply adding his arms to the family embrace while avoiding eye contact with his father.

"Kids, your father really earned this. He's been working so hard on his sculptures. He never gave up his dream. And now it's coming true." Tears of joy for Nathaniel and relief for herself streamed down Abby's face.

"Yay, Daddy!" Noah cheered.

"Yay, Daddy!" Abby echoed, still emotional at the thought that some measure of financial success would alleviate his resentment of her ability to pay the bills.

"I'm going to go change and then open a bottle of wine. I think this calls for a Margaux," she cheered.

She happily grabbed her cell phone off the counter, raced up the stairs, and turned toward the master bedroom. As soon as she entered, her gaze fell on the sculpture Nathaniel had done of her to celebrate their first anniversary as boyfriend and girlfriend nearly twenty years before. Unlike all the rest of his work, which was abstract, it was a highly detailed realist rendering of her, naked at eighteen. He'd captured her completely, down to the last curl on her head, which was turned as if looking at something off on the horizon. He'd started the sketches for the piece during a trip with her and her family to their summer home on Fire Island. Her überliberal parents had allowed them to share a bedroom, and they'd spent a blissful week picnicking on the beach by day and feasting on her mother's *moules marinières* around the rectangular kitchen table at night. Everyone had embraced Nathaniel except her dad. Though he never openly expressed dislike, in Nathaniel's presence his usual exuberance turned to distance and reserve. As much as she adored her father, Abby chose not to seek his opinion. She didn't want him to shake the faith she had in this, the love of her life. Over the years, in moments of difficulty in the marriage, she turned to this bronze rendering of her younger self. Most women had nothing to remind them of the depths of their husbands' youthful passion for them, of the days of boundless hope. Abby had only to look at the sculpture to know that though it may have changed, the love she and Nathaniel shared was permanent and indissoluble. Of course, sometimes she wished her figure had held up to its youthful prototype. The bronze also served as cruel reminder of how the mighty breasts had fallen, but some battles against time were unwinnable. As she removed her blouse, she played the first message on her telephone.

She was surprised to hear her own voice: "Hi, honey, it's me. Just reminding you my mom is picking Noah up from school. I don't think I'll make it back to the office."

Realizing she grabbed the wrong phone, she was about to head back downstairs when the second message began. Abby heard two giddy female voices: "Nathaniel, where are you? We're here, naked, waiting." More giggles followed and a voice in the background urged, "Hang up."

Abby slammed the phone shut and sat motionless on her bed. *Perhaps it's just pranksters,* she rationalized. Teenage girls having fun. She and Esme had made their fair share of crank calls as schoolgirls. But how would these women have known Nathaniel's name? She'd never fully believed he'd been faithful, but she'd always hoped he was and had assiduously avoided looking too closely at incriminating evidence. *When would he have the time?* she wondered. *Between the children and working on his art and installing pieces for rich patrons?*

"Mommy!" Rachel called from downstairs, giggling. "Come down. Daddy's tickling me."

*Marriage is about compromise. You have to put water in your wine,* Abby reminded herself as she rose from the bed. Her mother had always told her, "Perfection is too much to ask from any human being." *How right Mom is,* Abby thought. She looked again at the statue. Their love was flawed, but it was permanent, she insisted to herself. As she reentered the kitchen to rejoin her family, they saw nothing but a radiant smile on her face.

# *chapter six*

India sat at her desk composing the annual divorce summons from her mother to her stepfather and swilling water from a bottle of Vittel. She took mock "puffs" from her pen as though it were a cigarette. When stressed, she found it comforting to mimic certain human vices while not actually indulging in them. Puffing on her pen kept her from her chocolate drawer. Her phone rang.

"India Chumley," she answered.

"Did you forget our rendezvous?" Julien's soothing voice asked.

India cringed. She had intended to phone and postpone, but in the rush of events, it had completely slipped her mind.

"I'm so sorry. I got sidetracked."

"No problem," he answered reassuringly. "When can I expect you?"

"In another hour and a half. I'm waiting for my pro bono client."

"Your mother?" Julien inquired.

"No, a real case. This is the only time she can meet me. Please don't hate me."

"How can I hate you when you're helping people? I'll see you when I see you."

With that, he hung up. His patience warmed India's heart. She'd never been with any man so selfless. She had certainly grown up with the polar opposite, Richard Blythe, Mr. All-About-Me-and-My-Thriving-Ego. Her stepfather raised narcissism to an art form and disappeared more effectively than Houdini. He had miraculously managed to miss her mother's bout with breast cancer, her own emergency appendectomy, and her grandfather's passing, among other domestic disasters. Other families marked the passage of the year with Thanksgiving and gatherings at Christmas. For India, her childhood years had revolved around her mother's opening nights and her stepfather's absences and epic returns. It was no wonder that Julien's reliability and evenness of temper unsettled her.

There was a knock at the door. India crossed and opened it. Before her stood Khadija Udoje, a tall, solidly built woman with skin as smooth as black velvet, large eyes that sparkled like jet beads, and the chiseled features of an Ibo.

"I'm sorry to be late," Khadija said, revealing blindingly white teeth. "Pretty," she added, seemingly suddenly self-conscious about her gaudy acrylic sweater and tight jeans in comparison with India's elegant suit. India smiled back warmly, trying to put her at ease.

"What is the situation?" India asked, indicating a comfortable chair.

"I waaant to deeevorce my husband," Khadija answered in the syllable-stretching accent of her native Nigeria. "He went home to Lagos for three months. On beesiness," Khadija continued.

"What is his business?" India inquired as she scribbled notes.

"Leather goods. Puuurses. He sells them to the peddlers. I can get you a nice Louis Vuitton. Not the real thing, but good quality. You see, instead of a *V* they put a *W*," she explained, hoisting a plastic "feed bag" onto the desk. India nodded politely as she looked it over. It screamed "cheap street copy."

"It's lovely," India said, lying to spare Khadija's feelings. "But I don't have any room left in my closet. Handbags are my addiction," she confessed.

"Mine too. Anyway, on his last visit home my husband brought back a souvenir."

"A disease?" India ventured delicately.

"A ghell."

"Another woman? She's in your home?"

"Not yet. She's still in Lagos, but he married her."

"That marriage is invalid. Bigamy is illegal," India reassured her.

"Not back home. You see, we have three children. All ghells. So he finds someone young to give him a boy."

India studied Khadija's unlined face. She surmised she was in her late twenties, thirty at most. If this woman was old, then India was a fossil. Thank God, she didn't live in Nigeria, they'd have exiled her to the Natural History Museum as an exemplar of "early woman."

India reached reflexively for the box of Kleenex she kept for these occasions. Holding her head higher, Khadija waved the box away.

"I'm not going to cry. I want to keel him," she insisted. India handed her a diminutive boxing glove on a stick and a plastic man's head.

"Have this instead," she suggested. An hour of pummeling this gadget had saved many a client from committing murder.

India began to explain to Khadija the standard procedure for a divorce. It was clear from Khadija's well-timed nods that she followed perfectly.

"And you stand to receive half of any . . . assets," India expanded, certain there wasn't much to divide, "given that you've been married eight years."

"What about my citizenship?"

India's hand froze above her legal pad. The case had just gone from simple to disastrous.

"You're not a US citizen?" she asked, hoping against hope she'd misunderstood.

"He is. And he has been helping me get my papers. But he says if I deevorce him, he will stop," Khadija explained.

"He can't do that if you're already in process. We just have to sue for divorce on the grounds of cruelty." India breathed a sigh of relief and prepared to resume taking notes.

"No. That man is not cruel. That man is good. He never put a hand on me or my babies!" Khadija cried, outraged.

India assured Khadija that she needn't be so literal. There was mental cruelty. Had Khadija needed to seek professional help or take prescription drugs? No sooner had India posed the question than she realized how absurd it was. She knew full well that this stolid citizen of the "motherland" had never ingested so much as a microgram of Xanax, Prozac, or Halcion. She probably thought they were Christian names. Such pharmaceutical lifelines were the purview of the Pilates-and-panini set. This woman would no more have taken antianxiety medication than she would have paid five dollars for a prosciutto sandwich the size of a postage stamp.

"We may need to do a psychological evaluation of you, Mrs. Udoje," India explained.

"I'm not crazy," Khadija insisted, appalled at the suggestion.

"I know. Psychiatrists treat all kinds of people. I go to one," India reassured her.

Khadija eyed her suspiciously.

India could tell she was sinking rapidly in her client's esteem. Psychiatry was anathema to people from traditional cultures. Even Nana Chumley failed to understand why one would confess one's deepest secrets to a stranger and pay him for the privilege. India never discussed her shrink with Nana at their monthly lunches.

"You don't need a head shrinker! You just need to eat more rice. You're too teeen," Khadija counseled. India was delighted that even after a chocolate binge she still registered on the slender side. She was instantly ashamed of this vain impulse, but she couldn't help it. It often occurred to her that she could win the Nobel Peace Prize, but if she was tipping the scale above 135, she would feel like an abject failure.

"Mrs. Udoje, we need to demonstrate that he's caused you distress."

"No. You will not put me on the Hoprah Winfrey show with those crazy women!" Khadija insisted.

"Is going back to Nigeria an option?" India asked, trying another tack.

"No way. My last two ghells were born here. I want them to grow up in this country, where they can get an education and a job," she declared, determined. "If I go, he won't let me take them. And the youngest is nine months. I'm still breast-feeding her."

"Mrs. Udoje, if you want a divorce and your citizenship, you have to divorce him on the grounds of cruelty," India insisted.

"No, I will not denounce the father of my ghells. What will my grandmother say?" Up until this point, India had been ready to shake her out of her old-world ways with a "You in America now" speech. "Here, Khadija is not the prophet Mohammed's first wife, she's a character in the sitcom *Living Single*," she would have said. The mention of a black grandmother halted her course.

"What's your grandmother's name?" India asked, softening.

"Queen Victoria Igbokwe. She waas born under British rule." India smiled with recognition of the colonized's habit of naming their children after their colonizers' historic heroes. All of her late father's West Indian relatives bore the names of nineteenth-century British parliamentarians and military leaders: there were Gladstones, Nelsons, and Wellingtons galore.

"Does your grandmother live here?"

"No. Back home. But I cannot do anything that will disgrace her," Khadija explained.

"I understand," India rejoined. And indeed she did. Nana's lessons dogged and guided her every step.

"This is my grandmother. Judge Lydia Braithwaite Chumley," India said, indicating the framed photograph.

"She's pretty, too," Khadija said pleasantly, then after a moment she added, "My situation is no good, right?"

"You're not in great shape," India admitted.

"I shouldn't have wasted your time. My ghellfriend told me it was hopeless because I don't have my papers."

"No, it's never hopeless," India reassured her. "I'm going to help you," she offered, not certain how she could but determined not to let this lovely woman flail about on her own.

"You can help me get my papers?" Khadija asked, jubilant.

"No. I'm not an immigration lawyer," India explained. At this, Khadija's face fell again. "But we will figure this out, I promise," India added, boosting Khadija's spirits.

"You work as a housekeeper?" India asked.

"Yes."

"Is there any chance your employer would sponsor you?"

Khadija laughed and shook her head. India needed no further explanation. She met daily with clients who paid more for a fur shrug than they did to the women raising their children. It was unlikely she could really do anything to help Khadija, but she had to do something to level the world's playing field. And occasionally there were miracles.

"All right then. For the moment, stay where you are. Do not leave the domicile," India advised.

"I have no other place to go," Khadija said evenly as she gathered her belongings. "Have a gooood night," she said graciously as she exited.

India headed for the library to look up "asylum." Julien and his home-cooked meal would simply have to wait.

# chapter seven

It was a quarter of eleven as India's cab turned onto Beach Street and stopped in front of the converted sewing factory that housed the apartment she now shared with Julien. Looking at the uninspiring lines of the industrial exterior, she thanked God she rented herself that little brownstone pied-à-terre. All this downtown hipness would kill her. In her mind, only a descendant of generations of family wealth, someone who never once had to entertain the thought of any family member dipping below the poverty line and into a cold-water flat, could possibly have found it chic to live in a neighborhood of former sweatshops and tenements. It was like tours of third world countries, thrilling when you never suspected that if your ancestor had not been hauled off on a slave ship, or endured the hardships of the immigrant, you'd be peddling souvenirs by the roadside along with the other disenfranchised natives. Julien was not descended from extraordinary privilege. He hailed from four generations of chocolatiers. But he possessed the innate French willingness to follow his passions, wherever they may have led him. *Yes, if this relationship has any future, we will eventually have to move,* India thought as she walked through the tall glass and steel entrance door.

The rosemary-infused scent of roasting fowl warmed up the spartan vestibule of their landing. India opened the apartment door and was surprised to find Julien chopping onions behind the counter. At the sight of her, he beamed. Seeing him standing there, a sage-colored sweater setting off the jade green of his eyes, his lips full with the promise of pleasures to follow the meal—she had to admit he was lovely. Every time she walked into a room and found him, she felt peace gently lapping over her like a warm Caribbean sea. But was that true love and was it enough to build a life upon? *Shut up,* she told her hyperanalytic mind. Using a technique recommended by her shrink, she envisioned shutting off her mind as simply as a cell phone at the theater and surrendering to the moment. The only slight problem, one she had chosen not to share with her shrink lest he think her truly crazy, was that she never actually turned off the phone entirely, even at night, during sex. She merely put it on vibrate.

"*Salut, beauté,*" Julien greeted her in a soothing tenor.

"I thought you'd be in bed," India commented, happy in spite of herself.

"I should be, but someone couldn't make it home in time," Julien responded with a tender laugh.

"I'm so sorry. I had so much work to make up for."

"Ah, doing penance. Are you sure you're not Catholic?"

"Pure heathen, I promise. I wish one of my other clients was Catholic or born again. She just blew her divorce deal sky high."

"*Cherchez l'amant?*"

"How did you know?"

"There's always a lover in these stories," Julien asserted.

"What's wrong with these women?"

"Everybody needs passion, India. Especially if they marry a checkbook."

"Well, it's not worth ruining your life or your divorce settlement for."

"My little pragmatist. If you don't take risks in life, you'll never really live it," he said, tenderly cradling her chin. She kissed the warm palm of his hand.

"Those sound like the lyrics of a bad song," she teased as he continued to mince a green onion. She watched his fingers move nimbly over the cutting board. He had the grace of a pianist playing a Chopin nocturne; after all, the kitchen was his domain.

Nine months ago, during one of her semiannual visits to New York, she fell in love at first bite with one of his culinary creations: a dark-chocolate bombe filled with the richest and lightest Valrhona mousse she'd ever tasted. After devouring two orders of the heavenly dessert, she'd asked to meet the chef. Knowing Julien would be pleased to make the acquaintance of such a beautiful fan, India's waiter guided her to the kitchen at the back of the restaurant. She'd watched him wrap veal loins in pancetta with the delicacy of one swaddling a baby. He looked up, saw her, and nearly tripped over his sous-chef as he strode across the room to meet her. India hadn't expected a chef as edible as his dessert. Even beneath his grease-stained chef's jacket she'd divined the lines of a lean, powerful torso. Suddenly nervous, she'd sputtered a few stilted words of praise, then turned to race out. He'd gently touched her arm and asked her to stay and have a nightcap. She'd declined, but he hadn't taken that no for an answer and made her promise to return the next night. Luckily, she kept her word—and found he'd closed down the restaurant and planned an eight-course meal. She'd been relieved he'd stuffed her with so much food. Feeling like a fatted calf prevented her from sleeping with him that very night. For months he pursued her transcontinentally, fly-ing out to see her in Los Angeles at every opportunity. His tenacity, charm, and chocolate had worn down her defenses and inspired her to give him a chance.

Now, as she inhaled the aroma of onions simmering in extra virgin olive oil, there was no question in India's mind that she was fortunate to have met this man.

"What are we eating?" she asked, primed for a satisfying meal.

"Your favorite. Risotto with white truffles." India salivated at the mere thought. Julien smiled, pleased. He'd gotten her in her sweet spot.

"What's the occasion?" India demurred suspiciously. "You're not going to propose again, are you?"

"I'll make a fool of myself for you, but sometimes a truffle is just a truffle. We had some extra at the restaurant. We also had beautiful *poussins,* which are now roasting in the oven so the rosemary and the Pinot Blanc can sink into their flesh. And then for dessert—"

"I can't have dessert. I cheated, on myself and on you, with a Lindt bar," India admitted as though confessing the darkest of deeds.

"Then I guess I'll have to toss my soufflé au chocolat noir with passion fruit crème anglaise into the garbage, or feed it to the neighbor's cat."

"Don't you dare," India scolded.

She found herself crossing to Julien's side of the counter and easing herself into the warmth of his cashmere embrace. He kissed her tenderly on the top of the head and nuzzled her neck. She reveled in the softness of his touch.

"Worry less and enjoy more," he whispered into her ear. She's heard this before.

Normally, she had a thousand retorts to offer, ranging from her economic circumstances to her responsibility to her people, whoever they were, unseen generations of black Americans, Caribbean Americans, and impoverished English Cockneys. For this night, though, for once, she just nodded her head in agreement.

"I'll be right back," she whispered as she slipped from his grasp.

Moments later, she returned from the bedroom clad in his favorite evening ensemble: a silk charmeuse teddy the color of a Burmese ruby and nothing else.

"Will the birds wait?" she asked coyly, knowing full well the reply.

Slack-jawed with desire, Julien shut off every burner and the oven and grabbed her. He kissed her as her eyes shut and she caressed his hair. Keith's face appeared in her mind's eye in all its symmetrical beauty and the cerulean blue eyes she could never quite read. Were they laughing with her or at her? She shoved Julien away.

"*Qu'est qu'il y a?*" he asked, confused.

"Nothing at all," she said, grabbing him and leading him to the bed-room, but for the remainder of the night, she knew that after six years in exile, Keith had taken up residence again in the corner of her mind, watching and mocking her newfound domestic bliss.

# chapter eight

As Esme descended the white-railed staircase of her brick Colonial home, she saw nothing but compromise all around her. The walls were papered in conservative blue Regency stripes where she would have chosen magenta. The floor was carpeted in sisal that scratched the soles of her bare feet, whereas she would have covered them in Persian rugs. This was a traditional Greenwich, Connecticut, investment banker's home. And she, to her frustration, was a Greenwich banker's wife. She had picked Tim because he had been the polar opposite of all the South American and European cads she'd grown up around. He was loyal, handsome, and he loved her. He'd made that clear from the first night he met her at a mutual friend's party ten years before, when they were both eager young professionals of the Neo–Gilded Age. Overall, she knew she'd made the right choice in marrying him. But some days this life and his straitlaced New England propriety made her want to run off with the first Euro-trash Lothario who honked his Ferrari horn at her. Her little extracurricular adventures quelled that urge.

This morning she hummed as she sauntered into the spacious kitchen of the home she loathed and found her husband and her children seated at the table, enjoying their cereal and pancakes. Her whole being was flush with the energy of the rolling orgasms she'd achieved the night before with her Actor/Model/Waiter. He had given new meaning to "service with a smile."

"So this is the percentage of people with college educations," Tim explained to eight-year-old Esme Junior as he indicated a pie chart in the *Wall Street Journal.* Esme the Elder knew her friends wondered how she could cheat on this handsome, well-built, kind, thoroughly decent lover. What they failed to understand was that cheating had little to do with the attractiveness of one's spouse. It was about danger, risk, the new, and the unknown. She took the same pleasure in flirting that others took in hunting. She spotted a stranger across a crowded room. Once she'd caught his attention, she looked away to lure him. He kept glancing back until finally he just stared. Each of them recognized the lust gleaming in the other's eye. Then came the moment of triumph: he walked over, proffering his telephone number hastily scribbled on a scrap of paper. Sometimes she called, often she didn't, but the chase never failed to arouse her.

Any man grew dull when you lived with him day after day, seeing his foibles, smelling his farts. The finest foie gras grew dull to the palate if eaten every night, with the same Sauterne, on the same slice of lukewarm brioche. Variety was indeed the spice of life, especially variety of the sexual kind. Esme's little escapades brought freshness to her domestic life. Rather than weaken her marriage, they strengthened and renewed her commitment to her vows, she reasoned. Besides, if you let a man believe he had fully conquered you, you would end up the cuckold many times over, as her mother had. Esme had no intention of spending her life clinging to the twin consolation prizes of guilt jewelry and her own respectability while the humiliation of betrayal sucked the very marrow from her bones.

When she was eleven, Esme had accidentally found her usually emotionless mother sobbing on her knees in her walk-in closet, while clutching the Verdura Maltese Cross bracelet her husband had just given her. At that moment, Esme realized that new jewels heralded the ascendancy of a new mistress. Her father had given the precious pieces not as tokens of love, but as offerings tossed at the feet of a martyr to purchase indulgence for his sins. As she watched her mother convulse with sorrow, Esme vowed that she would never submit to such a fate or accept jewels from any man. Her father's philandering taught her that in marriage, a woman must always keep one stiletto-clad foot firmly out the door and her husband guessing. It was the only way to bind them to you, the only way to survive.

Little Esme looked up from the paper in amazement at a miraculous vision: her mother fully clothed before noon.

"Mama!" four-year-old Julio exclaimed with all the wonder of a believer witnessing an apparition of the Blessed Virgin.

"What are you doing up? It's only seven thirty! Is something wrong? Are you sick?" Little Esme asked with furrowed brow. Her mother tossed back her head and laughed.

"You act like I've never come to breakfast before," she chided.

"You haven't!" Julio exclaimed.

"Out of the mouths of babes," Tim commented with an amused smirk.

"Well, be grateful. At least I'm not boring," Esme scoffed as she poured herself a cup of coffee with cream and ladled in heaping teaspoons of sugar. "You know, you are all very lucky. You could have a mommy who thinks this stupid little corner of Connecticut is the center of the world, a woman who wakes up at five AM, packs your sandwiches, and drives you to school every day the same way, but she would be dull, and have no imagination, and always be in a bad mood."

"You're in a bad mood sometimes," Little Esme said sweetly.

"Well, not today," her mother responded, pulling her son onto her lap and stroking his hair as he caressed her neck.

"You got home late last night," Tim said, neatly folding his napkin. "I didn't even hear you come in."

Esme flinched for a moment but quickly recovered and instantly went on the charm offensive.

"No, and I even tried to wake you," she purred, leaning in seductively and caressing his thigh under the table. Tim struggled to contain his arousal. "But it was useless," she added, pulling away, and then challenged, "Maybe you'll be more alert tonight."

"Probably. Will you be home?" Tim said. Esme searched his hazel eyes for the answer. Did he know? Did he even suspect? In a year's worth of escapades, he seemed, much to her irritation, not to have noticed. He'd never directly confronted her. It only encouraged her to take greater risks, almost as a dare to his naïveté. It would have excited her if for once he let his rage fly and stopped being so damned civilized and contained. But it wasn't in him. He wasn't a high WASP like Abby's husband: he hailed from petit bourgeois aspiring WASPs. They did everything to be correct. Her father had been right; it took an aristocrat to have bigger-than-life emotions.

"Where else would I be?" she responded, throwing down the gauntlet and waiting for him to react, but he merely continued reading his paper.

"How did you do on the history presentation I helped you with?" she asked her daughter, by way of changing the subject.

"Miss Benson said it was very good, except the part about the Native Americans being the victims of genocide."

"That was the most important part!" Esme cried. "And it's completely true. Miss Benson needs to learn the history of her own people. Frankly, your Spanish conquistador ancestors did the same thing in South America. When they weren't shooting *indios*, they were raping them—"

"What's rape?" Julio interrupted innocently.

"Let's talk about something else," Tim suggested, glaring at his wife.

"They have to learn about reality at some point. I don't believe in all this sweeping under the rug, like your family," she said defiantly.

"You're right. Instead of sending him to preschool today, let's see if there's a seminar on the minds of serial killers," Tim answered sarcastically.

"Well," Esme answered, chastened, "at least I'm going to talk to that

Miss Benson and tell her she has a lot of nerve correcting my daughter for speaking the truth."

"No, you will not go to Esme's school and speak to Miss Benson. Remember what happened the last time?"

"They were mean to have those guards carry you out of the classroom, Mommy!" Little Esme said, indignant at the memory of her mother's "maltreatment."

"Thank you, *mija*." Esme stared at Tim, seething.

Zulma, the permanently stooped Colombian housekeeper, appeared in the doorway to the kitchen.

"*Perdón, señora, llego el* 'carpool.'"

"*Gracias.* Okay, mi amors, time to go to school. I'll see you later. *Dame un beso.*" The children clutched her in a passionate embrace.

"Mami, how come you never drive the car pool?" Julio asked.

"Mrs. Smithers says it's because you're too busy getting your nails and hair done," Little Esme added. Her mother took a deliberate sip of her coffee before commenting.

"Does she? Maybe she should get her hair done from time to time, and her husband wouldn't be having an aff—"

"Esme!" Tim scolded.

"I told her you didn't need to get your hair done because you are always beautiful," Little Esme declared proudly.

"Thank you. Thank you again. *Te quiero.*"

Zulma gently herded them toward the door. Esme whipped around to face her husband.

"Don't silence me in front of my children. What are they supposed to think of women when you do that?"

"What are they supposed to think of women when you start telling them about the neighbor having affairs? You're out of control, Esme," Tim responded, keeping his frustration in check.

"Oh, I'm sorry. I guess I should walk around saying 'yes, dear, no, dear' while I hold your slippers in my hand."

"Actually, I'd rather you had them in your mouth as you sat up on all fours," Tim said breaking the mounting tension. Esme smirked. *At least there's some fight left in him,* she thought. *He hasn't completely shut down.*

"You'll have to find someone else to be your little doggie, I'm going back to work. I'm up for some banking jobs." She smiled as she delivered the coup de grâce. Tim looked at her, stunned and wounded.

"When did you decide this?" he asked, incredulous.

"I started interviewing three weeks ago. But I've been thinking about it since Julio was born. For the past year, you've been telling me how bad the market is. You should be happy. Now you can stop complaining," she tossed out, thrusting her chin forward.

"And when exactly were you going to tell me? Or were you going to email from your new office?"

"You just want me barefoot and pregnant in this kitchen!" she yelled.

"No, actually I want you as far away from this kitchen as possible because you can't cook and, for the record, I prefer you in heels."

Esme was about to laugh when her cell phone rang. She froze, knowing that at that hour it could only be her most recent lover. She decided to ignore the call.

"Are you going to answer that?" Tim asked.

"No!" she snapped.

"What if it's the children?" he pursued.

"It can't be. They just left for school."

"Whoever it is wants to reach you. You should answer."

"Stop telling me what to do!" Esme screamed at the top of her lungs. They both stood, looking at each other for a moment in the wake of her explosion.

"Where the hell did that come from?" Tim asked, bewildered by the magnitude of her rage.

"It comes from the fact that I'm tired of you trying to turn me into the little Connecticut housewife of your dreams. I'm not one of those blond robots in a badly cut Talbots dress. And I'm certainly not your mother," she added to stoke his fury.

"Don't talk about my family," he warned her. While she respected him for not disowning his family, she wished he would join her in loathing them for their small-mindedness, pettiness, and prejudice.

"Why not? They talk about me. Don't they call me 'the spic'?" she taunted, using one of her classic techniques of dredging up other people's sins of the past. She knew full well it was reprehensible, but she couldn't resist hitting Tim's hot buttons.

"This is not about them," Tim answered defiantly. "This is about us! I'm trying to reach you. And sometimes you make it very hard. I don't want to stop you from going back to work, but we're supposed to be a team. I have a right to know what's going on with you." Esme looked away from him. She hated it when he was so calm and reasonable. Her sense of drama required someone who yelled as loud as she did. Tim was woefully miscast in the telenovela of her life.

The phone rang again. She bristled, then busied herself by leafing through the newspaper and ignoring both the phone and Tim as he tried to make eye contact with her.

"See you tonight," Tim said, as he kissed her on the forehead like one would a pouting child and exited.

Feeling genuine regret for her outburst, Esme started to go after him. Pride and a spite she herself didn't understand stopped her in her tracks. She tried for a moment to summon her sense of maturity and follow the pull of decency but instead turned to pick up her cell phone. She pressed the voicemail button and heard, "You have two new messages. First message: 'Hey, Esme, it's me. I just had to talk to you. Um, let me know when we can get together again. I have a pretty open week. Not a lot of jobs, fortunately or unfortunately,'" the Actor/Model/Waiter's voice said with an embarrassed chuckle. "I have to see you," he continued, his voice cracking slightly. Esme played the next message: "Hey, Esme, me again. Don't mean to bug you, but last night changed my li—"

Esme pressed the delete button and took a satisfied sip of coffee. For all his exasperation, her husband still adored her. Soon she'd be working in a city teeming with hundreds if not thousands of potential conquests of different ages, shapes, and sexual techniques. She planned to sample one or two, or a few, like an oenophile savoring the world's finest wines. She pitied girls like Abby, who clung to their virtues and those unrealistic marriage vows. "Forsaking all others"—ridiculous! How can any human being forsake fun for their entire adult life? *Girls who stay true to their marriage vows just don't know what they're missing,* she rationalized as she inhaled the aroma of her dark Sumatra roast.

## *chapter nine*

Every Monday morning at 9:00 AM, Abby and a half a dozen other upper-middle-class mothers and their children gathered at the West Sixty-seventh Street YMCA for Free to Be a Prodigy, a fashionable music class for the under-five set. Such enrichment classes were considered de rigueur for any self-respecting upwardly mobile New York toddler's formation. They had the added advantage of affording the mothers an excellent opportunity to gossip. Abby sat on the "mothers' side" of the bright yellow classroom, watching Noah and the other four-year-olds bang away enthusiastically on assorted drums and tom-toms.

"Half beats," their tall, broad-shouldered teacher, Sage, instructed. The children instantly obeyed, some keeping time with their fellows, others banging to a different beat. To her great annoyance, Abby was the only mother paying attention to the children's progress. She looked over at three others engaged in a New York alpha mom's favorite competitive sport: my-kid-is-smarter-than-your-kid one-upmanship.

"Sofia's ERB scores were off the charts. But Sanjay and I knew they would be," boasted Daria, a diminutive Indian woman with the clipped delivery and the drive of a four-star general. "We gave her drills every morning over breakfast. And of course, she's been doing puzzles since she was five months old."

"Mason got the highest test score in the history of her preschool," countered Liz, a washed-out brunette with a powerful lower jaw that bespoke smugness.

"When was her preschool founded?" Daria challenged.

"In 1966," Liz responded with a patronizing smile.

"Sofia solved the Rubik's Cube at two and a half. Her teachers think she may be a genius," Daria said, not to be bested.

"That's nothing," Abby interjected. "Last night my Noah solved the problem of cold fusion—in our toilet bowl."

Daria and Liz looked at her bemused, not certain if she was serious. Her humor was always lost on these inveterate climbers determined to bypass all other mothers and their offspring on the superhighway to New York private school glory.

Sage looked across the room and smiled at Abby.

*At least someone gets the joke,* she thought to herself. Ever since taking Nathaniel's cell phone by accident, she'd done her best to pick up her spirits by the bootstraps.

Undeterred by her interjection, Liz and Daria continued their verbal fencing match.

"Sofia's interview at Sibley is next week."

"Mason's is Friday. And our neighbor's girls go there. They've already sent a letter of recommendation."

"Sanjay's boss is on the board," Daria let drop.

"Careful what you wish for. I went to Sibley. I made good friends, but I'd never send my daughter there," Abby interjected.

"Why not? It's one of the best prep schools in the country."

"Yeah, it does a great job of preparing girls from uptight families for eating disorders, neuroses, and Valium addiction. Now, could we please listen to our children play music?" Abby begged. Liz and Daria put down their swords momentarily to join forces in a scowl of disapproval.

"It's okay, Mrs. Adams, this session of Free to Be a Prodigy is over. But next week, moms, please do respect the process. Values are caught, not taught. If you're good listeners, your children will be, too.

The only rule in this class is, Silence is golden, unless you're holding an instrument."

"Speaking of which, how much longer are you going to focus on these percussion instruments? I mean, I never heard of anyone getting into school because they know how to bang on a bongo," Daria protested.

"Mrs. Praterjee, I'm here to help your child understand the rudiments of music so she has something to enjoy for the rest of her life. I can't get her into Harvard for you."

"Well, that's it. I'm quitting the class," Abby joked.

"Sofia, come on," Daria snapped. "You have Mandarin in twenty minutes."

"I love the bongo," Noah exclaimed, beaming as Abby helped him with his coat.

A razor-thin sixty-five-year-old woman entered. Dressed in Levi's and a turtleneck, she had the runner's body, erect carriage, and zest for life of a woman half her age. Her long salt-and-pepper hair hung in a single braid down her back. Noah ran to her.

"Nana!" he exclaimed, jumping into her arms. She gave him a loud kiss on the cheek.

"There's Grandma's baby," she gushed. Abby was as pleased as her son to see her mother. She was the sort of confident, loving, optimistic person who made you believe that even if everything went to hell in a handbasket, in the end it would turn out all right. Abby strived daily to follow her mother's open, radiant example. Some days she succeeded better than others.

"Nice to see you, Sage," Eleanor Rosenfeld said, flashing him her trademark "life is beautiful after all" smile.

"Hi, Mrs. Rosenfeld," Sage answered, charmed by this frequent visitor to his classroom. Her calmness was a welcome counterpoint to the manic competitiveness of the caffeine-charged alpha moms.

"You would have been proud of your grandson today," Abby commented as she leaned to kiss her mother on the cheek.

"I'm always proud of both of you. So I'll see you back at the house tonight," she said. "Come on, big boy, let's get on the bus."

"Yay, we're taking the bus," Noah cheered.

"I'll walk you guys to the stop," Abby offered.

Suddenly she felt Sage's hand on her arm.

"Actually, Mrs. Adams," he said hesitantly.

"Please, call me Abby. When you call me Mrs. Adams, I feel like the original founding mother," Abby chided. Though behind the joke was the fear that she was beginning to look as haggard as her Revolutionary War namesake.

"Abby," he repeated. "I wanted to speak to you, privately."

"Sure," she responded, taken aback and plunking her overstuffed tote at her feet.

"Actually, not here, I was thinking we could grab a cup of coffee downstairs." Now she was truly confused and slightly intrigued.

"Oh." Abby pulled out her BlackBerry and quickly scanned her agenda. "Yes, I have a few minutes before I have to get to the gallery."

Abby's mother smiled at her conspiratorially. Abby wondered at her mischievous expression but hadn't time to question.

"Baby, I'll see you when I get home from work tonight," Abby said, kneeling to button Noah's jacket.

"Okay, Mommy," he answered. With those words, Noah bounded out of the classroom, holding his grandmother's hand.

"I just need to grab my stuff," Sage said awkwardly, running a hand through his auburn locks.

"No problem, I'll wait by the elevator," Abby responded cheerfully. She looked forward to having a moment to catch her breath.

She pulled a well-worn copy of *Middlemarch*, her favorite novel, out of her bag. She'd first been enthralled in a literature class at Sibley at sixteen by this saga of the brilliant, socially committed Dorothea Brooks, who marries an emotionally distant intellectual. Every few years she'd reread it, discovering a different significance each time. She'd picked it up again recently and, for the first time, had begun to see herself in the unfulfilled heroine. In years past, the fact that Dorothea's husband was old and sexually arid had obscured for Abby the parallels to her own situation. And of course, Abby was not crinoline-clad landed gentry in nineteenth-century England. She was a twenty-first-century working mom who shopped at Bloomingdale's. Yet the isolation of living with a resentful, tortured man whose every glance seemed like a reproach echoed her own feelings of late. She shuddered slightly as she read:

> But Dorothea remembered it to the last with the vividness with which we all remember epochs in our experience when some dear expectation dies, or some new motive is born. Today she had begun to see that she had been under a wild illusion in expecting a response to her feeling from Mr. Casaubon . . .

Abby reflected that her marriage to Nathaniel had begun, like his career, with such high hopes. In spite of the lovely moments, and his excellence as a father, sixteen years' worth of disappointments were slowly exhausting her faith and optimism. Though she was soldiering on, her recent discovery of his dalliance, or dalliances, was the final blow to her youthful illusions.

"Are you ready?" Sage asked. Abby looked up from her paperback to see him, satchel in one hand, leather jacket in the other flashing a welcoming smile. He held the elevator door open for her.

"After you," he said, bowing slightly.

"You're young to be so chivalrous," she commented, bemused at the treatment.

"I'm not that young, Mrs.—" He caught himself.

Abby smiled. "Abby."

"How old are you?" she asked, now truly intrigued at his motivation for asking her out.

"I'll be twenty-eight next month."

"That's young. But I thought you were even younger, maybe it's the dashikis."

"One of the reasons I love teaching music is I never have to wear a suit."

"I've got a husband like you."

"I know," Sage answered. Abby looked at him quizzically; he'd never even met Nathaniel. They walked out of the building and a few steps to the local Le Pain Quotidien, one of a chain of coffee houses built to have the rustic feel of a French country bakery with distressed mocha brown walls and large loaves of peasant bread displayed in linen-lined baskets. They settled at a wooden table by the window.

Moments later, Abby nestled a white porcelain bowl between her hands and savored the scent of the steaming brew.

"Mmmmm, is there anything better than the smell of a bowl of café au lait?" she asked. "I think they should make a perfume of it." Sage laughed.

"What did you study, in college?" he asked.

"English literature. Why?"

"Just curious. How did you end up running an art gallery?"

"That's simple. It's my family's. It's actually a tradition. My grandfather came to New York from Berlin in 1933. Right after Hitler came to power. Grandpa had read *Mein Kampf* and thought it would be a good idea to get out of Dodge."

"Smart man."

"He dealt in Old Masters paintings in Europe and just moved the business here. My father started in it and then discovered American art. And a little thing that came to be known as pop art. Grandpa thought pop was nothing but a bunch of vulgar cartoons, totally unworthy of representation in a gallery, so Daddy split off and started his own. But why am I telling you all of this?" She looked down into her cup and wondered when Sage would come to the point, whatever that was.

"Because I'm interested," Sage answered, looking her directly in the eyes. Startled by his answer, Abby prattled on.

"Well, I hadn't planned to join the business. I wanted to be a comparative lit professor but—"

"But what?"

"Life happened while I was making other plans. It's not my passion, but it's gratifying helping other people find theirs, in terms of the art they collect," Abby philosophized.

"Why is it so many women do that?" Sage asked.

"Do what?"

"Trash their own dreams to make everyone else thrive. It's not fair," Sage objected earnestly. Abby knew she couldn't ponder the truth of his words for too long or she'd dissolve into tears.

"Life isn't fair, Sage," she said evenly. "And who am I to complain? I have a lot to be grateful for, and I enjoy what I do."

"What about your husband?"

"What about him?"

"Isn't he an artist? He's doing what he wants to do."

Now Sage was hitting far too close to home.

"Sage, what is it you wanted to tell me about Noah?" she shot back, wanting to bring this tête-à-tête to a close, and to let him know his questions were out of line, if completely accurate.

"Nothing, actually," Sage bowed his head bashfully and picked at the golden cheese muffin he'd left uneaten on his plate.

"So why are we having coffee?" Abby asked, feeling unsettled.

"You want the truth?"

"Yes, why are we here?"

"I just really wanted a chance to talk to you. You're the nicest person I've met since I came to New York." His candor utterly disarmed her. She sat back stunned and, she had to admit, flattered. The music school strongly discouraged fraternizing between "faculty" and parents. It was a means of avoiding lawsuits and tamping down the neurotic mothers' innate "helicopter tendencies." Abby knew Sage was taking a risk by inviting her. Suddenly, she was eager to know more about the beautiful young man who seemed to take an interest in her. She allowed herself to take the full measure of his splendor, from his long, thick auburn hair, to his large hands and smooth alabaster skin. She'd never noticed the perfect cleft in his chin or how invitingly broad his shoulders were. Most arrest-ing of all were his eyes, which struck her as the very picture of Shake-speare's "windows of the soul." This soul was warm, honest, and kind.

"You're from Seattle, right?" she asked, trying to seem nonchalant.

"Yeah. It's nothing like this place. And you're different from all the other moms. They don't care about the music or the class. They just want me to turn their kids into—"

"Little prodigies. It is the name of the course," Abby said, complet-ing his sentence and noticing for the first time how large and mag-nificent his hands were. She told herself to stop immediately. This boy was young. He probably just wanted someone to talk to in the big bad lonely city. He wanted a big sister.

"That's the problem. People here are so busy 'achieving,' they have no concept of how fortunate they are, how fortunate we all are. I spend a lot of time in Africa—"

"That seems to be the trend these days," Abby chided good-na-turedly. Each generation had its bleeding-heart cause. For hers it had been the "living wage" for blue-collar workers.

"I've been going for seventeen years. My parents were missionaries. I'm not, but I've kind of followed in their footsteps."

Abby was taken aback by this information. Perhaps Sage wasn't just another starry-eyed idealist content to live on a do-gooder's salary until he met the girl upon whom he wanted to bestow a De Beers diamond.

"That's cool. Where have you been?" she asked, genuinely intrigued.

"All over: Eritrea, Tanzania, Congo, Benin. It just boggles my mind when I compare the conditions for most kids over there with what we have here."

Abby absorbed the comment. She hadn't heard such idealism ex-pressed since she sat in her college dining hall. And Sage was hardly a wide-eyed student. He was quite clearly a man. She took a gulp of her café au lait.

"Sage, you probably don't need or want the help, but there's a really cute girl who works at the gallery—"

"I don't want you to fix me up, Abby," Sage answered, cutting her off and looking her straight in the eye with more than teacher-to-parent interest. She pushed her chair back and crossed her arms, as if to deflect his erotic energy.

"Oh. Okay. Just trying to help," she said.

"Just sitting here is helping." Again, Sage looked directly into Abby's eyes. She found herself looking away, slightly flustered by the intensity of his gaze.

"I'm doing a concert in a couple of weeks," he added as he reached into his satchel and handed her a flyer. "Maybe you could stop by. If you have the time." Suddenly he rose and dropped some bills on the table.

"This is for the check. I've got to head back to the school. Thanks for having coffee with me." He leaned down and quickly pecked her cheek, then dashed out quickly on his long limbs.

Once he'd vanished from sight, Abby sat alone at the table. *What on earth just happened?* she wondered. She rose and walked out. After she took a few steps down Sixty-fifth Street, it dawned on her: she'd just had a date. Could that handsome young guy, ten years her junior, really have been looking at her with desire? She stopped and studied her reflection in the large window of the coffee house. She had great big blue eyes, and there smack in the middle of her face, a nose the shape of a giant Planters peanut. She looked fine, for her age. Thirty-seven. And married. She gently caressed her right cheek, the cheek Sage had pecked. Suddenly, she felt like Madame Olenska to his Newland Archer in *The Age of Innocence* or Dorothea to his Will Ladislaw. The thought rattled her and at the same time, it gave her a greater lift than the caffeine. Men still looked at her as an object of desire, not some product about to reach its sell-by date in the remainder bin at Sloan's Supermarket. Abby did a sudden U-turn on this mental road. May-October pairings happened in novels, not on Tuesday mornings on the Upper West Side to a nearly middle-aged woman whose husband might have been cheating on her. She hailed a taxi to the office and back to reality.

# chapter ten

As India jogged up the steps of the Fifty-first Street subway station, her phone let off a peal of church bells. It was her fifth call from Lucinda Diamond since she'd left the courthouse twenty minutes earlier. Reluctantly, she slid the bar and answered.

"India Chumley!"

"Where've you been? I have an emergency here!" Lucinda screeched at ear-splitting decibels.

"What happened?" India asked in the soothing tone nursery school teachers use to calm hysterical toddlers.

"I'm standing here at Chanel, trying to buy my suit and they're telling me my black card is canceled. Canceled! That munchkin schmuck! I want his balls on a silver platter, do you hear me? We're taking him to court!"

"Lucinda, this is just the reaction he wants from you. He's trying to scare you. You could put an end to it all by doing a few weeks of counseling."

"No way."

"It's one way of calling his bluff."

"I am not a drunk!"

"You know that and I know that, but sometimes you have to play the game. Lose the battle, win the war."

"Right now, I just want my suit. You tell my saleswoman I'm good for it," Lucinda demanded.

India had negotiated for many things in eleven years of handling divorce cases: second homes, yachts, even a lava lamp. This was a first for a bouclé suit.

"Lucinda, don't put the saleswoman on the line . . . Hello, Madeleine. Yes, I do understand your situation. Perhaps you could put the suit on hold . . . I realize you have a waiting list. Just for a day or two until we get Mrs. Diamond's situation sorted out. Thank you, Madeleine, I owe you. May I speak to my client? Lucinda, think about it."

"I don't need to think about the suit. I need it!"

"I mean going to court. You've got a lot more to lose there. Lucinda . . . Lucinda."

Lucinda had hung up. India had gone into law to help womankind, now she was pleading for designer suits. She looked down at her own Chanel jacket. She admitted to herself that losing the perfect purchase could drive any sensible woman over the edge. She tossed her phone back in her purse.

Through the window of San Pietro's, or Saint Pete's, as the regulars called it, she spotted Monique seated alone at a table in the very center of the room, ogling prey for all the bankers having power bruschetta at noon. She entered the revolving door and was greeted by the owner, Alberto, who bowed and perfunctorily kissed her right hand, as well-bred Italians did.

"*Buon giorno, signorina*," he said as though she came there every day.

"*Per favore*, must we be right in the middle of the room?" India asked as he led her to the table.

"I am following Ms. Sarmiento's express instructions," Alberto insisted with a smile and bow before withdrawing to tend to those who really counted in the New York restaurant world: his wealthy male patrons.

"Well, Miss Thing, you're on time. How can Esme be late to a lunch she's hosting?" Monique asked.

"Get used to it. Esme runs on *hora latina*."

"Oh, their version of CP time. Okay."

Monique chuckled, then pointedly said, "I'm just glad I finally get to see you. You've dissed all my invitations."

"I don't go out much. I'm a pathetic workaholic," India offered awkwardly, knowing full well Monique's accusation was accurate. She had avoided seeing her since the day of the ballet lunch and was not entirely pleased Esme, the pied piper, had chosen to include her in this get-together. Though Monique seemed to have mellowed, India's mistrust lingered. Just as it was impossible to forget one's first crush, it was impossible to forget one's childhood bullies. In spite of Monique's newfound kindness and polish, India could look into her eyes and still see the angry adolescent in beaded braids who scowled whenever she passed by and taunted her for not joining Sibley's Black Student Association, which had a grand total of five members. In an effort at reconciliation, their freshman year India had ventured into the cramped top-floor classroom where the group met. Four heads turned in unison to stare at her as Monique, the president of the group sneered, "What are you doing here?" India herself wondered, she grew nervous, as much an outsider to this group as she was to the "We winter in Lyford Cay and summer in Southampton" set. "I just wanted to see what you were all about," she stammered. Several girls snickered and whispered to each other while pointing at India's unruly coif.

"What do you think this is, remedial blackness? If you don't know what you are, we can't teach you," Monique had taunted. And with that, the girls turned their backs to her and continued their discussion. India was about to leave, but seized by her mother's "bugger them" spirit, she walked straight to the center of the room and recited Maya Angelou's "Still I Rise," which Nana had taught her, at the top of her voice. It was a ludicrous but effective gesture. When she finished, the girls sat in stupefied silence. India the mealy-mouthed mulatto had never stood up to tough-talking Monique, and who knew that she read black authors? As the girls looked to their leader to see how to react, Monique had bitten her lower lip in frustration. "So you know some poetry," she spat. "Good for you. Now get out." India turned on her heels and left, satisfied that though she was an oddball and the "authentic sistahs" laughed at her, no one could ever accuse her again of being confused about her identity or lacking pride in her black heritage. In spite of countless similar incidents during their youth, India felt obligated today to compensate for snubbing her erstwhile enemy.

"If you don't believe I'm a workaholic, ask my shrink," she continued.

"You're in therapy?" Monique asked scornfully. "You *are* a white girl."

"There you go again!" India said, only half-joking.

"Aha, now I know why you've avoided me. It's because I was a bitch to you when we were at Sibley, isn't it?" Monique challenged.

"Actually, yes," India admitted, stunned by Monique's bluntness.

"I'm sorry," Monique tossed out.

"You're forgiven," India granted, not entirely sincerely. "But what was your problem?"

Now Monique shifted uncomfortably. In Monique's reticence, India recognized her own hatred of revealing her hand lest someone else took advantage.

"I was scared. I hated that place." After a few seconds, Monique added sheepishly, "And you had everything."

"Oh yeah, that was me, the girl who had it all: a dead biological father, two certifiably insane parents, and the hairdo of a Troll doll," India joked, nonetheless touched by Monique's frank admission of jealousy.

"You knew how to act around those girls. And they were interested in you. They couldn't even remember my name. I might as well have been invisible, until I got into Princeton."

"I was an exotic curiosity to them, like a *National Geographic* photo come to life," India reassured her.

"But you went to their parties, and they included you in those Knickerbocker cotillions."

"Where I usually danced with the instructor's gay son because none of the mothers wanted me anywhere near their little fair-haired druggies. And by the way, can we stop this? We're old, and this is ancient history," India insisted.

"Yeah, it is. So can you forget the bitch that I was and see the fabulous person I've become?"

"I'll try," India conceded. It was comforting to discover that someone else walked the same rocky path. India knew only a handful of people who understood the world that shaped her. She felt a bond with every woman who attended Sibley in her form, even those she hadn't liked. Perhaps Esme had done her a favor by inviting Monique. With youthful insecurities behind them, perhaps they could form a friendship based on mutual respect and shared experiences.

"So how is it for your girls at Sibley?" India asked, genuinely interested.

"Fabulous. Sibley's so proud to have them, they think they have their own Sasha and Malia," Monique explained. "Wayne and I work day and night so that our girls can grow up and say, 'Kiss my rich, Ivy-educated ass,'" she added.

"Aim high," India said, thinking that Monique had earned the right to brag, having jump-started herself out of poverty on the power of her mind alone.

"Sounds like you and Wayne are a good match," India complimented.

"Well, I guess, but nothing's perfect," Monique said, her voice trailing off. She stared into space for a few moments then, as if shaking off a melancholy thought, did a little shimmy, squared her shoulders, and downed a sip of her Pellegrino. India didn't dare probe. Monique's pursed lips made clear she didn't intend to share any more confidences today.

"These girls better get here. I have a patient who's ready to pop. My beeper could go off at any time," Monique added briskly.

Abby entered, looking flustered and slightly disheveled. India constantly marveled at the freedom Abby felt to wear whatever she found in the closet, whether the item in question was in fashion or outdated, pressed or hopelessly wrinkled. Nana Chumley always told her, "Clothes may not make the man, but they definitely help the black person." India contrasted Monique's perfectly tailored pinstripe pantsuit with Abby's ill-fitting peasant skirt and blouse. It was obvious that though her mother was a fry cook, Monique had been raised on precisely the same principle: "Never let them see you sloppy." Nonetheless, at times, India did envy Abby her freedom, if not her actual clothing selections.

"Sorry I'm late, guys," Abby panted.

"Relax, Esme hasn't even shown up yet," India reassured her.

"She better make it before the check comes," Monique quipped.

"If she doesn't, I'll pick it up," Abby reassured her. "One of my biggest and least favorite clients is in town from Switzerland. She just bought two Claes Oldenburg sculptures I found her. My commission could feed India. The country, not this skinny bitch," Abby joked with forced cheer, pointing at her friend.

India saw most of the male heads turn in unison toward the door. Esme stood at the entrance wearing a skintight pencil skirt and matching Spencer jacket. She tossed a hot-pink cashmere shawl at an astonished waiter without once glancing in his direction, as if he were a coatrack.

"Good afternoon, Ms. Sarmiento," the waiter responded adoringly, watching her walk away like a forlorn dog whose mount just ran out from under him. The patrons' gazes followed Esme as she sauntered past their tables.

"Damn," Monique uttered in amazement. "Wish I could do that!"

"Girls, what have I missed?" Esme demanded as she tossed her fuchsia suede hobo bag to the floor and insinuated herself into the empty seat.

"Nothing. Why don't you tell us why you invited us all here?" Abby suggested.

"Well, I didn't ask you here just because it's my father's favorite restaurant, and when I come, then he can't wine and dine his *putas*," Esme responded.

"Stephen Covey calls what you're doing 'other centered.' Are you going to live your whole life as an act of revenge on your father?" Abby asked.

"Leave me alone with your self-help bullshit. I don't sit around constipated, thinking about my life, I just live it."

"You got that right," Abby snapped.

"I asked you all here because I got the job I wanted: I have just officially been named vice president in charge of client relations at Midas Capital, the hedge fund," Esme announced, ignoring Abby's dig.

"All right then," Monique cheered, raising her glass.

"Fantastic!" India cheered, raising her water tumbler. "That's a really hot firm. According to the *Journal,* they lost less than everyone else in the market meltdown."

"And let's talk about the fact that Senorita Thing managed to get a job—not just any job—but a good job in this economy. Esme, you got it going on. So what exactly are you going to be doing for them?" Monique added.

"What I do best: seduce people. I have to get companies and high-net-worth individuals to invest. I'll just start with my family's Rolodex," Esme said with a snap of her fingers.

"What does Tim think?" Abby pursued.

Esme remained silent and ripped a hot roll in two over her butter plate. In the awkward silence, India did a quick calculation in her head.

"But you asked us to lunch two days ago, before you knew for sure if you'd be hired."

"I knew. You always know. It's like a man or a fish. You know when you've hooked them," Esme assured her.

"When did you ever go fishing?" Monique deadpanned, surveying Esme's ensemble.

"Anyway, if they hadn't made me the offer, I'd be sitting here with my fabulous girlfriends cheering myself up. Either way, it was worth celebrating. Let's order. Success makes me hungry. I want pasta, lots of it."

Gianni, the young waiter, arrived at the table wielding a bottle of Dom Pérignon. Monique perked up at the sight of it.

"Excuse me, Madame. This is compliments of Mr. Alders," Gianni said to Esme.

"Who?" Esme asked loudly. India knew she was feigning ignorance. Anyone who'd ever glanced at the *Post's* Page Six or walked past a New York newsstand knew who Michael Alders was.

"The gentleman by the balustrade," Gianni explained. India and the others turned to see a distinguished-looking fifty-something-year-old, central casting from an ad for private jets: strong jaw, a full head of dark hair flecked with gray at perfect intervals, an impeccable bespoke suit, and hands that clearly received the weekly attentions of a manicurist. He nodded to Esme. She turned her back on him and removed her Spencer to reveal a diaphanous polka-dot chiffon blouse with a loosely tied jabot.

"Does your life always go like this?" Monique marveled. "Your champagne wish is their command?"

"Pretty much," Abby answered, biting into a breadstick.

"He's fine," Monique commented. "I thought George Clooney was the only white man I could ever sleep with, but I'd have to reconsider if Dom Pérignon came after me."

"You wouldn't want him to," India cautioned.

"Why not?" Monique asked, admiring Michael as he sipped his sparkling water.

"Because he's dangerous. He's been married four times. He's famous among divorce lawyers. He heads a vulture fund. And he behaves in his personal life as he does in his business—living to take over the distressed. He's the kind of man to avoid. Especially if you're married," India explained for Esme's benefit. The latter absorbed the information as Gianni filled her champagne flute.

"Gianni," she barked, snapping her fingers. "Stop pouring. Send the champagne back."

"Now?" Gianni asked, blanching.

"No, tomorrow. Of course, now!"

"It's too late. He already opened the bottle," Abby objected.

"I can't get my bubbly on anyway. I may be headed to the hospital from here," Monique lamented.

"The rest of us aren't. We'll order our own bottle," Esme responded. She turned to Gianni and added, "Bring us a fresh one and tell Mr. Alders we're not buying today."

Gianni stopped pouring and retreated, dreading the explanations he'd have to make to his patron and then to his boss.

India admired Esme's self-control. Most women could not have resisted turning around to gauge their victim's reaction to their rejection. Esme, on the other hand, had enough self-discipline to "shoot to kill" and never look back. India was dying to see the effect Esme's snub had had on the notorious Lothario. She noted to herself that Michael was a worthy opponent: his jaw clenched in frustration, but he quickly focused on his luncheon partner, refusing to betray any sign of having taken umbrage. Bad boy though he may have been, India could well understand falling victim to his charms. She was grateful that he was not after her. He could definitely have led her down the road to pantyless perdition. The deliberate way he licked his thin but well-formed lips signaled to her that this was a man who knew how to apply his tongue with surgical precision to precisely the spot where it was needed. She took a large gulp of mineral water to cool down and wash away the image of lying buck naked on a duvet to receive his oral attentions.

A cell phone played the tinny strains of a ring tone rendering of Ravel's *Boléro*.

"*Mierda*," Esme cursed as she looked at her Razor. "When will he leave me alone?"

"He who?" Monique asked.

"That waiter from the ballet. So clingy."

India reddened, remembering Esme slipping off into the elevator for a tryst with the beefcake Actor/Model/Waiter. She glanced at Abby, who sat tensely pursing her lips.

"He's called me ten times since the other night," Esme continued cavalierly. "'I came, you saw, I conquered.' Get over it. Girls, is anyone else in the mood for fried zucchini?"

"You are completely heartless!" Abby exploded. Monique stared at her, stunned. India put a reassuring hand on Abby's arm to calm her down.

"What are you talking about?" Esme asked, taken aback.

"Sleeping with people and then dumping them," Abby explained, seething.

"I only do it from time to time. As a pick-me-up," Esme explained, defensive.

"You want a pick-me-up, go have a tiramisu!" Abby snapped.

"Too fattening and not as satisfying," Esme responded with a shrug.

"Well, stop treating people like disposable treats. That waiter at the ballet was a human being. With feelings. Did it ever occur to you that maybe he really likes you? And what about your husband? Or doesn't he matter anymore?" Abby shouted.

"I care about my husband a lot!" Esme protested.

"You've sure got a unique way of showing it," Abby shot back.

"Listen, what I'm doing is saving my marriage. If I didn't have my little adventures, I'd be so bored I would have killed him by now!" Esme insisted.

"Oh, is that why you cheaters do it, to avoid committing homicide? Well, I've got news for you, there's still a victim, and it's still a kind of murder," Abby cried out.

"What's going on, Abby?" India asked, sensing the outburst had little to do with Esme's philandering or the abandoned waiter's "broken heart" and everything to do with Abby's own unpredictable husband. Abby paused.

"I think Nathaniel might be involved with some girls. I picked up his cell phone by accident. There was a message . . ." Abby admitted, as she sank into her seat. India absorbed the revelation. It horrified her, but it didn't come as a surprise at all. She'd always suspected Nathaniel of having a wandering eye and a taste for forbidden pleasures. On more than one occasion, at family brunch in a restaurant, she'd caught him staring at a waitress's bust or buttocks with more than artistic interest. Her instinct told her that the only thing preventing him from consorting with prostitutes was the fact he couldn't afford them.

"Girls? You mean more than one?" Monique asked, aghast.

"That arrogant son of a bitch, I'll hang him by the cojones!" Esme screeched, banshee style.

"I'm sorry, kettle, is the pot that black?" Abby yelled back in total disbelief at her philandering friend's double standard.

"My situation is completely different. I don't have a wife who gave up her dream and worked her behind off so I could continue doing my so-called art."

"It's not 'so-called.' The Azarian Gallery has just agreed to represent him," Abby said defensively.

"I've seen that saga before: build your career on a good woman's back, then stomp on it. Dogs, they're all dogs," Monique deadpanned.

"Absolutely, the old story, the minute the man makes a penny, he drops the woman who helped him get where he is. *Pendejo*! Hanging by the balls is too good for him!" Esme pounded a fist on the table.

"I hate to agree with them, Abby, but this tale is as old as divorce court," India added gently. "Do you want me to hire a private detective to see what's going on?"

"Good idea," Esme interjected before Abby had a chance to respond. "You need to find out what kind of mistress you're dealing with. My father always said there were three types: The disposable—the one-night stand you meet traveling, like the chambermaid at a hotel, for example. Then there's the functional—your assistant, convenient and accessible, but not so beautiful you fall in love with her. And, most dangerous of all, the *cocaina,* the one you would throw your marriage and your position out of the window for."

"I'm not hiring a private detective to shadow my husband. I'm not doing anything, for the moment."

"Yes, you are, you're sticking your head in the sand," India countered, frustrated at Abby's unwillingness to deal with the truth. *Why on earth,* she wondered, *do worthy women stand by these worthless cads who do nothing but heap dishonor and abuse upon them? No sex is that good. Well, perhaps it is,* she remembered as she watched Michael Alders absentmindedly suck a stray grain of risotto off his hand. *But at a certain point, the price is too high.*

"India, I've been with Nathaniel for nineteen years. I know every side of him. You don't throw away nineteen years of love on a hunch," Abby insisted.

"I know you love him, but what about you, your dignity, your pride?" India probed.

"Pride? Yes, it's very easy to be proud when no one else's happiness is at stake." India wanted to argue, but knew she couldn't. Hers was the vantage point of one who had chosen not to take the plunge.

"We have three children, whom he's doing a great job of raising. If their sanity costs me a little pride, so be it," Abby concluded. India had to admit that even she liked Nathaniel when he was around the children. In the summers, he would spend from dawn to dusk with them building a sand castle worthy of a museum exhibit. Last summer he'd helped them create a four-foot replica of the Frank Gehry–designed Guggenheim Museum Bilbao, then joyously joined them in smashing it. She also knew that Abby still loved Nathaniel in spite of everything.

"I have to agree with Abby's math. Nobody said marriage was a bed of roses. And if your husband is helping and he's a good daddy, you're ahead of the game," Monique added thoughtfully.

"So she's just supposed to look the other way and settle?" India asked, dejected.

"Nothing's perfect. And if you keep looking for that, the only date you're gonna have is with your flat-screen TV and a bucket of micro-wave popcorn. Hope you like those Woman's Channel movies about breast-cancer-slash-incest-survivors who get stalked by the mainte-nance man," Monique answered.

"Ladies, I'm sorry I brought it up. It's really not worth talking about," Abby stated, pulling herself together.

India stared Abby down. She knew the "brush it off and it will go away" routine.

"India, I'm fine," Abby responded to her silent admonition. "I didn't mean to bring you all down."

"You didn't bring me down. We're having fettuccine with butter and white truffles," Esme said with a smile as she gave Abby an affec-tionate squeeze of the hand.

"Ladies, a toast," Esme continued, raising a champagne flute. "To living life with passion and pleasure."

"To life," they all concurred. Abby mustered a smile to reassure them all that she was quite recovered from her outburst. India knew full well she was not.

Michael Alders approached the table. At six feet four, he towered over them.

"Ms. Sarmiento-Talbot," he said, inclining his head respectfully. "Congratulations on your new position at Midas. I'm sorry my firm couldn't tempt you." He spoke in the amalgamated accent of a Euro-pean who had learned English from British schoolmasters.

Esme looked at him defiantly, sticking out her chest like a breast-plate.

"I'm certain you'll make a much more interesting competitor than you would have an employee. Have a wonderful afternoon," he added.

"We will."

"I've no doubt. Ladies." And he turned and left the restaurant with the entire wait staff bowing as he made his way past them.

"Umh, umh, um, I love a man with an accent. You sure you're not gonna hit that?" Monique asked longingly.

"Not yet. That's the type you have to make work for it, so by the time he gets it, he's desperate," Esme said with a laugh as she took another swig of her champagne. But India noticed that Esme did turn to watch Michael walk down the street to his waiting car. *Everyone has a weak spot, even the master players of the game of love,* she thought. Personally, she was determined never to reveal her own weak spot again. The beeper attached to Monique's patent leather belt sent off its five-second-interval alarms. She glanced at it and leapt to her feet.

"The Cooper twins are about to make their 'de-butt' in the world. I'm not running out on the check, ladies, I promise," she joked, pulling bills out of her wallet. "Will eighty be enough?"

"Keep your money. I'm buying," Esme assured her, refocusing her attention.

"And before you go, the firm asked me to fill a table at a fund-raiser next Tuesday night at the Waldorf. Are you ladies interested?" Esme asked.

"I just bought myself a new Tracy Reese. It's the bomb, apple green silk charmeuse with a train. I'm there," Monique added, taking a final sip of her sparkling water and rushing out the door.

"What organization is this benefiting?" India asked.

"I don't know, somebody helping someone . . . poor. The firm just sees it as a chance to get more rich people to invest in the fund."

"I'll go. I could use a night out," Abby responded.

"I'm in too, even though this could be a fund-raiser for the American Neo-Nazi Party for all we know," India joked.

Esme's phone went off again.

"That's it," Esme announced at the top of her voice. "It's time to change my number. Some people don't know when a love affair is over." She tossed her Razor into her water glass.

Though India thoroughly disapproved of Esme's philandering, she did wish she had just a bit of her devil-may-care chutzpah.

# chapter eleven

At 7:35 on the evening of October 25, India pushed her way through revolving doors into the lobby of the Waldorf-Astoria, site of the Bright Futures gala. She carried her bulging briefcase in one hand and a diminutive evening purse in the other. Her hair sat perched atop her head in an unkempt "had to cancel my hair appointment" bun. Her makeup consisted of the faded remains of that morning's concealer and eyeliner pencil. She had decided to change at the office to save time but neglected to pack her makeup kit or any hair products. Flyaways crowned her head like a halo, sticking out in every possible direction. As she caught sight of herself in a mirror, she reminded herself of nothing so much as Woodstock, Snoopy's bird.

*Remain calm,* she told herself. *It's a fund-raiser for education, not the Miss Black America pageant.* The crowd would consist of bankers and corporate types, not fastidious fashionistas.

She looked up at the hotel's glorious glass-paneled ceiling. Entering the lobby of this New York landmark was like walking onto the set of an Astaire and Rogers musical. It was impossible not to feel a spark of romantic hope and longing. The magnificence of the Art Deco architecture confirmed the appropriateness of her wardrobe selection: a bias-cut gown of ice blue satin. If people focused on her dress and not her face, all would go well.

Once the elevator doors opened on the third floor, she made her way across the deserted anteroom, through a corridor, and into the cream-and-gold ballroom ringed with three tiers of seats. The cheapest occupied the upper tier, nearest "heaven," where the nonprofits exiled their staffers in their knockoff gowns machine beaded in Hong Kong.

*Perhaps it is true that the meek will inherit the earth,* India observed, *but only after enduring years of bad seating at charity functions.*

It didn't take India more than a moment to spot Esme in a ruby red velvet strapless gown that hugged every minute of her hourglass figure. She chatted with a handsome twentysomething-year-old India didn't recognize: a strong-jawed all-American prep-school hottie with an athletic build and a great head of hair. Silky and thick, it was the sort of hair India loved to run her fingers through. India brought her salacious thoughts to a screeching halt. After all, she was nearly old enough to have been this boy's teen mother, she was here to meet her boyfriend, and she looked like hell. She had no business even fantasizing about any man but Julien. A few seats away from Esme and "Lolito," she spotted Esme's husband, Tim, handsome and stoic in his Brooks Brothers tuxedo.

*Someone should call Pope Benedict about him,* India thought. *Never mind Pope Pius XII, that anorexic Nazi sympathizer, here is a true candidate for sainthood.*

"There you are!" Esme gushed as India approached the table. Julien leapt to his feet to greet her.

"Here's your makeup," he whispered as he discreetly slipped a cosmetics case into her free hand. India smiled at him, touched. She had merely mentioned over the phone that she'd look a complete wreck because she'd forgotten her toiletries. Relieved and grateful, India gave him a warm hug. He kissed her neck and whispered, *"Pas de quoi"* in return.

"Hey, what about the rest of us?" Tim said, rising and extending his arms.

"Tim, watch it, you're going to burn in the fires of eternal damnation. Anything more than a handshake is considered an orgy in New England, where he grew up," Esme explained to Julien. "Affection is a crime against those purple laws."

"The blue laws. And I believe we should break as many of them as possible," India jested.

"Especially when your friends are as pretty as India," Tim shot back, giving her an affectionate squeeze. India and he had liked and respected each other from the start. Like so many other men, he had been smitten with Esme at first sight. India had admired the caring and consistent way he courted Esme without falling dead at her feet. It was indeed this ability to cherish her yet not roll over like a begging dog that had earned him Esme's respect and ultimately her hand in marriage.

"You know almost everyone," Esme commented.

Wayne Dubois, Monique's portly, bespectacled husband approached. "India, you look as great as ever," he said in a jolly tone. India remembered him now from around campus, but he had been slim then. Now he wore his protruding belly unapologetically, having reached the level of financial success that, in men, was accepted as a substitute for a great body.

"Thank you, Wayne," she answered, unable to return the compliment.

"We met your man," Monique said with a wink. *"Oh là là!"*

"He's French, not deaf," India chided.

Abby raced in, trailed by Nathaniel, who looked miserable in an ill-fitting tux with frayed lapels.

*Probably a hand-me-down from his grandfather, Winthrop Adams, the last member of Nathaniel's clan with any money,* India surmised. She watched as they stopped in the middle of the room to have one of their typical heated exchanges. Nathaniel, on the attack as usual, thrust his face forward as he snapped at Abby. The latter flinched at first, then held her ground and shot back a response. *What had set Nathaniel off this time?* India wondered. The prospect of spending the evening with Abby's friends, most of whom he couldn't stand? The way she adjusted his bow tie? He had so many insecurities it didn't take much to send him into a rage. When India asked her how she could be so patient with him, Abby always offered the same justification: "In a marriage, someone has to be the bigger person." India saw Abby tenderly caress Nathaniel's cheek. Once again, she'd obviously apologized to appease her angry man. His fury subsided. He bowed his head like a child embarrassed at having thrown a tantrum. Abby composed herself and they approached the group.

"Sorry we're late," she apologized.

"I'm not," Nathaniel grumbled. "Some hedge fund schmuck just mistook me for a waiter."

"You're in good company, happens to me all the time. What you need is a better tux," Wayne said, laughing, then introduced himself. "Wayne Dubois. What firm are you with?"

"I'm not with any firm. I'm an artist," Nathaniel snapped.

"Oh, really. Have I ever heard of you?" India was taken aback by Wayne's smugness. It was of a piece with his rich man's paunch.

"Wayne is married to Monique, who went to Sibley with us. Remember, I told you," Abby pointedly reminded her husband. He dropped his rabid guard.

"Oh, nice to meet you. What are we doing here?" he asked.

"Having fun," Esme fired back. "But that's a foreign concept to you. You're so busy working on your . . . pieces," she added contemptuously. Nathaniel glared at her; she stared back defiantly.

"I'm with Nathaniel. These events are a pain," Tim concurred in an attempt to effect a truce. His wife's disdain for Nathaniel was well known to him.

"I love parties like this," said the handsome twentysomething-year-old with fabulous hair seated to Esme's left. "I'm Patrick, by the way, Patrick Herzog. Glad our boss couldn't make it and gave me this ticket," he continued, devouring Esme with his eyes.

"So you work with Esme at Midas," Abby concluded, reassured to know that Esme hadn't stooped to picking up stray boy toys in the street and flaunting them in front of her husband.

"Yeah, I work with Esme. But I'm on the trading side. Esme reels in the clients. Just the job for her, man," Patrick responded, looking longingly at his colleague.

His palpable lust startled India. To her relief, Esme seemed to take no notice of the young stud. Nor did Tim.

*For all Esme's insanity, she certainly did pick the right husband,* India thought. She prayed she didn't foolishly throw away her domestic happiness. India had resisted discussing the subject with her, but as a good friend, she resolved to do so at the first opportunity.

"So, how do you know Esme?" The prep-school hottie fired the question at India before she'd even had the chance to place her napkin on her lap. India had come across men like him before, ruthless baby wolves of banking, with the cockiness of the young, Ivy-educated, and untested. He'd quickly learned the Manhattan placer question: "How do you know so-and-so?" It was posed not as a query, but as a challenge because one seemed—to the narrow-minded asker—out of place in a certain social set. Special emphasis on the *you* was code for "show me where you belong on the socioeconomic food chain." One's answer allowed the rude and socially ambitious to decide whether or not one was worth their conversational effort. India was tempted to give her stepfather's favorite answer: "We used to fuck."

Instead she smiled and responded, "You wrestled. At Princeton, class of 2000. You graduated from HBS last year."

"Wharton actually. But everything else is right. How did you know?" Patrick asked, astonished at her grasp of his curriculum vitae.

"Lucky guess," India answered. In fact, she reflected to herself with satisfaction that being a perpetual outsider had given her the gift of observation and an ethnographer's knack for "classification." Just as Henry Higgins could place a regional accent to within a one-mile radius of the person's hometown, India could detect people's ethnic

origins, social castes, and even personality traits. Great hair notwithstanding, this one had no charm. "Will you excuse me?" she added,
rising.

Julien sprang to his feet to pull out her chair.

"Dude, chill," Patrick admonished. "You're making the rest of us
look bad."

"If you're less than a gentleman, it's not my problem," Julien responded, smiling.

"I'll be right back after I do some reclamation work on my face,"
India whispered in his ear.

"You look beautiful just as you are," he assured her.

"In a Bride of Frankenstein way," she joked, giving him a peck on
the cheek.

India made her way down the brightly lit corridor, the thick carpeting muffling the sound of her steps so that she moved quietly as
an angel. She looked up, admiring the moldings and the bas-reliefs of
pseudo-Grecian revelers in diaphanous togas. She sensed someone had
stopped right in the middle of the hallway and was staring straight at
her. She looked down from the crown moldings and saw Keith Wentworth, her former fiancé. She gasped and froze in her tracks. Keith's
mahogany locks framed a chiseled face completely unchanged by the
hands of time. Beneath his tux, his six-foot-three frame was still a
V-shaped marvel of anatomy. Once India resumed breathing, she tried
to read his expression. Was that shock? Had the color truly drained
from his cheeks? He had never had much to begin with, much to the
delight of his light-skinned mother.

*No doubt I've turned him to stone with my middle-aged office Me-
dusa grooming,* India thought with despair. *The closer he gets, the
luckier he'll feel that I called off the marriage.*

Keith started to walk toward her. Through the fluid wool of his
bespoke tuxedo, each slow and deliberate step suggested the outline of
a different perfectly defined leg muscle. India's heart pounded in her
chest. It was too late to turn and run in the other direction. Perhaps she

could pretend she was someone else, a homely India Chumley look-alike. As he drew closer, she forced a smile, well, at least a constipated grin. At last he stopped, inches away from her, his endless lashes rising to unveil huge indigo eyes that stared directly into hers. He flashed a half smile revealing teeth so white and even they could have passed for cultured pearls. At thirty-eight, he was still a statue of a Roman god brought to devastatingly beautiful life. Was it any wonder she had almost been razed Carthage to his conquering Scipio? "How's it going, Chumley?" Keith said nonchalantly, the way one might have greeted a colleague, not the girl one had nearly married and with whom one used to have sex that would have registered 10 on the Richter scale.

"Good evening, Keith," she managed to eke out woodenly.

"Whoo," he answered trying to lighten the mood, "Felt the breeze on that one."

India couldn't think for the conga drum beats of her heart. She laughed nervously.

"There's no breeze, Keith," she reassured him.

"Could have fooled me," he bellowed in a "hail fellow well met" voice. "Anyway, water under the bridge," he added with a wave of his perfectly formed right hand.

"What are you doing here?" India asked awkwardly.

"Didn't you read your program, Chumley? I'm the honoree, the Bright Futures Torchbearer of the Year," he answered nonchalantly.

"Oh, I'm so sorry. My hostess didn't tell me," India sputtered, mortified. Now she'd compounded her haggard appearance with ignorance and stupidity. "Congratulations," she hastened to add.

"For what—being the check magnet of the year? This isn't about me, they just needed rich, corporate, nonwhite," he joked.

India had always loved Keith's ability to cut through society's euphemisms and hypocrisies. Now she smiled in earnest and wide.

"There it is, that's my smile," Keith said quietly, smiling back with his whole face. India paused to savor the moment's warmth, then remembered she shouldn't get too comfortable. This was, after all, the man who had demolished her heart. And she had moved on to another more worthy of her affections.

"The organization is fortunate to have you, whatever the reason," she said with formality, to reestablish a boundary.

"Yeah, and I'm damned glad to meet you, too. So what are you doing here? You're supposed to be in LA."

"I moved back just a few months ago."

"Hard to keep track of your moves. You don't give people much advance notice . . ."

India refused to take the bait. She would never admit to Keith that their breakup had caused her to go to Los Angeles in the first place. She strongly suspected he knew. Like most beautiful men, he was fully aware of his power over women.

"Bigger opportunity at the firm here. They made me a partner."

"That was bound to happen. You're good," Keith tossed out. The offhand compliment stunned India. Keith had never been generous in his praise.

"Maybe we can have lunch sometime," he suggested, as he took a step or two away from her.

"Yes, that would be nice," India found herself answering and, to her shame, wishing he would pull out his BlackBerry on the spot. She wanted to kick herself for letting down her guard but then rationalized that befriending him was actually a sign of how far in the past her feelings belonged. Platonic friendship—that was all that remained, in spite of his flawless good looks and edible body.

Keith stared at her, taking in all the planes of her face. India allowed her eyes to meet his. To her shock the cerulean blue irises conveyed affection. Just as she began to settle in for another moment's silent exchange with the man she'd nearly married, she heard a lilting female voice cry, "There you are, sweetie. I've been waiting for you."

At the door of the ladies' room, a sinewy, chiffon-clad creature appeared, like a wood sprite in an ancient myth. She was diminutive, five feet three or four, at most, with the fat-free lithe body of a dancer or a gymnast, a flawless complexion, big bright doe brown eyes, and flowing dark hair. She rose on tiptoe to kiss Keith full on the lips then turned her pep-squad smile on India, who wanted nothing so much as for the earth to open up and swallow her whole.

India looked to Keith for an explanation. He flinched for a moment, but without skipping a beat, slipped an arm around the apparition's minuscule waist. *It was not measured in inches,* India thought, *but in ring sizes.* Who was this nymph, this Tinker Bell to her hideous Captain Hook? Suddenly India felt the lines of her forehead gape like Grand Canyons, revealing the continental divide in their ages. How old was she? Not more than twenty-six with a soul and spirit as unblemished as her complexion, no doubt.

"Serena," Keith said warmly. "This is India Chumley."

"India. What a pretty name," Serena uttered in a tone of sheer amazement. "I've never met anyone with that name."

*Of course you haven't. You're eight years old. I, on the other hand, am a contemporary of Queen Victoria's,* India wanted to answer but smiled instead. Clearly Keith had never even mentioned her to this child. But then, why would he have? Maybe she was just a passing fling, a wife for the evening, or a holdover from the weekend. Yet scrutinizing her fresh-faced sorority girl demeanor, India had to admit she looked like the "to wed" type, not merely the "to bed" type. Something about her carriage, her perfect, prim posture suggested Wellesley BA, with honors, less than five years before.

"India, this is Serena Charles, my fiancée."

The last word hit India like a knockout punch. Everything afterward turned blurry and vague like an out-of-body experience. She had expected anything but this. Why hadn't Monique warned her? For that matter, had Monique known Keith would be there all along?

"When did this happen?" she managed to muster, instantly regretting having asked. She might as well have added the word "disaster."

"Three days ago!" Serena gushed. "Can you believe it?"

"That is . . . wonderful. Really. Best wishes to you, Serena. Congratulations, Keith. Well done." When in doubt, offer a good British turn of phrase.

*"Well done?" God, what a clunker.* India willed herself to do an about-face and walk away from the happy pair, completely forgetting that her original destination was the ladies' room. She hoped she'd turn invisible as she walked away.

# chapter twelve

As Keith stood at the podium delivering his acceptance speech, India listened, stiff as a figure on Mount Rushmore. She felt about as attractive as George Washington, he of the beakish nose and oversize forehead. She didn't dare turn toward the table at the center of the room, Keith's table. She didn't want to see his mother, Livia Wentworth, the Mama Vampire embracing her future daughter-in-law, a malleable near-virgin whose blood she could suck with ease. And yet in that moment, she wanted to offer her own blood for sacrifice. But Livia wanted sacrificial lamb, not sacrificial mutton.

*That could have been me,* kept repeating in India's mind. *Yes, but you didn't want it,* her reason answered. But the beat of impulse was undeniable. She wanted to rush the stage and throw herself at Keith. Thank God, a ballroom full of people, the world's biggest chastity belt, stood between them. She downed her glass of ice water.

"People credit me with being a success," Keith's voice boomed. "The fact of the matter is that I stand on the shoulders of two giants, my mother and father, Livia and Elihu Wentworth." The room burst into applause, everyone having read his parents' humble-to-fabulous success story in *Forbes* and countless other business publications. Livia leapt to her feet and waved to the crowd, as though she were Queen Elizabeth during a royal progress. Behind her stood another candidate for canonization for time served with such an unmitigated shrew, her husband of forty years, Elihu Wentworth. At seventy, he still qualified as a light-skinned pretty boy. He wasn't as strong a candidate for a halo as Tim Talbot because India suspected him of many a dalliance. Given his wife's dragon-lady ways, she couldn't blame him. A story had gone around Washington, DC, that she had bribed a hairdresser to substitute lye for hair relaxer when doing one of his mistresses' hair. The girl ended up bald and dumped. One couldn't cross Livia Wentworth and expect to remain standing. In such a contest, India knew she would have suffered and lost.

From the stage, Keith continued, "As Eleanor Roosevelt once said to Katherine Dunham, 'No one does anything alone.'"

*I taught him that quotation!* India mentally exclaimed. *He's taken my quotations and is using them to marry another woman. Plagiarized and dumped. Wait, I wasn't dumped, I dropped him,* she reminded herself. What if she had looked the other way from his philandering? Would she now be sitting at the table, her arm around their four-year-old son?

"That's what it means to me to be a torchbearer: to have the humility to remember no one does anything alone," Keith continued.

"Humility? He doesn't even know how to spell the word," Abby whispered over Patrick to India, who was taken aback by the observation. Hadn't Keith earned his arrogance, given his credentials? In fact, India rather liked his air of "I will run them off their feet" superiority, beating his white counterparts at their own game. Most Caucasians mistook him for a member of their club, but he never for a moment forgot his true origins. *And men who make love the way he does have no reason to be humble,* India remembered with flushed cheeks.

"We in this room must take the time to help those coming up behind us. As the saying goes, 'Each one, reach one.'"

"But he does," Esme said in a stage whisper to India and Abby. "He's reached out and touched thousands of women!"

"Esme!" Tim chastised. She stuck out her tongue at him in reply. India watched Patrick smirk approvingly. India appreciated Tim's admonition of his wife. She was in no mood to make fun of Keith Wentworth tonight. Julien placed an arm on India's shoulder. She brushed it off, much to his confusion. Then, realizing her gaffe, grabbed his hand affectionately. In an effort to turn the page once and for all, she had never told him about Keith. Telling the story would have served only to reopen the wound.

"Thank you, thank you for this honor. I will do my best to live up to the title of Torchbearer. God bless you all," Keith concluded to enthusiastic applause and to India's relief. Now she'd be spared the sight of him and the regret it inspired.

"Thank God, that's over," Esme raved. "Did he talk that much in bed? No wonder you left him," she whispered to India, who ignored her.

"Ladies and gentlemen," a British voice bellowed. "The moment you've all impatiently awaited, our live auction. Remember, every penny goes to this wonderful organization. You are saving the world by spending."

"Jesus Christ," Nathaniel groaned. "These people never miss a chance to show off the size their wallets."

"That's because they have something to show off," Esme taunted. Nathaniel glared at her. Abby took a deep breath. Did Esme have to go there? Now she'd have to hear about this all night.

"Our first item, a magnificent Russian sable stole, valued at twenty-five thousand dollars. I'll start the bidding at five thousand," the auctioneer called out.

Esme thrust her paddle in the air.

"Esme, we're barely out of a recession. And you don't need that," Tim reminded her, annoyed.

"Who shops because they need? I want it!" Esme insisted.

"You'd look gorgeous in it," Patrick said with barely concealed horniness.

Ignoring him, Esme continued to bid, standing up for emphasis each time she stabbed the air with her paddle.

"Six thousand, five hundred, do I have seven?" Paddles went up.

Suddenly a male voice intoned, "Forty thousand dollars!"

"*Qué*? He can't do that!" Esme yelled.

"Did you say forty thousand, Sir? Bless you. Forty thousand once, twice, sold to the very generous gentleman at table thirteen."

Esme threw down her paddle in disgust.

"Now somebody's tacky Russian mistress is going to be walking around in my fur!"

"I think that's a sign for us to go home," Tim said, rising. "We have a long drive."

"No we don't. We can stay at my parents'," Esme sulked.

"Esme, I promised our daughter I would go over her math homework with her in the morning."

"You can do it by phone. From bed," she said seductively, removing her evening shoe and caressing his ankle with her silken foot.

He removed his foot from under hers, then commanded, "Esme, we're leaving."

"No, I'm staying," Esme answered, setting her lower lip.

"Esme, please," Tim said sotto voce, turning shades of crimson.

"I'm not going back there. I want to stay in town and get a decent night's sleep without hearing crickets chirping and the other stupid sounds of nature!" she hissed.

India and the others did their best to ignore the discussion. Abby dragged Nathaniel onto the dance floor. Patrick watched the exchange with the intentness of a predator. Tim composed himself, clearly tamping down his frustration in order to avoid a scene.

"I'm going home. Good night, all. Thank you for joining us," Tim announced as he withdrew from the table.

"Esme, you should follow him," India urged in a whisper.

"Why? The party has just started."

"You're driving him away," India begged.

"What do you know about keeping a man or about marriage? You've never even had the guts to try," Esme struck back in a hushed tone. *Cruel but accurate,* a stung India acknowledged in silence. She sat back in her seat, retreating. Her life was no shining example of personal relationship success. Julien notwithstanding, she sometimes feared she was on her way to becoming a sad statistic: the six-figure earner with no real emotional life.

"It is rather late. And I have to be at the fish market by four AM," Julien said in an attempt to help the situation. India knew his kind motivation but had no desire to budge either.

"*Chérie,*" he said turning to her. "*Tu es prête?*"

*I'm anything but "prête,"* she thought. She looked longingly toward Keith's table, drawn to her seat as though by a magnetic force. She admired the back of his neck, the beautiful broad shoulders she used to caress for hours. Across her own table, she spotted Monique, who smiled and nodded at her. Feeling caught, India jumped to her feet.

"Yes, let's go," she answered, taking Julien's hand.

"If you're all going to abandon me, I'm going to have to leave. You are all party poopers," sulked Esme.

Instantly, Patrick rushed to Esme's side to pull out her chair. "I'll walk you to the coat check," he offered. She nodded in acceptance, taking a good look at him for the first time all evening. She liked what she saw.

"So you learned something tonight," Julien commented to Patrick.

"Yeah, thanks for the etiquette lesson," he said dismissively.

The two couples walked together to the coat check crowded with departing guests eager to get to their waiting town cars, and for the less fortunate, to be the first in the taxi line. A young volunteer in an evening gown far too short for her gawky frame approached Esme.

"Miss Sarmiento?" she asked tentatively.

"That's me," Esme answered, tossing back her lustrous locks.

"Great. A gentleman told me to give this to you. We don't usually let people go home with their items the night of the event. But he was very insistent. He said it's a gift from a friend." She handed Esme the sable stole. Esme caressed it lovingly.

"Who's the gentleman?" she demanded to know.

"He asked me not to say," the staffer answered cagily.

"Come on. You're dying to tell me. And I'll never tell him how I found out."

"Mr. Alders," the girl admitted sheepishly, looking around nervously to make sure no one had overheard her. India's eyes widened with shock. Esme's lips curled with satisfaction. She was beginning to reel in her big fish. She rubbed the amber-colored fur against her cheek and ran her hand over the satin lining. Suddenly, she thrust it back into the stunned staffer's hand.

"Tell Mr. Alders I'm not interested." With that, she grabbed her own coat, delighted with this checkmate. It would keep Alders off-kilter, where she wanted him.

"Are you sure you don't want to come for a drink?" Esme asked India and Julien.

"Another time," he answered with a chivalrous nod.

"Okay, see you soon." Esme kissed India and Julien each on both cheeks and flounced out, trailed by Patrick.

India overheard him say, "I'll get you a taxi."

"Why not?" Esme answered as they disappeared down the escalator.

"It's sad," Julien commented to India. "She's very beautiful and very angry."

India had never thought of Esme that way: Esme, the mischievous ringleader who believed in living for the moment, consequences be damned. Even now, India thought of what flip reply Esme would have spouted in answer to his analysis, "Yes, I'm angry you didn't bring a magnum of champagne, and you call yourself a restaurateur." Just at the moment, India had a more pressing problem than psychoanalyzing her spoiled friend. She had to figure out what to say to Julien to get out of going home with him. She pulled her iPhone out of her evening purse and scrolled through emails.

"Oh no," she said, summoning all her suppressed thespian powers. "I have to go back to the office."

"Tonight?" Julien asked, flabbergasted.

"Yes, there's something new on one of my cases."

"Surely it can wait until tomorrow morning."

"It can't. I'm sorry. I'll get home as soon as I can."

Julien sighed in exasperation but refrained from speaking. India eyed him nervously.

"What's wrong?" she asked, knowing full well the answer. "I can't help it, it's my work," she offered feebly.

"I know. I understand, as always," Julien snapped. Then catching himself, he said more gently, "It just would be nice to feel like a priority from time to time."

India looked at him crestfallen. Her conscience gnawed at her. Julien was kindness personified, but right now she needed time alone to convince herself that she hadn't made the biggest mistake of her life six years ago when she walked away from the man she'd loved. Not daring to look Julien in the eye, she pecked him on the cheek and jumped into a waiting taxi.

# chapter thirteen

After trudging up one flight of narrow town house stairs, India unlocked the door of her one-bedroom hideaway. With its deep mahogany wainscoting and its walls covered in dusty rose acanthus leaf paper, it reminded her of the cozy hotel rooms in London she had stayed in with her mother when she was doing a play in the West End. Through the closed window, she heard the strains of a live female voice singing "Un Bel Dì" from *Madam Butterfly*. *An aspiring opera singer,* India surmised. *She's probably just come home from working the late shift at Fiorello's restaurant where she doles out the daily antipasto to the very Met Opera patrons she hopes one day to astonish with her voice, rather than her waitressing skills.* Tonight, the city seemed full of "dreams deferred."

India caught sight of her reflection in the full-length cheval mirror by the bed. To her surprise and relief, she was not the shipwreck she felt herself to have been by comparison with the little dreamboat Serena. Her figure looked long and lean. Her face, though slightly marked by lines, was still a dramatic face. So what did this girl, this Serena, have that she didn't, other than a flawless complexion? "Obedience training, from the local kennel," came her mother's voice in her head. She'd probably learned to greet Keith with a wagging tail whenever he returned from his adventures, professional or otherwise. She probably didn't have a single opinion of her own, and if she did, she never expressed it.

India considered calling either Abby or her mother to share her confusion but didn't dare. Neither one would have sympathized. They both thought that she could do better than Keith. And so did she, until tonight. Six years' worth of logical objections to the relationship had crumbled at the sight of him. She felt the same breathtaking shock tonight as she had the afternoon she had first laid eyes on him in the stacks of the Langdell law library when they were twenty-three. He'd asked her out on the spot and they'd spent three hours nursing the same cups of cappuccino in the basement of Café Pamplona. The conversation never ceased, wending its way from his family history to their con-law class, to her work at a clinic for battered women and his disdain for dull-as-dirt European movies. Maybe that was his hold—they met so young, when everything still seemed possible.

From under the bed, India pulled a tin box faux painted to look like birchwood. Her mother had purchased it in London when she'd first become a hit in a revival of *Look Back in Anger.* India opened it and inside found dozens of letters written in longhand on yellow legal paper: her correspondence with Keith during the first summer they were together, and every year thereafter. The missives mixed legal musings and erotica, in their case the two being inextricably linked. For them, debate had always been either an extension of sex or a preamble to it, the most titillating foreplay India had ever experienced. No one before or since had ever so ignited both her mind and her passions. She had managed to bury the memory until the Waldorf. She unfolded one letter and read:

I don't think your defense of racial quotas in the Michigan
case holds even a teaspoon of water, and kindly recall the ugly
applications of numerical formulas to race questions (Plessy v.
Ferguson). Nonetheless as I read your argument, Counselor, I can
see you lying on my bed in your g-string, that crazy bush you call
a hairdo falling all around you.

The letter still smelled faintly of Grey Flannel, the slightly sweet cologne Keith wore back then.

That was the summer he'd worked in New York, she in Chicago. That was the summer he'd introduced her to satin sheets, all the positions of the *Kama Sutra,* and the proper application of ice cubes. He'd bounced her on his tireless thighs while delaying his own pleasure until she . . .

She tossed the letter back in the box and recalled that she had strongly considered making a bonfire of these writings on the evening she'd caught Keith with the other woman, but as she started to burn, she started to read and couldn't bring herself to destroy them. And so she had locked them away for future reference. She knew it was dangerous to reread them now. It was like throwing a bucket of kerosene on a fire one claimed to want to douse, yet she wanted to wallow in the delicious ache of longing.

She allowed her mind to wander down a road she had closed off when she walked away from the man and the impending marriage. Instead of sending him a fax saying, "I saw you, it's over. Never come near me again," what if she had met with him to discuss the situation? It was obvious from following him that fateful night that he had taken the trollop to a room and slept with her, but what if she had been the only one, and what if it had been the first time? Had she given him a chance to explain, would he have thrown himself at her feet and promised never to do it again? Was he now faithful to Tinker Bell? Having learned the lesson of loss, had he now reformed, and was he prepared to be the husband she would want? When she could tolerate the thoughts no longer, she headed to the refrigerator and found a promising green and yellow Teuscher chocolate box. Oblivion awaited her in high-octane cocoa form.

She nestled onto her bed, a festival of pillow shams and eyelet-covered neck rests, and flicked on the remote control. Turner Classic Movies was showing *Duel in the Sun,* the Jennifer Jones tearjerker about a half-caste Mexican torn between good boy Joseph Cotten, who wanted to teach her to read and raise her to the dignity of white Christian womanhood, and his brother, bad boy Gregory Peck, who treated her like a sexual serf, ravishing her on the dirt floor. As India shoveled one miniature champagne truffle into her mouth after another, it dawned on her she had become the incarnation of Monique's dire prediction: "You'll be snuggling up to a bucket of popcorn, watching a cable channel movie." The only difference was that she was watching a better movie and eating finer snack food.

She could not let her existence come to this. She shut off the television and picked herself up off the bed. She went to the bathroom and furiously brushed her teeth, then gargled with Listerine to erase the telltale signs of her cocoa binge. Grabbing her coat, she exited her apartment to go face Julien. Jennifer Jones might end up dead for love and lust of Gregory Peck, but she was going back to her Joseph Cotten, to live a life of purpose and dignity. Romance was, after all, greatly overrated. Where had it gotten her mother? Or Abby, or Cio-Cio-San for that matter? But would the longing ever end? Or would she be eighty-five, in a walker, and still ready to fling herself naked at Keith whenever their paths crossed? He'd probably stay youthful forever and his wife preternaturally lovely. The poet lied. It was not better to have loved and lost than never to have loved at all. It was hell to have known ecstasy and compare every other situation with its ashen remains.

## chapter fourteen

At 11:45 PM, Esme and Patrick stumbled, laughing, out of the glass doors of the Jean Georges restaurant at One Central Park West. They exuded the beatific glow that a few rounds of cocktails bestowed. Nonetheless, Esme's focus remained clear. She held her liquor as deftly as she managed her dalliances with men: she knew how to indulge without letting it go to her head.

"Walk down the stairs backward for me!" she challenged her young, slightly less sober companion. Patrick did not hesitate. He turned to face her, and without losing eye contact, dutifully descended the staircase, much to Esme's delight. This new one could have been just what she'd been craving: a young, ambitious, and horny buck. He was not looking for meaning and true love. He was just looking for fun and fabulous fornication. In short, he was a married woman's dream.

"You're not as drunk as I thought," she complimented him as he cleared the final step without tripping.

"I'm in full possession of my faculties," he riposted. Esme descended the five steps slowly and deliberately, her sheared mink flying open to reveal the crimson velvet beneath and her exquisite olive skin. Patrick took it all in appreciatively. She stopped in front of him and looked up. They were nose to nose. He leaned in to kiss her; but she slipped coyly under his arm and ran across the street.

"Fuck you!" he yelled.

"I'd like you to, but you have to catch me first!" she taunted. He started to cross the street, but the light changed and he jumped back onto the curb to avoid the oncoming cars. Taxis honked frantically at him. Esme laughed at the near catastrophe and crossed the next street. Patrick would not let fear or traffic deter him. At the first opening, he made a dash for the roundabout, then ran across Broadway. He looked around and saw Esme, bathed under the bright lights of the Mandarin Oriental Hotel, smirking at him. She dashed into the lobby.

"Evening, Ms. Sarmiento," the doormen said with a bow. They merely nodded discreetly at Patrick when he entered. Esme was pleased. She had them well trained and in check. It was amazing what a little charm and bribery would do for a girl.

The elevator arrived and Esme slipped in. Patrick ran to catch up with her and was squashed by the sliding doors. He had her cornered, or so he thought. He lunged for her. She ducked and slipped to the other side of the elevator. Finally he pinned her arms against the wall. Esme breathed deeply, inhaling his scents. This for her was one of the most delicious junctures in any seduction: the anticipation of the first kiss, that moment when she and a man were drawn to each other with heat-generating force, and it all began with the lips. This exquisite tension could never be recaptured after several years of marriage. Even Patrick sensed that the magic would be lost if he rushed. Esme pressed her mouth to his, slowly opened it, let a breath pass, but withdrew as impatience overwhelmed Patrick and his warm tongue thrust forward.

"Ah, ah, ah. This is just the prelude to act one. Act two happens inside," she murmured. He followed her. She looked him over: he was eminently trainable with natural sensuality that just needed to be harnessed and properly guided. With a little work, she would make him into a master lover. He had all the right raw material and the willingness to learn. It was written all over his face. She hadn't noticed him more than in passing at the office, but there she was focused on work.

Now she could mix business with pleasure of the most orgasmic kind.

Esme unlocked the door to the apartment and opened it to reveal a panoramic view of Central Park and the East Side across the way.

"Where are we?" Patrick asked, astonished at the splendor of the surroundings.

"Heaven," she answered, laughing.

"I mean whose place is this?"

"My father's," she explained, tossing her mink on the low, white Roche-Bobois sofa. "This is where he takes his mistresses."

"Whoa, that's Freudian and weird. Should we even be here?" Patrick asked, slightly sobered by the concept.

"If you want to leave, leave," Esme dared him, reclining on the couch and resting her head on her arm. Too mesmerized to move, Patrick merely shook his head.

"No, I don't want to leave," he said robotically. Esme smiled and rose. She didn't think so. Patrick followed her with his gaze as she crossed to the bar. She retrieved a bottle of Perrier-Jouët Fleur de Champagne from the little refrigerator and two rock crystal flutes from a shelf. She poured deep purple crème de cassis into the glasses, then expertly popped open the champagne bottle and filled the flutes to the brim. The foam bubbled over the edges of the glasses. She offered the sparkling libation to Patrick.

"What's this?" he asked.

"A Kir royal. You've never had one?" she answered, intrigued by his lack of sophistication. This truly was one she could mold.

"No," he admitted as he took a sip.

"There's a first time for everything," she commented, removing his tuxedo jacket. She ran her hands over his shoulders, appreciating their breadth and power. His buttocks she noted were taut and muscular. *This is so delicious, like opening a new gift at Christmas,* she thought. After the first kiss, she loved seeing a man naked for the first time, particularly one with a beautiful athlete's body like Patrick. This boy was clearly in his prime.

"Nice soft cotton. Pink's?" Esme asked, fingering the collar of his shirt.

"How did you know?" Patrick answered, amazed and more than a little aroused.

"I know my custom-made shirts." She unknotted his bow tie and tossed it to the floor, then removed the first two evening buttons.

"We'll have to be careful with these," she said, cradling them in the palm of her hand. She delicately kissed them and placed them on the coffee table. The promise of cradling to come was not lost on Patrick. As he swallowed hard, his Adam's apple bobbed up and down.

"I'll be right back," Esme promised, running a hand down his chest and withdrawing it just as she reached his fly. She turned and exited to the bathroom. There she ran water in the tub, mixing a concoction of amber-scented bath oil, lavender salts, and Chanel No. 5. She tossed the empty perfume bottle into the wastebasket. Whichever of her father's chippies the bottle belonged to would simply have to go out and buy a new one. The room filled up with steam, fogging up the mirror, and Patrick appeared in the doorway, holding his drink and hers.

"You forgot this," he said, trying to appear suave and unruffled as he handed her the champagne flute. She drained it and placed it next to the sink, then carefully unbuttoned the rest of his shirt. He whipped off his cotton undershirt. With her long fingers, she caressed his smooth alabaster chest, free of any hair. She ran the back of her hand over the firm ridges of his washboard stomach, anticipating the punch these abdominals would pack when called into action in just a little while. She unbuttoned the top button of his trousers, and then the rest. His penis bulged like a tent pole from his boxers. Their duck pattern offered a childlike contrast to the weapon of pleasure they barely managed to contain.

"Take them off," Esme commanded, removing her hands.

Patrick obeyed and stood stark naked before her. Moisture trickled down Esme's thigh at the sight of his beautiful body fully revealed.

"Get in," she ordered, and Patrick stepped into the tub, never taking his eyes off this exotic woman, so different from the overeager Seven Sisters types who besieged him at bars and mixers.

Esme backed away from Patrick and the foaming waters, slowly unzipping her dress from behind. She turned her back on him and stepped out of the gown. She could hear his breathing quicken. She loved the effect the first sighting of her naked body had on every man she'd ever teased, taunted, or screwed. She could understand the delight some strippers took in their work. A man was never again as vulnerable as he was in the minutes before he penetrated you. She started to unhook her black satin corset top, then paused and faced Patrick again. He leaned forward over the side of the tub, as if moving closer would hasten the moment of total disclosure. Esme took a sip of his champagne, snapped open one garter, then the other. Putting her arms behind her back, she removed the corset entirely, revealing her slim waist, slightly rounded belly, and her full, generous, and utterly authentic breasts. Their rose nipples stood erect with arousal. She dipped a toe in the water. Patrick extended a hand and helped her enter, step by step into the warm depths of the perfumed pond.

"Now for act two," Esme whispered as their open mouths met and her tongue fell into the warm folds of his. Frothy mounds of bubbles spilled silently onto the floor as the waters began to churn.

## chapter fifteen

India entered conference room B, a cavernous wood-paneled room fit to intimidate the enemy, even when that enemy was the notorious José Feldman, the greatest divorce lawyer of his generation. She found her client, Robert Winston, quietly absorbed in reading a used-looking copy of *Siddhartha*. The book's ragged condition was of a piece with Robert's ill-fitting tweed sport coat, brown cotton shirt, and tie that hung like a noose around his neck. His good looks were somewhat diminished by his air of sadness and defeat. He rose as soon as he saw India. She smiled warmly at this overgrown Berkeley boy lost in New York's Darwinian jungle.

"Is this a good sign that they've asked for this meeting?" Robert inquired with a desperate tremor of hope in his voice.

"We've definitely scared them. Clearly, what motivates your wife is money. She'll do anything to avoid forking over a quarter of a million for your legal fees."

Robert bowed his head and winced at the comment. India instantly regretted her blunt, if accurate, assessment of his soon-to-be ex. However horridly his wife had treated him, he didn't want to hear anyone speak ill of her. He'd made that clear at his very first meeting with India. His gentleness of spirit reminded her of Julien's. It made her wonder if such extreme kindness in men brought out the worst in their women, turning potential pussycats into cruel viragos.

India's musings were interrupted by the arrival of the virago in question: Paula Winston, the Queen of Green, trailed by José Feldman.

"You tell Glenda I can't do the shoot on Thursday," she barked into her cell phone's headpiece, which was made to resemble a twig. "I've got a meeting with the mayor about the Earth Day Gala . . . No, I can't move it, I'm the goddamn honoree, and it's the mayor! Do I have to hire a cleaning crew to airlift the wax out of your goddamn ears! Just fix it!" she screamed, then ripped off the headpiece, shut her eyes, and let out a loud meditation "ohm." India was pleased to see her display her claws so early in the game. If they did end up in court, she would be very easy to rile in front of a judge, a big point in their favor.

"Miss Chumley, José Feldman," the fifty-nine-year-old legend said suavely. At five foot nine and a little over two hundred pounds, he was not traditionally handsome. But his ease of manner and the twinkle in his eye disarmed and seduced. He had the unhurried confidence of the perpetual victor.

"How is your grandmother?" he asked India.

"She's well, thank you. You know her?" India asked, intrigued that he'd made the connection. Feldman was famous for digging up as many details of opposing counsel's life as possible in order to find chinks in their armor. India thanked God she had never been drunk at an office Christmas party or at the annual Bar Association holiday mingle.

"Who doesn't know Judge Lydia Chumley? She made history. No doubt you will too. Just not with this case," he chided, letting out a hearty laugh.

"Are we here to have a tea party or to discuss why that lazy blood-sucker keeps trying to stick his hand in my cookie jar? I work my a—" Paula Winston interjected.

"Paula," José said, cutting her off politely but ever so firmly. Robert looked down at his hands, no doubt in an attempt to forget the banshee his wife has become. *It must be painful for him to remember the young woman she was when they first met as students at Berkeley,* India thought. She reflected with a wince that marriage and money could make bloodthirsty monsters of the once madly in love.

"So, you've applied for two hundred and fifty thousand dollars in additional fees," José said with an admiring smile. "I'm getting dizzy just thinking about it," he added, casually popping a diminutive mint into his mouth and looking at India as if to say, "Your move."

"I'm sure we'd all rather settle this out of court," India volleyed, smiling back.

"You would, Ms. Chumley, because you know with a judge in the picture, Mr. Winston stands no chance whatsoever of getting the children. Or the child support and alimony that conveniently come with them," Feldman parried.

"My client is not principally interested in alimony," India said, containing her fury at the suggestion of venality as one of Robert's motives. His wife had become the grasping mogul. He remained the "sensitive new age" guy he had been at twenty. He just wanted to raise his children, read his Hermann Hesse, and cultivate his organic garden.

"So he's asking for something in which he has no interest. Novel approach," Feldman answered with barely masked sarcasm.

"Mr. Winston made career sacrifices so that the children could thrive—" India pointed out.

"Sacrifices?" Paula scoffed, "What? His two-dollar-a-week beat at the *Village Voice*? We'd be living on the street on his salary."

Paula furiously scratched her neck beneath the enormous white cowl of her top. It framed her face like a twenty-first-century Queen Elizabeth's ruff. *She certainly could defeat an invading armada, though none of her soldiers would have a testicle to his name,* India observed.

"How'm I supposed to wear hemp when they make it so itchy?" Paula whined.

"Mrs. Winston, Mr. Winston has every intention of returning to work," India baited. Mrs. Winston stopped her scratching, intrigued. José eyed India warily. "Once your youngest, Oliver, is in school full time, which will be in two years. Therefore, Mr. Winston is willing to reduce his number of alimony years from the eight I recommended, to three. It will give him the time to get back on his feet," India continued.

"That's awfully generous of your client," José commented. "What does he want in exchange?"

"Full custody," India answered calmly.

"Not on the table," José said, rising to leave, buttoning his Brioni suit coat.

"José!" Paula snapped, pushing him back down in his seat. "Go on."

Just as India was about to make her pitch, Una's voice came over the intercom, "Sorry to interrupt, it's your mo—it's Ms. Blakely. She says it's urgent."

José folded his hands and leaned back, thrilled at the interruption. "Mommy's calling," he explained to his client for India's benefit. India seethed at her mother's timing and at Jose's uncovering Una's bluff. But she'd done her own due diligence and she'd learned that José's modus operandi was to maintain a devil-may-care demeanor while turning opposing counsel into raging bulls. India was determined not to become a blind bull to his picador. Though José fixed her with his gaze, she refused to even glance in his direction.

"Put her through on my cell, please, Una," India said, speaking into the intercom.

"This will only take a moment," India assured Robert, ignoring José and Paula.

"I'm timing this because this is costing me!" the latter yelled, exasperated both by the intrusion of a call and India's refusal to kowtow to her, one of the most important businesswomen on the planet. Out of the corner of her eye, India caught José's smirk of approval at the deftness of her move. He removed another mint from his silver pillbox and slowly and deliberately placed it on his tongue. *He probably knows his way around the bedroom as well as he does the courtroom*, India deduced from the sensual gesture.

She moved off into a corner of the large room so as not to be overheard. Within moments, Elizabeth's voice bellowed in her ear, "Darling, I hope I'm not interrupting anything important." Without giving India a chance to respond, she barreled on. "Richard hasn't responded to the summons. I've heard nothing, not a phone call, not a telegram, not a note by carrier pigeon, and it's been six weeks."

"Actually, he's refusing to be served," India explained, dreading the response.

"What? Why in heaven's name would he do that?"

"Maybe because this is the tenth time you've served him with divorce papers in nine years. It's your version of Valentine's Day," India whispered into the phone.

"How is he managing to evade the server?" Elizabeth asked, flabbergasted.

"By not admitting that he is who he is when asked."

"But that's illegal," Elizabeth objected.

"I know, but can we talk about this—"

"Well, have him arrested, then!" Elizabeth commanded.

This suggestion stunned India. She turned to Robert and Paula. "I'm going to step out for a moment," she said, and walked out into the hall.

"Mom, do you really want me to have your husband of thirty-two years arrested?"

"I have to bring him to his senses somehow," Elizabeth answered.

India thought to herself that only in her family could an arrest warrant have been considered an appropriate means of "bringing someone to their senses." Her family and perhaps one of those inbred clans that appeared with frequency on *Jerry Springer*.

"Mum, I want you to think about this," India urged, knowing her mother had moved into charging rhinoceros mode and would not be stopped.

"The time for thinking has passed. It's time to screw our courage to the sticking place and take action," Elizabeth insisted.

"Remember as you say those words, Mother, where they led. Macbeth and Mrs. Mac-B died hideous, bloody deaths."

"But weren't they glorious in their gore? Onward!" Elizabeth cried.

"This is also getting very expensive. He is in Scotland after all," India objected.

"What's a pound or two in the name of love?" Elizabeth scoffed. *Of course, Mother can afford to be cavalier; she's not the one footing the bill,* India mused in frustration.

"Have you checked the exchange rate recently?" India reminded her.

"Bother the exchange rate! Do it, Beauty, do it for Mummy." And with that she hung up.

"I hate my family, I hate my family, I hate my family," India repeated like a soothing incantation. She stopped, took a breath, and opened the conference room door to return to the relative peace and calm of the *Winston v. Winston* debacle. Yes, this was why she had become a divorce attorney, to prove to herself that her family did not hold the monopoly and the patent on insane behavior. She reentered to find Paula speaking loudly into her cell phone.

"Tell Glenda I can't wear Pucci. It's not green!" she screeched, still scratching her neck. She hung up.

"All is well with the family, one hopes," José offered with a look of completely insincere concern. India chose to ignore the comment and addressed herself directly to Paula.

"Mrs. Winston, it's full custody with allowances for unlimited visitation. The children would be available for any photo shoots or public appearances they might need or indeed want to make with you. Say at the Earth Day celebration, for example," India offered, knowing this last suggestion would pique Paula's interest. Indeed, she perked up at the mention of the opportunity for shameless self-promotion. "They'd probably look pretty cute on the Vanishing Arctic float. Last year I think they used the Jolie-Pitt rainbow tribe, but what has little Maddox ever done for our melting ice floes? He's been photographed more than once tooling around in a plastic car. Why not have the heirs to an eco-friendly fortune? Your three socially conscious children who—as you pointed out so beautifully in that article in *Parents* magazine—play only with wooden and other biodegradable toys," India continued.

Paula listened intently and even took notes. India could hear her next conversation with her publicist: "Get my kids the ice float gig, now!" Like José, India did her opposition research. She knew that Paula's principal concern in life was presenting the proper airbrushed image to the world. Robert looked up at India in utter surprise, and José nodded as if to say "You're good."

Paula's eyes gleamed at the prospect of hoarding more of her precious fortune. "We'll take—" she started to say.

"We'll think it over," José said, cutting off his client at the pass. "This has been very productive. We'll call you," he said with a courtly bow. He led Paula out of the room.

"Where'd you come up with that?" Robert asked India.

"I read the characters. He wants to go to court; she wants to save her money. Trust me, they'll be back."

"I don't care about the money. I just want my kids. When Oliver has a nightmare, he needs you to rub his back in a circular motion ten times. Paula doesn't know that," Robert explained. India envisioned him perched on the edge of a trundle bed, caressing his three-year-old's Elmo-pajama-clad back. She could imagine Julien doing the same with their child one day. Men like Robert and Julien were all heart. *So how can a woman tire of such a man and want to leave him?* India wondered. *Women simply don't know what's good for them,* she concluded. She wished she could hold a town meeting on the subject. She'd pull out a bullhorn and yell, "Ladies, snap out of it! Stop screwing and start thinking!"

"You'll be putting the kids to bed again before you know it," she assured Robert. He offered a wan smile, the first sign of joy she'd ever seen from this unfortunate man.

India's phone buzzed, announcing the arrival of a text message:

RU free for dinner next Friday? Wayne and I are having a few friends over.

Possibly. I'll have to check with Julien, India typed in reply.

May want to leave Frenchie at his restaurant. Keith is coming.

India's heart pounded with terror and exhilaration. She composed herself and replied,

Then count me out. And why didn't you tell me he was going to be at Bright Futures?

Didn't think you cared. He'll be disappointed. He asked me to invite you.

What? When?

India typed, her heart now racing. She would never have guessed from Keith's cool response to her at the gala that he had any desire to see her again.

Gotta run. See you Friday. Look pretty, Monique replied.

India decided she must go. If only so Keith could see that she hadn't totally fallen apart in middle age. She looked up from her phone at Robert.

"So sorry," she said. "Another client. Let me walk you to the elevator." She escorted him out, her spirits floating on a cloud at the prospect of seeing Keith again.

# *chapter sixteen*

"You know you're too old for a place when they card everyone else at the door but you. We're like den mothers in here, Abby," India commented as they entered the seedy Lower East Side bar known as Guthrie's Garage. *Why on earth,* India wondered, *had she allowed Abby to drag her here?* Yes, rock-and-roll legends like Bob Dylan and Cat Stevens had once graced the stage, but the place reeked of five decades of coagulated beer to prove it.

From across the way, a tall, handsome young man spotted them and flashed Abby a smile.

"Is that Sage?" India asked, intrigued.

Abby nodded, beaming.

"He's bringing up the standard," India offered as she took in Sage's athletic six-foot-three frame, a rower's body. She'd loved rowing since freshman year of college, when she had seen her first scull gliding across the glass-smooth surface of the Charles River at dawn.

"Abby, you made it!" Sage cried, looking at Abby with the adoration of a pilgrim who, after a long, arduous climb, had arrived at last at the shrine of his saint.

"Sage, this is India, my best friend," Abby explained.

"Hello, best friend. Glad you could make it, too. I've got to get backstage. Damien here is going to take care of you ladies," Sage said, indicating an androgynous person as slender as an exclamation point with the telltale pallid skin and dark eyeliner of a goth. The only sure indications of his sex were his goatee and huge feet clad in combat boots that could snuff out a rodent in a single stomp. That skill could come in handy in this dump.

"Good evening, ladies," the exclamation point said with the courtliness of a Park Avenue boy at a cotillion. Perhaps he *was* a Park Avenue boy who had fled screaming from the 10021 ZIP code to breathe free in the downtown air.

"Just water for me, please," India answered, clutching her purse against her like a shield.

"I'll have a Corona. No glass," Abby said to tweak her prissy friend. Damien withdrew with a bow.

"What are we doing here, Abs, reliving our teen years?" India challenged, remembering nights of misery spent going from one dive bar to the other with her sheltered Sibley classmates. To them, it had been a thrill to take a walk on the wild and dingy side. To India, it had been a terrifying reminder of the seedy life she might have led had her mother not made her way out of the slums of Liverpool, England.

"I just had to get out of the house. Nathaniel is out until midnight most nights, sometimes later. And he has a new cell phone. We know what that means," Abby explained.

"Have you tried talking to him?" India pressed.

"When you ask questions like that, it's so obvious you've never been married," Abby answered with more than a hint of exasperation. India didn't feel that her friends lent enough weight to all she'd learned from observing the dysfunctional marriages around her: her mother's and those of all her clients. She hadn't lived it literally, but, boy, had she seen. A doctor didn't have to suffer a venereal disease to know its cure, after all. Nonetheless, India chose to take a more self-deprecating approach in the hopes of getting through to Abby before she made a further mess of her life.

"Well, from the Old Maid comes the question; can we get out of one situation before getting into another, however studly? This is not like you. You've never even looked at another man," she reminded Abby.

"I see. And are you following your own advice?" Abby countered, thrusting her jaw forward.

"What do you mean?" India asked, feeling guilty. She hadn't canceled dinner with Monique, Wayne, and . . . Keith, but she hadn't told Abby about that date. She refrained from doing so now. It would not help her make the case against dabbling with the young and the restless.

"You just seemed very . . . perturbed by seeing Keith the other night. Has he contacted you?" Abby pursued.

"No. Nor should he. He's engaged," India answered.

"At least you know where that relationship belongs—in the past. I don't know where I belong anymore. Sometimes you have to stare temptation in the face so you can make a decision, one way or another," Abby added, admiring Sage, who stood at a distance near the stage.

"That's true," India replied, thinking Abby had provided her with yet another justification for accepting Monique's invitation.

"I thought if I came here tonight, I might understand better why Nathaniel cheats," Abby explained. India looked at her, stunned. She'd never heard Abby admit the truth about her husband. Abby smiled wistfully while twisting the simple gold wedding band on her finger. Like India's client Robert Winston, Abby probably wondered how her marriage came to this crossroad. India could have predicted this nineteen years ago, but Abby never would have believed her. She had been too much in love with Nathaniel, whom she saw as a brilliant, tortured soul, an abused little boy crying out for help. Just as Abby couldn't rescue her husband from his demons, India knew she wouldn't get through to her friend by bludgeoning her with the facts. What Abby wanted tonight was fun and an escape.

"Oh, please, let's not get all psychologically twisted. You came here because that boy is 'foine.' If you hadn't seen him first, I'd be fantasizing about him," India teased to lighten the mood.

"Get your own object of lust," Abby chided as Damien returned with the drinks and set them down on the table.

"How much do we owe?" Abby asked.

"No, no, ladies, these are on Sage."

The house lights dimmed and everyone went quiet, except for a group of five young men incongruously clad in Paul Stuart suits. An androgynous question mark—Damien's fraternal twin, perhaps—approached the microphone.

"Hey, everybody, thanks for coming, remember this is a smoke-free environment. That goes for chronic, too. If you got any, take it outside. Now put your hands together for Sage McAllister and The Winds of Justice."

The moth-eaten black velvet curtain rose to reveal Sage holding a guitar and flanked by a United Nations of musicians: an African on the keyboard, an Indian on bass, and a classic made-in-Seattle Chinese-and-black kid on drums. After what seemed to India like an endless instrumental intro, Sage launched into an earnest ballad about "Willy the Low-man," the forgotten, medically uninsured American yearning for a living wage and an affordable HMO. His voice was full and pleasant, but the lyrics struck her as a parody of socially conscious folk music: Tracy Chapman à la *Saturday Night Live*. She turned to Abby, who stared at Sage intently, drinking in each word as she sipped her beer. The song ended to enthusiastic applause from all but India and the rowdy preppies in the corner.

"They're pretty good," Abby said.

"You've got to be kidding," India answered, incredulous.

"Well, okay, the lyrics need . . . work. But at least these songs are about something. Something of our time," Abby insisted.

After staring at Abby for a moment, India blurted, "That's the biggest load of crap I've ever heard, Abby Rosenfeld." Abby couldn't help but laugh.

"You are so gone," India continued.

"Hey, I listen to Benjamin's music, and I have to tell you that by comparison—"

"This musician is much more screwable?"

"Sshh. They're starting another number."

Sage gently strummed his guitar, looked up at the ceiling, then launched into a cry of "Why?" The query echoed India's own: *Why am I here?* After the tenth "Why?" he sang, "Why do your Janjaweed ride through my town tonight, spreading hate, blood, death, and spite?"

India stifled a laugh.

"This is not funny. It's about Darfur!" Abby whispered, glaring at her.

"I know it is. But he's singing about it. *Darfur: The Musical,*" India quipped.

"He actually went!" Abby defended, still in a whisper.

"To Darfur?" India asked, impressed, thinking she stood corrected.

"Well, to the march in Washington."

India rolled her eyes, another heart bleeding from the comfort of the developed world.

"But he did help build a school in Eritrea when he was in college," Abby told her triumphantly as the song came to a plaintive close. The table of rowdies burst out laughing, not at the song, but at some off-color joke. There was a shifting in the crowd, and male heads turned in unison, one or two female heads as well. A woman in a gray, knee-length pencil skirt and sky-high heels wound her way to the yahoos' table.

"Esme!" India called in a stage whisper. Esme turned, delighted and surprised to see her pals.

"What the hell are you two doing here? In this pit that smells like peepee?" Esme asked, laughing.

"We could ask you the same question," Abby countered.

"Simple, table in the corner, the cute one with the blue eyes," Esme answered nonchalantly.

"That's the boy from the event," India commented, stunned.

"He may look like a boy, but he works like a man. What's your excuse for coming here?" Esme responded. Abby and India looked at each other. Esme instantly sniffed a cover-up.

"One of you is up to something, either the Mulatto Virgin of Manhattan or the Should-Be-Mad Housewife. I'll find out," Esme said with a smile. Abby did her best to appear nonchalant so as not to pique Esme's curiosity further. The latter started to walk away, then turned back with an afterthought.

"India, is anybody using your apartment? The one Julien doesn't know about."

"I'm the only one who uses it. And that's rare," India answered pointedly.

"Great. My father's mistress is back in town, so I can't use his place. And you see those wild men? Those are Patrick's roommates. He has five of them. In four rooms. We need some privacy. He's a screamer."

The night of the Bright Futures function India had guessed that Patrick would have been Esme's next plaything. Still, the casualness of Esme's attitude stunned her.

"You want to borrow my apartment so you can get it on?" she asked with eyes wide as saucers.

"No, so I can read him the Ten Commandments. Come on, yes or no, are you going to help an old friend?" Esme answered, testily.

"Is it helping you?"

"Ssshh, you guys, this is rude, there's a performance going on," Abby whispered, then continued, "and India, don't give her the key."

"So?" Esme asked, extending a hand. India looked from her to Patrick, who tossed his head back, laughing, and winked at Esme. There was nothing India could do to stop this train wreck. She unzipped the inside pocket of her purse and handed Esme the apartment key on its brass Veritas key chain, a gift from the Harvard development office for her volunteer work on her fifteenth reunion.

"The address?" Esme asked.

"One forty-nine West Seventy-fifth. Apartment Three."

"Ooo, it's in one of those seedy brownstones. Is there even an elevator?"

"No, but it's just one flight up."

"To paradise. *Gracias, querida,*" Esme crowed as she tossed the key into her hobo bag, which India surmised must have contained a negligee and sundry sex toys. Esme sauntered away.

"Thanks for not telling her why we're here," Abby whispered to India. "She'd never let me live it down."

"Why are we here?" India demanded. "We should go, Abby. This is dangerous."

"I need a little danger," Abby admitted.

"Well, I'm leaving," India insisted.

"Please," Abby begged. "If you go, my cover is blown. And I'll be more prone to do something stupid."

The last reason appealed to India's conscience. She had already served as an accessory to cheating for Esme and against a man she liked and admired. She may as well have absolved her sins by serving as the guardian of Abby's virtue. Even at the price of listening to a song about the Amazon rain forest so sickeningly earnest it could have driven the most dedicated tree hugger to grab an ax and start chopping. As that dirge ended and Sage began a ballad about redeeming love, India settled in for a long night.

## chapter seventeen

"You are from India?" the cab driver inquired in a singsong Punjabi accent as he leered at India's reflection in the rearview mirror. Julien looked at her expectantly, awaiting her response as their taxi careened up Broadway to Monique's town house in Hamilton Heights, the Park Avenue of Harlem. While the driver's nosiness irritated India, she took the question as a sign that her blow-dry was strand perfect.

"No, I'm not, sir," she answered, choosing not to elaborate further. She wanted to concentrate on composing herself for the evening ahead. She was eager to see Keith's reaction to her carefully chosen ensemble: not so buttoned-up as to appear prim, not so revealing as to seem desperate, a last-ditch mating signal from a woman who feared her eggs were rapidly turning to powder.

"Where you from originally?" the driver persisted, skeptical at her response. "Because you look Indian."

India knew that if she didn't give him the full genealogical picture, she would never have her moments of peace.

"My mother is English, she's white. And my father was black, from Trinidad."

"Your father black?" the driver repeated, turning around and nearly annihilating a pedestrian in the process.

"Monsieur, please watch the road," Julien admonished.

"Yes, I'm half black."

"Hmm. But you look Indian." India didn't care if she looked extra-terrestrial as long as she looked leave-him-panting beautiful. *It's not that I care what Keith thinks of me at this juncture in my life,* she told herself. She merely wanted the satisfaction of making him realize, in the course of a two-hour dinner and by means of a perfectly fabulous outfit and coif, everything he had missed by betraying her.

"He your husband?" the driver interjected.

"Who?" India asked, momentarily confused.

"I think he was referring to me," Julien reminded her. "Not yet," he reassured the driver, with a wink to India, who smiled uncomfortably in response. The taxi lurched to a stop in front of a five-story limestone town house with a bay window. It was turn-of-the-century by India's estimation.

"*Nous voilà,*" Julien paid the driver, who practically crossed the divider to get a closer look at India, the object of his fascination.

"You not married. How old are you?" he asked, dropping the final straw on the back of India's patience.

"None of your damn business!" she snapped. The driver recoiled and Julien helped India out of the backseat.

"You look Indian!" the driver yelled out the window before speed-ing away.

India and Julien walked up the three steps of the house's neo-classical portico and rang the bell.

"You are beautiful tonight," Julien declared appreciatively as they waited. The compliment failed to calm India's nerves. Julien would have found her exquisite in a mud mask, bathrobe, and fuzzy slippers. Compliments from a man so thoroughly accepting rated much lower than those from more withholding types, like Keith. India chastised herself for the thought but could not extinguish the feeling: she hoped her appearance would dazzle her former fiancé.

After a few moments, she heard girlish falsettos calling, "We'll get it!"

The large oak door opened. India and Julien looked down to see two girls of about seven or eight with neatly plaited hair, wearing matching pink robes. The robe of the taller sister read "Madison," and the other's robe read "Tiffany." India wondered if this was their mother's homage to the places she could now afford to shop.

"Don't stand there signing for the deaf, girls," Monique called from the top of a wide carved wood staircase. "Say 'good evening,' or in the case of Mr. Julien, *'bon soir.'* Show Mommy she's not wasting her money on those expensive French lessons at *l'Alliance.*"

*"Bon soir, Monsieur Julien,"* Tiffany and Madison said in unison, sounding like Madeline and her fellow boarders.

"Say, 'Welcome to our home,'" Monique commanded.

*"Bienvenus à notre maison,"* they recited, giving a literal translation.

*"Merci,"* Julien answered.

"My girls!" Monique cheered as she descended from her perch. Julien went down on one knee to greet the girls at eye level.

*"Je n'ai jamais vu deux princesses aussi belles,"* he said tenderly as they squirmed and turned pigeon-toed with coyness. India never ceased to marvel at his rapport with children and his genuine interest in them. He reminded her of Abby's father, who would always take the time to tell the girls stories and make them feel that their every utterance was worthy of an adult's attention. It would be a wonder for a child, a girl especially, to grow up with a father like that. She felt certain her real father would have been that kind and attentive, had he lived past her second birthday.

From upstairs, she heard Keith's deep belly laugh, the kind that burst out of him whenever she said something insightful and witty. It had always given her great pride to have elicited that response. It had meant more than an A from a professor. *Who has garnered the coveted guffaw?* she wondered.

"Let's go on up," Monique beckoned. "Everyone's waiting for you," she added suggestively.

India's pulse quickened to double-time. She forced herself to stay a pace or two behind Julien. They arrived on the landing of the parlor floor and followed Monique across the shining parquet squares to the center of the yellow room. Through half-open pocket doors, India saw the dining room, the table elegantly set for supper.

Keith stood with his back turned to them, his right arm casually slung over the diminutive Serena's shoulder. India's eyes traveled over the limited length of Serena's body. She wore an inexpensive pair of slim-fitting black trousers, probably from H&M, or some other shopping mecca of the newly minted college graduate. The inexpensive pants were incongruously paired with a sumptuous N.Peale cashmere sweater set in coral and matching headband, trademark Keith Wentworth gifts. He'd given India a nearly identical set in pale blue. On Serena's left hand, which caressed Keith's taut waist, sparkled a diamond as clear as an ice cube and nearly as large. India never counted carats; she found such calculus crass and venal. If one measured the worth of a marriage proposal by the size of a fired-up lump of coal, one might as well have walked the streets for a living. Nonetheless, this gem was easily five or six carats, twice what Keith had given her. India was ashamed to compare, but it was impossible to ignore a doubling in size for someone half her age and height.

"Hey, nice to see you," Wayne called out, looking up from Serena.

"Serena, Keith, you've met Julien and India," Monique tossed out.

"You could say that," Keith offered wryly.

"Not touching that," Wayne joked. India's eyes opened wide with surprise. But then she reassured herself that she was reading far too much into the comment. Forcing the corners of her mouth up, she gave her best "all is well" smile.

"Nice to see you again, India!" Serena gushed. "Nice to meet you, Julien."

India was relieved yet annoyed that Wayne's reference had gone right over Little Miss Sunshine's head. She was either completely ignorant of her past with Keith or diabolically cunning at masking her knowledge. Then again, why should Keith have told her? She hadn't shared the information with Julien, other than to describe him as a former law school classmate. It wasn't an attempt to hide the past, just one to move forward. *Perhaps Keith is attempting to do the same,* she surmised.

"What can I offer you to drink?" Wayne asked. "We've got everything except Ripple, and Monique mixes a mean margarita."

For the first time in her life, India longed for a double Scotch, no ice. Instead she asked for a glass of red.

"I'll open the Opus One. It's a '98," Wayne boasted, "their best year on record."

"Opus One! Phh. That wine was created for overpaid Negroes like you," Keith chided.

"You would say that. You've barely graduated from wine coolers. But let's ask an expert. Don't you own some kind of restaurant or snack joint, Julian?" Wayne asked, purposely anglicizing Julien's name. India cringed, awaiting Julien's reaction to the belittling remark. Julien merely smiled knowingly. India relaxed, noting that he was too secure a man to respond to such petty jabs.

"Don't you think Opus One holds up against any Bordeaux?" Wayne continued.

"I would not say any. But certainly it's very good. I'll try the hostess's famous margarita," Julien answered.

"If Opus One is so damn good, why are you opting for tequila with limonade?" Keith taunted. Wayne laughed. India knew their game: "The white boy is in our world tonight so let's swat him around like a squash ball and see if we can make him squirm."

But Julien remained unfazed. He studied Wayne and Keith for a moment, then answered, "I happen to like margaritas. Especially when they are made by beautiful women." Monique pulled her shoulders back and shimmied with glee.

"*Merci,*" she said.

"Watch out, you're in the man's house. Don't hit on his wife. This ain't France," Keith challenged.

"Frenchmen hardly hold the monopoly on infidelity," India blurted.

How dare Keith accuse another man of inappropriate behavior? Keith glared at her, his right jaw pulsing with tension. Wayne and Monique exchanged "it's getting thick in here" looks. Serena looked around at all of them, wide-eyed with confusion. Julien's gaze traveled from Keith to India.

Realizing she'd brought the banter to a screeching halt, India plastered on another smile and tried to fill the conversational hole.

"What were you talking about when we first came in? Whatever it was, it must have been funny," she said chattily.

"We were talking about Serena's upcoming exhibit," Keith answered calmly as he caressed the top of his fiancée's head. India wondered if he was putting on a display of affection for her benefit, in response to her jab.

"Oh, are you an artist?" she asked, thinking Serena, with her unimaginative perfect-little-wife attire certainly didn't look like one. At best, she was a graphic artist, designing ads for modern furniture outlets that sold tacky leather sectionals.

"No, I'm an assistant curator at the Museum of Contemporary Art, and this is my first."

This was not the answer India had expected, and it was as unsettling as the six-carat diamond. Not only did the little sprite have a magnificent engagement ring, she had an impressive job as well. This was growing more irritating by the moment.

"I love that museum. What is your specialty?" Julien asked, genuinely interested.

"I work in the contemporary painting division, but this exhibit is actually about censorship. I'm comparing the Giuliani administration's crackdown on the Sensation exhibit at the Brooklyn Museum in '99 with the NEA's stifling of the Corcoran Gallery for showing Mapplethorpe's homoerotic photographs. I don't know if you remember that incident."

*Of course I do,* India thought to herself. *I was actually reading by then; you, on the other hand, were a fetus.* She took a gulp of her Opus One, annoyed not just by Serena's youth, but also by her obvious intelligence. It had been a good deal more reassuring to think of her as a second-rate graphic artist.

"It actually happened when I was really little, but my parents kept all these clippings and it always fascinated me. I'm writing my PhD dissertation on it," Serena said in a tone so soft and mellifluous, she sounded like she was discussing fellatio, not a PhD thesis. India had never mastered the come-hither whisper, the voice so feminine and soothing that it held all men and dogs in its thrall. Whatever she had to say, she said it loudly and absolutely. Maybe that's where she'd gone wrong in life. What man wanted to come home to Bella Abzug and her megaphone?

"When is it going to open?" Julien asked. "I'd love to see it."

"Not until May. But you're all invited!" she said cheerily, as though asking them to a pep rally.

"So you're gonna be planning a wedding and an exhibit? Scared of you, girl," Monique commented with feigned admiration.

"Baby, what are you talking about? You planned our wedding while finishing your residency," Wayne reminded Monique, less from a desire to compliment his wife than out of unwillingness to be surpassed in any area of his life.

"Please, we had fifty people in at the meeting room of Abyssinian. This is the extravaganza that's gonna be the cover of *Ebony* magazine and *Town & Country Weddings.*"

"Actually, Mrs. Wentworth is handling it," Serena explained.

India laughed inwardly at the thought of Serena's mother-in-law-to-be from hell. She remembered wrestling with Mama Gorgon, she of no daughters and only one highly prized son. She had even wanted to help select India's wedding gown. She'd sent clippings of dresses she deemed appropriate for a "Wentworth bride." India's mother had mailed them back to her with a note that read,

Dear Livia, You'd look lovely in any of these creations, except the one with yards of tulle. A bit Miss Havisham at our age, don't you think?

"So have you set a date yet?" Wayne asked provocatively.

Keith looked at him as if to say, "Did you have to bring that up?"

"That's one small problem," Serena said in a mock stern voice. "Mrs. Wentworth and I can't pin my honey down," she explained.

"That's how they are," Monique piled on. "That's why some sisters go for brothers in jail. You want to talk to them, they can't escape."

"So, Julien, what do you do?" Keith volleyed, giving Julien the once-over.

"As Wayne mentioned, I own a restaurant. Unfortunately, that short answer is not going to save you from the conversation you're trapped in."

Monique winked at India, pleased at Keith's obvious discomfort. India shot a nervous glance at Julien to make sure he hadn't seen the exchange.

"I want to hear more about Serena's thesis," India interjected, hoping to shift the course of discussion. Serena stared back blankly, not certain where to begin.

"Why don't we all make ourselves comfortable," Wayne suggested, leading the way to the seating area of the parlor. He settled into a large club chair like a man preparing to watch his favorite sporting match. Keith lowered himself into a seat opposite Wayne.

"Go on, honey," Keith barked at Serena, who jumped like a startled fawn. "Tell India about your thesis. She wants to hear all about it," he added sharply. Serena perched herself on the arm of his chair and caressed his shoulder like an obedient concubine.

"Well, I've only written four chapters . . ." she began.

Julien took a seat beside India, who reluctantly clasped his outstretched hand. As Serena prattled on, India kicked herself for accepting this invitation to "death by awkwardness."

# chapter eighteen

The candles on Monique's rectangular table had dwindled a full inch and a half in height. India sat wishing the barely nibbled slice of sweet potato tart with butter pecan coulis prepared by Raya Jean, caterer extraordinaire to Harlem's buppie-ocracy, was a chocolate mousse, a Lindt chocolate bar, hell, a Sara Lee brownie. It might have given her something on which to obsess other than Keith, who held all the women spellbound with a tale of visiting a potato chip plant in Idaho, a hotbed of the white supremacist movement. Wayne leaned back in his chair fingering the stem of his wineglass and looking around the room. Keith, his best client and fellow Boule Club member, had bored him with this story before. India forced herself not to stare at Keith's face, the color of heavy cream in the candlelight, and his full, rosy lips so versed in talents not usually displayed in public. Monique's seating was almost diabolical. Had she put Keith and India right across from each other on purpose? India practiced the art of looking around the room while someone was speaking, without appearing rude.

"Didn't he know who you were? You have your daddy's last name," Monique asked, taking a large, lustful bite of tart.

"We weren't doing the buy through Wentworth Foods. We were using a subsidiary. So he's taking me around and there's a brother operating the fryer. He tells me he's been 'eliminating them.' 'We may have a nigger in the White House, but when I'm done, the only way a nigger will get in this plant is as dirt on a potato,' he says."

The women all gasped. Monique shook her head in dismay and added: "The Obamas have taken us many steps forward, but they've also got those crazy Klan types fired up."

"I don't believe it," Julien uttered, horrified, and then gave a sympathetic squeeze to India's hand as if to apologize for the racism of certain American whites.

"So what did you say, Keith?" Monique asked, riveted. Wayne groaned.

"First, I said a prayer in my head: 'Dear Lord, please help me find the strength and the wisdom not to kick the shit out of this motherfucker.'"

They all laughed, even Wayne.

"Then I got him to keep on talking. Found out he wasn't just a randomly hating fool, he was part of a Klan cell. Like Monique said, electing a brother has them fired up. I told him I thought he really understood the world and asked him to take me to a meeting."

"Man, you're crazy," Wayne scoffed.

"Had to be done, Wayne. So we drive out in the middle of the night to this house, could have been anywhere. And all these dudes are sitting around talking about Jews taking over the world and how to repackage their message so they don't come across like the violent, humanity-hating sons of bitches that they are."

"Baby, we are all for saving the world, but what if they found out what you were?" Monique interjected, serving herself more tart.

"He could have been killed," Serena said with a shudder. India could have throttled her. Didn't she realize Keith was the ultimate survivor and could get himself out of any scrape? If she was to be a true partner, she'd have to be less melodramatic. To India's satisfaction, Keith completely ignored Tinker Bell's outburst and continued.

"They thought maybe I was 'eye-talian'; I told him I was black Irish. Anyway, the long and short of it is, I listened, and I recorded. We sicked the feds on their asses and had the manager and his buddies arrested for conspiracy to commit hate crimes. That's how you win the war against racism."

"Just like Walter White," India said, mentioning the former NAACP leader who had used his ability to pass for Caucasian as a weapon in the early struggle for civil rights.

Keith whipped around to stare at her. She knew he was amazed she remembered, but how could she not. Walter White was his hero.

"Keith has me reading *A Man Called White*. His crusade against lynching was amazing," Serena commented, doe-eyed with wonder.

"The point is," Keith continued, once again disregarding the wood nymph's contribution to the conversation, "God made me this way, a 'stealth bomber.' I've got to use it."

"Lord, now you're gonna go messiah on us, the great *passant blanc* hope. It's definitely time for some cognac," Wayne snorted. "Personally, I think the color of victory is green. You gotta make enough bank so people can't mess with you or your children, or your children's children," he concluded.

"Amen," Monique concurred, raising her glass, then draining its contents swiftly.

"It's a two-pronged battle. You gotta change how people think, and you gotta let them know what they can't get away with," Keith insisted. India found herself nodding in agreement. Along with his physical splendor, Keith's idealism had always affected her like the world's most potent aphrodisiac. The warmth rose to her cheeks, and she shifted in her seat.

"Like every other brother who graduated Harvard Law School in the nineties, you're just mad Barack beat you to the presidency," Wayne chided.

"He broke the ceiling, but it doesn't solve the whole problem. Besides, no shame in being the second," Keith shot back, laughing. "At least in politics," he added, glancing toward Julien, who at that point bent over to pick up his fallen napkin. India blanched and looked desperately to Monique, who nodded as if to say "I got it, I'll get this back on track."

"Keith, you're a rich boy. For those of us who grew up with nothing, we don't want to change hearts and minds. We want bank and for people to leave us the hell alone," Monique stated, stabbing the air with her monogrammed silver fork for emphasis.

"I don't understand your American racism," Julien suddenly said. Everyone at the table turned to look at him. India waited with bated breath to see how Keith would respond. The latter took a slow, deliberate sip of his wine, then fixed Julien with his gaze.

"Really? Well, we don't understand your French *racisme*," Keith answered. "Seems to me a few years back the natives were getting restless and burning down Paris. Looked like Los Angeles in '92."

"I'm not defending our treatment of North Africans and other immigrants. But the situation is different."

"Racism is racism," Keith retorted.

"But it's so *absurde*. You are not really black," Julien rejoined. Monique, Keith, Wayne, and even sweet little Serena stared at him in stunned silence.

"Oh no, he didn't," Monique muttered under her breath. Like a towering dunce cap, Julien's comment singled him out as the lone racially naïve white person in the room. India wanted to die of mortification. After all, it was she who had brought "the Great Clueless One" into their midst to trample their sensitivities with his ignorance.

Sensing a pall over the table, Julien turned to India. "What is the problem? Did I offend someone?" Before India could answer, Keith jumped in.

"For your information, Julien, my ancestors didn't fly here on Air France. They came from Africa in the belly of a slave ship. They were bought and paid for."

"I just meant to say—"

"We know what you meant," India snapped. She glared at Julien to indicate no further comment on his part was necessary or welcome. Keith refused to let the matter drop.

"You French think you're so liberal just 'cause you love jazz and Josephine Baker. But you're as bad as any American redneck," he accused, swirling the Bordeaux around in his glass before polishing it off.

"That's not true," India found herself objecting to this low and undeserved blow. Keith looked at her as though betrayed. "France has treated the North Africans horribly, but their treatment of blacks overall, particularly people from the West Indies, puts our system to shame. The chief of police in Paris at the time of the 2005 unrest was half Martinican. And Sarkozy's minister for human rights is a thirty-two-year-old black woman from Senegal."

"You just like the French because their mouths don't drop open every time you introduce your white mama," Keith said, going for the jugular.

India sat up stunned. She couldn't believe he would make such a personal reference in front of everyone. She should have let the remark go, in the hopes that it would drift away unnoticed in the conversational current. But she couldn't; she had to address it.

"That quality alone indicates an ability to see individuals, not just stereotypes. Not to mention something that has yet to happen in this country, in spite of the DNA evidence in the Thomas Jefferson case: an acknowledgment that miscegenation happened, that we are a nation of mongrels."

"Speak for yourself, Pinkie," Keith answered, tauntingly using his old pet name for her. "Both my parents are black."

"By way of a few visits from the master of the big house. Check a mirror, Adam Clayton Powell," India rebutted. Keith flashed a smile, touché.

An awkward silence fell over the table until Serena ventured the question, "How do you two know each other anyway?" Monique stifled a laugh.

"You stepped in it now, brother," Wayne said sotto voce to Keith, slapping him on the back as he rose from the table. His tone struck India as cruelly gleeful at his handsome friend's predicament. India waited on tenterhooks to hear Keith's response. She feared he'd reveal the truth yet hoped desperately that his answer would betray some trace of feeling. Julien looked from Keith to her and took another sip of his wine. After what felt to India like a century, the oracle spoke at last.

"Chumley and I were in law school together," Keith explained dispassionately. "A long time ago." He then put his arm around Serena and kissed her full on the lips. She melted into his enveloping arms.

*So this is what I amount to,* India surmised, *a footnote in the story of his life.* Why had he insisted to Monique that she come? Was it to parade his impending connubial bliss in front of her, the ultimate payback for her having walked out on him? Perhaps Monique had lied, and it was her idea, not Keith's, to force them into each other's company tonight.

"Will you excuse me?" India asked after a decent interval, during which the conversation buzzed around her like so many bees whose signals she couldn't decipher. She turned to Monique.

"Where's the powder room in this palace?"

"Down the steps, to the right."

Julien rose to pull out her chair. India hummed a funeral march in her head to slow her pace as she exited.

The powder room was a soothing coral. With a cinnamon-orange-scented candle burning, it offered the perfect sanctuary. India closed the mahogany toilet seat cover and collapsed onto it, hugging herself. Keith's words echoed in her mind like an endless loop of news footage. "Chumley and I were in law school together, a long time ago," followed by the soulful kiss. What had she expected? Had she thought he would stand up and declare, "It's been lovely, Serena, but it's always been India and no one else," then burst into the opening lyrics of "And This Is My Beloved"? Of course not, but then again, it would have been nice. Neither her vaunted discipline and self-restraint nor her efforts at demonizing his memory could stop the pull he exerted on her heart. In spite of everything, she still wanted him, and she hated herself for it. She found herself uttering the four words in the English language that most repulsed her: "I can't help it." She wanted to slap her mother and her other clients when they made such professions of powerlessness and emotional defeat. And now she had joined their pathetic, white-flag-waving throng.

*Perhaps that is what I need, a good loud smack across the face,* she thought, rising. *A splash of cold water perhaps?* Better to keep it figurative—she didn't want to ruin her makeup or wet her hair and have it frizz, God forbid. It was bad enough her emotions were in shambles. She didn't need a hairdo to match. She could not—she would not—turn into everything she despised: a weak-willed, emotionally disheveled woman looking for bodice-ripping Barbara Cartland love. A victim. The late Princess of Wales served as proof of where fairy tales led.

Staring at her reflection in the mirror, India made a mental vow never, ever to revisit this situation again. So what if she still cared? She must act as if she didn't, and eventually her wanton heart would follow her back to the realm of sanity and good judgment where women she admired, Constance Armstrong and Nana Chumley, dwelled. And with that resolution, she flung open the bathroom door. Two large male hands grabbed her and pinned her against the wall. Keith's mouth was inches from hers. She shoved him away.

"What are you doing?" she asked, galled as much by the thrill she felt at his touch as by his forwardness.

"I haven't stopped thinking about you since that night at the Waldorf. I asked Monique to invite you. I had to see you again." So it was true. This revelation tamed her fury, at least a bit.

"What do you want from me?" she asked, attempting nonchalance though her every nerve stood at attention.

"It's not finished between us," he answered. Her heart leapt, but she forced it to heel by envisioning him kissing Serena, and then his floozy of six years before.

"Yes, it is. You're engaged," she managed coldly. "And I'm not some cheap blonde ready to screw you in a rented room at the Harvard Club," she added.

"Damn! Are you ever going to forgive me for that?" he pleaded.

The memory of seeing him with the other woman was still so vivid she could choke him. And yet she wanted to fall into his arms.

"We've both moved on," she said, the softness in her tone belying her words.

"No, we haven't," he retorted, leaning in.

"You arrogant shit," she whispered. He caressed her right cheek with his hand. She batted it away. He grazed her left cheek. Again, she batted his hand away. He grabbed her wrist tightly and lowered his mouth onto hers. She started to push him away, but her hand fell on the firm mounds of his pectorals. They flinched under her grasp. Her grip loosened, becoming a caress. She melted into this kiss, the most potent she'd had in years. It was the kind of kiss that used to begin on a Saturday night in the vestibule of Keith's apartment and continued until they reached the bedroom, where he'd switch on the Luther Vandross with the remote control, a cheesy but effective move.

"Let me hold you tight, if only for one night," Luther's voice would croon. She savored the nuclear attraction, inhaling the familiar scent of his warm, satin-soft skin.

"Isn't this cozy?" a strong female voice intoned.

Keith and India disengaged and saw Monique standing at the foot of the stairs.

"Don't worry, I don't talk," Monique said, relieving their suspense.

"Excuse me," Keith sputtered, abruptly turning and bounding up the stairs two by two. India was stunned at his departure. Then again, it was of a piece with his behavior of six years ago. *What lies will he tell his wood nymph?* India wondered, fuming. *And the little twit will probably believe him.*

"Nice work," Monique commented. "Quick too."

"Monique, that's not my style. He kissed me," India insisted.

"Oh yeah, and you looked like you were hating it. A few more minutes and ya'll might have ended up doing it over the sink in the powder room." The blood rushed to India's cheeks. She knew she was guilty as charged.

"Don't worry," Monique continued. "Like I said, I don't talk. And I want you to get him back. Who wants to see him marry Miss Pep Squad with the gravity-defying titties and the PhD in esoteric art of the twentieth century? He needs a real woman."

India thrilled to Monique's words while telling herself it was wrong.

"Monique, you shouldn't speak that way," she cautioned.

"Fine. I won't talk about it, and I won't find opportunities for putting my two favorite people together. Since you don't want me to." India's heart pounded, but she didn't bite. She still didn't understand why Monique wanted to see her "get the man." Could she really have been that fond of her?

"But there is one thing you can do for me," Monique said coyly.

"What is it?" India asked warily.

Monique tossed a glance up stairs, then murmured, "Lend me the key to your apartment, the one Frenchie doesn't know about. Please."

India's jaw literally dropped. Et tu, Monique? Of all the women she knew, she didn't expect cheating and dallying from practical, no-nonsense Monique.

"Why?" India finally summoned the wherewithal to ask.

"Come on. You've seen my husband. You think Wayne knows how to give the kind of kiss you just got from Keith?" India tried to envision Wayne, a man with the physique of a beached walrus, in a passionate embrace. Her sympathies went out to Monique, as they did to so many of her clients. It seemed half the married women in the world led lives of quiet sexual desperation.

"He was never Dr. Love, even when we first met at the Black Ski Summit twelve years ago. He was poetry in motion on the slopes, but it didn't translate between the sheets."

"So why did you marry him?" India asked, truly baffled. Monique looked at her in exasperation.

"You can't pick a husband with your pussy. If you find somebody who's got the important things going on, you work with what you got." Monique grabbed India's arm and moved her further away from the staircase, presumably out of earshot of Wayne and the others. "But ever since we had the girls, he hardly touches me," Monique admitted in a whisper. "Eight years."

"You haven't had sex in eight years?" India asked, horrified. She'd never had the misfortune of dealing with impotence, and certainly none of her dry spells had lasted nearly a decade.

"Maybe once a quarter. And it lasts about a minute."

"Have you tried counseling?" India asked tentatively. Monique let out a derisive "Ha!" India instantly regretted suggesting the "white liberal" solution to the problem. She'd seen enough couples to know that most straight men hated therapy, and that straight black men would rather go to war than share their problems with a shrink.

"I can't live like this anymore. I can live with bad sex but not no sex. It makes you wonder, 'Am I that ugly?'" Monique continued.

India absorbed the revelation, and for the first time in thirty-two years of knowing Monique, she saw the deep pain that lay beneath her "don't mess with me" toughness.

"I'm sorry, Monique. That must be awful," she offered sympathetically.

"I don't need you to feel sorry for me, Miss Thing. I need the key to that apartment," Monique snapped.

"I just don't feel right about it. I know Wayne. I'm a guest in your home tonight. This is wrong, not to mention supremely rude. You don't arrange trysts for the wife of a man who's served you his best wine," India replied, taken aback by Monique's desperation.

"Girl, this isn't a garden party. This is my life. After all these years, I have somebody who wants me. He came after *me*!" she said. It dawned on India that Monique couldn't believe someone actually found her attractive.

"So are you leaving Wayne?" India inquired, softening.

"Hell, no. Who said anything about leaving?"

"Well, if it's been so bad—"

"The sex is bad. There is no sex. But our marriage is fine. Yeah, ever since he started making serious bank, he can be an asshole sometimes, but he's smart and funny, and he's my girls' daddy. They're not growing up without him," Monique said as if stating the obvious. India was thoroughly stunned by Monique's apparent ability to compartmentalize. It was hardly the first time she'd seen a woman justify maintaining more than one relationship, but it still threw her.

"If he's so important, how can you be cheating on him?" she insisted.

"I guess I could ask you the same question about Julien." India recoiled, stung.

"I'm not married to Julien. And again, Keith kissed me."

"And you loved it."

India averted her gaze, crimson rising to her cheeks again.

"Because he has the touch," Monique continued, knowing she was speaking for both of them. "It's a gift. Some men have it. Most don't. My Hector has it. He doesn't have much else, but between the sheets, he's a god."

Without knowing anything else about this Hector, India sensed that in him Monique had encountered that rarest of creatures: a sexual virtuoso. Such lovers could divine exactly what a woman wanted without being directed from point to point. They slowly but surely coaxed a woman to the very heights of ecstasy, making sex a sublime, transcendent experience. They worked a woman's naked body like a prodigy played the keys of a piano, expertly varying their rhythm from pianissimo to scherzo to crescendo. Most of a woman's life was spent at the mercy of amateurs who had no instincts or finesse, but just banged away, hoping for the best. Among the men India had slept with, she had encountered only two erotic geniuses: Sam, the dumb-as-a-post dentist in LA, and, of course, Keith. Just as she had to renounce the latter, she felt Monique should avoid continuing this dalliance that would only make her current situation more untenable.

"Monique, you're jeopardizing your marriage," she insisted.

"Do you know what it's like to feel ugly? I do. Every night my husband lies next to me, snoring. If I can't have my afternoons with Hector, I'll lose my mind. And then I really will do something stupid."

The last argument, while thoroughly depressing, convinced India that helping Monique arrange her trysts was the lesser of two evils. She reached into her purse and handed her the key. Esme had sent it back to her via messenger with an accompanying note that read: "Thanks for loaning me to the key to paradise. Sex is better when you can make some noise. Hope the neighbors didn't complain." Instead of a period, she'd marked the end of the sentence with a smirking smiley face.

"A Harvard key chain, classy touch," Monique commented as she fingered the key, then added sincerely, "Thank you. I owe you." She flounced up the stairs.

India stood alone in the hallway, reluctant to return to the dining room. There was no doubt she would have found Keith snuggling with Serena, and poor, unsuspecting Julien waiting for her with open arms. She'd settle in beside him and find herself wishing his every caress was Keith's.

# *chapter nineteen*

Julien and India sat in the backseat of a dilapidated sedan from a cheap car service heading back downtown. India looked out the window at the changing cityscape, trying to make sense of the night's events. Julien interrupted her reverie.

"India, I did not like the way you cut me off at dinner. I felt like a naughty child being silenced."

*You might as well have been,* India thought to herself. She hadn't realized until tonight how little Julien understood of American racial politics. Then again, they hadn't really ventured much outside the conversational cocoon of his restaurant and apartment. What a difference one outing made. This was always the ultimate question for her lovers: could they fit into all the worlds through which she moved? Most failed miserably. There had been the music executive in LA who thought Sophocles was a venereal disease. Next came the talent agent who found her family too theatrical and crazy. In point of fact they were, but accepting her meant accepting them, straightjackets and all.

*Will Julien ever understand the challenges I face as a woman of color?* she wondered. Granted, she waged her battles for equality in gleaming boardrooms and at the counters of overpriced luxury good stores. Nonetheless, she wondered if she could travel the road of life with a color-blind Mr. "We Are the World."

"You said yourself, India, that Keith has white blood," Julien reminded her.

"I can say that. You can't," she answered, irritated at having to explain.

"Why not, since it's true?"

"You were insulting him."

"You're very protective of his feelings, I see," Julien said pointedly. India feared he would probe further into her past with Keith. In her current state of emotional disarray, she did not feel up to the task of appearing unperturbed while discussing the object of her deepest desire. Like an evasive politician, she stuck to her original point in order to dodge the true question looming in the air.

"What you said was insulting," she repeated.

"So it's an insult to tell someone they look white? Are we that disgusting?"

"That's not the point. In this country, one drop of African blood makes you black. It doesn't matter that my mother's so pale she makes you look like an aborigine. In the eyes of the Census Bureau and the law, I'm black," India corrected.

"Do you think that's right?" Julien challenged.

"Maybe not. But it's the way it is. If we had children, what do you think they would be?"

"Beautiful," he said simply.

The statement disarmed her. In her heart, she did find racial classifications arbitrary and ridiculous. But she couldn't admit that to Julien at that moment. It would have meant giving him a chance. And she had chosen to live in the United States where these issues mattered.

"I want to understand, India. But you have to help me. Please explain," Julien pleaded.

*There it is again, the request for how-tos,* India reflected with exasperation. At one point, India had thought of writing a manual to hand out to all romantic prospects: "The Care and Feeding of Your Mulatto." That had been one of the many joys of her relationship with Keith. He didn't need an instruction booklet or a symposium. He just got it.

As they exited the town car, the wizened black driver called out to her, "Miss! Sister!"

"Yes." She turned to him as he rolled down his window.

"You gonna marry that white boy?" the man asked.

"Maybe," she answered curtly.

"If you do, you're gonna wear yourself out trying to educate him. Find one of your own kind," the driver warned.

"If my parents thought that way, I wouldn't be here," she said, and walked away.

As Julien unlocked the door of the apartment, India rushed in, tossing her coat in the closet.

"I have a little work to do. I'll come to bed when I'm done," she announced.

Julien shook his head. He retreated into the bedroom. India winced, knowing he was angry and hurt. She would tend to his wounded feelings later. She ran to the little cubicle off the kitchen. She turned on her computer, her twenty-first-century confession booth, and sent Abby an instant message.

Abs, just got back from dinner at Monique's. Keith cornered me and kissed me. I kissed back. Monique saw. Don't know what it means.

What were you doing there to begin with?

Tempting fate. Dumb, dumb, dumb.

Don't be so hard on yourself. I slept with Sage.

India was stunned. She typed

What? After I spent a night in that smelly dump. When?

The night of the concert.

You mean I spent two hours listening to that shitty, self-righteous do-gooder music for nothing?

Yes! No! It isn't shitty. Although the other adjectives are accurate.

But we shared a cab.

And I went back. And he took me home. It was awesome.

This is a mess.

But it feels really good. Gotta go. Husband ready for bed. Call ya tomorrow.

And with that, Abby signed off. India thought she'd seen it all at work, among her clients, but now her best and oldest friends had succumbed to being statistics out of *Cosmopolitan* magazine.

"You've got mail!" the computerized male voice announced. At the top of her new emails she spotted "KWentworth@WentworthFoods .com, re: no subject." She stared at it a moment, then unable to resist, clicked to open it.

Pinkie,

I need to see you. We have to talk. Say when and where and I'll be there.

KW

India closed her eyes and imagined sitting across from Keith at a corner table of the bar at the St. Regis Hotel. *It's only fair to let him have his day in court,* India mused before shaking off the thought. No good could come of such an encounter. She summoned all her resolve and pressed the delete button. She shut off the computer and went to the bedroom, tiptoeing in past Julien, who slumbered on his side of the bed. He'd left the lights on low so she could see.

As she undressed by the closet, he asked, "How long did you go out with Keith?"

India stopped in her tracks, her dress down around her ankles.

She thought when he didn't bring it up again on the ride home that he hadn't suspected there'd ever been anything between Keith and her. She'd underestimated Julien.

"Who told you we went out?" she asked.

"Everything. It's obvious."

*What else is obvious?* India wondered nervously.

"I was waiting to see if you would admit it," Julien continued. She looked at him as she formulated the appropriate answer, one that was truthful without betraying her current state of confusion. In the courtroom and in life, India found playing for time a useful strategy. Rushing to speak always led to disasters.

Julien broke the silence. "India, I don't care who you dated or slept with. Or how many lovers you had before me."

"You don't?" India responded, taken aback.

"No. I hope you had many and that they were very good. You can't appreciate my talents unless you have something to compare them to," he added, laughing. "I'm not possessive. You can do as you please."

"Are you giving me permission to sleep with other men?" India asked, seizing the opportunity to move off the topic of Keith, the lumbering elephant in the boudoir.

Julien smiled and shook his head.

"If you don't want to tell me anything else about Keith, that's okay," he said, calling her bluff. His perceptiveness surprised and excited her. He hadn't read the Great Books. He could not argue fine points of constitutional law with her, but his awareness of the foibles of human nature inspired respect. An hour ago, she was ready to dismiss him on the grounds of his racial naïveté. Now she wanted nothing so much as to snuggle up beside him. She approached the bed, tentatively. He extended a welcoming hand and drew her close. With great relief, she rested her head on his chest. *There are worse places, by far,* she thought.

"The only thing that would hurt me, India, is if you lied."

India swallowed hard. She'd already lied about the apartment. Well, that wasn't a lie, more of a fib of omission. Was this the moment to confess its existence? She thought better of it. The lease was only a year. By then, they could be married or at the very least engaged. The lease could slip into obsolescence without his ever having known. Even Nana Chumley, a federal judge, had told her, "No man should know everything about you. Keep something to yourself." And so, for that night at least, India decided in all good conscience, she mustn't say a word.

## *chapter twenty*

"Let me get the key in, baby," Monique shrieked, playfully batting away the hands of her young stud. He stood five feet ten with a solidly built boxer's body, caramel skin, and close-cropped hair. Around his thick neck he wore a gold link chain with a charm that spelled "Hector." The door yielded. Monique flicked on the lights, and they looked around India's Victorian studio apartment.

"What do you think? Doesn't this beat the utility closet at the hospital?" Monique asked.

"Not bad. But I like the way the smell of ammonia makes you go all super freaky," Hector said, smacking his wad of Big Red gum as he caressed her left buttock with his large hand.

"I don't need ammonia to make me freaky, baby," Monique purred to him, already weak at the knees.

"Whose crib is this, anyway?" He strutted around the expansive room, examining every corner.

"A friend of mine's," Monique said evasively.

"What time is she coming home?"

"She's not. This is just her extra pad."

"You got rich friends," he said, whistling again as he picked up a Lalique crystal bird that sat poised for flight on a spindly side table. He slammed it back down, nearly toppling the table, steadying it just in time.

"Hey, we don't have much time before we have to get back to the hospital," Monique reminded him, eagerly whipping off her jacket and lunging for him. He stopped her, removing her hands from his chest and gently placing them back at her sides, much to her confusion.

"Slow down," he whispered in her ear as he nuzzled her earlobe and then her neck. She melted at his warm, electrifying touch and reached for him again, but again he stopped her.

"What's the rush? We're not in the utility closet," he reminded her as he sat down on the edge of the bed with his legs spread. Monique's breath quickened at the sight of the huge bulge in his pants. As usual, he was ready for action.

"Stand back," he commanded. "I want to check out my baby."

Monique, suddenly self-conscious, took a few tentative steps backward. Hector never had seen her fully naked, since their trysts took place in dark, cramped corners of the hospital. Two trips to labor and delivery had left the skin on her belly slightly wrinkled and sagging, for all her sit-ups and sensible eating. She panicked at how he would react when he got a good long look at this "elephant flesh." She often wondered if the sight of it cooled what little ardor Wayne had in the first place.

"I think we should turn off the lights," Monique suggested, wrapping her arms around herself to hide her flawed midsection.

"No, let Hector see you, all of you. Take it off for me. Slow, Mami," Hector murmured, leaning back and rolling his wad of gum around his mouth with his tongue. Monique knew she had no choice. There was no place to hide. If seeing her naked drove him screaming from the room, then that would be that. She took a deep breath, doing her best to suck in her tummy and with eyes shut, unbuttoned her blouse. After a few moments, she removed her pants. She stood still, with eyes firmly closed, awaiting a reaction but heard nothing. She opened her eyes, and found Hector gaping at her, dumbfounded.

*Shit,* she thought to herself, cringing, *he's wondering how the hell he can get out of here.* Mortified, she wished she could just evaporate.

Suddenly, she heard him say, "Damn, you're beautiful."

She looked up at him, stunned. No one had called her beautiful in years. In this moment she had to admit that even though she didn't think of herself that way, it was glorious to hear the words. She pulled her shoulders back with pride, sucking her belly in some more.

"No, no," he pleaded, drawing her near and caressing the wrinkled folds of flesh. "Don't suck it in. It's the belly of a real woman. That's what Hector loves, Mami," he groaned as he began to kiss and lick her belly button. Monique felt the burgeoning orgasm rising within her, born as much of his compliments as of his warm caresses. Within moments, he whipped off his Members Only jacket and pants. Stark naked, he pounded her with a steady, rhythmic grace that made the bedsprings squeak and lifted her to the orgasmic stratosphere.

# chapter twenty-one

It was par for the course that on the night India had to go from her office to her mother's dress rehearsal, she found herself trying to hail a taxi at rush hour in a deluge worthy of the last scene of *The Tempest*. No one warned of impending rain, not even trusty Al Roker. So she had left the house wearing a cashmere coat and her favorite crocodile pumps. She struggled to keep her makeshift rain hat—a plastic bag from the local Barnes & Noble—on her head with one hand while waving madly with the other. Finally, in the distance, she spotted a ray of hope, a taxi with its light on, indicating availability. It signaled to her with its blinker, but as the car approached and the driver got a closer view of India's brown face, he swerved away, splashing India with brackish water. India took off after him, running as fast as her rain-sodden pumps would take her, yelling, "Son of a bitch!"

She caught up to the taxi and tried to open the door.

"I'm not going to Brooklyn!" the African driver shouted through a cracked window.

"Neither am I! Take me or I'll report you!"

Dismissing the threat with a wave of his hand, he sped off, illuminating his "Off Duty" sign. India rifled through her puddle of a purse for a pen, and hastily scribbled his license number. In her blind fury, she hadn't noticed that the wind blew away the only thing standing between her and "bushwomandom." She watched the bag floating off in the gutter and felt the rain pouring down her cheeks, matting her hair to her face. A black Lincoln pulled up beside her.

"I don't take gypsies!" she yelled without stopping to look inside the car as she walked away.

"India, get in!" a familiar baritone commanded. Turning, she saw Keith standing beside the back passenger door under the shelter of an umbrella the size of a parachute. She smiled with relief, then remembered she was angry with him for kissing her, angrier still that he had emailed and phoned every day since.

"No, thank you! I don't need a lift!" India walked on, trying to project an air of dignity in spite of her dishevelment.

"Just get in!" Keith repeated, this time grabbing her by the arm and sheltering her with his handheld awning. She glared at him defiantly as raindrops ran down her face like tiny rivers.

"Are you going to make me stand out here all night?" he challenged. Realizing she was risking contracting pneumonia out of sheer stupid pride, she relented and slipped through the open door. The car was warm and comforting. She settled into the backseat. Keith glided in hurriedly beside her.

"Manuel, hand me some paper towels please," he demanded.

"Yes, Mr. Wentworth," the driver obliged, handing him a roll from the front seat.

"Now we're in business," Keith said, dabbing her face, her hair, and her neck. India thrilled to the touch of his warm hands through the paper. She was relieved she couldn't see what she looked like, as she was certain the effect was that of a drowned Pekinese.

"So, your phone and email aren't working. Or is your assistant not giving you the messages?" Keith challenged.

"You have a fiancée. I have a boyfriend. We have nothing to talk about," India answered firmly. If she had been looking more attractive, she might have been tempted to ask him to the St. Regis Hotel for a drink. Fortunately, she was not and she could stick to her moral guns. With homeliness came virtue.

"So that's it?"

"That's it," she repeated, as much to convince herself as to deter him from further overtures.

"Okay. Where are you going?"

"To my mother's rehearsal. Forty-fourth Street between Eighth and Ninth please."

"You can't go like that. You'll get sick," Keith protested.

"One of the dressers will dry me off or give me a change of clothes. I'll be fine. I'll just have to walk around in a toga for the rest of the night," she offered in a wan attempt at humor that she hoped would distract him from her less than alluring appearance.

"What tragic figure is your mother playing now, Lysistrata?"

"Lysistrata is a comic figure, actually," India corrected him.

"You know me, I was an econ major. The classics were your department," Keith explained with a shrug.

India smiled at the memory of his self-professed ignorance of anything vaguely literary.

"She's playing Medea," she informed him.

"She's done that part about a thousand times. But I guess if the crazy role fits—"

"What is that supposed to mean?" India bristled, getting back on the high horse from which she had momentarily dismounted.

In the years they had been together, his derisive comments about her mother's career had infuriated her. Keith could claim descent from four generations of proper professionals: doctors, lawyers, and schoolteachers. Like many of his cornbread-aristocracy caste, he had regarded actors as one step above carnival barkers and circus performers. To him, her mother might as well have been the bearded dwarf at Ringling Brothers.

"My mother may be stark raving mad, but at least she's kind," India wanted to scream. What right had he to criticize when his own mother was the living incarnation of Clytemnestra, a viper in St. John knit clothing?

"Nothing, India, it doesn't mean anything," Keith responded. He sighed with exasperation and slid over to his window.

*Take your petty bourgeois snobbism and go back to Serena, your adoring ingénue,* India thought, fuming. Her mother probably had some deadly dull career he needn't be ashamed of: a school administrator or a dental hygienist. They rode in silence, each looking out their respective windows in the rain. The car came to a stop and India looked up at the marquee of her mother's theater as she gathered her belongings. Keith placed a hand on her soaked arm.

"Do you really want to go?" he asked, looking her directly in the eye.

India imagined her mother onstage, pulverizing the scenery and her costars like a human Cuisinart. She could hear her spitting out the lines India had known since nursery school: "'O accursed children of a hateful mother, may you perish with your father and the whole house collapse in ruin!'" *Yes, just another fun night with Mom,* she thought. And then of course, she couldn't wait to see, for the umpteenth time, her favorite scene of all: Medea's entrance after murdering her children. How would they convey the carnage this time? With the usual—a bit of ketchup on the hands? Or her personal favorite—two tiny severed heads wielded like evening purses for today's infanticidal woman? She could only say to herself with Kurtz, "The horror, the horror."

She sat for a moment, unable and unwilling to move, looking forlornly at the poster announcing "Elizabeth Blakely IS Medea" plastered on the brick wall of the theater.

"I have to go," she said at last, grabbing the door handle.

"When are you going to stop babysitting your mama and lead your own life?" Keith asked. India reeled around, livid. She started to launch into a defense but realized that anything she said would come across as the lady protesting too much. He stared her down, daring her to argue the point.

"Nice to see you haven't changed. You're still a shit," she answered icily as she prepared to exit the car. He shut the door, pulling her back inside.

"Don't go," he insisted.

"Why? So you can insult me and my family some more?"

"Stay with me!" he begged, putting a hand on each of her shoulders.

"No bloody way!" She tried to loose her shoulders from his grasp.

Manuel discreetly exited the front seat and waited outside.

"Don't leave me again!" Keith implored. India stopped struggling, bewildered at his sincerity. "Don't leave me," Keith repeated in a whisper as he buried his head in India's chest. Slowly, she folded her arms around him. Her hands caressed his back. She felt his muscles taut and palpable beneath his trench coat. Her body relaxed, relieved to surrender to its impulses at last. As Keith's full lips met hers, India Chumley's mind went blank with pleasure.

# chapter twenty-two

Spent and glistening with perspiration, India lay on her bed looking up at her little three-pronged chandelier. Its crystal strands swayed gently as if offering a wave of approval for the passionate acrobatics witnessed from above. In her postcoital daze, India reflected that this must have been how water felt when the dam holding it back gave way and it was released to follow its natural course at last. She hadn't realized how much she'd pent up until she let it go. She looked over at Keith, who'd fallen into a deep sleep after round five. She listened to the ebb and flow of his rhythmic breaths and savored the delicious calm.

She heard the peal of church bells and thought at first the clarions of Saint Luke's were tolling the hour. With a start, she realized it was in fact her cell phone. She lunged for her bag and retrieved the source of the tintinnabulation. The words "Julien Des Forêts" flashed across the screen. She braced herself, then glided her finger over the bar to answer.

"Hello," she whispered.

"India? Where are you? Why are you whispering?" Julien asked testily. India cast a nervous glance at the still slumbering Keith and slipped into the bathroom.

"India?" Julien's voice called through the phone.

"I'm here," India answered in the most chipper tone she could muster as she shut the door. Hopefully, she'd erased all traces of the bedroom from her timbre. There was silence on the other end.

"What's going on? Is something wrong?" Julien asked at last, sounding doubtful, India might have even said suspicious.

"No, everything is great, I feel great," she assured him, mortified at how true her words were.

"Good," Julien said a bit less gruffly. "Where are you?"

India froze. She'd lied before about her whereabouts when she had been in her little hideaway, but she'd never been there for such a treacherous reason.

"I'm at the office," she mumbled dreading his response.

"Oh, I just tried you there and you didn't answer," he answered nonplussed. She panicked for a moment then collected herself.

"I'm in a conference room, the library," she fudged, staring at the toilet and lowering the seat Keith had obviously raised.

"You work too hard, India," Julien said in a softened tone. Guilt now washed away all remaining traces of the beatitude she had felt only minutes before.

"Really, I don't. I promise you," she assured him, taking cold comfort in the fact that at least these words were true.

"Let's get off the phone, so I can get home," she added cheerily.

"I love you, you know," he responded, as if reminding her of a forgotten fact. The words struck her like a flagellant's whip. She hung up and wondered what to say to him when she walked through their door. What if he wanted to make love? She would plead fatigue. He was never one to push. She stared at her face in the mirror: mascara streaked her cheeks, her hair stood in a coiled mass, like underbrush in the wake of a tornado. This was the face of dissolution, the face of an adulteress. She grabbed a washcloth to scrub it clean, but no amount of Lancôme Ablutia Fraîcheur would remove the stain of the fallen. She reentered the bedroom, grabbed her stockings and skirt from the chair, and hurriedly put them on. Keith groggily sat up. As he did so, every muscle in his washboard stomach flexed and revealed itself. India took a deep breath. She'd had her share of good lovers but none like him. Just by running his index finger down her naked back he made her entire body want to yield. If she didn't get out of there, she'd compound her original sin. He was someone else's, not just boyfriend, fiancé.

"Where are you going?" Keith asked, his eyes half closed, like a child awakened after a long drive. India wanted nothing so much as to cuddle him.

But another man waited in another bed. And a perfectly innocent woman waited, pining for Keith. As she imagined Serena alone and worried, India didn't see Keith as a groggy little boy, but as a serial cheater. And now she had made herself his partner in crimes of the heart. She walked briskly to the door.

"India!" Keith called out.

"We can't do this," she answered, desperate to maintain her resolve.

"We just did. Stop fighting it."

India's eyes traveled over the lines of his naked torso. No jury would have convicted her for falling into those arms. It was forgivable, but just this once.

"Keith, that was once for old times' sake. It can never happen again." She meant it as a dictum, but it came out as a desperate plea.

"It will. You know it will," he insisted. She turned her back on him and walked resolutely out the door.

Once out in the street, it dawned on her she had just left him alone in her apartment. It didn't matter; the door locked automatically, she reminded herself. Then she remembered her mother, whose rehearsal she had missed. She could only deal with one source of guilt at a time. She decided not to go home to Julien, not yet. A taxi sped past and she yelled for it. It screeched to a halt and she climbed in.

"Take me to 375 Park Avenue," she commanded. A night of shredding old papers in her office would help wash away her shameful deed and give her time to concoct an alibi. She heard a male voice bellowing her name. She looked out the back window and saw Keith, standing in the middle of the street, shirt unbuttoned, holding his jacket in his arms as he watched her taxi drive away from him.

# chapter twenty-three

Abby checked her watch as she rushed down Forty-second Street toward Madison Avenue. She wasn't accustomed to walking fast in high heels. From the catacombs of her closet, she'd resurrected a pair of Manolo Blahnik stilettos with a "dominatrix by way of Madison Avenue" ankle strap. She'd sausaged herself into a tight black slit-skirt Esme had forced her to buy at a Dolce & Gabbana sample sale. Her hair sat piled atop her head in a chignon precariously held together by a lacquered red stick, the better to unravel at the appropriate moment.

She looked at her watch again as she turned the corner: 5:20. Knowing she was uncharacteristically late, she started to jog but stopped after half a block. Her hair was beginning to fall off its perch as a result of the bouncing motion. And besides, she didn't want to come across as a complete perimenopausal desperada. Nor did she want to greet her young lover in a puddle of sweat. She slowed to a brisk walk and as she crossed Forty-first Street, she spotted Sage pacing. Abby paused and channeled Esme's femme fatale saunter. Sage looked up and noticed her. An enormous smile instantly bloomed on his face. His eyes shone with warmth and unabashed approval of what he saw. His gaze was so different from Nathaniel's, whose ambiguous stare so often made her squirm and wonder what error she'd committed. Where once he had greeted the sight of her with delight, he now wore a look of permanent dissatisfaction. She had often told herself not to take it personally, that it was the natural erosion of enthusiasm brought about by years of marriage. She just had never believed it would happen to her. She smiled at her naïveté.

Drawn by the sight of Sage, she dropped her "wicked city woman" hip rolls, walked briskly, and threw her arms around him. The lacquer chignon holder tumbled to the ground. Both Abby and Sage stooped to pick it up, butting heads in the process. As she straightened up, Abby heard the sharp sound of fabric ripping. She reached back to feel and, sure enough, the zipper had torn away from the seam of her skirt. Abby clutched her swing coat around her, mortified. She had been going for Rita Hayworth. Instead she was Lucille Ball, maybe even Roseanne Barr. Sage sensed something was amiss.

"What's the matter?" he asked, genuinely concerned.

"Nothing," she assured him, smiling more brightly still as she laced her arm through his. His powerful hand clasped hers. He stopped to caress her palm, then leaned down to kiss it, sending a shiver down her spine.

"Where are you taking me?" Abby asked, primed. This was, after all, the neighborhood for cute boutique hotels. Maybe he'd booked a room. Of course, she wouldn't have wanted him spending a huge chunk of his weekly salary on a tryst. She would have insisted on paying the bill. And once she would have ripped her clothes off, she could have explained the tear in her skirt and not admitted its true cause.

"I hope you'll be surprised," Sage answered with a mischievous grin. He had a devilish side Abby hadn't noticed before. She liked it. It tempered the saccharine of his do-gooder, "don't care if I ever make a dime" sincerity. They approached the Library Hotel but kept walking. Now Abby was confused. They reached Thirty-seventh Street, and Sage led her left to the mausoleumlike entrance of the Morgan Library.

"Come on," he said as he led her up the steps. *What corner of this building are we going to do it in?* She wondered. She hadn't had sex in the stacks of a library since college. Arriving at the glass atrium, they took a seat at a table nearest the window and Sage ordered tea. Abby perched gingerly on one hip, hoping not to tear the back of her skirt further. Already she felt the draft traveling up the length of her thong underwear.

"Can I take your coat?" he asked, his warm hands on her shoulders.

"No!" she snapped. Then more calmly she added, "Thank you. It's a little chilly."

"We won't be here long," he assured her. *Thank God,* she thought as she looked at her watch. Only an hour and forty-five minutes before her absence from home would begin to look odd to her children and Marta, the housekeeper. Sage took her hands and rubbed them to warm them up. Abby bit her upper lip as if to contain the desire welling up within her.

"So, is this where you take all your girls?" Abby asked, making light of her discomfort and doing her best to ignore the air current making its way up to her bottom.

"I don't have a lot of girls, Abby," Sage answered guilelessly.

"Come on. In all your travels, there have probably been one or two or twenty. I'm just curious."

The waitress set down a tea caddy laden with scones and little porcelain pots brimming with ruby red jam and thick clotted cream. Abby longed to devour a scone smeared in both condiments, but remembered her seam-bursting hips.

"Have one," Sage offered, proffering the plate. Abby stared at the biscuit-shaped delights, fresh from the oven. Their slightly sweet aroma filled her nostrils. Impulsively, she grabbed one. Steam rose from the inside as she broke it in two and shoveled an index finger full into her mouth.

"Have some cream," Sage insisted. Abby stabbed the content of the pot with the butter knife and lifted out a heaping teaspoon's worth. She slathered it over one half of the scone. Sage ladled the preserves over the white cream, then lifted the scone and held it for Abby to take a bite.

"Mmm," Abby moaned with pleasure.

"I knew you'd like it," Sage commented, proud that he'd struck a gastronomic chord.

"So, how did you know about this place?" Abby prodded.

"The Morgan Library?" Sage asked, incredulous.

"No, this. The tea spot. It just doesn't seem like a real guy thing."

Sage sat back with arms crossed to contemplate Abby.

"I'm getting this 'I don't trust you' vibe from you, Abby."

"I trust you," Abby insisted.

"No, you don't. And that's actually why I brought you here."

"It is?" Abby was completely baffled.

"Yes. I brought you here to show you I don't just want to screw you."

"You don't?" Abby asked, hoping the drop in her voice didn't betray her deep disappointment.

"No!" Sage answered with indignation. "I mean, sure I'd like to spend the whole day making love to you. It's awesome. But I want more from you than that."

Abby was at a loss to figure out what that something was. She suddenly felt quite tawdry in her tart manqué getup.

"So what are we going to do?" she asked.

"A friend of mine worked here as a researcher, and he is going to let us see some of the works close up. He's pulling Thoreau's manuscript of *Walden Pond*. That's the first book that changed my life. And I saw you were reading some George Eliot the other day. They have some of her letters. I thought you might like to see them."

Abby had heard of "Let me show you my etchings" seductions, but this guy meant it. She'd come prepared for an early evening of steamy, illicit sex, and instead this poetic soul in a hottie's body wanted to have a meeting of minds.

"Sage, this is the sweetest date I've ever been on," she told him.

"I'm not a boy, Abby," he stated with a look so open it demanded her complete honesty in response.

"Sage, you need to know I'm not in a fit condition to go anywhere. My skirt is about to rip wide open."

Sage smiled and reassuringly stroked her hand.

"I can fix that," he said, removing his jacket and then his shirt. He stood in the middle of the atrium, sturdy chest muscles covered only by his Fruit of the Loom undershirt.

"This should work. Come on."

He led her to the ladies' room and handed her the shirt. When she emerged, wearing it over the skirt, he whipped off the belt holding up his pants.

"May I?" he asked.

"Sure," she answered, puzzled. He knelt before her and circled her waist with the belt. The sliding of the leather against her body felt almost like his hands caressing her. Abby's body relaxed at the tenderness of Sage's gestures as he cinched the belt, placing a thick finger between the buckle and her belly to make sure it wasn't too tight. Finally, he looped the end over so it stayed in place.

"There. You ready?" He looked up at her.

"Yes, I am," she answered, meaning it. This was neither what she had planned nor had expected and certainly not what she had fantasized, and yet it couldn't have been more perfect. She surrendered to the joy of walking arm in arm with a man who cherished her completely.

## *chapter twenty-four*

India walked at a clip down Park Avenue. Though it was merely days after Thanksgiving, the wide street was already gaudily bedecked for Christmas. Every glass office tower was festooned with a red bow. As India listened to the speaker on the other end of her iPhone, she mouthed a little prayer of thanks. In the birthplace lottery, she was grateful to have pulled the "educated, from North America" card as opposed to Khadija Udoje's "poor, from sub-Saharan Africa."

"Right," India said into the tiny tube-shaped speaker. "I just want to be prepared in case we need to seek asylum. Two of her children were born here and one's still nursing. No, she can't afford that, but whatever she can't pay for I'll backstop. Okay. Take care."

She pressed the screen and disconnected. *Is it possible that the great democratic United States rips immigrant mothers from their citizen children?* she wondered. It was inhuman. But her outrage at the injustice of the system abated when she spotted a handsome businessman with thick, wavy hair. She envisioned her own hands running through Keith's luscious locks as their pelvises thrust toward each other with the full-throttle frenzy of lust unleashed. Their bodies merged faster and faster until India smacked herself on the cheek.

"Hey, be good to yourself, sistah!" a bike messenger yelled out as he peddled past.

India frantically scrolled through her list of iBooks. Had she ever downloaded the *The Scarlet Letter? Ah,* she thought as she scrolled to *The Age of Turbulence.* Alan Greenspan on globalization. That should douse the flame of desire.

"On September 11, 2001," the former chairman of the Fed's professorial voice intoned as India reached Madison Avenue. There the shops were truly tarted up to celebrate the birth of the Savior and an uptick in sales. Giant nutcracker soldiers stared out of every window. *Can't they take a breath before jumping from one holiday to the next?* India thought with disgust. Then it dawned on her that her actions were no less tawdry than the merchants'. She had gone from Keith's bed back to Julien's after a mere twenty-four-hour "hiatus." She hadn't made love to Julien, of course. Nonetheless, in her own estimation, she had joined the morally dubious ranks of the hoochies, of women with something to hide. If a sidewalk Santa yelled "Ho, ho, ho," as she passed by, she would have thought he was calling her name.

Through the floor-to-ceiling windows of Saint Pete's, India saw Esme presiding over their usual "give the eight-figure men something to ogle" table. And indeed, the largely male and over-forty clients of the establishment stole sly glances at the little "multiculti" assortment of female pulchritude. Alberto opened wide the door to two bespoke-suit-clad sexagenarians. The scent of his fern-based cologne battled the cold air for India's attention.

"Signorina!" he cried as though India were a long lost relative. "Your friends are waiting for you." From the table, Abby spotted her and waved. Both Esme and Monique teasingly consulted their watches.

"Miss Punctuality finally breaks her record." Esme laughed as India took her seat. Esme munched matchstick-thin zucchini strips fried to golden crispness.

"You look tired and stressed," Abby noticed.

"Actually, you look like hell. I've never seen you look so bad," Monique added.

"Thank you, ladies, for the support," India grumbled in response. To her further annoyance, her friends had never looked better. Monique's skin glowed. Esme's thick hair shone like a black stallion's newly brushed coat. Abby looked as though she had dropped five pounds, and her mood was buoyant.

"Seriously, what happened to you?" Abby pursued, taking a sip of Pellegrino.

"Nothing! I feel great!" India announced defiantly. And she did, somewhat. After six years of wondering, she knew that Keith had never forgotten her. He had been pining . . . at least some of the time. Presumably he hadn't thought of her when he had asked Serena to be his bride. But India chose to ignore that thorny detail for the time being.

"And I'm going to look a lot better to all of you in a second," she announced rifling through her knockoff Kelly bag. Her passion for purses notwithstanding, she had never allowed herself to succumb to the bank-breaking temptation of purchasing the genuine article. She handed each of them a small cream-colored envelope. Esme ripped into hers immediately and pulled out a golden key.

"What's that?" Monique asked.

Esme put two and two together. "This is the key to your garçon-nière," she gloated.

"Her who?" Monique asked.

"Her sex studio," Esme explained. "Thank you. I need this. My father's place is getting harder and harder to use. His latest mistress is the sticky type. They were together four times last week. But wait a minute. Why do you two need keys?" she asked, suspicious. Abby and Monique looked at each other guiltily.

"Sage," Abby confessed.

"Brava! It's about time! What's good for the cock is good for the hen," Esme cheered.

"It's gander and goose," India corrected.

"Whatever. I'm happy. And it feels good, doesn't it?" she asked Abby. Abby's cheeks flushed, and she sighed with a relief India recognized from her own recent surrender to desire.

"It does," Abby admitted.

"And you?" Esme pursued, looking to Monique.

"Hector," Monique admitted dreamily.

"Hector?" Esme repeated, smiling.

"I call him the 'ever-ready man' 'cause he can go and go and go," Monique crowed.

She and Esme high-fived. The latter pulled out her BlackBerry.

"Girls, let's coordinate when we use the love shack. I'd like Mondays and Wednesdays."

Without skipping a beat, Monique consulted her BlackBerry.

"That works for me because Hector and I have been doing Tuesdays and Thursdays, and the occasional Saturday when I'm on call," she explained.

"I'll take alternate Saturdays. Every other week, Mom takes the kids to a museum for the afternoon," Abby jumped in. "Sage's apartment is all the way in Brooklyn. The commute really cuts into . . ." She trailed off, embarrassed. Monique finished the thought.

"Screwing time?" Abby nodded sheepishly.

"For two people who are new to this game, you certainly got comfortable quickly," India commented, taken aback. *How easily does one adjust,* she wondered, *to juggling two men?*

Monique and Abby looked at each other, then refused to acknowledge the statement.

"Shut up, Miss Morals, you're ruining the fun," Esme retorted. "So, Monique, yours works at the hospital? Is he a gynecologist, too? I like them. They know what to do with our equipment."

"You've slept with a gynecologist?" India was shocked. It seemed every time she had been with Esme, the list of her lovers grew.

"Two. One was a disaster. He kept naming my parts as he touched them. I said, 'Shut up, guapo, I want an orgasm, not an anatomy lesson.'"

Monique burst out laughing. Abby tried to suppress a giggle but couldn't. Esme watched her with the satisfaction of the devil signing on a new soul. India looked at all three of them with dread. *Are we just careening down the road to perdition, me included? Will we all reach the point where we have no self-control whatsoever?* she wondered.

"My Hector drives an ambulance," Monique declared with the pride of someone describing a Nobel laureate. India couldn't believe a woman of her intelligence could be so taken with someone who had barely made it through high school.

"Ooh, I'd like to do it in an ambulance." Esme smacked her lips.

"Overrated," Monique responded matter-of-factly. "If your man packs any power, those little cots crash to the ground."

Gianni, the waiter blanched and made the sign of the cross as he passed the table.

"Ladies, a little discretion." India winced, indicating poor, mortified Gianni.

"And Abby, will you stop staring at me? I get it. I need an extreme makeover," India snapped.

"Why are you giving us the keys to your apartment anyway?" Monique asked pointedly. All eyes turned to India, who swallowed hard. In spite of growing up with an actress and an inveterate philanderer, she'd never truly mastered the art of the lie.

"I want you ladies to have the key so I can't use it," she admitted with embarrassment.

"What are we, your designated hos?" Monique asked.

"You slept with Keith, didn't you?" Abby surmised after a moment.

India nodded. The revelation stunned Esme into silence. She sat staring at India, looking over every inch of her.

"Hallelujah, there is a god!" Monique cheered, lifting her Bellini glass as if to toast the event.

Esme looked at Abby with a raised eyebrow. Abby nodded and winced. She remembered all too well the pain of India's breakup six years earlier. Abby placed a reassuring hand on India's shoulder. India turned away, fearing that if she looked Abby in the eye, she'd dissolve into a puddle of emotion in the middle of the restaurant.

"This calls for champagne!" Monique continued, gleeful. "This round is on me. Waiter, a bottle of Cristal!"

"Are you all right?" Abby quietly asked India.

"I'm fine. Really. Let's just not make a federal case out of it. Or a funeral," India answered brusquely. It mortified her to have reached this moment. It was one thing to have crossed the moral line; it was another to admit her transgression to a jury of her friends. It made the "sin" more real and redoubled her sense of shame.

"Funeral? Honey, I've got to start shopping now for what to wear to the wedding," Monique replied.

"Whoa, Nellie. Who said anything about a wedding?" India protested.

"I guess talking wasn't really the point, huh, Miss Morals," Esme commented at last with a sardonic grin.

"Let she who is without one-night stands cast the first stone," India shot back, stung. Esme tossed back her hair, defiant.

"At least I haven't spent my whole life telling everyone they should cross their legs and act like they don't have a vagina. I've been honest: I love to fuck!" she cried.

"Now that every man in here wants your business card," Abby said, hoping Esme would calm down or at least lower her voice. The diners at the adjacent tables craned their necks to get a better look at the self-proclaimed wildcat.

"Who cares about these men? And you, viejo, stop staring and go get your Viagra prescription filled," Esme scoffed at an aging ogler at the next table. The prune-skinned object of her admonition retreated behind his menu, mortified. Esme continued her rant. "I'm just glad Miss Perfect has finally come down to earth. Now maybe she'll stop acting like such a hypocrite. I always knew deep down inside you were just like me: a gourmande for fucking," Esme insisted.

"Excuse me, I don't need to install a condom dispenser next to my bed," India retorted, uncomfortable at the thought that if she had let herself go, she would probably have accumulated lovers with alarming speed.

"Actually, a candy dish of assorted sizes is better—easier access,"

Esme advised, not backing down. "You'll have a lot more fun and a lot less regrets if you stop trying to be something you're not: a nun."

"Look, last night was a fluke. A 'for old times' sake' moment that will not be repeated. Ever!" India said emphatically though she feared she wouldn't be able to live up to her own words.

"It was that good, huh?" Monique deadpanned.

"God, yes," India confessed. While it was painful to face the truth of her actions, it was a relief to admit to her friends and to herself just how good it was: blinding sell-your-grandmother-to-experience-it-again pleasure. Orgasms of the sort India had with Keith made her understand drug addiction. And it was such a massive relief to follow her true desires, rather than bottling them up and struggling to keep them from exploding.

"You got yourself a one-stop-shopping man. Bank, bling, and booty," Monique commented, delighted.

"But what about Julien?" India asked.

"He is a very nice guy. Don't drop him," Esme concurred.

"Are you following your own advice?" India was floored at Esme's double standard.

"I never said you should marry Keith. You marry the nice ones. They treat you well," Esme declared.

"And in return, you screw around on them," India countered.

"Yeah, by screwing the bad boys?" Abby asked, trying to make sense of Esme's byzantine logic.

"Absolutely. You did it backward, Abby Adams. That's why you're having problems," Esme pointed out.

"I beg your pardon?" Abby scoffed.

"Okay, I'm sorry," Esme added. "I'll leave your husband out of this. For today."

"Esme does make a good point, though. Amid all the twisted, sicko ones, Julien is a great guy. Don't just kick him to the curb," Abby stated.

"I'm not! Anyway, we're not married," India protested.

"Yet," Abby cautioned.

"I wouldn't do what I did if we were married," India insisted. Esme let out a guffaw.

"Ha! You're fooling yourself. Cheating is cheating. If you can do this to Julien before marriage, you would do it after," she warned.

"That's not true." But in spite of her insistence, India feared that it was.

"She's not gonna marry Frenchie. Why marry a man when you know you're going to cheat on him?" Monique interjected.

"Isn't that what you did?" India countered.

"No! I didn't plan for Hector. He just happened," Monique answered honestly, then brightening, she added, "Ladies, I have to show you the watch I bought Hector for Christmas." Monique pulled a red leather Cartier box out of her bag. She opened it to reveal a gold watch encrusted with diamonds.

"That must have set you back," Abby commented, then continued, "And isn't that a little risky? I mean, it does show up on the credit card bill."

"Separate man, separate card. The bill comes to my office, never to the house."

"Excellent. That's just like my phone system. I have one cell phone for my *amantes*, and I change it whenever anyone gets too clingy. That's how I got rid of that wimp from the ballet. New number, *adios muchacho*. I make them evaporate," Esme explained with a snap of her fingers.

India felt slightly repulsed at this laying out of the rules of cheating, and yet she listened with rapt attention knowing she might need to employ some of the techniques.

Abby ventured a question: "What do you do when you come home from seeing your—"

"Lover! Just say it!" Esme prodded.

"Your lover. And your husband is suddenly very amorous?"

India felt truly sick to her stomach and yet eagerly awaited the reply since she couldn't pull an all-nighter every night. Aside from being exhausting, they were no beauty treatments.

"I haven't really had that problem," Monique ventured awkwardly. "My Wayne is usually fast asleep when I come home." Her voice trailed off.

India watched Abby and Esme to see if they would read between the lines of Monique's comment, but a sexually inactive husband was an unfathomable notion to them both.

"You've got to play the tease. I put on a very sexy negligee. For you, Abby, that means going out shopping. I lie down and say 'I'm ready for you, after you shower.' By the time he comes out, I pretend to be asleep. It gets you out of having sex and makes your husband even crazier for you. Men always work harder for what they can't have," Esme explained.

"That's cruel!" Abby cried.

"It keeps them interested. With men, it's kill or be killed," Esme said.

That was precisely why India had left Keith the first time. She hadn't wanted to spend her life in a marriage where she would have had to use Sun Tzu's *The Art of War* as a relationship manual.

"Is this how we want to live our lives? Lying and scheming and hopping in and out of bed with men not our husbands?" India asked, despondent.

Monique, Esme, and Abby paused to ponder the question a moment, then answered "Yes!" in unison.

"I haven't felt this alive in years," Abby admitted. "I understand your client who was ready to risk fifty million for a great night."

"Nothing's that good," Monique commented. "Oh, by the way, India, on the night of the thirteenth, I'm at your mama's opening with you, okay?"

"That's so nice of you to come," India answered, genuinely touched.

"I'm not coming. You're my alibi," Monique corrected.

Now India really felt she'd sunk to the level of a petty criminal. She knew it was useless to protest, so she merely nodded. *What's one more sin, if you're doomed to hell anyway?* she wondered.

"Don't look so sad," Monique protested. "You might need me to return the favor." India shuddered to think Monique might be right.

She noticed Esme staring at the entrance to the restaurant. India turned and saw Michael Alders with a blond glamazon on his arm. The woman wore an exquisite sable stole draped over 36D-cup store-bought breasts. Spotting Esme, Michael leaned in to give his voluptuous companion a deep kiss. India watched Esme's back go stiff even as she feigned nonchalance, sipping her wine.

"Isn't that Dom Pérignon, your man?" Monique indicated Michael with her chin.

"Yes, and that's the stole he tried to buy me," Esme answered in a tone of insouciance.

"He was going to give you a sable?" Monique was deeply impressed.

"I turned it down," Esme boasted, taking another sip of her wine.

Alberto led Michael and the glamazon to the table right next to Esme and the girls. Esme sat up straighter, running a hand through her jet-colored mane.

"Guess he's moved on," Abby surmised.

"No, he's trying to make me jealous. It's the oldest trick in the book," Esme corrected.

"What are you going to do?" Monique asked with the breathlessness of someone watching the match point at Wimbledon.

"Ignore him. Nothing drives a man like that crazier," Esme said, taking another long, slow sip of her Sancerre.

*And nothing drives women crazier than seeing a man they lust for with another very pretty woman,* India thought as she observed Esme tensely crossing her legs. *In Michael Alders, Esme seems to have met her match at last. Is it possible to face one's match and not be broken?* she wondered.

## chapter twenty-five

India sat at her desk eating a penitential salad of grilled chicken with romaine lettuce, no dressing. Three days of chocolate indulgences brought on a slight battle of the bulge, at least by her "live a size six or die" standard. She had refused to answer Keith's phone calls for an entire week, but her hunger for him had to find its outlet somewhere. And it did in an orgy of truffles, Rochers, and pralines. She wore her phone headpiece and tried every few moments to get a word in edgewise as on the other end, fast-talking Feldman rattled on.

"But, José," she managed to interject at last. "My client is taking the kids to school, picking them up, feeding them dinner, and bathing them every day as it is. For their sake, can't we just move this along and formalize the custody arrangement?"

"I'm not going to rush my client into anything; this is an emotional time for her," José answered in the earnest tone of an undertaker.

*Emotional time, my bloated ass,* India thought. *Paula Winston, the Queen of Green, wouldn't know an emotion if it fell on her like a pile of unrecycled garbage.* This was all a stall to inspire desperation and capitulation in India and her client, Paula's long-suffering husband. It wasn't unlike the mating dance between men and women, people seeing who could be maneuvered into the first move. India decided to call José's bluff.

"José, you can drag this out as long as you like. You won't get us into court," she said sweetly.

"Divorce is a long proposition," José responded, dropping all pretense of charm as he hung up. India ripped off her headphones and tossed them on her desk. This was the worst part of her job: the waiting game during which she felt utterly powerless. And in fact, she was. It also killed her to think of Paula's three children, pawns in the cold war between their parents. She flung open the chocolate drawer. Ripping off the top of a Lindt chocolate assortment box, she sank her teeth into a hazelnut praline. She stopped herself midbite. At the rate she was going, she'd have no man, no clients, and an ass the size of Texas. That which she could not have, she would destroy. She grabbed a letter opener and furiously stabbed at the remaining chocolates, then dumped them handful by heaping handful in the wastebasket.

"What have we here? The immolation of the chocolates?"

India looked up and saw her mother poised in the doorway. As usual, Una stood behind her, mouthing, "Sorry." A bad day had just gotten worse.

"Oh, I do apologize for interrupting. I only rushed over here to see if you were still alive since you've not returned any of my calls. Or attended a single rehearsal," Elizabeth reproached.

"Mum, I'm sorry. I've just been really tied up," India responded.

"To a bed, I hope, and not this dreary desk. You haven't made it even once. It's unlike you."

India looked away. Her mother had an uncanny ability to detect shifts in her emotions. But India did not want to reveal her current state of confusion. She didn't need the advice of a woman whose emotional life qualified as an unmitigated disaster.

"You look pale. And tired. Is everything all right?" Elizabeth pursued.

"Everything's fine," India insisted.

"Convince me," her mother demanded.

"Mother, if you're here about Richard—"

"Your stepfather? I haven't given that man a moment's thought in days. Weeks, in fact!" she announced grandly.

"Did they arrest him?" she continued.

"Yes."

"Good."

"But they couldn't hold him."

"Why not?"

"Because they didn't have any grounds. He accepted the summons, and they had no choice but to let him go."

"So that's that," Elizabeth capitulated, collapsing into the chair facing India. She'd played her hand and her opponent had left the table. Una returned carrying an arrangement of yellow roses.

"India, this was just delivered," she explained.

"How thoughtful of Julien!" Elizabeth exclaimed. India knew for certain they were not from him. He always sent his own handmade chocolates, never flowers. What's more, yellow was the color of jealousy. India reached for the card and tore it open. Its contents did not surprise her: "When will I see you again? KW."

India smiled involuntarily, then blushed. She quickly folded up the card and slipped it into the pocket of her slightly snug pants. Elizabeth studied India, who squirmed under her mother's laserlike gaze.

"May I see the card?" she asked, extending her hand.

"No, it's none of your business," India protested. "You need to go, Mum."

"Why are you acting so strangely about flowers sent to you by Julien? Because they aren't from him, are they?" Elizabeth pursued.

"No, they're not. Say good night, Gracie," India answered, leading her mother to the door by the elbow.

"India Chumley, are you two-timing that enchanting Julien?"

India stalled. She hadn't expected her mother to guess so accurately.

"You are, aren't you? I'm ashamed for you."

"Mother, don't be dramatic."

"Don't be dramatic? My dear, I raised you better than this. And whoever this other person is, I'm absolutely certain he can't hold a candle to Julien."

"Mom, you don't know what you're talking about, and I don't even know what's happening with Keith," India blurted. She covered her mouth, as if she hadn't intended that bit of information to tumble out. And yet the urge to speak his name was irresistible, as if some part of her wanted to confess her "dark deed."

"Keith? No! Not that albino creature with the middle-class Medusa of a mother! Have you gone mad?" Elizabeth cried.

India had pondered the same question several times during the last few days, but coming from her mother, Prima Lunatic, she couldn't accept the verdict.

"A life without passion isn't worth living. Isn't that what you taught me, Mum?"

"Yes, but passion with the right person. That Keith had all the passion of a black adder. Remember, you brought him to see me in *Long Day's Journey into Night* and he actually complained that the play was too long," Elizabeth said, shuddering at the memory.

"News flash, Mother, it is too long! Do you have any idea how many boyfriends I've lost to Eugene O'Neill?" India asked.

"Well, good riddance to them all. Unpoetic souls. O'Neill understood longing, love, and drinking. The pillars of the human experience!"

"The pillars of your experience. Not mine," India yelled.

She heard someone clearing her throat. To her dismay, she turned to discover that Constance Armstrong had entered the room. India wondered with panic just how much of this unseemly exchange her boss had witnessed. Constance surveyed the trail of chocolate bits and brown paper cups surrounding the wastebasket. India started to lean down to pick up this incriminating evidence, then realized it was best not to draw further attention to the disarray. She knew she must take control of the situation.

"Ms. Armstrong," she said with dignity, "I don't know if you've met my mother, Elizabeth Blakely."

"I've never had the pleasure," Constance answered woodenly.

Elizabeth's back went up. She arched her right brow as she extended her hand. India recognized the gesture: it's how she extended her hand to the actor playing Sir Walter Raleigh to her Elizabeth the First in a stage production of *Fire over England*. It may have convinced the audience at the Theatre Royal Plymouth, but it was doing nothing for Constance Armstrong.

"I've seen you perform. At the Public Theater. My husband serves on the board," Constance explained.

"Really? Well, perhaps he should tell the other cheap bastards to get off their pennies. They wouldn't let us bring the *Mahabharata* there. Claimed it wasn't commercial enough," Elizabeth scoffed.

This time, it was Constance who raised an eyebrow. India glanced at the picture of Nana, solid, reasonable Nana, to steady herself. Constance turned to India.

"I came to see how the Winston case is progressing. You spoke with Feldman today, didn't you?"

"Yes," India answered, wondering how to spin total stalemate into a positive without lying outright. "Um, they're still mulling over our offer. I expect them to make a decision soon."

Constance absorbed the information. India knew she could read between the lies.

"Don't let him string you along," Constance advised. "If he senses any weakness whatsoever, you will be dead. I expect you to win this one, Chumley," she continued, sounding like General Patton rallying the troops. "Lovely to meet you, Ms. Blakely. No doubt you'll be leaving soon," she added as she exited. India dug into her chocolate drawer and pulled out a Cadbury bar.

"What a dreadful woman," Elizabeth commented as she watched Constance depart.

"She's dreadful? Really, you think so? There are a few other people I'd put in that category." India chomped on the thick bar, unleashing her aggression on its chunky squares.

"I suppose you want to grow up to be just like her. Iron Lady, the Margaret Thatcher of New York divorce attorneys. Anything not to become like your crazy old mother," Elizabeth said, suddenly trembling.

India surveyed her stooped form. She looked thin and old, like someone just hanging on by a thread. Her histrionics were a little bag of tricks to get her through, but underneath, she was lonely and terrified.

"I didn't say that," India offered gently.

"You didn't have to. It's written all over your face," Elizabeth said, resigned. And indeed, it was true. India knew too much about her mother. She was not a role model she longed to emulate, but a cautionary tale she wanted to avoid.

"Will I see you at the opening?" Elizabeth asked, gathering her things.

"Yes," India answered.

"You'd better have Julien on your arm, not that that . . . glowworm, or I won't even speak to you."

India wanted to shout "One lives in hope!" but she held back. Her mother swept out of the room. She would let her mother go to her grave without ever telling her what she really thought. She didn't need to devastate her any more than life already had.

## chapter twenty-six

The Niedermeyer Theater was a little turn-of-the-century jewel box tucked between Sardi's and the Helen Hayes on Forty-fourth Street. India sat in the middle of the orchestra section, surveying the gathering crowd. The house vibrated with the energy of opening night when hope ran high. There were cries of "Darling!" as Broadway veterans greeted each other across the aisle, proud of their membership in the genteel yet raucous cult known as the Theatre. She recognized Bruce Wagner, the *New York Times* reviewer; Clyde Barrow, the scruffy gray eminence from the *Daily News*; and John Wyman, the misanthrope from *City* magazine, pad and poison pen in hand. Now that her mother's breasts sagged, Wyman was certain to rip her to rags and declare: "Given Ms. Blakely's physical decrepitude, one understands Jason's abandonment of this shapeless harridan who calls herself Medea." *It is a man's world,* India thought to herself, *when an old, flabby-bottomed misogynist can pass judgment on a woman whose pinkie packs more talent than his entire arrogant person.*

Suddenly India spotted a familiar-looking man walking up and down the aisle. She recognized Manuel, Keith's driver. Upon spotting her, he gave a nod and made his way toward her.

"Hello, Miss, how are you tonight?" he asked, inclining his head respectfully.

"I'm fine. Are you here to see the play?" she inquired, surprised to see him.

"No. Mr. Wentworth asked me to deliver this," he said, handing her an envelope. Not wishing to appear overeager, India placed the envelope in her clutch and snapped it shut.

"Thank you, Manuel. I assume you had to buy a ticket to get in here."

"Mr. Wentworth bought it last week," he explained. India could barely believe her ears. She wondered what it was Keith had plotted with such care and effort. The envelope was burning a hole in her handbag. She forced herself not to flip open the bag and pull it out.

"Have a nice night, Miss," Manuel offered with a bow before withdrawing. India watched him make his way up the sloping aisle. Once he was completely out of sight, she tore the letter open. In it, she found a plastic key card from the George V hotel in Paris and a note that read:

Is this the key to our future? Come with me next week to the City of Light and find out. The plane leaves Kennedy Wednesday night at ten. Be on it and I'll be the happiest man alive. K.W.

India stopped reading to catch her breath. She reread the letter. She hadn't hallucinated. Keith was inviting her to Paris. She feverishly perused the postscript:

In the meantime, good luck to you on your mom's big night. Hope she breaks a leg.

Keith never cared about her mother's career during the years they were dating. In fact, he had shown some disdain for a life in the theater. He finally seemed to have grasped how important it was to Elizabeth and therefore to India. And he had invited her to the most beautiful city in the world. This must have been what it felt like to be crowned Miss America or win an Oscar. It was as if the gods had selected you above all others to experience the greatest exhilaration on earth.

India watched Abby making her way down the red-carpeted aisle on Sage's arm.

"Hey, there! You remember Sage," she crowed as they reached India's row. India was still too stunned to register the boldness of Abby's parading Sage in public.

"Nice to see you," India responded, dazed. Sage leaned over and kissed India on the cheek.

Taking her hand and looking deep into her eyes, he said, "I'm really honored to be here. Abby's told me about your mom's amazing career. I looked her up online and I was blown away. That review for her *Medea* at the Public Theater in 1975 is unbelievable. And you look just like her."

India brightened. Sage just went up twenty points in her estimation. In her thirty-seven years, she could count on the fingers of one hand the number of people who had had the openness of mind to look past coloring and see the resemblance between her and her mother.

"Abby, I'll be right back. I have to go to the washroom," Sage said as he exited.

India wanted to blurt "Keith invited me to Paris" but forced herself to refrain. She would savor the secret until she could properly decide whether or not to accept. The mere invitation made her feel anointed among women. But she must remember, it was an invitation from a man betrothed to another. For that reason alone, she had to keep it to herself. She had to endeavor to be in the moment, and she had just registered that her best friend had chosen this opening to flaunt her fresh young thing.

"Doesn't he have the most beautiful ass you've ever seen?" Abby marveled as she watched Sage walk away.

"Yes, but that beautiful ass should not cloud your judgment. Are you crazy, bringing him here?"

"We're not going to make mad, passionate love in the aisle. We'll save it for the after-party," Abby teased.

"I'm serious. What if you run into someone who knows you and Nathaniel?"

"What if I do?" Abby set her jaw. "It's not like he's noticed or even seems to care. He's not around much these days. Too busy getting ready for his show."

"It's not like you to be vengeful," India observed.

"I'm sorry I'm not living up to your high moral code."

"It used to be your code, too."

"Well, we've both loosened up a bit, haven't we?" Abby rebutted. Given that she was considering going to Paris with Keith for a weekend, India had to concede the point. Keith's invitation suddenly struck her as sordid. It wasn't much different from being asked to tryst at a motel for the afternoon. It was just more expensive: a five-star version of Back Street. And yet the opening line of his note tantalized her with its promise of permanence: "Is this the key to our future?" Those were not the words of a man simply seeking a booty call.

"Stop frowning," Esme's voice called out to them. Abby and India turned to see her sashaying down the aisle gingerly, perched atop a pair of peep-toed pumps.

"Why do you both look so serious? The play didn't even start yet!" Esme shouted joyfully. Tim trailed her, admiring her behind as it swayed from side to side. She was a vision in a fitted fuchsia dress with a sweetheart neckline that framed her ample décolletage to perfection. "Come on, girls, smile. I'm on time for once."

"Only because I drove," Tim explained. "And dragged her out of the house before she had a chance to accessorize."

"I do feel naked," Esme commented about her arms devoid of bangles. "But that can be a good feeling," she quickly added, running a hand down Tim's arm. He blushed in spite of himself. *She must have had a tryst with someone else very recently*, India surmised. Only a guilty conscience could drive her to such sex-kittenish displays with her husband, the better to mask his cuckoldry. She was lavishing affection upon him the way cheating husbands showered their wives with expensive jewels as distractions from the sins at hand. What's more, on this particular night Esme's ploy was working. Tim had the mile-wide grin of a man who knew he was in for a sexual spoiling from his Maggie the Cat wife, perhaps even involving lingerie or edible panties. Although, India never understood the appeal of Fruit Roll-Ups applied to one's private parts.

Sage returned from the men's room. Esme instantly spotted him and, not knowing he was Abby's paramour, gave him an appreciative once-over, connoisseur of fine male flesh that she was. He approached the group and extended a hand to Tim.

"Hi, I'm Sage McAllister," he declared looking Tim straight in the eye. Esme turned and looked slyly at Abby as if to say "Well done!"

"Tim, Esme, this is Sage, um, Noah's music teacher. He's very into all forms of the performing arts, and since Nathaniel couldn't make it, because he's working late . . . again . . . I thought, why waste the ticket and invited him to come," Abby babbled, an overflowing tub of infor-mation.

"Don't explain too much," India heard Esme whisper in her ear. "It makes you look guilty." India nodded in agreement. Unfazed by the presence of the strapping young stranger, Tim extended his hand.

"Tim Talbot, glad to meet you. This is Esme, my wife," he added proudly. An awkward silence fell over the group as Abby stood won-dering what path to lead the conversation down next. India rescued her from her confusion by suggesting they find their places, as the show was about to begin.

Just as everyone settled into their narrow red velvet seats, a deep female voice intoned, "Ladies and gentlemen, please take a moment to silence all cell phones, pagers, and other electronic devices." Julien slid into his seat beside India. He kissed her on the neck, but she barely took notice, because to her great horror she spotted Wayne Dubois, Monique's husband, across the aisle, scanning the auditorium.

"Shit!" India cursed.

"I'm happy to see you, too," Julien said, bewildered.

"*Allô*, amour," she quickly rejoined, offering him a perfunctory kiss on the cheek as she continued to watch Wayne, who spotted her and waved. She leaned back in her seat, hoping against hope he didn't notice her looking right in his direction.

"Fuck!" she said to herself.

"Do you have Tourette syndrome?" Abby asked her in a whisper.

"Wayne's here! And Monique is . . . not," India whispered back. She rose from her seat to make a mad dash to the ladies' room to phone Monique, but eerie Philip Glass music began to play and the curtain rose on the spare black set. She instantly sat back down.

The first act passed in a complete blur as India tried to figure out how to climb over the ten people flanking her and race to the lobby at intermission to warn Monique that Wayne was in the house. She knew the play so well she could recite practically every line, certainly all her mother's soliloquies, which she used to practice with her as a child. As the curtain came down on her mother letting out a bloodcurdling scream, India leapt out of her seat, catapulted by the twin springs of panic and fear.

"Where are you going?" Julien asked as she shoved past ten pairs of knees to reach the aisle. Once on its carpeted ground she took off at a sprinter's pace for the ladies' room. Monique's cell phone rang, but the voicemail picked up. India redialed maniacally until, at last, Monique herself answered in a bedroom voice laced with the irritation of coitus interruptus.

"Why the hell are you calling me?" Monique asked languidly.

"Wayne is here!" India screeched into the mouthpiece.

"Where?" Monique's disoriented voice questioned.

"At the theater. At my mother's opening," India explained, fearing that any moment now, Wayne would appear before her looking for his bride.

"What is he doing there? He never goes to the theater! He hardly ever leaves his damn office," Monique asked, clearly snapping out of her fornicator's fog.

"Well, he left his office tonight. What am I supposed to tell him?"

To her complete irritation, India heard Monique squeal with delight. She could have killed Monique for putting her in this predicament. Then again, it was her fault for not just saying no. "Monique, focus!" she shouted into the mouthpiece.

"Yes . . . um, tell him it's a baby, hospital, premature labor. Three weeks early. Twins. Probably will last all night, 'cause that's how long my baby can go." Monique laughed.

"Monique, do you want your husband to find out what you're up to?"

"No, I don't," Monique answered, sobering up once again. "I really don't."

"Then I need your help. I'm not a great liar."

"Oh, yes, you are. You've been lying to yourself for six years. And you've got Frenchie fooled, too. You can handle this."

India resented this assessment, mostly because it was the truth.

"I better go," she said.

"Listen, I owe you. Big-time," Monique offered conciliatorily.

India pressed the "end call" bar and walked out of the bathroom. She found Julien waiting for her in the lounge.

"What's going on? Why are you so upset that Wayne is here?" Julien inquired. India tried to decide how much information it was safe to give him. Her internal debate was interrupted by the arrival of Wayne, breathless from descending two flights of stairs.

"Hey, India, I've been trying to catch up with you. Where's my wife?" he panted.

"She couldn't make it. Got called away to deliver twins who came early. Which I understand is the norm with twins," India explained, nervously.

"I was hoping to surprise her. Isn't it always the way? You try to do something nice, but you don't get any credit for it? You'll vouch for me that I was here, right? Because she won't believe me. She thinks I spend too much time at the office," Wayne said, clearly disappointed that his romantic plan had been foiled. India suddenly felt very badly. Wayne was gruff and arrogant, but clearly he still cared for Monique. This grand gesture might have been too little too late, but at least he was making an effort.

"Definitely, I'll let her know you were here. And give her a hard time for not making it. Please, feel free to come to the party afterward," India offered with forced cheer, as she did everything in her power to avoid looking Julien in the eye.

"No, thanks. No offense to you or your mom, but I'm gonna skip the rest of this thing and head back to work," Wayne answered, then lumbered away.

Julien stared at India. She decided to try the charm and cleavage routine that seemed to work so effectively for Esme. She moved in close and nuzzled Julien's neck.

"Don't play coquette. I don't like it," Julien said, pushing her away gently but firmly. "Everything you just said to Wayne was bullshit, wasn't it?" he accused, looking at her intently. India looked away. Julien continued to scrutinize her, waiting for an answer. Unwilling to spin another web of deceit, India remained mute. Julien was far too perceptive; she could not take the risk. "Look, India, it's not my business what your friend Monique does. That's between her and Wayne," he continued.

"Then what are you upset about?" India asked, jumping at the chance to shift the discussion.

"You lie very easily."

"No, I don't! I'm the worst liar on the planet. I swear," she said, raising a hand as if taking an oath of office.

"You just did an excellent job. I'll ask you again: please never lie to me." Yet again, India looked into his large, honest eyes and wondered if this was the moment to come clean, to admit everything, the apartment, Keith. Yes, at that point there was something about Keith to admit. She started to speak, but the self-preservation instinct silenced her. She preferred to live with guilt rather than risk losing Julien by revealing the truth. She told herself that her confusion about her own feelings justified the continued deception. And yet she would not compound the situation by promising Julien honesty.

"I should go see to our friends. Make sure no one's running for the exits," she joked, changing the subject. He stared at her, clearly not amused. "I'll see you upstairs," she added, abruptly heading for the staircase. She didn't dare turn back to face his questioning gaze.

## chapter twenty-seven

On the ground floor of Sardi's restaurant, India's mother sat on a burgundy leather banquette, brandishing a wineglass and receiving the steady stream of admirers paying homage. At her side stood Charles Wainwright, the director who, like India, was a "member of the tribe": the black child of a white mother. Until her death, his mother would show up at his productions with homemade rugelach for the entire cast. He always looked at India as if to say, "Baby, I understand." She felt safe in his presence, like someone in the world that knew she grew up in a mental institution, surrounded by the certifiably loco.

Elizabeth reached for the wine bottle to pour herself yet another glass. To India's great relief, Charles delicately swept it away as he ushered forth another fan. He winked at India, who sat with Esme, Abby, and their respective dates some distance away, taking in the scene. Tim had his arm firmly planted on his wife's shoulder. Sage tried to remember not to touch Abby at all, and finally clutched his beer bottle to prevent his hands from wandering.

Julien, still somewhat stunned by India's dishonest ways, kept his chair a good two feet away from hers while continuing to show the utmost gallantry. She wondered how to bring him back from his self-imposed Siberia.

"So you grew up going to things like this?" Sage asked, awestruck as he watched the legendary director Hal Prince bow to Elizabeth and kiss her hand.

"Yes. I did my homework in this room more times than I care to count. My mom and stepfather weren't big on babysitters. That banquette my mother's sitting on was my second bedroom," India recollected.

"What a cool childhood," Sage gushed.

"Nice to visit, but trust me, you wouldn't want to live there. I prayed every night my parents would magically turn into certified public accountants with really boring lives."

Julien dropped his guard and offered a sympathetic smile. India smiled back, relieved at the beginnings of a thaw.

Just as she was about to apologize for their earlier exchange, Elizabeth bellowed, "Beauty! Beauty! Come here, I need you!" India jumped out of her seat, ever the enabling child catering to her unstable parent's whims.

"Excuse me," she tossed over her shoulder as she hurried to her mother's side. "What is it, Mum?" she asked.

"You must bring me home tonight and tuck me in. I'm quite undone," Elizabeth sighed, leaning backward as though on the verge of fainting.

"Fabulous, Elizabeth," a debonair eighty-year-old with a walking stick exclaimed as he ambled past.

"Wasn't I?" Elizabeth said, brightening. Then, once her fan had made his way past her, she resumed her maudlin pose.

"I can't bear to be alone tonight!" she cried, clutching India's hands.

"Mum, I've got Julien," India protested. She could not pass up making amends to go babysit Medea.

"Oh my, how unspeakably selfish of me. How could I forget that lovely man? Just stay until you've put me to bed and then go. I wouldn't dream of asking for more."

India started to object. Suddenly, the double doors of the restaurant flew open and a tall man with a full head of thick, wavy salt-and-pepper hair entered. He exuded sexual magnetism in spite of his slightly bloated physique and rumpled clothing. He had all the dash of Lord Byron, senior citizen.

"Woman born of Adam's rib!" the man declaimed across the expanse of the room. Both India and her mother turned like dogs hearing their master's voice: Richard Blythe, the prodigal, had returned.

"Woman born of Adam's rib!" Richard repeated. "Heed the voice of thy love and master!"

"Who claims the name of love and abandons me to the darkness?" Elizabeth answered, rising from her perch, miraculously restored. India rejoined her friends to make way for the evening's real performance: the reunion of her mother and wayward stepfather.

"Is this a continuation of the play? I don't remember him onstage," Julien whispered to India, utterly bewildered.

"Meet my stepfather," India explained flatly.

"The one who's been in Scotland?" Julien asked.

"Yes, welcome to our family circus," she replied, making light of the chaos she had striven all her adult life to overcome. Elizabeth and Richard strode toward each other with the deliberate steps of eighteenth-century duelists in Hyde Park.

"You curse my action when you toss me to the gallows?" Richard reproached.

"And there you should have remained, cur!" Elizabeth shot back.

"Only if I could drag you there with me to strangle you, wench!"

"Who uses 'wench' in a sentence?" Abby commented to India.

"Bastard!" Elizabeth cried.

"Whore!" Richard replied. Several party guests gasped.

"Cuckolder!" Elizabeth spat back, unfazed.

"Termagant!"

"I wish you dead. I loathe the very ground you tread!" Elizabeth cried. India sighed. She had heard all this repartee before. It was excerpted from *Scenes from a Very Bad Marriage,* the epic drama of their lives. Once nose-to-nose, Richard wrapped his arms around Elizabeth and dipped her in a long, slow kiss. The guests burst into spontaneous applause and let out cries of "Bravo!"

"So that's what it was like at your house," Tim surmised.

"Every night was dinner theater, either my mother's one-woman show or this," India commented evenly. Julien lovingly folded an arm around India's shoulder. India gratefully took his hand. It was a relief to be with the polar opposite of the madman who raised her.

"No wonder you don't want to get married," Esme blurted.

"Esme!" Tim chastised.

"What? It's the truth. This is a loony bin. This makes my family look like *The Cosby Show*," Esme insisted. India didn't resent the assessment. It was the observation of a kindred spirit: another woman haunted by the home horror movies of her parents' dysfunctional relationship. Richard swept Elizabeth up in his arms, faltered slightly as a result of his bad back, but managed to steady himself and carry her out. Charles came running after them.

"Don't you want to wait for the reviews?" he asked.

"Bugger the reviews!" Elizabeth cried as she threw her arms around Robert's neck, leaving her guests and her accomplishments to oblivion. In Elizabeth's willingness to forgo reading the reviews, India took the true measure of her mother's obsession with Richard. And it was only getting worse.

"I'm sorry I didn't get to meet him," Julien offered sweetly.

"Don't be," India said with a resigned smile. It was a miracle her mother wasn't weaving baskets in an asylum. Yet for all their insanity, at least her parents were living life, perhaps not rationally or sensibly, but certainly to the hilt. The only problem with that sort of passion was all the victims it left in its wake.

India spotted a familiar-looking man walking back and forth in front of their table. She recognized his height and his long hair but could not quite place him.

"I'm going to the ladies' room!" Esme announced. "Don't go chasing after some cheap starlet," she warned Tim as she leaned over and kissed him full on the lips.

"Hurry back," he answered, patting her rounded bottom. As Esme hopped up the stairs, India saw the familiar-looking man follow her.

"Will you all excuse me?" India asked, then made her way to the second floor. Right outside the ladies' room, she found Esme backed into a corner by the man with the long hair. For once, fear replaced smugness on Esme's face.

"Didn't you see me onstage?" asked the man India recognized as the Actor/Model/Whatever from the ballet, the one Esme summarily dumped after one tryst.

"I didn't. You were wearing a mask," Esme answered.

"But couldn't you see my eyes? I played every scene for you."

India knew then he was a prime candidate for the funny farm. He had been an extra onstage, unrecognizable in a black hood and unitard.

"Good performance, now get out of my way," Esme said through gritted teeth.

"Didn't our love mean anything to you?" the man asked, a tremor of rage and desperation in his voice.

"Love? That was just screwing. Get over it," Esme spat.

"I can't," the AMW said, grabbing her by the arm. Esme whirled around and stomped on his foot with the full force of her massive heel. He doubled over in pain. India grabbed Esme and they dashed into the ladies' room.

"Tell security to take that man away!" Esme ordered the attendant, who exited quickly.

"Are you okay?" India asked Esme.

"Fine," she responded, regaining her "what the hell" equipoise. "I know how to get rid of old lovers," she tossed off as she disappeared behind the pink metal door of the stall.

As India emerged from the restroom, there was no sign of Esme's AMW. He had been swept away like a dust bunny from the floor of Sardi's and from Esme's life. India's cell phone rang. She answered.

"Well, are you coming with me to Paris?" Keith's baritone challenged. The question stopped India in her tracks. Panicked, she started to hang up.

"Don't hang up on me!" Keith's disembodied voice commanded. She placed the phone back at her ear.

"Please, Keith, I can't talk right now. And how did you get this number?"

"I have contacts at AT&T." This struck India as slightly stalkeresque and yet strangely appealing. He was so desperate to reach her that he would go to any length. Still, she reminded herself she had Julien downstairs.

"I have to go, Keith," she said weakly.

"I need to know. Tell me," he insisted.

"No. The answer is no," she answered resolutely. It was Keith's turn for stone silence. India held her breath, awaiting his reaction.

"India, don't do this to me," he pleaded. "For once in your life, stop thinking and live. Let me take care of you."

"We can't do this," she protested feebly.

"We have to or we'll spend the rest of our lives wondering what might have been." With this statement, he dealt the coup de grâce to the paper fortress of her resolve. She closed her eyes. "Please, India," he continued, "just say 'yes.'" India took a breath. She felt the same way she did as a little girl just before diving into the frigid ocean: terrified but eager.

"Yes," she whispered into the mouthpiece.

"You won't regret this," Keith promised. India hoped he was right as she clicked her phone off. She had just taken a step in the direction of her parents' rocky road. But perhaps without the alcohol and the histrionics, she and Keith had a real chance.

# chapter twenty-eight

It is a tradition at Broadway opening-night parties to wait up for the reviews, hot off the presses. As soon as she was old enough to read, India was drafted into service as her mother's official "filterer." She was to look at the articles and tell Elizabeth all the critics' accolades and suppress all their negative comments. Was it any wonder she aced reading comprehension on the SATs? Still, it was a tradition India was determined to uphold, if only to postpone the moment of facing Julien alone. And so, at 2:00 AM, after all the other guests had gone home, she, Charles, and Julien huddled in the corner of the banquette, nursing lukewarm cups of watery coffee.

"Baby, take this man home. He's exhausted," Charles said to India in reference to Julien.

"I'm fine," Julien insisted. "I'm staying as long as India does." *Must he be so chivalrous?* India thought. It made her betrayal of him all the more reprehensible. Her guilt mounted with every passing hour, but it did not diminish her desire to go to Paris. Keith's words rang in her ears: "We'll spend the rest of our lives wondering what might have been." As important as it was to follow her reason, it was equally important not to have regrets. And besides, exploring the situation would help her make an educated choice. So in a way, going on the trip was the reasonable course of action. *Now I'm a casuist,* India chastised herself. *I'm using the twisted logic of cheating spouses everywhere. I sound like Esme.*

The oldest waiter, Red, arrived with a stack of newspapers to deliver India from her personal mental hell. She and Charles practically knocked him over to grab them.

"I'll take the *Post,* you do the *Times,*" Charles suggested.

"Great. But I should really read all of them myself, because you know Mom, she wants details," India insisted. They sat on either side of Julien poring over their respective publications.

"The *Post* calls your mum the best Medea since Diana Rigg," Charles informed India.

"She won't like that. She hates Diana. I'll leave that out," she answered as she went back to her study of the *Times.* "This is good: 'Elizabeth Blakely utterly convincing as a woman on the brink of insanity.' Of course, she's convincing; she *is* on the brink of insanity," India commented.

Charles tossed the *Newsday,* the *Sun,* and the *Daily News* to the floor. India knew what that meant: they panned Elizabeth. Uh-oh, that would send her mother on a bender. She would have to hear about it ad nauseam, then spend three days digging her out of the hole of depression. Thank God, Richard was back to distract her, if not to comfort her. And because he was there, she wouldn't have to deliver the bad news tonight. Richard's return had earned her, the unlucky messenger, a brief "stay of execution."

"Okay, it's 'Good Night, Irene,'" Charles insisted. "Bedtime for Bonzo." The waiters stripped the tablecloths off the tables, confirming it was time to go. India steeled herself for the task ahead.

She and Julien walked out onto Forty-fourth Street. The pavement shone brightly with the reflection of all the lights from the theaters on the block. Little had changed on the street over the years except for the shows playing. Julien put an arm up to flag a taxi. India stopped him.

"Let's walk," she suggested.

"India, it's almost three o'clock," Julien reminded her.

"I know, but I love these streets at this hour," India responded. Julien offered his arm and they made their way across Shubert Alley, past life-sized photographs of the cast members of *A Chorus Line:* gorgeous young men and women with lean dancer bodies, smiling megawatt smiles from under the golden marquee. "I'm sorry, Julien, I'm sorry about the whole evening, the thing with Wayne," India led off.

"Forget it. I overreacted," he said conciliatorily. In point of fact, he didn't overreact, given that at that precise moment India fervently hoped she could live up to his accusation that she could lie easily. She looked at the front of the Lyceum Theatre, where her mother once played Cecily in *The Importance of Being Earnest.* It was time to discover the merits of being duplicitous.

"I have to go away," she blurted, "to a conference." She paused as she considered the next part of the fabrication. She shouldn't name Paris because he would suggest she look up his friends and relatives. "A conference in London," she concluded.

"Oh, okay. When?"

"Next week," she stated.

"I'll miss you," he said, giving her a kiss on the cheek. India waited for him to pry further. But no other questions came.

"You see, the firm is trying to expand its international—"

"I understand," he said, interrupting her.

India recalled Esme's advice to Abby: "Don't overexplain." She was not certain whether it was his fatigue or her abilities, but Julien had bought her story, hook, line, and sinker. That was it. She didn't need to go further.

"Can we take a taxi now?" he asked gently.

"Of course," she answered, giving him a tender kiss on the forehead. She felt relief and a rush of exhilaration at having gotten away with her deception.

# chapter twenty-nine

The Paris sky was white veined with pale gray and suggested the cottony silence that preceded a city's full awakening. In the backseat of the Mercedes sedan, India snuggled up against Keith with the freedom of anonymity. High-rises crowned with neon signs advertising electronics companies—the French version of low-income housing—gave way at last to the soaring white domes of the Sacré-Coeur basilica. For India, this marble monument held all the promise of Paris: streets that seemed plucked from an Impressionist painting, history at every street corner, and an abundance of chocolate in its most glorious forms.

"That church is so magnificent, it's hard to believe the French built it to atone for the sins they thought led to their defeat in the Franco-Prussian War. They built it to appease God," India marveled. Keith looked at her unimpressed. *There I go again,* she cringed to herself. Like so many children raised among intellectuals, she constantly felt like a font of utterly useless information.

"Who cares?" Keith teased as he lowered his mouth onto India's. She savored the warmth of his tongue on hers and ran her hands freely over the silken expanse of his custom-made Charvet shirt. She fingered the initials delicately embroidered over his left pectoral: K.W. II. Keith's muscles flinched and he groaned, fully aroused. The scent of the backseat's fresh leather upholstery mingled with his amber cologne. This embrace was the culmination of a seven-hour flight's worth of fondling and foreplay under a blanket in first class. India wallowed in the delicious languor of these unhurried moments. These were not the stolen kisses of a furtive tryst between appointments in New York, but the preamble to two days of uninterrupted consummation of pent-up desire. If she had had pom-poms, she would have waved them.

As soon as the car reached the Seventeenth Arrondissement, which marked the entrance to Paris, the horns of the special police force blared their singsong "Pin-pon! Pin-pon!" India and Keith sat up and collected themselves. They ran their hands over their clothes to smooth them. India tried to think of dry topics that would take her mind off of what she planned to do to Keith once they were alone and naked. The best she could muster was reciting the opening lines of the Declaration of Independence in her head. But once she reached the line about the "pursuit of happiness," it evoked the particular brand of happiness she planned to experience this weekend, over and over again.

Within minutes, the Arc de Triomphe loomed before them. Napoleon was correct to think it would inspire awe. At the Champs-Elysées, the wide boulevard of fame, the Mercedes took a sharp right, past the geometric lines of the Louis Vuitton flagship boutique. The car came to a halt in front of the George V, the Art Deco palace they would call home for the next two days. The driver knocked on the curtained glass partition.

"*Nous sommes arrivés*," he announced.

An army of attendants surrounded the car. A tall young man tipped his cap at them as he opened the door, while two porters whisked away the luggage.

"*Bienvenus aux Quatre Saisons*. Welcome to the Four Seasons. Welcome back, Monsieur Wentworth. *Bonjour,* Madame," the doorman said with a discreet bow.

India and Keith passed through the revolving doors into the gray and pink marble expanse of the lobby. India adored the retro Parisian coziness of hotels like the Ritz and the Trémoille, but something in the bald majesty of this space, with its inlaid marble floor in shades of gray, blue, and white, appealed to her very core. Huge bouquets of orchids arranged in cylindrical vases so clear they were almost invisible filled the air with a soothing scent. Trailing Keith, India floated to the front desk. Keith treated this "for pay" palace like a second home, nodding to various employees as he passed like the returning prince. India did love his arrogance. It made her stand at attention, much like the lobby. After years of flagellating herself for even daring to think that Prince Charming existed, she felt as if she had walked into a fairy tale.

As Keith completed the room form, India's phone let off its peal of bells. She searched the bottom of her mock croc tote. Keith scowled at her. As she pulled out her agenda, her iPhone crashed to the marble floor and skidded halfway across the lobby. India ran to retrieve it. After picking it up, she tried to reactivate it, but to her dismay, the screen had gone completely black. She frantically pushed the stop-start button at the top of the contraption to no avail.

"Where can I get this repaired?" she asked the elegant fifty-year-old man at the concierge desk. Keith came up behind her and swiped the phone from her hand.

"We'd like a new one. Have it ready for the twenty-fifth," he said, consulting the date on his Rolex.

"But that's the day we're leaving," India protested.

"Exactly," Keith confirmed. India was stunned at his self-centeredness. She had almost forgotten how insistent he was on being the sole focus.

"I can't be phoneless," she objected.

"Why? Who are you expecting a call from?" Keith challenged.

"The office, for one," she bristled. The concierge's head moved from one to the other as if he were watching a ping-pong match.

"And so? What are you going to do for them from here?"

"I have clients, Keith."

"Right now you also have me. And I want your undivided attention. Otherwise we might as well have stayed in New York. But at the end of the day, I can't tell you what to do," he conceded. India softened at his acknowledgment that he didn't have the right to control her actions. She also knew he was right. If this was a romantic getaway, she should "get away." She worried that she never gave Una the hotel information; she did not want to implicate her in the deception. But, on the other hand, it would be a relief not to have to lie to Julien transatlantically.

"As Monsieur instructs," India told the concierge.

"Put it on my bill," Keith tossed over his shoulder as he happily grabbed India's hand and kissed it.

"Would you like to see our suite?" he asked.

"It's ready?" she responded, stunned. Like all seasoned travelers, India knew check-in time was 3:00 PM for everyone but VIPs and those willing to pay for an extra night.

"I booked it from last night so it would be. I wanted you to be able to rest as soon as we got here," he said, tenderly tucking a stray strand of hair behind her ear. Rest was the furthest thing from her mind. And also, she was quite certain, from his. But the gallantry of the gesture aroused her. Yet another of her defenses dropped like a stripper's garter belt. They took the walnut-paneled elevator, which smelled of an intoxicating combination of vanilla and cedar, to the seventh floor.

Once they arrived at their suite, Keith opened the heavy cream-colored door. He led India down a marble-floored corridor to her idea of hotel heaven: a bright sitting room with French doors that opened onto a terrace. The eighteenth-century reproduction furniture was upholstered in a soothing Dresden blue that matched the pattern on the potpourri bowl atop an inlaid wood and marble credenza. Floor-to-ceiling damask curtains framed the enormous picture windows. India couldn't resist running her fingers through the thick ropes of their silk fringe. The fabric was so lush it could have inspired her to follow Scarlett O'Hara's example and turn the drapes into a ball gown. As she looked around, she noticed that cut crystal vases filled with long-stemmed roses adorned every conceivable corner. She stooped over one arrangement to smell the fragrant blooms and looked up to see Keith smiling at her with deep satisfaction.

"You ordered all these?" she asked tentatively, unable to believe he'd gone to all the trouble.

"Yes," he admitted, lowering his head bashfully. India recognized the gesture. Keith was always capable of romantic offerings, but they embarrassed him.

In the middle of the room, a round table was set for breakfast with blue and yellow Limoges china and gleaming silverware. Keith crossed to it and pulled out a chair. India sat. He proffered a basket of freshly baked croissants, brioches, and her favorite, pains au chocolat. Her teeth sank into the buttery flakes of mille-feuille pastry and then the dark chocolate paste in the center. This was the most sinful and most delicious of breakfast treats. As she slowly swallowed, she looked out the French doors and spotted the gilded dome of the Baroque Hôpital des Invalides, built by Louis XIV for the veterans of his many wars.

"I asked for a room with a view. Unfortunately, the one that looks out on the Eiffel Tower wasn't available," Keith apologized.

"This is much, much better," India assured him.

"So you're happy?" Keith asked, like a little boy seeking an approving pat on the head from his mother. Her opinion had always mattered to him, though he was loath to admit it to her.

"This is a beautiful room," she reiterated. In truth, at that particular moment, she would have found a room at the Motel Six palatial. With passion like this, it didn't matter where you were. She closed her eyes to enjoy this taste of nirvana: a luxury hotel room, chocolate croissants, and Keith, all in one. It was hard to believe she was not dreaming.

"I never know what's going on in that mind of yours," Keith said. "Are you going to let me in one day?" he demanded, barely masking his frustration. India was taken aback. She didn't think of herself as inscrutable; in fact, she felt ridiculously transparent. Realizing that Keith felt more vulnerable perhaps even than she, she crossed over to him and kissed him. He rose from his chair, swept her in his arms, and carried her into the bedroom.

# chapter thirty

The Frette sheets enveloped India's naked form like an eight-hundred-thread-count cocoon. She heard Keith's deep voice from the other room and slowly opened her eyes. She had forgotten what deep sleep rolling orgasms induced. It occurred to her that Keith Wentworth could have single-handedly cured insomnia and Valium addiction in the American female population. As India rolled over, she found his side of the "Louis the Never" bed empty. She caressed the indentation left by his body, then rose to follow the sound of his baritone into the sitting room. She didn't bother to clothe her nakedness in a bathrobe. Her body retained the delicious warmth of the duvet and the atomic lovemaking. As she ambled into the room, she found Keith bare-chested in his pinstriped suit pant. She didn't need to drag herself to the Louvre to admire the statuary. Even a Greek kouros couldn't rival the masterpiece before her. Keith paced as he spoke animatedly into the handheld.

"How could they screw up these numbers?" he shouted. India stood in the doorway, admiring his stomach, each transverse and oblique muscle delineated with the clarity of an anatomical sketch. She moaned with pleasure remembering how these muscles rippled with every thrust of his pelvis. Unable to control herself, she threw her arms around his waist. He abruptly shoved her away. She was stunned and started to object, but he held up his hand as a sign she stop. Rather than smack him, she turned on her heels. He grabbed her hand and pulled her back toward him as he continued his conversation.

"I'm not paying them to be incompetent! I'm paying them to get it right! Tell them to get their asses out of bed and start over!" he yelled into the phone. His machismo was irritatingly appealing. She wanted nothing so much as to fall to her knees and unbutton his trousers. She hated to admit that Nietzsche's advice to the men of the world was disgustingly brutish, but, in her case, completely accurate: "When you go to woman, bring your whip."

Keith placed the handheld back on the reproduction *bureau plat.*

"We're spinning off one of our subsidiaries, and the bankers screwed up the books . . . I'm sorry," he added under his breath, looking away. Knowing his congenital inability to apologize, she couldn't help but be moved by this one, even if it was a mumbled afterthought.

"Words are cheap. Why don't you make amends to me in front of the mirror?" India answered, unbuckling his belt. He grabbed her hands to stop her, already aroused.

"Can't right now. I've got to go down to the business center and look over the new books. They're faxing them within the hour." India wished she had Nietzsche's whip to throttle Keith.

"You wanted my full attention so you could spend your time at the business center?" she shrieked.

"Look, it's not my fault the bankers screwed up. This is work, India."

"Right, work. What do I know about that? I live off that huge trust fund that my mother, the semiemployed theater actress, and my stepfather, the poetry professor, created for me. I'll never have to worry where my next Happy Meal is coming from," she said sarcastically.

"You don't seem to get it: we're about to do an IPO. We're going out to institutional investors on Monday."

"You don't seem to get it: I have a full roster of clients with pending cases, and you made me ditch my cell phone! That's my lifeline."

"Could you stop acting like a child and get on the bus?" he snapped.

"Because your work is so important, but I, on the other hand, can just drop everything."

"Oh, Jesus!" Keith snorted, exasperated.

"What? What's the problem?" she challenged.

"You! You're a fucking pain in the ass! You always have been, and you always will be!" he yelled.

"Then why do you bother with me?" India yelled back, wounded.

"Because I love you!" Keith blurted.

The words struck India motionless. Her shoulders relaxed as she absorbed their full meaning. Even back when she and Keith were a couple, she could have counted on the fingers of one hand the number of times he'd managed to say "I love you." It was an admission he would whisper in her ear in the dark, so she couldn't see his face. Yet she had collected each and every such moment in her memory. Each one was precious because she knew how difficult it was for him to express his emotions. He had just stated it out loud, in broad daylight. She wanted time to stand still to burn the moment into her soul. Keith grabbed her, bent her head back, and kissed her.

"I love you, too," India whispered in his ear.

"I know," he whispered back. His cockiness infuriated her, while also making her want to lie down and scream "Take me now!" Keith gently pushed her away.

"I gotta get moving," he said, grabbing a flawlessly pressed shirt off the back of a chair. "The driver's downstairs. He's yours all day. Anywhere you want to go," he explained.

"When will I see you?" India asked.

"Tonight," Keith said, as he suckled her neck. "I'll make it up to you. Trust me." With a gentle pat on the bottom, he prodded her toward the bedroom. "Off with you!"

And India Chumley, crusader for women, advocate of sensible choices in men and careers, obeyed.

## chapter thirty-one

At the dainty marble-topped table next to India's, two sixty-year-old Parisiennes sat sharing tea, cigarettes, and confidences. They wore the classic uniform of well-to-do women from the Sixteenth Arrondissement: tweed pencil skirts, scoop-neck cashmere sweaters, and equestrian-themed Hermès scarves knotted artfully around their necks, a chic and cost-effective alternative to plastic surgery. Their heavy gold link bracelets clinked against their porcelain cups as they dropped ashes into the Café Angelina ashtrays. The smoke from their Gauloises didn't bother India a bit. She smiled at these quintessential French-women whose handsome, lined faces bespoke wisdom, confidence, and a matter-of-fact acceptance of life as it came.

She felt she was perhaps on her way to becoming one of them, albeit the New York version, which meant that when the time came she would actually have to spring for the face-lift. She watched children run around the Tuileries gardens across the way as she dropped a heaping dollop of whipped cream into her cup of Angelina's peerless hot chocolate. It was thick as molasses and dark as ebony. She took a sip and savored the richness of the cocoa and the drink's silky consistency. Keith had admitted he loved her. Only an hour before, she had been ready to walk out on him. Now she would follow him anywhere.

She spotted a man chasing a skinny little girl of five or six around a statue of Mercury. As the father caught his child and scooped her up in his arms, the little girl threw her head back, giggling uncontrollably. India delighted in the sight, but then doubt clouded her enjoyment: *Would Keith ever play with our daughter or son? Would he ever take off an entire afternoon to bring them to the park? Or would he just offer the perfunctory pat on the head as he moved on to more important matters: his work and conquering the world, one food company at a time?* For India, the elation of hearing that he loved her was tempered with sadness at being shipped off to spend the day alone. But that was Keith.

Life with him would probably always be a roller-coaster ride. Yet without the bargain basement lows, how could one appreciate the dizzying highs? He was certainly more stable than Richard, and her mother wouldn't have traded life with that human cyclone for anything, not even a Tony Award. The father across the street knelt to brush some dust off his daughter's shin. *Something Julien would do,* India reflected. She stopped herself. She couldn't ruin her holiday with thoughts of someone who was not there. She dropped six weighty Euro coins into the diminutive check tray. As she exited the tea house, even the low winter sky couldn't dampen her mood.

The driver, Alain, opened the back door of the sedan, and she gracefully slid into the seat. The scent of the Cordoba leather filled her nostrils. It was a virile, masculine scent that reminded her of Keith, alpha male of her dreams.

"Monsieur Wentworth would like me to bring you somewhere, Madame," Alain informed her.

"Where?"

"It's a surprise."

India fastened her seat belt and sat back, intrigued. They drove down the rue de Rivoli, past the Jeu de Paume museum, housed in Napoleon III's squash court. Alain made a right as they passed the neoclassical Crillon hotel, then another onto the rue du Faubourg Saint-Honoré, the paradise and the purgatory of shopaholics from the four corners of the globe. Every luxury good purveyor—Chopard, Gucci, Gianfranco Ferré, Tod's—beckoned those of weak will and soaring credit limits. Alain pulled up in front of the enormous Hermès flagship boutique. Hoisted atop the building like a wood carving on a ship's bow, the statue of a man on horseback heralded the shop's past as saddler to kings, queens, and assorted nobility. The brightly lit window displays reflected its modern preeminence as purveyor of the ultimate objects of purse envy. Dainty handbags in iridescent pale pink and sherbet green crocodile dangled from invisible threads over a floor strewn with glistening Swarovski crystals. Women waited for as long as three years to receive the holy grail of accessories: a Kelly or a Birkin. For the true believers, no substitute would do, no Gucci, Ferragamo, or Prada could console the true Hermès seeker.

"Here we are," Alain announced. "You are to ask for Antoinette," he stated as he helped India out of the car. India's heart beat faster. Her Imelda Marcos–sized collection of purses did not boast a single Birkin, Kelly, or Bugatti. She had never permitted herself to exceed the $2,000 mark for such a purchase. *There's a first time for everything,* she thought to herself. She was ready to join the sacred sisterhood of the overpriced handbag.

India rushed across the street. As she entered the shop teeming with eager buyers, saleswomen in Hermès slacks, silk blouses, and belts with shining golden *H* belt buckles greeted her courteously. Once she mentioned Antoinette's name, however, they snapped to attention as though she had uttered the secret code that raised her above the madding crowd. Their newfound solicitousness indicated to India that Antoinette was a queen in this beehive, assigned to deal with VIPs: Very Important Purchasers. A young woman who had merely nodded politely at the door feverishly led her through the throngs of silk-scarf-seeking tourists to a desk tucked in a corner.

Antoinette came from behind the table to greet India. She was a well-preserved fiftysomething with an angular body, darting eyes, and the pronounced features of a bird of prey. Her dark hair was swept up in an immaculate French twist.

"I've been expecting you," she said in a seductive Lauren Bacall

drawl. "Would you like to have a look around, Mademoiselle Chumley?" she said, jangling a dozen keys on a giant circular key holder.
India nodded and they began their odyssey through the maze of glass
cases where the purses were illuminated from above, like rare jewels.
They passed an irate Manhattanite who wore her Birkin Madison Avenue style: with the flap tucked in, the better to display the word Hermès
stamped in gold inside and declare its authenticity to the world.

"But I ordered the bag a year ago. How long do I have to wait? It
took me less time to find a second husband!" the woman screeched.

"I understand your frustration, but bags of this quality take time,
Madame," a courtly young salesman patiently explained.

India's attention was drawn away from the altercation by the sight
of gold link bracelets similar to the ones she saw the elegant Parisiennes
at Angelina wearing. A junior salesperson silently trailed her and Antoinette. She became the human hanger for the bags India selected.
Seeing the poor girl weighted down with assorted wares, India offered
to carry a few. Antoinette refused with a peremptory "She's fine" as she
looped another Bugatti on the young woman's overburdened forearm.
A black crocodile envelope caught India's eye. Antoinette identified the
proper key on her enormous ring and delivered the bag from the case.

"I think we have enough. At least to get started," India suggested as
Antoinette's minion looked to her with gratitude. When they returned
to the table, a navy blue felt cloth had already been laid out, the better
to offset the treasures. Antoinette donned a pair of white cotton gloves
and proffered a pair to India.

"We mustn't scratch them," she advised with the seriousness of a
Mother Superior instructing a novice on the proper conduct at com-
munion.

India dutifully donned her gloves before picking up the little crocodile envelope. Its skins gleamed and were as pliant as rubber. India had
never seen reptile so magnificent. It made her crocodile bag look like
"pleather."

"How do you get them so soft?" she asked.

"They are the finest skins taken only from the belly of the crocodile before it has reached two years of age. Elsewhere they use . . . refuse."

"How much?" India dared to ask. Antoinette quoted a number equivalent to a down payment on a car, and not a cheap one. India decided to turn her affections to the leather selections. There was a dove-gray feed bag made of two separate pouches that joined together, a royal-blue miniature Bugatti, and most enticing of all, a hot pink rectangle with two elongated handles. She could imagine herself walking to the office with it slung over her shoulder. It would add a touch of whimsy to a proper work outfit.

"Now that you've amused yourself, let me show you what Monsieur Wentworth has chosen for you," the Mother Superior said. From behind a counter guarded with the intensity of a vault, she pulled a large brown felt bag emblazoned with the trademark *H*. She unfastened the chocolate brown silk cord and uncovered a classic Kelly bag the color of cognac. India touched it, it was stiff as wood. The effect was elegant, sensible, and utterly unoriginal. It was the bag of every banker's wife from Park Avenue and Sixtieth to Carnegie Hill. The bag seemed stamped with the word India's mother hated most: proper. And in spite of the fact India had rebelled all her adult life against her parents' "dance with wolves" teachings, a part of her recoiled at being cast in a role. She wanted to howl at the moon. The woman who carried this purse lived her life with the express intention of "fitting in." She carried this purse to prove to the world that she belonged to the right "set."

"I'd rather have the pink," India ventured.

"This is the bag Monsieur Wentworth has selected for you," Antoinette insisted with a pursed-lipped smile. India considered purchasing the pink herself, but then envisioned herself paying the astronomical duties once at customs in the United States, to say nothing of the bank-breaking credit card bill. She thought of the women at Café Angelina. They would have carried this purse and made it chic with a scarf tied around the handle. *Originality is all in the attitude,* she reminded herself.

"I'd like to look at your *carrés,*" India asked. She carried her Kelly as they crossed the floor, passing the irate woman from New York.

"That's my purse!" the New York woman screamed across the floor as she ran to accost India. The latter was startled and almost prepared to hand the bag over. "That's the purse I ordered. Give it to me!" she yelled, hyperventilating. A security guard discreetly sidled over to her.

"It's not yours, Madame," Antoinette responded with icy formality. "It was ordered especially for this lady," she added, indicating India.

"When? I want a date!" the woman demanded, as Antoinette led India to the safety of the scarf counter.

"When did Mr. Wentworth order this?" India asked, uneasy. Antoinette smiled impassively.

"Is it that lady's purse? Because if it is, I cannot accept it," India protested in a whisper, so as not to be overheard and subsequently murdered for the item.

"It's yours, Madame. You have my word of honor. Now, let me show you our most recent scarf designs. I think you will be pleased," Antoinette assured her. India decided to stop inquiring. It was a handbag, not someone's husband. With the uneasy feeling of acquiring something that didn't quite belong to her, she began to sift through the silk scarves.

"This one is special. It's called 'Carpe Diem,'" Antoinette said unfurling the foulard like a sail in the wind. *Indeed,* India thought to herself. Enough worrying and fretting. She was in Paris. She had to seize the day and the purse that came with it.

## chapter thirty-two

India swept through the wide corridor leading to her hotel suite, brandishing her Kelly. She hummed as she slid her plastic card key into its slot and pushed the door open. From the living room, she heard Keith's voice speaking on the phone. She loved his deep baritone, inviting as a black mink coat. Soon, that seductive voice would be whispering in her ear as they ravished each other for the umpteenth time. She tiptoed over to the doorway, the better to surprise her beloved and model the sine qua non of accessories. Should she strip naked? The better to set the Kelly off. She could place it strategically over certain body parts, like a fig leaf. She stopped suddenly when she heard Keith utter the word *Serena*.

"Serena will do whatever you tell her to do, Mother," she heard him say. The words struck India with the force of a smack across the face. She stood stock-still. "I told you why I'm here," Keith continued in a tone of irritation. "Nobody, Mother! I'm not here with anybody . . . Yes; I'll take care of it. Good-bye." India stood in the vestibule for a moment to collect herself. *What an apt expression that is,* she thought. She did feel as though shattered bits of her heart lie scattered all over the floor. Once she felt ready, she walked into the living room. Upon seeing her, Keith broke out in a smile.

"There you are. I was wondering when you'd make it home. I missed you," he bellowed joyously. He had just hung up with his mother, talking about his fiancée. Now he was greeting her like the long-lost love of his life. His nonchalance made India's blood boil. How stupid did he think she was? She hurled the Kelly, four thousand dollars' worth of calfskin, directly at his head. He deflected the designer projectile with his arms. The Kelly tumbled to the floor.

"What happened to 'Thank you'?" Keith demanded, furious.

"Fuck you!" India yelled.

"What the hell is your problem?" Keith asked, utterly baffled.

"'Serena will do whatever you ask her to, Mother,'" India parroted. Keith blanched and looked away. "'Nobody, Mother. I'm here with nobody!'" India continued in epic harridan mode.

"That's enough!" Keith commanded. Crazed with fury, India grabbed a porcelain ashtray and raised her arm to launch it. Keith lunged toward her and wrested the would-be lethal weapon from her grasp.

"You lying son of a bitch!" India screeched. Keith dropped her wrists, picked up the receiver, and handed it to her.

"Here, go ahead. Dial Julien right now and tell him where you are. Come on!" he dared her. India stared at him, then at the phone, stunned. She had banished Julien from her mind. Or rather, all thoughts of him had been washed away in the Wentworth Sea of Rolling Orgasms. Suddenly, Julien's honest face surfaced. She imagined telling him, "By the way, I'm at a hotel in Paris with Keith," breaking his heart with the casual cruelty of a pedestrian squashing a cockroach. She recoiled from the phone.

"Now who's full of shit?" Keith taunted.

"I'm not going to tell him over the phone," India replied.

"So you're going to do it in person, face-to-face, when you get home?" Keith persevered, now firmly on the offensive. India didn't respond. She hadn't given any thought to what she would tell Julien. He thought she was at a legal conference in London, staying at a hotel whose phone number she couldn't quite dig up before she left. He had probably been dialing her cell phone in vain. The thought and image of him became suddenly unbearable.

"Well, what are you going to do?" Keith badgered. "Or do you have your alibi ready?"

"Like you do?" she spat.

"Face it, India. We're exactly the same!" Tears welled up in India's eyes as the truth hit her: she had become what she once condemned. Devastated, she slumped into a nearby bergère. Keith crossed to the French doors to look out at the golden dome of Les Invalides; it glowed beneath a gray sky. "What am I going to do with you?" Keith asked wearily. *Do with me? I'm not a Limoges ashtray,* India thought to herself, tempted to hurl one at his head.

Instead, she controlled herself and said, "We should never have come here."

"Thanks a lot," Keith retorted, clearly upset.

"You know what I mean," India insisted.

"I know you need to make up your mind."

"Me?"

"Yes, you. Until you kick Frenchie to the curb, I'm not doing a thing."

"So Serena's your insurance policy?"

"Step to me and I'll step to you. I put myself on the line before and I got kicked in the teeth."

"You cheated on me!"

"Fuuuuck!" he yelled so loudly India jumped back. "I didn't give a shit about that woman!"

"So if I screw other people I don't care about you'll understand?"

"I've let you have Frenchie, haven't I?" he retorted.

She lunged for him, pummeling his ironclad chest. He grabbed her wrists. She struggled to wrest them from his grasp. Each time she pulled away, he yanked her back toward him. They fell to the floor, wrestling.

"I hate you!" she screamed in frustration.

"It's mutual!" he answered, then lunged for her mouth with his. She slapped him. Then kissed him back. He devoured her neck. She writhed with pleasure and stopped resisting. The embrace turned tender.

Lines from *Gigi* and various paeans to agonizing love rang in her ears coalescing in the admission: "I'd rather be miserable with you than happy with someone else." She felt more alive and fulfilled having a screaming match with Keith than she did lying peacefully next to the adoring Julien. Try as she might to keep her true nature in check, she was her mother's child. As she and Keith melted into each other, she knew that for every strong woman, there is one man who brings her to her knees. For India it was, always had been, and probably always would be Keith.

## chapter thirty-three

Esme looked around her oval dining room table at her assembled "guests": her mother-in-law, "Big Terry"; sister-in-law, "Little Terry"; and her poor, unfortunate father-in-law, who was as lanky and taciturn as his shrew of a wife was overweight and loud. Esme felt certain she had died and gone directly to hell where her customized punishment was to spend all eternity with these terminally suburban, small-minded women.

"That pot roast was delicious. Must be nice to have a maid who does everything for you," Big Terry said with a venomous smile. Esme felt certain the woman had been a reptile in a former life. And this incarnation was an evolutionary step down. She chose to ignore the comment.

"How's your company culture changing now that you've been acquired by First American Title?" she asked her father-in-law. He smiled appreciatively, but before he could answer, Little Terry, Barracuda in Pearls Junior, brought the conversation back to Esme's culinary ineptitude.

"Did you at least make the salad?" she challenged, as if not cooking were tantamount to devil worship.

"No," Esme answered nonchalantly. "I'm too busy with work and, of course, my sexual affairs." Big Terry's and Little Terry's eyes widened to the size of butter plates. Their jaws dropped in unison. They looked at each other and gasped.

"Affairs?" Big Terry managed to repeat aghast.

"I'm joking!" Esme reassured her in a tone of exasperation, all the while looking at Tim to gauge his reaction. To her frustration, his face remained an imperturbable blank.

"What's an affair?" Julio asked, his mouth full of peas.

"Never you mind," Big Terry told him. "See what you've started," she hissed to Esme, who would have liked nothing better than to dump the entire bowl of pureed peas on her head. Esme forced herself to look out the window, lest the temptation of staring at said bowl grew too strong. She spotted a male figure dashing past. Thinking she must have been mistaken, she looked again. Staring at her through the window was her AMW. She let out a gasp and dropped her wineglass, spilling its contents all over her end of the table and her skirt.

"What is it?" Tim asked.

"Nothing," she answered brightly. "I just made a mess. Excuse me." She ran out into the kitchen and through the back door into the back-yard, which was illuminated only by the night's quarter moon.

"'Let me not to the marriage of true minds admit impediments,'" a plaintive voice recited. Esme felt a hand on her shoulder, and she turned to see her AMW, naked. She jumped back.

"I'm sorry," he murmured. "I didn't mean to scare you."

"What are you doing here?" she whispered.

"Declaring myself to you, my love," he said, falling to one knee.

"Get up! You look ridiculous!" Esme snapped, turning away. It was not entirely true. She had to admit to herself he did have an awfully nice body. One could scrub an army's worth of laundry on his fat-free stomach.

"I can't live without you, Esme. I need you!"

"You need to get out of here!" she hissed, pulling him away from the French doors leading to the dining room.

"How did you find me anyway? I'm unlisted."

"I followed you home the night of the performance. I had to see you again."

"Well, you have. Now go," Esme barked, reaching for the cell phone in her pocket and dialing 911 behind her back.

"I can't. I won't. 'Maid of Athens, ere we part, give oh give me back my heart!'" he yelled.

"Shut up," she said, then, into the phone "Police, I have an intruder at 828 Willow Avenue!" Undeterred, the AMW continued to recite his poem. "Maid, beautiful maid."

Tim arrived, running, trailed by his mother and Julio.

"What on earth is going on?" Big Terry bellowed.

"This man came into our garden," Esme explained to Tim, doing her best imitation of a damsel in distress.

"Don't pretend you don't know me, Esme!" the AMW yelled.

"I don't even know his name," Esme insisted, and it happened to be true. She had never bothered to find out. She never did with a one-night stand. To learn the man's name was to admit that the sex had some sort of meaning beyond orgasm. Knowing a name was the beginning of attachment, something to avoid at all costs. Tim wrestled the AMW to the ground. Esme heard sirens moments before several paunchy police officers arrived and surround the naked man.

"That man has a big penis!" Julio blurted. Little Terry covered his mouth.

"Do you know this man?" Big Terry asked Esme, her eyes narrowing.

"Put your hands up and come with us," the police ordered. The AMW obeyed, trembling as they lead him away. He looked back at Esme longingly.

"He acted like he knew you," Big Terry commented suspiciously.

"Mom, that's enough," Tim silenced her. "Please take Julio back inside."

"Your wife obviously spends too much time in the city," Big Terry said, unable to resist the opportunity to toss a barb Esme's way. Esme braced herself for a confrontation with her husband. Her blood pulsed with the adrenaline rush of uncertainty and danger. She anticipated a heated battle of words followed by steamy make-up sex.

"Are you all right?" Tim asked, nonplussed.

"I'm fine."

"He didn't do anything to you, did he?" he continued. *He fucked my brains out in my father's apartment,* Esme was tempted to answer, but refrained. She studied Tim's face, hoping for a sign of suspicion. But there seemed to be none. "Okay, then," Tim concluded. "Glad everything's all right." He exited back into the house. Either he didn't know or didn't care. Esme panicked at the latter thought. She couldn't lose her hold on him. It had never occurred to her before now that she might. Feeling suddenly very chilly, she rushed back inside.

## chapter thirty-four

Dragging her rolling bag behind her, India stepped out of a town car in front of the glass-and-steel tower of her office building. Its industrial chill and a baptismal spray of New York gutter water courtesy of a speeding cab reminded her she was not in Paris anymore. Her eyes were beet red from lack of sleep. Her hair was a rat's nest, and she felt as if she had just been run over by an MTA double-length accordion bus. Yet life had to continue. Inside, the elevator soared toward the twenty-third floor. She shook off her exhaustion and donned her "bring it on" office face, prepared for battle with O'Donnell and the other "anuses on the masthead." *I'm ready to face the day, I'm ready to face the day,* she told herself, stepping into the reception area of Hallingby and Hallingby. If negative self-talk brought us low, surely the reverse could catapult us to the zenith of joy. Just as she was starting to feel mildly buoyed by her own pep talk, O'Donnell reared his ugly bulldog head.

"There she is, the messiah herself. You were MIA the other day and we needed you. What happened?"

"Good afternoon, O'Donnell," she answered, choosing to kill him with kindness. As she reached her office, Una pounced, peppering her with questions.

"Where've you been? You haven't answered a single one of my messages. Why haven't you called Julien?" India reeled. Three days' worth of orgasms had drained her of all manic energy, and she reacted like one emerging from pitch black into the blinding noonday sun.

"Una, stop. Breathe. My cell phone broke."

"So? You couldn't get another one? We had situations here. Before I tell you, phone Khadija, she's at the Starbucks around the corner."

"What's she doing there?" India asked, concerned.

"She showed up with her baby. I know if you meet the kids, you can't represent her anymore. She left her husband. Something about how he brought his other wife to live with them."

"Great, now we have a case. She can divorce him, and we can force him to continue with her naturalization process. She probably needs a place to stay. Call the SoHo Shelter for Women and ask for Sophie. Tell her Khadija's a client of mine. Then arrange a car to take her down there. On me," India said, feeling charged. Romance was lovely, but she got almost as great a high from being able to help those unable to help themselves.

"Boss, that's the good news," Una warned. "The Winston people wanted an emergency meeting at the end of the day Friday. You weren't there, so O'Donnell covered and now it's going to court," she concluded, wincing.

India's blood pressure rose into the high triple digits. Her adrenaline pumped and her fight-or-flight responses switched into full readiness.

"Get Mr. Winston on the phone now, please!" she barked. "And tell O'Donnell I want to see him right away."

"Before you see him, Ms. Armstrong wants to see you. Immediately." India's blood ran cold.

"Right now?" she asked, fearing the worst.

"She said in her office as soon as you got in."

India pulled her shoulders up and back and headed in the direction of Constance's office, the Bataan death march relocated to a law office high above Park Avenue. Constance's assistant, a whisper-thin WASP who had kept her hair in the same shoulder-length bob since the Ford administration, ushered her in.

"Ms. Chumley," she announced in the subdued tone of the court-ordered executioner about to administer the lethal injection. India mused that she neglected to add "object of your boundless wrath."

"Welcome back, Chumley," Constance said without looking up from her tome. India didn't quite know where to situate herself. She decided to stand directly in the line of fire, smack in front of Constance's desk. She'd take this verbal execution like a woman. "Sit down," Constance ordered, still not looking up from her reading. India obeyed. During the ensuing moments of silence, the mahogany walls of Constance's office seemed to grow closer and darker. Time expanded when one stared death in the face, thus victims of earthquake swore the tremors lasted ten minutes when in fact they took up all of ten seconds. Thus India felt she'd waited an hour rather than a few scant minutes for Constance to lower the proverbial boom. Looking up at last, Constance inquired: "Where have you been?"

"I was away on family business," India fudged.

"Your mother is an actress, your stepfather a poet. I was unaware your family had 'business' that would prevent you from fulfilling your duties here," Constance commented dryly.

"What I mean to say is that I had a family crisis," India elaborated, feeling sweat form on her brow.

"Is anyone dead?"

"No, ma'am."

"In need of a kidney transplant?"

"No." India sensed with dread that this line of questioning led directly to the guillotine.

"Then you must excuse me, Ms. Chumley, but I fail to see what could possibly prevent you from answering your phone for two full business days. The *law*," she said, emphasizing the word as though it were a synonym for God, "requires total dedication." India half expected to hear the instrumental version of "Climb Ev'ry Mountain" piped in from the walls. "Our problems and emergencies come second to those of our clients. If you're not the woman I thought you were, please tell me now. We need focus, discipline, and reliability."

India's heart sank. She had obliterated an adult lifetime of focus, discipline, and reliability with seventy-two hours of folly. She rose in her own defense.

"Ms. Armstrong, I think the record will show that I have never—"

"The past has no bearing," Constance cut her off. "You have failed your client, you have failed your profession, and you have failed this firm," she intoned. There it was, the dreaded *F* word. It was a term India never once heard in twenty-four years of schooling. She certainly felt like a failure in her personal life, but she had devoted her adulthood to never making a misstep in her career. Now Constance Armstrong attached the label to her like a glaring scarlet letter. The wages of sin were death, and perhaps even worse, professional derailment. "Bottom line, Ms. Chumley, I'm not interested in explanations or excuses. You will go to court and you will right this wrong," she proclaimed.

"Yes, Ms. Armstrong," India assented, knowing no explanation would ever suffice. Constance bowed her head to return to her reading, the sign for India to withdraw. As India reached the door, Constance delivered the coup de grâce. "I cannot imagine your grandmother, Judge Lydia Chumley, behaving in this manner," she declared.

India turned to look at her, stung. Constance had buried her head back in her book and didn't even deign to look up. India stepped out of the office. Before she could take a step, O'Donnell appeared from around the corner, nipping at her heels.

"So, what did the boss say? She was pissed at me, but I heard she was saving her big guns for you," he said snidely.

"O'Donnell, to paraphrase Mark Twain, 'Better to remain silent and be thought an asshole than to speak and remove all doubt,'" India volleyed back.

"Sexual harassment goes both ways, you know?" he yelled after her. "That's creating a hostile work environment, you b—." He stopped himself just in time.

"We'll discuss your lawsuit when you come to my office in ten minutes to tell me exactly how you botched the Winston case," she fired back as she walked away.

"I botched it? It wasn't my case to botch. You stole it!" His accusation rang in her ears. This was what happened when you dabbled in things that didn't rightfully belong to you. She did something terribly wrong and she deserved every bad consequence that ensued.

## chapter thirty-five

"You need to call Julien," Una counseled as India reentered her office. Now India's intestines tied themselves in a bow, but she knew she must speak to him sooner rather than later. She picked up the receiver and composed the number. His warm voice came through the wires.

"*Allô, ici Julien,*" he said happily.

"*C'est moi.*" India tried to sound cheery. There was dead silence on the other end. India panicked.

"Julien, are you there?" she asked nervously.

"Yes," he answered coldly. India knew she had pushed him too far. Desperate to atone for her mistreatment and to ease her own conscience over her duplicity, she launched into her explanation.

"I'm so so so sorry not to have called in the last few days. It was insanely busy at the . . ." she searched for the word, "conference and every time I went to call you, it was way to early or way too late and then, can you believe it, my cell phone broke?" she babbled lamely.

"And there were no other telephones in that backward place you were, what's it called, London?" he asked with more than a hint of sarcasm. India fell silent knowing there was no justification for her behavior. A wave of sincere regret washed over her.

"I won't do that again," she said. "I'm really . . . sorry," she continued, barely getting the words out as she broke into quiet sobs. For a few moments, Julien remained silent, then broke in with: "India, I'm not trying to attack. It's what I've told you before. I would like to feel like more than an afterthought."

"I know," she assented. "You're right."

"At some point you have to decide . . ." He trailed off.

"Decide what?" she asked, petrified.

"Decide if you want to be in this relationship," he said quietly. India's heart sank. And of course, he had hit the nail on the head. She couldn't go on straddling two relationships indefinitely. But if she left Julien, what would her future with Keith be? He had made no promises, just a declaration. Who knew that a trip to Paris was the gateway to emotional inferno?

"But we're not going to solve that question now," Julien reassured her in his soothing voice. Her guilt quadrupled. She didn't deserve such mercy, especially in light of the Winston debacle. Robert Winston's three little children would probably have to spend the next ten years with their wicked witch of a mother. And it was all India's fault.

"When are you coming home?" Julien continued.

"Not until very late. I have a crisis on a case. I've got to get cracking on it."

Julien didn't respond.

"It involves kids. And I screwed up big-time," she elaborated. Another long silence ensued as Julien took in the information.

"Are you sure there's nothing you want to talk about?" he asked. India's alarm bells went off. No good could come of a full confession at this point. And she couldn't bear the thought of hurting a man so dear any more than she already had.

"I'm sure. Don't wait up for me," she insisted, buying herself some time.

"Okay, I won't. And India . . ."

"Yes?" India asked apprehensively.

"I love you, even though you are a lunatic," he admitted in a tone of resignation, and then hung up. *I love you, too,* India thought, *because you're not a lunatic.* There was no time now to dwell on her "torn between two lovers feeling like a bitch" dilemma.

"Una!" she called and the latter appeared, pad in hand. "Get José Feldman on the phone and requisition all of Paula Winston's financial records, particularly her travel expenses over the past twenty-four months. Before you do that, get Mr. Winston on the phone for me. I've got to grovel and hope for forgiveness." Una smiled approvingly. She knew the boss was back and in fighting form.

# chapter thirty-six

At 1:00 PM on a glorious winter day, the buildings clearly delineated against a robin's egg blue sky bright with the promise of spring, Abby walked briskly up Central Park West. With each step, she was naughtily aware of her new Aubade lace brassiere and matching tanga with its corseted waist. The eight pounds she'd lost since the start of her *liaison délicieuse* had given her a new taste for the form-fitting as opposed to the flowing. And while Sage loved her in Billy Joel terms, just the way she was, Abby took a new delight in the attention she received from random men everywhere. It was as if the gods had doused her in pheromones. At Seventy-first Street, she turned left toward Columbus Avenue. She put her hands in her pocket and ran her index and third fingers over the now well-worn key to India's *garçonnière*. In another five blocks, she would be there and in the arms of her beautiful young beloved for their bimonthly Saturday tryst.

While walking, she admired the stately brownstones that lined the street. Most were occupied by single families with children. She spotted a woman wrestling with a Bugaboo Frog stroller and helped her navigate the ascent to the sidewalk from the "garden floor." She smiled to herself as she thought of the contrast between this block and the inhabitants of Dancer's Row: struggling artists striving to hone their skills and hang on to a life in Manhattan. It is *La Bohème* vs. *thirtysomething*, Upper West Side style. What a difference a few streets could make. Abby felt proud to belong to both worlds: that of the free and the passionate, and that of the bourgeois and family oriented. She congratulated herself on managing her two lives brilliantly.

As she turned the corner onto Columbus, she looked up to admire the Art Nouveau building on the corner of Seventy-second Street. Then her eye traveled over the Z'Baby boutique, which evoked fond memories of the tie-dyed onesies her babies wore. The Betsey Johnson boutique already displayed flirty cotton dresses for spring. She quite fancied the one adorned with what appeared to be cherries. Sage would have liked it. She started to cross the street to get a closer look but stopped upon spotting a couple sitting at a window table of the Cuban-Chinese restaurant on Seventy-first Street.

Nathaniel sat tenderly holding and caressing the hand of a young blonde easily ten years Abby's junior. Ten years were not much in light of eternity, but in the life of a woman's beauty, they could mark the dividing line between a shining young mane and the creeping grays, smooth skin, and smiles that created all manner of crags and crevices about the eyes. Abby studied the woman from head to toe. She was obviously tall, very lean, with a tennis player's body. In short, she was everything Nathaniel insisted from the moment they met that he found utterly boring and forgettable. She had the flawless features of a soap-opera, old-money American aristocrat, only it was obvious from her flat chest that her ski-slope nose was passed down through generations of genetic perfection and was not the result of intervention by a skilled surgeon. A gold ring shined discreetly on her pinkie finger, probably a family crest ring, Abby surmised. And how fitting, with her peach-colored cashmere sweater casually tied around her shoulders and her bracelet of beautifully patinated gold links, she looked like someone with some forgotten forebear's last name for a first name: Crosby, or Kendall, or Brooksie. No doubt her surname was chiseled into the marble of a gymnasium at one of the Seven Sisters. And she wore it all as easily as the sweater. It was just part of her wardrobe.

Nathaniel was so fixated on this vision of high WASPdom, he

did not notice the waiter had arrived to deliver what appeared to be dumplings. Once Nathaniel saw them, on the table, he picked one up and tenderly fed it to Crosby Very-English-last-name-engraved-on-every-building-of-an-ivy-covered-campus. He then quickly grabbed a napkin and dabbed away at something invisible to Abby's gaze that had trickled down the goddess's chin with the same care and attention a loving mother showed a toddler. The goddess blushed. Abby turned away. The ten years her affair had lifted off her seemed to return many-fold. The corset stays tightened around her like the bars of a prison, and the brassiere felt like all that stood between buoyancy and her breasts crashing onto the filthy pavement at her feet. Should she have turned back, squared her shoulders, and faced the illicit pair? What would that have accomplished, other than creating a hideous scene out of the soap opera being filmed at the ABC studios a few blocks down the street?

Abby turned to look again. Nathaniel continued to feed his blond goddess, the embodiment of everything anti-ethnic. She could have passed for one of Nathaniel's cousins, from the still-moneyed side of the family. How had he managed to beguile this flawless creature? Women like that rode off into the Southampton sunset with solvent hedge fund managers. Perhaps now that he was poised to become a famous artist, that was the allure. He offered a slight walk on the wild side without too much risk since he was beginning to have cachet, and she probably had enough money for both of them, just as Abby once did. Now, Nathaniel probably wanted to move into an even higher income bracket. Perhaps all of Nathaniel's claims of disdain for the women of his own caste sprung from his fear that because his family was penniless, none of them would deign to marry him. They would sleep with him, of course, but not take his name, as Abby had proudly done on that day some sixteen years before.

A rage rose within Abby at the betrayal; she suddenly wanted to risk the traffic and run across the street to smash the window and make glass rain down upon the happy pair. She started across the street, but a bus whizzed past and she retreated to the sidewalk. When the bus moved away to once again reveal the restaurant, Nathaniel turned to look in her direction. Now it was she who felt like the intruder on a private moment between two perfect people. She turned on her heels and hurried back up Seventy-first Street. She would not cross into bohemia today, or perhaps ever again. She would go home to face her life and what remained of her marriage.

She pulled out her cell phone and composed a text message to India:

Love affair over. Back to reality.

## chapter thirty-seven

The New York Bar Association building on West Forty-fourth Street was the sort of marble and gilt confection erected at the turn of the nineteenth century when America felt certain of itself and its unassailable moral character. As India waited in the cavernous dining room, she mourned the days when she too felt certain of her destiny and the virtues by which she'd earned it. How the mighty and chaste had fallen! Now she sat reducing a stale sesame breadstick to crumbs with her thumb and forefinger, an embarrassment to the law and to womankind. Her iPhone buzzed, announcing the arrival of a text message. She discreetly slipped it out of her purse, under the table. Technology was verboten in these august halls of justice, as it was in many private clubs of another era. She strained to read the message from Abby on her lap.

*What happened?* she typed, only with typos it read, *qhar happened?*

I will explain later.

As an ancient waiter ambled past the table, India slipped the phone back into her bag. Abby had decided to return to the path of virtue, she who had more excuse than anyone to stray. *What is my problem?* India wondered.

The arrival of her luncheon partner roused her from these self-degrading musings. As Judge Lydia Chumley made her way through the tables, several diners stood to greet her as though a bailiff had bellowed, "All rise." It had always been India's dream to command that degree of respect. Now she'd be lucky to command rotten fruit projectiles. Nana Chumley greeted her with the warmest of smiles and a gentle pressing of her powdered cheek. India braced herself to make a full confession and accept the consequences. She decided to wait, however, until they'd finished their meal to demolish Nana's image of her as a woman of accomplishment, discipline, and high principles.

As they ate, India admired Nana's "uniform": a trim navy blue gabardine skirt suit with burnished gold buttons, Ferragamo bow flats, wrist-length gloves, and an old-fashioned rectangular purse with a metal frame. "No woman should ever leave home without one. You might as well go out in your unmentionables," Nana would admonish India when she passed from the age of pinafores to the age of pumps. In homage to Nana and her years of sage advice, India carried the purse Nana had given her for her Sweet Sixteen. When India reached the dregs of her Clam Chowder à la Institution, she mustered the courage to say what was on her mind.

"Nana, there's something you need to know," she ventured.

"I was wondering how long you were going to let me drone on about my flower beds," Nana commented wryly. She pursed her full lips and looked down her aquiline nose at her granddaughter. Her strong features led people to describe Nana's face as "handsome." To India it was quite simply the most beautiful face in the world, belonging to the person whose opinion she prized above all others. Looking Nana in the eye, she chose to begin with the least heinous of her sins, though in her mind both transgressions had earned her a spit roasting in the fires of eternal damnation.

"I let down a client. I missed an appointment, and as a result we're going to court. A nasty custody case. The father deserves the children. Now, because of me, he probably won't get them. I've ruined four peoples' lives. And three of those people are under ten." India looked to Nana for a reaction, but her grandmother remained utterly impassive, Her Honor waiting to hear the full case before passing judgment.

"Constance Armstrong told me I had failed my profession and the firm," India continued. At this comment, Nana's cheek twitched, but she maintained her poker face.

"Why did you miss your appointment?" she asked at last.

"Because I'm seeing two men." India stared penitent at the bottom of her soup bowl.

"Only two? I was hoping for something juicy," Nana said, nonplussed.

"Nana, I don't mean 'see,' as in have an ice cream soda with. I mean—"

"You're getting busy with them." Nana enunciated every consonant with staccato precision.

"I've never done anything like this before."

"Well, it's high time." India looked up from the soup bowl, stunned. Nana had always been the voice of reason and decorum. Yet she seemed to advocate throwing caution and undergarments to the wind. And it was not the influence of alcohol because she was sipping seltzer water.

"I desire some apple pie," Nana declared as she hailed the waiter. Even though she had grown up in New York, Nana sometimes borrowed the florid language of her South Carolina–bred mother. "Come along. We're going to take a little constitutional," Nana insisted, rising from the table.

She laced her arm through India's and led her out. They walked arm in arm toward Sixth Avenue, passing the Harvard Club, a Georgian pile dwarfed by surrounding skyscrapers. India paused for a moment. Through the paned glass windows of the double doors, she could see the fireplace in front of which she had spotted Keith preflagrante with his peroxide tart six years before. In the days after the incident, she forced herself to return to the scene of the crime and stare at the spot. She wanted to brand the memory of her humiliation into her mind and, more important, her heart, so she would never put herself in such a situation again. At first, she had been unable to look upon the fire grate without weeping, but eventually the wound callused, and she became numb to the pain. As she looked at the spot, unchanged by the passage of six years, her stomach tensed with a dull stabbing pain. History might repeat itself. She turned to look at Nana, who gently squeezed her arm and pressed her onward.

"The past will kill you if you dwell on it," Nana counseled evenly as she admired the galleon window of the New York Yacht Club. Their trip down "WASP Power Row" ended in front of the Algonquin Hotel.

"Do you know what this is?" Nana asked once they'd settled into a cozy booth in the mahogany paneled Blue Bar, which was so dimly lit it should perhaps have been renamed the Darkness at Noon Tavern.

"This is Dorothy Parker's hotel," India answered.

"True, but it was also the scene of your grandmother's disgrace," Nana said suggestively. This piqued India's curiosity. She never would have uttered Nana's name in the same sentence with the word *disgrace*. Knowing she'd hooked her listener, Nana continued. "I had just passed the bar exam. I was dating Jimmy Lee Bailey." Nana's voice dropped an octave and turned sultry as she uttered the name. Sixty years on, the man's memory stirred the embers of desire. "Jimmy was tall and lean with skin the color of toffee. He could have any woman he wanted from Harlem to the Bowery. And did."

India didn't dare ask, "Did he have you?" though she longed to know. Instead she asked, "What did he do?"

"He was a numbers runner. The biggest in Harlem."

"A numbers runner?" India repeated, shocked. Grandpa Chumley had been a respected internist. She'd only ever imagined Nana being courted by educated men from traditional professions.

"Mmmm, he was baaaaaad." Nana stretched out the last syllable with lusty relish. "Jimmy Lee and I had come to hear Miss Ella Fitzgerald, who was singing in that room right over there," she said, pointing to the Oak Room, a nightclub incongruously fashioned after a wood-paneled library in a Tudor manor. "I was so giddy about passing the bar, hearing Miss Fitzgerald, and spending the night with Jimmy Lee that I just kept ordering cocktails. Jimmy tried to slow me down, but it was no good. Unaccustomed to liquor as I was, I was a cheap drunk. After two pink ladies, I was standing on a chair belting out 'My Funny Valentine.' That's when Jimmy Lee dragged me out." Nana paused to take a sip of her water, then asked, "Have I shocked you?"

"You mean, this is all true?" India asked, incredulous. She could not imagine Nana, the personification of dignity, drunk and disorderly anywhere, let alone in an elegant nightclub.

"Of course, it's true," Nana bristled, annoyed at the suggestion she would lie.

"But it can't be. You're Nana," India insisted like a seven-year-old who had discovered how she was conceived and wanted to cling to the stork theory.

"I wasn't always a judge, baby. I was twenty-four."

"What's my excuse? I'm thirty-seven."

"That's your problem. You've been holding the steam in for too long. It's bound to blow the top off the kettle if you don't let a little out from time to time."

All these years India thought she was impressing Nana with her intellect and propriety, and all along she'd known she was a tramp trapped in a prude's body. It was a relief to be understood, although she was somewhat ashamed that Nana saw the person she was rather than the ideal to which she aspired.

"How did you know?" India asked. Nana chuckled.

"I practically raised you, child," she took another sip of her water and gave India a reassuring wink. "Anyway, as Jimmy Lee and I were leaving, I noticed an elegant white-haired man who looked familiar: he was the judge I'd just started clerking for."

India gasped. "What did you do?" she asked.

"Tried to pretend I hadn't seen him. And hoped he hadn't seen me. But of course, he had. He didn't say anything, but for the next six months, he gave me all the dreariest assignments, obscure tax codes, torts. I did it all like I loved it. Finally, one day he came in and said, 'Your penance is over, just don't ever let me catch you getting smashed again.' The point is, there's no mistake you can't recover from if you work hard enough."

"But did you ever recover from Jimmy Lee?" India asked boldly. Nana's lips curled in a cryptic Mona Lisa smile. She paused for a moment.

"Let me tell you a little bit about your boss, the great Miss Constance Armstrong, Esquire," she said in a complete non sequitur. "That rock-solid marriage of hers? He was her boss, had been married for twenty-two years, and she stole him."

Suddenly Constance's Benthamite aphorisms rang in India's ears with new meaning: "Someone is always the winner and someone always the loser in love. Just make sure you represent the winner in the end." Little had India imagined that the embodiment of female professionalism's philosophy was an apologia for her own floozy past.

Nana savored another bite of her apple pie, which lay in a pool of melted vanilla ice cream.

"People who try to appear as perfect as Constance usually have everything to hide," Nana philosophized. Still, India was not comforted by being a sinner among fallen idols.

"I can't go on seeing two men forever, Nana. It's got to stop."

"Whom do you love?" Nana challenged.

In the rush of secrets and lies, India hadn't stopped to ponder that central question and yet the answer spilled out of her, to her own surprise.

"Both! But I'm in love with Keith. You think he's bad for me, don't you?"

"It's not my place to say."

"Please, I'm asking."

Nana smiled with profound understanding. "Love is anything but simple," she said.

"It would be if I found someone like my dad," India countered wistfully. Nana put down her fork and spoon very deliberately. She delicately dabbed her mouth with the white linen napkin.

"He was my son," she said, willing the tears from rolling down her cheeks. "But don't build a shrine to him. He had his faults just like anyone else. No man is perfect." India's eyes welled up. She needed her father to shine as a beacon to guide her. It was intolerable to think that he too had feet of clay. Sensing India's discomfort, Nana chose not to elaborate. Instead, she said, "Many women marry the man they're in love with and find to their eternal disillusionment they make the worst possible husbands. Others marry a man they don't love who makes them so happy they love him in the end. More than they could ever have imagined. Every woman has a choice: to have a husband and a career, or to make keeping her husband her career. Do you want to be a handmaiden to greatness or be great yourself? I made my choice; you will have to make yours. Just make sure the bed you choose at thirty is the one you want to lie in at eighty."

India rolled the film of her life forward several decades. She imagined herself leaving Julien babbling about truffles in the chef's kitchen of the downtown apartment she loathed as she went off to address a conference of recent law school graduates on balancing career and marriage. She knew that when she returned, she would find him waiting for her with dinner, a bottle of wine, and a warm embrace.

Now she turned her mind to life as Mrs. Keith Wentworth II. Her heart leapt at the thought of where Keith's ambition would have brought him: the pinnacle of international business, a cabinet post in a Democratic administration. She imagined herself at a state dinner, bending the ear of the president, their close personal friend, about women's and children's rights. The reality she saw in Paris intruded upon her fantasy. Would she be at the state dinner with him or sitting alone in the living room of their floor-through on Central Park West, overlooking the park? Not only would she be there alone, but she would also have a face stretched more tightly than the sail of a catamaran and collagen-inflated fish lips. It would be a desperate surgical bid to woo Keith away from the latest in a succession of comely assistants who all happened to have been runners-up in their hometown beauty pageants.

"Stop whining and fretting. Stop being afraid of making mistakes. Do what you came to do!" Nana snapped, as though reading India's mind.

"Whatever became of Jimmy Lee?" India asked.

"He made a pile of money, turned legit, and married the president of the Links, New Rochelle chapter. Had a passel of babies," Nana answered, betraying neither joy nor regret.

"Did you ever see him again?"

"No. Didn't care to," Nana said with equanimity. She remained silent for a moment, staring in the direction of the Oak Room. "But from time to time I come here, order a pink lady. And remember."

India's heart sank. Nana eschewed marrying her bad boy, but she'd obviously never quite gotten over him. For all the joy and peace the "sensible choices" brought, they could not erase the memory of the passionate love of one's life. Was it not better perhaps to take her mother's path and follow one's heart, even to the grave?

## chapter thirty-eight

It was near closing time as India finally arrived at L'Oasis, Julien's French-Asian bistro nestled between a Dunkin' Donuts and a bar with a blinking neon martini glass for a sign.

"Glad you could finally make it," Cora, the angular Blapanese hostess commented with a scowl as India passed her station. India felt the full force of the reproach.

"Nice to see you, too, Cora," she responded cordially, aware that as she removed her coat, Cora sized up every millimeter of her person, assessing her shoes, the cut of her pants, the width of her ankles. Cora could probably detect the pound and three quarters India had gained as a result of a few nerve-induced truffle binges. India had always suspected that Cora dreamt of replacing her at Julien's side. Since their first meeting, she had greeted India with all the warmth of a growling Cerberus welcoming a dead soul to the underworld. India detected an increase in Cora's watchfulness since the inception of her—she didn't want to label it "dalliance"—her slippage with Keith.

"*Voici la belle!*" Jean-Luc, the bartender, called out to India. He was a more handsome version of Trotsky, minus the goatee. Cora's back stiffened at his warm greeting. She shut her reservation book with an angry slam.

"Where is Julien?" India asked.

"I'll see if he's still here," Cora said with a cold stare.

"It's okay, I'll find him." India made her way past the brass railings separating the ebony booths from the aisle. She found Julien tucked away in the last booth, poring over menus. His passion for food and exploratory recipes was boundless. He could study a cut of meat or the relative merits of orzo versus Israeli couscous the way other men zoned out in front of a football game. It was this among other qualities that drew India to him. With him, she would never have to suffer through the nacho-and-beer-laden high holy day of American masculinity known as Super Bowl Sunday. It had never been celebrated in her home growing up, and she had no desire to adopt the ritual. If she ended up with Keith, she would have to. And he probably would want her to bear the brood of boys who could join in the festival of brawn. In fact, Keith was the sort of man who would insist his wife have babies until she produced a male heir, a Keith Wentworth the Third. If Keith stopped phoning, she would be well rid of him.

"Novelties on the menu?" India asked to get Julien's attention. He rose instantly and smiled as he kissed her.

"My sous-chef found the most astonishing new algae in Borneo. They carry it in a few tiny shops here. We can't decide whether to serve it as a salad because the texture is so extraordinary, like squid. Or whether to make a soup or a sorbet because the flavor is sour-sweet."

"I vote for the salad," India suggested.

"Enough about the menu. I have a surprise for you," Julien said, clearly pleased with himself.

"You know I don't like surprises." In over a year of being with Julien, she had found it very difficult to allow him to take the lead on anything but supper. Julien took her hand in his and looked into her eyes. For a moment she feared he was going to utter the dreaded M words: "Marry me."

"I don't think we've spent enough time together recently," he offered gently. "We need to get away alone together to see where we are. I love you, you know." India gulped. Was this the moment to tell all, whatever the consequences? Was she being a loving person by his definition: "Letting someone be who they are even if it means being away from you." Before she could form a confession, he continued.

"I'm taking you away."

"Where?"

"You won't know until we get to the airport. And you will need your passport."

"Is it someplace I've been before?" India pursued, her curiosity piqued.

"I won't answer any more questions," Julien teased. His evasiveness alarmed her. She suddenly envisioned herself in a mosquito-infested rice paddy in Cambodia, or worse, trolling for seaweed in some forgotten corner of Borneo. Her desire to confess vanished, supplanted by the urgency to save herself from a misadventure in ecotourism.

"Just one warning, Julien. If this involves hiking shoes, bug spray, and energy bars, I'm not your girl. Never have been. You've described some of your trips canoeing down the Amazon with your ex-girlfriends. My idea of hell is to be more than a mile from the nearest Four Seasons. I see no poetry in sleeping on a tatami mat, and my Nana Chumley did not become the first black female federal judge in this state so that I could use an outhouse on holiday."

"India, I know who you are. I live with you. I see you and I accept you. I promise, no tatami mats. Why would I want to change perfection?" India smiled and basked in the glow of Julien's complete acceptance. Their future stretched promisingly before her: no Super Bowl, no vacations virtuously devoid of a shred of luxury, and a husband who did not harbor a godlike desire to remake her in his own image. He really was as perfect as his chocolate Valrhona cake.

"I saved something for you," Julien said tauntingly.

"Chocolate?" India's taste buds moistened with anticipation.

"You'll see."

India's cell phone played the Hallelujah Chorus. She couldn't resist looking down and instantly recognized 646-555-2887, Keith's number. Her heart pounded.

"A crisis?" Julien asked, sensing the rise in her blood pressure.

"No." She plastered on a smile and tamped down the insistent urge to answer. Julien leaned over to kiss her. She forced herself to focus on the kiss, not the phone. Mercifully, Julien left her to fetch her "gift." India pressed the "answer" bar.

"Hello!" she practically panted into the phone.

"I have to see you," Keith's deep voice beckoned.

"What did you have in mind?"

"Can't now. Too much going on. But everything's changed since Paris," Keith answered abruptly. India longed to ask what had changed: His feelings? His status? She wouldn't allow herself to show such desperation, especially since he'd put her off. She had to, in the words from *Gone with the Wind*, "remember herself." She would not stoop to conquer. Perhaps that was why she was still single and the more pliant Serena was officially at Keith's side, a doubting voice whispered. India silenced it instantly and donned her armor of dignity.

"It's not a good time for me either. Won't be for a while," she lied.

"Where are you right now?" Keith asked.

*Ready to jump into the nearest taxi to come meet you,* she ached to answer, but instead she said, "At a coffee shop. In my neighborhood." She waited for Keith's cross-questioning. He knew full well she loathed greasy spoons. It was a source of endless frustration to him in their student days that he could not entice her to even set foot in Elsie's sandwich shop, the most popular diner in Harvard Square. To her surprise, he accepted the implausible explanation of her whereabouts. *Does his lack of curiosity indicate a lack of caring?* she wondered. She then reminded herself of what many men had told her: don't parse our statements. Only women and Bill Clinton spoke in such coded terms. The male mind simply wasn't so complex.

"I'll call you," Keith promised huskily. She pressed the end call bar, then clutched her phone like a precious relic. She looked up to see Cora staring her down from behind the ebony and brass partition. Cora moved away like Madame Defarge counting another victim for her guillotine. India panicked for a moment that Cora had overheard the conversation. Had she been lurking in the vicinity all along? India tried to remember all that she had said to Keith. It was her tone and body language that gave away the nature of the exchange. She hadn't said anything particularly self-incriminating. Besides, even if Cora heard it all and reported every word of it to Julien, he loved India too much to believe the worst. India sighed with the relief of having dodged a bullet.

Julien emerged from the kitchen, holding large tinfoil containers and a white paper bag.

"I need your client Khadija's address," he said.

"What for?"

"I made some food for her and her family. I know it's a difficult time and I'm sure they don't have much money. You said there were three children? A baby, a four-, and a six-year-old?"

"Yes," India answered, stunned at his powers of recall. She had mentioned Khadija's children to him only once.

"I have little surprises for them." He pulled meringues shaped like gazelles out of the white bag. "Not the tastiest," he offered apologetically, "but at least they will amuse them. And there's a huge pot à la crème to satisfy their appetites. So where am I dropping it off?"

India couldn't speak. In spite of her neglect of him over the course of weeks, Julien reached out to help a family he didn't even know for her sake. Perhaps it wasn't about saving the world on a grand scale, from a perch of power like Keith's. Perhaps it was about such small daily acts of kindness that brought a smile to a child's face and reminded them that there was still good in the world.

"I'm not sure this isn't a breach of attorney-client privilege," India responded at last, fighting back tears of gratitude at his kindness.

"Who's going to report you to the New York Bar? You didn't ask me. It's my restaurant's Good Samaritan program. We do it all the time," Julien said with a wink. India scrolled through the addresses on her iPhone. The numbers blurred through the undulating screen of her gathering tears.

# *chapter thirty-nine*

As the Lincoln Continental from the budget car service sped across the Triborough Bridge, India sat beside Julien, reading a text message from Abby:

Don't worry about me. Walking wounded, but I'll live. Just enjoy your trip.

Email if you need me, India typed.

"I see I'm going to have a rival during this trip," Julien sighed.

"No. I promise I won't use it." India slipped her iPhone back in her purse. Julien looked at her skeptically.

"It's an extension of your arm," he joked.

"Not this trip." Indeed, she had told Keith she was going on a business trip and wouldn't be bringing it. She needed neither hope nor fear he would reach her. The silence would help keep her focused. Julien deserved her full attention.

"I'll love you even if you break that promise." Julien leaned in to kiss her. She couldn't help but contrast his patience with Keith's insistence she focus on him and him alone. And Julien was a very nice lover overall. He didn't make her see the sun, moon, and stars, as Keith did, but marriage was about trade-offs. The women India knew who'd married their best orgasms ended up quite miserable in the end. She needed only look to Abby and her own mother to see where strato-spheric ecstasy led. *If you want to see the sun, moon, and stars on a regular basis, go to the planetarium,* she told herself.

Julien caressed her foot with his, a reminder he was not without his talents. India looked forward to long sultry afternoons on the beach. He had insisted she pack all her bikinis. It was so exciting that he'd taken charge. India was tired of the driver's seat and relished the notion of being a passenger. Of course, she would have booked a better car service than this one with its surly drivers, ten-year-old vehicles, and the coils of the springs practically protruding through pleather seats patched with masking tape. Nonetheless, at the end of the day, she wasn't a material girl. As she had learned from watching countless clients, it was better to be with a kind man with fewer creature comforts than a bird in a bedazzling cage.

The car sputtered up the ramp of Kennedy International Airport, the Air France terminal. India swallowed hard, then reassured herself of the multitude of destinations that airline offered its passengers. They were probably on their way to the Seychelles, or Morocco, or Madagascar. Julien smiled enigmatically as they pulled their suitcases up to the business-class counter. Now India was certain they were going a long distance. Business-class travel was not really in Julien's budget.

"Nice of you to fly us in style," India said warmly.

"Only the best for you." Julien kissed her on the top of her head. India knew how much this cost him. He worked for every penny he had. A gesture from such a man meant more than an eighteen-carat diamond from a multimillionaire who, in the end, had to make no sacrifice to purchase it. India felt a sudden rush of gratitude and adoration. Julien inspired something greater perhaps than the excitement she felt in the presence of Keith: respect and warmth that made her want to open her heart and reveal it fully.

The woman at the counter greeted them cordially. "Two for Paris," she chirped as she scrutinized their tickets. India's heart stopped.

"Paris?" she managed to repeat.

"Not very original, I admit," Julien explained, "but it is the most beautiful city in the world, for the most beautiful woman in the world. I was going to take you to Madagascar until you said what you did about ecotourism. So you will see Paris, my Paris."

*Why, oh why, did I have to go on that pampered black American princess tirade about my aversion to roughing it?* she thought, ready to strangle herself for sheer stupidity.

"Wonderful," India said wanly, her mind racing over every detail of her weekend with Keith. Mercifully, so much of it was spent holed up at the hotel that she really hadn't ventured anywhere she would be recognized.

"What's the matter?"

"Nothing at all. I love Paris!" she answered gaily.

"I'm going to take you to my favorite place for tarts, and you'll meet Pierre Hermé. He's going to make you a special tasting of his *macarons*. We're going to dine at La Serre, we'll go to Poilâne at five AM and taste the croissants just as they are pulling them out of the ovens."

"It all sounds heavenly. But don't fatten me up too much," India joked to cover her mounting panic.

"I'd love you anyway you came." Julien slipped his arm around her waist. They stood at the counter as the woman printed off their boarding passes and tagged their luggage.

"But there you are again! With another fabulous outfit!" a male voice boomed.

India looked up to see the chatty Martinican mulatto who checked her and Keith in the night they left on their tryst. He'd gone mad over her Chanel pantsuit and mock croc tote. And of course, he'd gone mad over Keith, who reminded him of one of his light-skinned cousins. He was so thrilled to be dealing with a chic black couple that he'd talked their ears off for twenty minutes. India looked away as she tried to find a way out of the hole. Her panic turned to anger at the indiscreet boob. Couldn't he see she was not with Keith? She thought the French were noted for their discretion. Surely she was not the first "tryster" to fly this airline. It should probably have been renamed Air Paramour.

"*Mais oui, c'est bien vous.* Don't you remember me? I helped you a few weeks ago. You were with, oh, not with him," he said, noticing Julien at last.

"I remember!" India said by way of shutting him up. Julien looked at her perturbed.

"You were just here?" he asked. "When?" The Martinican gate agent finally saw the tangled web he'd shone a light upon.

"*Oh là là,*" he gasped as he beat a whip-fast retreat to help another passenger.

Julien looked to India for an explanation. She considered lying to him yet again. Staring into his eyes, she could not bring herself to deceive him. After months of dodging, the moment of truth was upon her. She steeled herself and began, as calmly as she could.

"When I took that trip last month. Remember, to London?"

"Why were you flying Air France to London?"

"Why not?" India bluffed. She could tell from Julien's serious expression he was not buying.

"What's going on, India?" he asked with the calm that comes with resignation to hearing bad news.

"I didn't go to London last month. I went to Paris." India took a long beat before delivering the coup de grâce. "With Keith," she whispered.

"Oh, merde." Julien doubled over as though he'd just been punched in the gut. India cringed at the blow she'd dealt him. Having been the cuckold, she knew the pain the discovery of betrayal caused. She'd never thought she'd be the one crowning someone she cared about with a pair of humiliating horns. She instinctively reached out a hand to place it on Julien's arm but pulled it back before it ever pressed his flesh, knowing she'd forfeited the right to touch him at will. It would have been a violation of his dignity to do so at that point.

"Why?" Julien asked, turning to face her, tears welling up in his eyes.

"To try to figure things out. It was wrong and selfish, and I'm so sorry!"

"I believed you when you said you were going to London, that you lost your phone. *Quel idiot!*" he shouted, suddenly pulling himself upright and walking away from her and back toward the seats by the exit. India followed him. He turned on her. "Do you love him?" Julien's eyes betrayed a glimmer of hope that she'd answer "no." India fell silent, not wanting to speak the truth.

"Merde," Julien said again in a tone of sheer agony.

Desperate to ease the pain, India blurted, "I don't think I know what love really is!" Tears now welled up in her eyes.

"Don't give me your intellectualizing bullshit!"

"It's not bullshit. It's true! You've seen my family!" A seventy-five-year-old married couple sat one chair away from them. They listened to this exchange and cast pitying looks at India, or so she thought. Yes, they probably believed she was an idiot who'd royally screwed up her life. She could have been calmly married like them and instead, she had chosen to risk everything.

"Don't blame your family," Julien cried. "They didn't make you lie. And you lied to me, after I told you what that would mean!" His words cut deep. Her heart suddenly felt the burden of having broken another. India wished she could erase the last six months.

Julien collapsed into one of the leather-and-chrome seats by the revolving doors, burying his head in his hands. India knelt beside him, throwing her arms around him and caressing his back. She held him as though doing so would put his shattered heart back together. The elderly married couple had the grace to move away and give them their privacy.

"I'm sorry, I'm so sorry," she repeated desperately. And so they sat as eager travelers rushed past them until at last, Julien looked up and rose to his feet.

"Come with me," he commanded suddenly.

"Where are we going?"

"Just come." He dragged her enormous suitcase with him. He walked her to the door and stepped out. On the ramp, he hailed a taxi.

"What's going on?" India asked.

"I'm sending you home. I'm going to Paris." India absorbed the finality of the decision. The fun and games were definitely over, and she'd officially made a mess of things.

"When will you be back?" she asked.

"I don't know. I need time by myself. I can't even look at you anymore," he answered in a tone of defeat.

"I understand," India said, holding back her own tears so he didn't think she was trying to manipulate him when at that moment all she felt was immense regret at the damage she'd done. Julien opened the door and extended a hand to help her into a taxi while averting his gaze.

"Thank you," she said, hoping he'd realize she meant "thank you for everything, for being kind and tender and always a gentleman."

"Good-bye, India," he said hoarsely as he shut the door and rushed back inside. India watched him go and wondered if she'd ever see him again. She was suddenly terrified that she wouldn't.

## chapter forty

Esme stood in the black-and-white-tiled bathroom of India's studio, pinning a blond Marilyn Monroe wig to her head. She tugged at it to make sure it would withstand the "climax yank." Satisfied, she dropped the bag of bobby pins into her toiletry kit. She opened the medicine cabinet and pulled out an atomizer of vanilla spray she kept stored for such occasions. She ran the spray over the length of her body, then turned to admire herself in the full-length mirror on the door. The cream-colored satin slip fit her like a shining second skin. She filled it out like Elizabeth Taylor did hers in *Cat on a Hot Tin Roof.*

"Are you ready?" she called out toward the bedroom. She threw open the door. Patrick, wearing nothing but his Brooks Brothers boxers adorned with diminutive whales, lay on the sea of eyelet-covered pillows waiting for her. The bulge in his pants rose at the sight of her.

"Whoa!" he exclaimed. She sauntered toward him.

"You like it?" she purred.

"I like everything. The outfit, the hair. Where'd you get the hair?"

"No man wants to sleep with the same woman all the time. No woman wants to sleep with the same man every time," she quipped.

"Come here, baby," Patrick begged, rising to his knees, his penis so erect it protruded from the slit in his boxers. This was Esme's favorite miracle, the parting of the "cotton sea." She stopped at the edge of the bed. Patrick crawled toward her.

"Oh, the vanilla spray. Shit, I love that stuff," he moaned. Esme ran her hands through his mass of auburn hair, relishing its silken feel. Her hands moved down his neck to his shoulders. Suddenly, his BlackBerry buzzed and they both leapt off the bed and ran to his jacket that hung on one side of the cheval mirror. Esme beat him to it, grabbing the device.

"Give that to me!" he barked.

"No! Let's see who's calling!" she taunted as the device continued to buzz. "Oh, A. J. Honeycutt. Sounds like a girl. Should I answer?"

"Don't!"

"Aha, it is a girl. Who is she?"

"Just someone I met," he said defiantly. The BlackBerry stopped buzzing.

"Did I say you could sleep with other people?" Esme warned, arching her left eyebrow for effect.

"What the fuck are you talking about? You screw someone else all the time. You're married." The BlackBerry buzzed again. Patrick lunged to grab it from Esme, but she ran to the other side of the room.

"Oh, it's A. J. again. She's persistent," she commented. Patrick grabbed her arm and flipped her onto the bed. He wrested the buzzing device from her hand. "If you answer, you will walk out now and never see me again!" Esme threatened from her pinned position. Patrick panicked at the thought. "A. J. can't do what I do. Nobody can. I'll bet she uses her teeth when she does fellatio, like a cheese grater."

"She does," Patrick said, laughing. He handed Esme the BlackBerry, and she tossed it onto a nearby armchair. Patrick leaned in to kiss her, but she put a hand on his rosy mouth.

"Ah, ah, ah. Not so fast. You have to beg my forgiveness," she instructed.

"I will. And I know exactly how," he said with a cocky grin. He glided down the length of her body and pushed the satin slip upward. Esme shut her eyes as his warm tongue delicately encircled her swelling clitoris. He had learned fast, and oh, oh, oh so well. Her hips rocked slowly backward and forward to meet his mouth. "AAAw! OOOh," she let herself moan, lost in the feeling of her hands on his silken hair, his warm tongue on her, the smell of his slight perspiration. Suddenly, he stopped.

"What are you doing—" Esme started to yell, but Patrick placed a hand over her mouth.

"Listen," he whispered. They heard the door unlock and someone shoving against the chain lock.

"Who's there?" Patrick yelled, leaping off the bed and assuming a defensive stance.

"I'm sorry. I forgot," a female voice answered.

"It's India!" Esme cried. The door slammed shut. Esme rolled off the bed and ran to the door. She unlocked it and flung it open.

"India!" she called at the figure beating a hasty retreat down the hallway. India stopped and turned, strangely relieved to see Esme.

"What are you doing?" Esme asked.

"I'd ask you the same question, but it's pretty obvious," India answered in a lame attempt at lightheartedness. "Sorry for interrupting."

"Why aren't you on a plane with Julien?"

"We broke up, I think," India answered, her voice quivering. Esme put her arms around her. They stood holding each other in the middle of the hallway. Esme's gesture allowed India to give full vent to the sadness welling up since Julien placed her in a taxi.

"I'm sorry," Esme said.

"I deserved it," India answered. "I was a horrible girlfriend."

"Stop it. You weren't married," Esme insisted.

"No, it's like you said. 'Cheating is cheating.'"

"I was just being hard on you. It's not the same," Esme argued. India wished Esme was right, but having spent her life watching a cheater, she knew she was wrong. Her own past as a victim only compounded her sin. There was in her mind absolutely no excuse for what she did to Julien. It was quite simply unforgivable.

"I'm fucked up, Esme. Utterly and totally fucked up," she said at last.

"Esme! What are you doing out there?" Patrick called from inside the apartment.

"You should go back inside."

"No, I'll get rid of him. You and I will sit and have wine and cry."

"No. I only came here because I couldn't face his place. I need to go there. Pack up my things."

"So it's really over? It can't be," Esme said with agitation in her voice.

"If you were he, would you forgive me?"

"No, I wouldn't." India bowed her head, resigned to the bad news. "But I'm a bitch, he's not. I think he would. I know he would. He loves you the way Tim loves me. Without holding anything back," Esme added pensively. She wrapped her arms around herself as though suddenly ashamed of her near nakedness.

"Thanks," India said, embracing her before she turned away.

"India," Esme called after her. "The real question is: Do you want Julien to forgive you?" India was stunned at Esme's insight. As India watched her reenter the apartment, she wondered if Esme were speaking for herself as well.

## chapter forty-one

India sat at her desk, devouring a Lindt Crème Brûlée chocolate bar. She started by breaking off dainty pieces, but eventually tore off huge slabs with her teeth. She rolled her eyes as she listened to Mrs. Diamond's voice screeching over the speakerphone.

"I'm down to my last fifty grand in cash. I'm destitute here!" Lucinda cried. *All is relative,* India surmised. To Khadija, her pro bono client, fifty thousand would have been the start of a new, prosperous life. To Lucinda Diamond, it put her well below the Park Avenue poverty line, amid the squalor of knockoff designer purses and costume jewelry. India remained silent to give Lucinda a moment to calm down.

"Hello, are you there? Or have you hung up because he's not paying you?" Lucinda whined.

"I would never do that. Now, you're not going to want to hear this, but there's only one way out of this game."

"I've told you fifty times, I'm not going to rehab," Lucinda snapped.

"If you don't, your husband's just going to drag this out until you're clipping coupons. Now I've found a place. It's called Chrysalis. It's in a Malibu mansion." India took another bite of her Lindt as she heard Lucinda pause and consider her proposition. After months of stalemate, she actually appeared to be on the verge of a breakthrough with her navel-gazing client.

"Do I have to share a room?" Lucinda asked, disgusted.

"No. You have a fifteen-hundred-square-foot suite, decorated with a butterfly motif," India assured her. She too was a "five-star hotel or bust" prima donna, but she could not imagine worrying about such trifles when your children's happiness hung in the balance.

"Room service?" Lucinda pursued.

"Yes, and they offer mani-pedis," India added enticingly.

"In the room?"

"And during the therapy sessions."

"I just hate to give in to that pig," Lucinda protested. India took another enormous bite of chocolate to prevent herself from lashing out. The most persuasive argument of all occurred to her.

"Lucinda, this place has been written up in *Vogue*, *W*, and *Allure*. Every drug abuser who's anyone has been there, all the A-list coke addicts . . . I hear the Windsors considered sending Prince Harry there." *This will get her,* India thought to herself. If nothing else, Lucinda would have visions of snagging Prince Harry as an honorary cochair of one her many charity benefits: the eating disorder ball, food allergy casino night . . .

"So they must have a royal suite," Lucinda surmised, brightening.

"Probably."

"I'll take that," Lucinda said.

"I'll email you the numbers. They're holding a reservation. Call them tonight," India answered, hanging up. When she undertook the case, her sympathies were squarely with her client. Since then, she'd seen so many different sides of Lucinda that she didn't know if she was achieving anything by winning the case. It had become as muddled as her personal life.

An hour later, at 10:15, India lumbered out of the front doors of her office tower, lugging her laptop in its case. As she walked down the steps leading to Park Avenue, she spotted a familiar-looking town car. Keith leaned against it.

"Working late?" he called out. She stopped, dismayed and excited to see him. *It is not fair that any human being can look so consistently perfect at every single hour of the day in their thirty-ninth year,* she thought, taking in the imposing length of his flawless body. She, on the other hand, was the very portrait of a woman in shambles: hair piled in a Scrunchee on top of her head, faded makeup, and chocolate on her breath. If he could find her attractive in that moment, then he must have loved her.

"It's nice to see you," she said, trying to hang back so he couldn't take in her dishevelment at close range.

"So you come back to town, but you don't call, you don't write," he reproached.

"I'm sorry, I was going to phone you tomorrow," she said, lying. She didn't know when she would have called him. She wanted to do proper penance for her sins before falling into his powerful arms.

"Let me give you a ride," he said, opening the car door. Her Carmelite nun code told her to refuse his offer. But deep in her heart and soul, she wanted more than anything to snuggle up to that rock-solid chest. It was as natural as breathing. Deny it though she might, he rocked her to her core. And so she acquiesced. Once in the backseat, he rubbed her neck with his huge, smooth hands. "Is your man waiting for you, or can you come with me to the St. Regis?" he whispered in her ear, his warm breath sending a shiver down her spine. "Let's have a little Paris in New York," he added.

India looked him in the eye. "He's not my man anymore." As soon as she'd said it, she felt naked. With Julien, she had a shield against Keith and something to hold over him. How would he react now that he had no competition? India instantly regretted taking the risk of telling him and awaited his reaction with trepidation.

"Now we have to go to the St. Regis, to celebrate," Keith gloated, caressing her face. She removed his hand and placed it at his side.

"You shit." She was ashamed of her own excitement at his invitation.

"What do you want me to do, lie?" Manuel, the driver, discreetly exited the car. "It killed me every time you were going home to him. I hated it," Keith admitted, bitterly.

"Well, I hate that you're with Serena."

"Fine, then, it's over."

"What?" India asked, stunned.

"I'm going to break it off," Keith stated.

"That's easy to say," she challenged. She wanted so very much to believe him, but their history put her on her red alert. How many times in one life could a woman let a man make a fool of her?

"I'll prove it." He stepped out of the car and whispered something to Manuel. They both reentered a moment later and the car sped up Park Avenue.

"Where are we going?" India asked.

"Just shut up and trust me for once," Keith ordered.

"There's an irresistible invitation. Did you learn that at the Stanley Kowalski school of charm?" India quipped, but Keith looked straight ahead and didn't answer. India's curiosity and excitement mounted with every passing block. The car turned left on Fifty-ninth Street and tore up across Central Park South. At Columbus Circle, it veered right. India's heart pounded as they pulled up in front of 15 Central Park West, Keith's building. India couldn't believe her eyes. He was taking her home. Keith stepped out of the car and extended his hand. The doorman opened the door and tipped his hat.

"Good evening, Mr. Wentworth," he said with a bow.

"Hello, Jim," Keith answered. India did her best to look down and away, a bit like a newly arrested felon who didn't want her face shown on the evening news. She felt certain the doorman was looking her over with disapproval. No doubt Tinker Bell had them all wrapped around her delicate fingers. India forced herself to dismiss the unpleasant thought. This was her moment. She needed to savor every microgram of joy.

As she and Keith walked down a long marble hallway into a waiting elevator, she allowed herself to fantasize that they were returning to their home. Keith pressed 15. The walnut-paneled car lifted off like a rocket, silently shooting them into the sky. Seconds later, the doors slid open. Keith gently pressed the small of India's back. They stepped off the elevator and made their way in silence down a corridor with chocolate-brown carpeting so thick India longed to lie down on it. Keith slid a key in the door and guided it open. To India's shock, he scooped her up in his arms and carried her over the threshold. India was grateful he hadn't carried her long enough to compare her leaden weight to Serena's feather weight. He set India down before an enormous picture window. The buildings of Fifth Avenue twinkled in the distance. Central Park lay at their feet, a dark expanse dotted with streetlamps that glowed like tiny diamonds scattered on black velvet.

"Could you be comfortable here?" Keith asked, knowing only an ascetic monk or a masochist could answer no. India didn't dare reply for fear of seeming too eager or, worse, desperate. For once in her life, the situation had robbed her of the power of intelligent speech. Sensing India's hesitation and mistrust, Keith took her by the hand. "Let me show you around," he offered.

With a flick of the sleekest silver remote, he turned the lights on to their mellowest, most seductive level. India's eyes scanned the expansive living room. Furnished in the finest custom-made contemporary pieces by Knoll and Roche-Bobois, it had the expensive but impersonal feel of a designer-decorated corporate apartment. This was the room of a man who had every intention of becoming king. The tabletops were bare. There was not a photograph of Serena anywhere. This oversight both reassured and unsettled India. A man who was madly in love would have had a large framed photograph of his fiancée prominently displayed. This was the living room of a man who sought to keep his options open and his private life private. But would he ever have a photograph of any woman?

On the large wall above the daybed hung a map of the world on parchment. Dots marked a route from Portugal to the West Coast of Africa to the New World. India crossed to inspect it at closer range, as well as to make certain that the small silver frame on the inlaid side table did not contain a photograph of Serena. As she approached, a quick glance revealed it was a photograph of the redoubtable Livia, Keith's mother. Was she ultimately the woman of his life? India refused to dwell on this slight evidence of emotional dysfunction. She turned her attention to the map, studying it in earnest.

"It's a slaver's map from the 1600s," Keith's voice came behind her. "I bought it when I became CFO to remind me of where I came from and where I plan to go." India turned to face him. His sense of manifest destiny always left her weak at the knees. She could well imagine sacrificing her own ambitions at the altar of his future greatness. But she refrained from capitulating just yet.

"I need to use your loo," she said. He pointed her toward the master bedroom.

"In there," he said simply. "Light's to the right of the door."

India gingerly entered the master suite, which was reached by a little corridor. Again, no photograph of Serena presented itself as evidence of his feelings. She flicked on the bathroom light. Keith's bathroom was the size of most New Yorkers' living rooms. It was done in black and green marble with gold fixtures. India shut the door and looked around. Unable to resist, she opened the medicine cabinets above the double sinks. There she found the telltale evidence of Serena's presence in Keith's life. Stored upon its milk glass shelves were hair products, Lancôme face creams, and various declensions of the youthful fragrance Trésor. India shut the cabinet, flushed the toilet, and ran the water in the sink in case Keith was listening. She reentered the bedroom and crossed toward the closet. Again, it was the size of an entire room, rather than the usual alcove. As she had suspected she would, amid the double rows of bespoke suits and Hermès ties, she found a section housing Serena's H&M pants, and a rainbow display of cashmere sweaters in all the saccharine colors of the Care Bears. These were not a few items left over from the occasional weekend; this was the full-fledged wardrobe of a girlfriend who practically lived there.

India heard footsteps. She turned and saw Keith standing behind her. He looked at her, then at the incriminating clothing, and knew at once the visit had backfired. She stared him down, and he looked away, running a well-formed hand through his shining hair. A flood of expletives sat ready to pour forth from India's mouth. To let them out would only be ridiculous. She knew he was still engaged when she walked into the apartment. She had no claim on him. She rushed past him. He ran after her and barred the door. She tried to push past him and grabbed the doorknob, but he was blocking her path. He grabbed her by the shoulders and shook her.

"Listen! Listen to me!" he yelled. She tried to wrest her shoulders from his ironclad grasp.

"What? You're hoping that Serena will come home and we'll have a three-way?" India joked.

"Goddamn you, India Chumley! For once in your life shut up and listen!" Keith yelled, releasing his grip. He looked her dead in the eye. "Give me some time, a few weeks, a month at the most, and I'll get out of this. And then you and I will be free to see what we are. What we might be. Please. I'm asking you to be patient." India knew he wasn't bluffing. While she felt like an intruder in this apartment, his words had quelled her desire to run out. She looked at him, praying he would give her further reason to trust him. "India," he whispered, "I've never felt like this about anyone else. Ever. God, I love you." As India heard these words, an emotion rose up in her she hadn't felt since she and Keith first met: faith in passionate love. "I don't want to lose you again," he continued, "but Serena deserves—"

"Take the time you need," India said, meaning every word. She knew from personal experience how devastating it was to smash a pure heart. Part of her shuddered when thinking of the moment in which he broke it to Serena. She could see Serena's huge eyes welling up with tears, feel her shortness of breath at the realization she'd been living a lie. Indeed, India would be patient. How could she not be magnanimous when her greatest hope was about to be realized?

## chapter forty-two

The chipped mahogany chair rail molding of Family Court room B-42 was of a piece with the paint curling off the walls. India and Mr. Winston occupied the battered rectangular table to the right of the bench. Its shellac, like the paint, had seen better days. India noted that Paula Winston was not in her usual fresh-from-the-window-of-Barneys green attire. Instead, she wore a conservative skirt suit that looked like she had bought it at Escada, boutique of choice for proper corporate wives. *Feldman has costumed her,* India surmised, *for this command performance as the devoted mother.* New-age clothing would not have played well with this conservative judge. José calmly read the *Post* while his client paced.

"I can't believe they won't let us bring cell phones in here. How are we supposed to get any work done?" Paula complained loudly to Feldman. He whispered something in her ear. Paula sat and pulled a brag book out of her purse and began leafing through the images of her children. *They don't call Feldman "Mr. Razzle Dazzle 'Em" for nothing,* India observed. She said a prayer invoking judicial brilliance. It would take her best skills to win this one. Mr. Winston sat fidgeting like a nervous schoolboy while pretending to read his latest book, *Hegel and Me.*

"This judge is always late," India reassured him. "He's known for it. It doesn't mean anything." India looked at the clock. Judge Leonard Trafalgar was keeping them waiting longer than usual. India could hazard a guess as to where he was: on the links. He was known as Tee-time Trafalgar because of his predilection for golf and his tendency to wear his knickers under his robes. Woe to the plaintiffs who made him miss a round.

After an interminable wait, a wizened sixty-five-year-old sporting Coke bottle glasses ambled slowly to his bench.

"All rise," the bailiff cried. The assembled dutifully obeyed. Paula was the first to leap from her seat and flash the judge an enormous saccharine smile. The judge took his seat. He removed his glasses and rubbed them clean with his robe. He wore an expression that said, "Frankly, I'd rather be on the eighteenth hole at Winged Foot." He opened the folder before him and gave it a cursory glance, then rapped his gavel on the table.

"Case now in session. Ms. Chumley," he called out with world-weariness. "Do you have all the documents I requested at discovery?"

"Yes, Your Honor," India answered with such gusto it caused the judge to stare at her.

"Humph," he uttered. "Mr. Feldman, have you gathered all the documents I requested?"

"Yes, Your Honor," José answered, running a hand along the lapel of his hand-stitched suit.

"Counsel, approach the bench. What are the issues before us?"

"My client, Mr. Winston, is petitioning the court for full custody, Your Honor," India ventured.

"That's highly irregular," the judge answered, peering over his thick glasses the better to scrutinize Mr. Winston. José cast a "don't you worry about a thing" glance at his client. His smugness only fueled India's determination. "I must tell you, Ms. Chumley, in thirty years on the bench I have never once granted custody to the father. Frankly, I can't see why any man worthy of the name would want the bother of taking his wife's place. Countless studies and centuries of human history suggest the woman is the better primary parent," Judge Trafalgar grumbled.

"No doubt, Your Honor, all that you say is absolutely true," India assented, buttering him up. "But there is always the exception that confirms the rule. Mr. Winston is that exception. I submit Exhibit A, the record of Ms. Winston's travels in the past eighteen months." José Feldman turned beet red, struggling to contain his fury.

"Objection, those records were obtained for the purpose of establishing lifestyle and expenses, not to call into questions my client's lawful right to raise her own children."

Feldman had stalled as long as he could in giving the travel records to India. She'd ultimately sweet-talked his paralegal, invoking her legal right to them to establish Mrs. Winston's net worth.

"Your Honor, these travel expenses are directly related to our case because they present the record of Ms. Winston's frequent absences from the home and from her children. We have chosen not to subpoena witnesses who are in Ms. Winston's employ and would therefore be compromised by having to testify against her."

"I'll allow it," Judge Trafalgar barked, pulling a rumpled handkerchief from his pocket and blowing his nose with a honk. India handed him the monumental stack. The judge leafed through the papers.

"As per these records, Ms. Winston was absent on average for two weeks of every month of the year except for December," India explained. Paula squirmed. The judge frowned, clearly disapproving.

"Were your children with you on these sojourns, Mrs. Winston?" he asked, peering over his glasses at Paula and taking her in for the first time.

"No, I was working. And I didn't want to take them out of school. Education is paramount in my house," Paula said in a studiously softened voice she'd clearly rehearsed for hours.

"Your Honor, the youngest just turned three and didn't attend school last year. Even if he had been in preschool, missing a week or two would not have affected his future. No toddler's life has been ruined because they missed Introduction to Pasta Collages," India countered. The judge chuckled, amused. José refrained from objecting because it would only cast him in the role of the killjoy. India forced herself not to smile back at the judge. She was leading him to the tipping point and didn't want to appear too certain of victory.

"Ms. Winston, remind me, what is it you do?" Judge Trafalgar said, staring down at her.

"I own a company that makes organic stationery," Paula answered in her studied "soft" voice.

"All stationery is organic. It's made from trees, for Lord's sake, you can't get more organic than that," the judge snapped, thoroughly irritated at having to live in this brave new world of inattentive mothers, fathers who want to raise their children rather than golf, and organic everything.

"Most paper is made with bleach, from bleached wood. Mine is made from elephant dung, a renewable resource. We are saving the world's forests and an endangered species." Paula said in her saccharine earth-mother tone. "My company is called Zakan, which is Sanskrit for 'dung.'"

"Sounds revolting. How do you get rid of the stench?" Judge Trafalgar barked. Paula opened her mouth to respond, but the judge cut her off. "Never mind! Who stays with your children when you're off making greeting cards out of fertilizer? A grandmother, their aunt?" he pursued. Paula hesitated, sensing the judge would not like the answer.

"Their nanny," she responded at last.

"You leave your children for weeks at a time in the care of a paid employee? I hope she's legal."

"She is, Your Honor, and has the highest qualifications, a master's in education from—" José interceded.

"Hogwash!" barked the judge, cutting him off. "A nanny is not a mother! Children need a parent, not a paid custodian with a PhD. What is this mania? We pay people to water our lawns, walk our dogs, carry our children in their wombs. And then we wonder why the delinquency rates are through the roof. I'd take up arms against my fellows too if my mother was off combing the jungles of the world for exotic dung!"

India quietly rejoiced. This was better than she expected. Paula seethed.

"Your Honor, if I may—" José ventured.

"You may not!" Judge Trafalgar snapped. "This is my courtroom. And since Mrs. Winston is too busy rescuing the trees of the world to mind her own brood of . . . three, is it? I'm inclined to take a good long look at Mr. Winston."

Paula struggled to retain her composure. She tapped her pen on the table and glared at the judge, clearly ready to leap up and throttle him. José placed a calming hand on her arm, forcing her to cease tapping. Her foot went into overdrive under the table.

"Your Honor, we can prove that Mrs. Winston was forced to go to work against her will because of Mr. Winston's unwillingness to earn a decent living," José offered smoothly.

"What?" India blurted, outraged. Then, catching herself, "I apologize, Your Honor."

"It is our belief, and the facts will show, that Mr. Winston seeks custody in a cynical bid to take a larger portion of his wife's hard-earned fortune," José Feldman declared.

"My client is prepared to forfeit his claim to any portion of Ms. Winston's fortune," India retorted. Paula looked up, stunned. Robert Winston nodded to let her know it was no bluff.

"I'm not sure he should!" the judge exclaimed. "I think you may be right, Ms. Chumley. Mr. Winston may well be the exception that confirms the rule. Let's hear more about him."

Mr. Winston looked at India with true elation. India nodded to assure him that the case was going as well as he thought. With all the injustice in the world, somewhere, sometime there was a pony. Most important, Mr. Winston would have the opportunity to raise the children he loved.

## chapter forty-three

India nestled in the backseat of the taxi speeding down Ninth Avenue to Nathaniel's long-awaited opening at the Azarian Gallery. Not wanting to support Nathaniel in any of his endeavors, she'd originally declined the invitation. She'd relented when Abby, who feared that his girlfriend would make an appearance, had begged her to come. It pained her to think that a friend so worthy of every happiness and respect should find herself in such a twisted marriage. To take her mind off of Abby's domestic misery, she indulged in a favorite pastime from her twenties: listening to the same schmaltzy song over and over in celebration of her love of Keith. In this case the hymn to passion playing on her iPhone was Janet Jackson's breathy nineties hit "Again." As Janet's dulcet tones filled India's ears, the sights of this particular stretch of Ninth Avenue filled her with the magic of New York at night. Even the tenements of Hell's Kitchen struck her as charming. The little dive restaurants looked fun and inviting, the perfect spots for cozy tête-à-têtes with Keith after long days at the office. They drove past Jezebel's, the hangout of black fashionistas since the eighties. Once again, she and Keith would sit under the ferns hanging from macramé plant holders and feed each other spoonfuls of peach cobbler dripping with syrup and thick whipped cream. Now they brought to their love the passion of their youth and the deep appreciation of those who had been broken and suffered loss. She remembered Julien with a pang, not of longing but of guilt. The truth was, her heart, body, and mind, were so full of Keith she didn't miss gentle Julien at all. She was relieved he hadn't tried to reach her.

The taxi pulled up in front of the converted glass-and-steel building that housed Azarian's Chelsea outpost. No self-respecting art dealer could afford to merely be uptown or downtown anymore. Chelsea was the new SoHo, and would no doubt be replaced once too many retail chains opened in the area by some formerly contemptible neighborhood in Brooklyn. The beau monde and the hedge funders in Manhattan would then rush to that destination across the bridge in their chauffeur-driven SUVs, the limousines of the twenty-first century. As she contemplated the sterile glass structure, India was relieved that she no longer had to live in a "hip" neighborhood. She could be a visitor to downtown postmodernism, not a permanent resident. Keith shared her predilection for unabashed luxury. No minimalist Le Corbusier, Bauhaus, or Meier for them. In their home, crown moldings would not be outlawed, but required.

India checked her watch. It was only 6:15 and already the room was crowded with a Whitman's sampler of New York art scene characters. Right by one of the sculptures, five elongated wrought-iron stick figures holding hands in a semicircle, stood two androgynous women, pads of paper in hand. India surmised they were critics, probably from a small downtown publication. One of them drained her glass of wine and eagerly seized another from a passing waiter's tray. Penniless intellectuals could not afford to pass up free food and liquor. A tall British woman in a fresh-from-the-runway Alexander McQueen skirt suit led a slightly plump couple in their early forties through the crowd. The husband murmured incessantly into the mouthpiece of his cell phone, which he held in his right hand like a prayer book.

"This is it. Nathaniel Adams has arrived. Buying him now is like buying Damien Hirst in 1989. Bloody brilliant," the expensively dressed British art consultant cooed.

"This could be nice in the nursery," the husband said of the sculpture of five figures, which India noted was titled *Family One*.

"But how do we babyproof it?" his wife asked.

"There's a solution to every problem," her art cicerone in the pencil skirt reassured her. The woman's consulting fee mounted before India's eyes. She had the perfect victims: young, newly rich, and desperate to purchase prestige at any price. India continued to scan the crowd and finally spotted Abby, looking drawn and forcing a smile while she talked to an older woman with enormous round glasses that made her look like an owl. Rachel held her mother's right hand and listened to the conversation above her head, while Noah clung to Abby's left thigh as though it were a floating log in a rushing river. A few feet away, Benjamin hunched over a Game Boy, oblivious to everything around him.

"How are my favorite niece and nephews?" India asked as she reached the group.

"Aunt India!" Rachel exclaimed gleefully as she ran to embrace India.

"How are you holding up?" India asked Abby with genuine concern.

"Greaaat!" Abby responded in a tone of such false bravado that Noah looked up at her with furrowed brow.

"Mommy, why are you sad?" he asked.

"Mommy's not sad. Mommy's peachy keen. Why don't you and Rachel go talk to Nana? She's over by the giant ladder that's supposed to represent Mommy."

"Why did Daddy turn you into a ladder?" Rachel asked.

"Because that's what happens in life . . . and in abstract art," Abby answered in a tone of resignation as she pondered her demotion from naked goddess cast in bronze to functional tool. Would Nathaniel's mistress suffer the same fate eventually?

"But it doesn't make any sense," Rachel insisted.

"Actually, it's completely accurate. Go on, go surprise Nana."

"I want to stay with you," Noah protested.

"Mommy's right here. Go on," Abby reassured her youngest. Though she had shared nothing with any of them, Noah's protective instincts had flared. Rachel detached Noah from their mother's leg like she was removing a piece of Velcro.

"Come on," she said as she led him across the room.

"So?" India asked once the coast was clear.

"So, my husband admits to nothing, won't talk, has buried himself in getting ready for this. And I'm contemplating addiction to prescription drugs. Got any Vicodin on you?" Abby reeled off.

"Did you tell him about Sage?"

"No. Why would I? It's over. And anyway, he hasn't given me enough time to say more than 'Have a nice day,'" Abby commented wistfully as she looked over at Nathaniel. He stood on the other side of the room, explaining his Abby ladder sculpture to a group of middle-aged women. India noted that they listened with rapt attention, hanging on his every word, following his every gesture with their eyes. It was like watching Von Rothbart, the seductive sorcerer from *Swan Lake,* beguile a ballroom full of noblewomen. These art patrons stared at Nathaniel with stupefied expressions that said "You can turn me into a ladder anytime." Viscerally, India had always understood why Abby fell for him, though logically she thought it was as catastrophic a choice as the Princess's to follow Von Rothbart into his cave. At the end of the day, the most intelligent women completely lacked common sense. *And therein lie the seeds of their destruction,* India mused.

"What the hell is this shit?" Esme's voice boomed as she made her way toward them.

"Sshh," Abby scolded. "There could be critics or buyers around."

"And they'll see with their own eyes this isn't art. It's bars for your ground floor window, to keep out the robbers," Esme declared with contempt.

"Esme, you've got a lot of nerve showing up here to rip everything apart. If you hate it so much, go home, or go screw one of your boy toys. Who died and made you Holland Cotter?" Abby snapped, then stormed off.

"What's wrong with her? I came to support her," Esme asked, genuinely baffled.

"She's still enough in love with her husband to resent your insulting his life's work."

"Life's work? He needs a new life. Look at that ladder. What the hell is that? My God, Julio could build that with his Tinkertoys. Then he has the nerve to call it *Abby*. She shouldn't defend him. She should shove that thing up his flat ass." India struggled to keep a straight face. She shared Esme's low opinion of Nathaniel and his art. "Come on, Miss Goody Two-shoes," Esme coaxed. "You hate Nathaniel as much as I do. She never should have married him in the first place."

India didn't dare answer because, in fact, she agreed completely with the assessment, she'd just never said it out loud. But she had thought it every day of Abby's nineteen years with the lying egomaniac.

"So, what about you? Any word from Julien?" Esme inquired.

"No, but something else is happening." India's cheeks flushed.

"Ah, that expression. It can only be the mulatto," Esme deduced.

"Keith is not mulatto."

"Mulatto, white, purple! He's just another Nathaniel." Esme shrugged. India was floored by this assessment. In her mind, two people could not have been more dissimilar: the degenerate scion of a once noble, now decrepit WASP clan and the robust heir to generations of black strivers. They had nothing in common but their sex.

"What are you talking about?" she challenged.

"He's completely selfish. He doesn't know how to love a woman. That's why you didn't marry him the first time," Esme elaborated. "Don't let your biological time bomb push you to marry him now."

"It's biological *clock*," India corrected, disturbed by Esme's character analysis. Part of her wanted to delve further, but the "sensible" part of her dismissed her friend's opinion. It would be madness to take relationship advice from the female version of Casanova. *Besides, Esme was blinded by resentment of her father,* India thought. Her insights had to be taken with a boulder of salt.

"Ah, I knew there was a reason to come out tonight," Esme said looking toward the door with relish. India turned and saw Michael Alders making a beeline for Esme, while feigning nonchalance. He nodded vaguely to people, bestowing a "hello" here, a "nice to see you" there, clearly remembering no one's name.

"I thought he was trouble," India reminded Esme.

"Tonight, I'm in the mood to play with fire." Esme gleefully watched Michael make his way to her.

"Ms. Sarmiento, apparently this trip downtown is not a complete waste of my time after all." Michael flashed his pearly whites and planted himself right in front of her.

"I was thinking the same thing. You didn't bring your accessory tonight?" Esme taunted.

"Which one?" Michael answered, chuckling.

"You probably have so many, you can't remember them all," Esme challenged.

"No. I discard those that bore me," Michael commented as he surveyed the crowd. It seemed to India he purposely avoided looking at Esme, the better to reel her in.

"Heartless," Esme teased, unconsciously dipping her head to the left and nibbling her upper lip.

"I couldn't entice you to come work for me instead of Midas, but I hope you won't decline an invitation to dinner. Don't break my heart twice, Esme. Even though you're under the mistaken impression I don't have one." Michael turned the full force of his gaze on Esme. She looked up at him and then took a step back.

"When?" she asked, titillated.

"Now . . . unless you feel compelled to look at more of the . . . 'art.'"

"I've seen all I need to see," she answered, never taking her eyes off of him,

"Let's go."

She started to lead the way, but he stopped her, took her by the hand, and pulled her along. Esme threw a backward glance at India and gave a delighted thumbs-up. They disappeared into the enveloping throng. India was relieved that with Keith, there would be no temptation to dally. He had her body and soul. *And no,* she told herself, *he's nothing like Nathaniel.*

"India, what are you doing here?" India turned and was stunned to see Serena, bright-eyed and beaming. Her warmth merely heightened India's feelings of sympathy and guilt. Serena's 5-carat ring still sparkled on her slender ring finger. It no longer inspired resentment in India. It served as a painful reminder of the impending smashing of Serena's youthful hopes. "All that glitters," she wanted to warn the poor unsuspecting creature.

"What are you doing here?" Serena repeated innocently.

"Nathaniel's wife and I are best friends. We've known each other since kindergarten," India explained.

"So amazing. He's going far. My boss thinks he could be the next Henry Moore."

"What do you think?" India asked, hoping this awkward encounter would soon come to a close. She found it difficult to look Serena in the eye since she had been having regular assignations with her fiancé in her Seventy-fifth Street love nest.

"I don't know if a postmodern audience wants a Henry Moore. And my question is: is this work derivative of or intertextual with some of the great modern masters? It's a fine line. I'd like to watch him develop," Serena responded.

*So she isn't just a toady,* India thought. *She's not afraid to differ from an authority figure. Yes, she will find a lovely husband somewhere. Perhaps in this thicket of art-collecting superstars. She could give them class and they could give her cash. She could finally get out of the H&M trousers.*

"By the way, you are coming next week, aren't you?" Serena asked.

"To what?"

"Keith's and my engagement party. I haven't seen your name on the RSVP list."

The news hit India like a knife in the gut. She had to catch her breath. Perhaps this was a clever, vicious, mind game on Serena's part. But looking into Serena's large innocent eyes, India knew it wasn't. "Tinker Bell," unlike the vicious winged sprite after whom India nicknamed her, was guileless. India's mind reeled as she thought of the nights she'd spent with Keith, listening to him declare undying love.

"I've been so busy. I haven't looked at my mail," India vamped. "Will you excuse me? I have to take this call," she said in the wake of total silence from her cell phone. She pushed her way through the crowd. She didn't even notice Abby, who tried to flag her down as she rushed past in a blind fury.

Out on the street, night had fallen. India dialed Keith's office number and hung up when she got voicemail. She pressed his cell phone number. Again, voicemail answered.

"To leave a message . . . " India scrolled through the numbers on her electronic address book. She found it, *Iglesias, Rosario,* Keith's trusty assistant. She pressed the number.

"Hello," Rosario answered after five rings.

"Rosario, I'm sorry to bother you after hours. It's India," she said urgently.

"No problem, Miss Chumley. What can I do for you?" Rosario inquired cheerfully. India wondered how Keith had trained her to juggle both her and Serena. And who else was on the trip to Paris and souvenir Kelly bag list? She wanted to kill him, and she wanted him to tell her it was all a mistake. She wanted him to say he'd tried to tell Serena and she just wouldn't let him go. She knew in her gut that was not the case.

"I'm trying to find Mr. Wentworth. He's not answering his cell," India explained to Rosario as she tried to subdue the slight tremolo that had crept into her voice.

"He's in a board meeting tonight."

"Well, it's very important. Is there any way you can patch me through?" India asked, doing her best to sound even-keeled as her stomach churned. There was silence at the other end of the phone. "Rosario?" India pursued.

"Well, I'm sorry, Miss, but he said not to interrupt him," Rosario answered woodenly.

"This is an emergency. Please, Rosario, I have to speak to him," India pleaded. India wasn't certain whether it was the crack in her voice or her palpable desperation, but Rosario relented. She was probably not the first to place such a call. And she certainly wouldn't be the last.

"All right. Hold on," Rosario said. India took long, deep yoga breaths in an attempt to recover some measure of sanity. After what seemed like an hour, Keith's voice came loud and strong through her earphones.

"I'm in a meeting. What is it?" he asked testily.

"How could you be having an engagement party in a week?" India attacked. Keith fell silent. "Answer me!" India screamed through the phone.

"I can't talk about this now. I'm in a meeting. I'll call you back later," he answered flatly, and hung up. India pressed the number furiously over and over again. Each time, Keith's voicemail answered. She cut it off, pressed the number again. As she was engaged in this manic and futile exercise, the doors of the gallery flew open. A beautiful, leggy blonde ran out, followed by Abby in hot pursuit, wielding the iron ladder.

"Who am I? I'm his wife, you fucking bitch. His wife!" she screamed as the girl practically hurled herself in front of a yellow cab to stop it and scrambled inside. India stopped her manic speed dialing to watch. Seeing her best friend chasing a woman down the street using a sculpture as a deadly weapon had the effect of a bucket of cold water splashed on her face. She and Abby had become everything she pitied: insane, screaming banshees desperately seeking the attention of unworthy men.

Nathaniel arrived on the street and wrested the ladder from Abby.

"What are you doing? Are you trying to ruin the most important night of my life?" he yelled.

"Oh, is this the most important night of your life?" Abby hissed. "I thought it was the night we got married or perhaps the night Benjamin was born, or maybe now it's the first night you fucked your teenage, blueblood mistress. Is she as stiff in bed as she looks?"

"You don't even know what you're talking about. And you're the one who's been fucking someone else!" Nathaniel accused.

"Yes, I did, and I loved every minute!" Abby yelled. Nathaniel stepped back, stunned. India realized he was bluffing. He hadn't really thought Abby had had more than a flirtation. He faltered, as if stricken. Abby looked at him with compassion. India marveled at the fact Abby could show any kindness to the man who'd humiliated and hurt her for years. "I've told you the truth," Abby said, no longer shouting. "Please admit to me what's going on."

"I don't have to explain anything to you," Nathaniel spat.

"Then there really isn't anything left to talk about. Go sleep at your studio. I'll send over your things in the morning." And with that, Abby pulled herself up to her full height and began to walk away from her first love. He stood in the middle of the sidewalk, looking lost and terrified. He started after her.

"Abby, don't go," he said desperately. She ignored him and kept walking. He caught up to her and grabbed her by the elbow. "Please, don't do this to us," he begged.

"Leave me alone!" Abby yelled in a voice that came from the bowels of her fury. Nathaniel recoiled. "It's over!" she added. He remained stoop-shouldered before her, like the beaten child he'd once been, bracing for the next blow. Within mere moments, however, his blue eyes turned to ice and he called after her.

"Colby wasn't the first! There were lots of others!" Nathaniel hurled the words at Abby like a grenade. Abby paused for a moment, but then chose not to look back. She knew his method of last resort: wound others more than they can wound you. At least that way, they would remember you. Even in hate. Nathaniel watched her walk away for a moment, then turned to head back into the gallery. India emerged from the doorway in which she had taken refuge and ran to catch up with Abby.

"It's over," Abby said with a strange calm.

"I saw the whole thing," India admitted.

"I'm glad you did," Abby said, grabbing India's hand. "You were there for the beginning. You might as well bear witness to the end. And someday, when my children ask you, please tell them I did try."

"I will," India promised.

"I'd better go get them," Abby said, turning back toward the gallery. "It's time to go home." As India watched Abby reenter the frigid structure, she wondered how a woman faced the future with confidence after devoting nineteen years, half her life, to the wrong man.

# chapter forty-four

Twenty-eight dizzying floors above Fifth Avenue and Fifty-ninth Street, Esme sat in Michael's oval dining room draining the last sips of Château Margaux from a Saint Louis crystal goblet so massive it could have doubled as a paperweight. Michael admired her from across the English Regency table magnificently set with Limoges china and silk damask napkins custom made in Florence. His dwelling was a festival of opulence, a shameless display of the riches he'd amassed over the course of more than three decades. Esme felt at home as soon as she entered the triplex palace in the sky. It was not unlike the homes she grew up in, and the homes of all her parents' friends, and their friends' friends. Her family made it a rule never to associate with anyone of inferior net worth. While she'd rebelled against their social strictures by marrying "beneath her" into the upper middle class, she did miss the freedom of environments in which excess was the norm, indeed an expectation. It was heaven to sit in such a setting with a man who, unlike most billionaires, looked like a matinee idol instead of like Yoda. This evening was the ultimate deliverance from Esme's stiflingly bourgeois Connecticut existence. While strong, steadfast, decent Tim had offered a welcome change from all the cads she'd known growing up, ten years of marital stability had made her long for uncertainty and adventure. Though she'd tried to reject the material and emotional excess in which she'd been raised, the craving for it was in her blood.

"A woman with a good appetite for food and drink. I like that," Michael commented appreciatively as he signaled to the houseman to refill Esme's wineglass. The houseman silently obeyed, pouring the deep ruby liquid from a faceted crystal decanter with a gleaming silver top.

"Bordeaux like this, it's a crime to leave in the glass," Esme explained when really she'd downed three glasses through the main course of veal escalope just to steady her nerves. She was stunned at her own state of disarray. Whether with her husband or a boy toy, she was always in command. Yet the unwavering, hazel-eyed gaze of this distinguished Adonis was turning her into proverbial mush, putty for his beautifully formed hands to mold. And she relished feeling off-balance, for once. She could tell that he was a phenomenal lover from the way he cupped a water goblet, from the slow, deliberate up and down movement of his jaw when he chewed. Then there was the sensual way he let each morsel of meat linger on his tongue and savored its full flavor before swallowing it. Some men knew how to coax unheard sounds from the keys of a piano; others could take a plank of wood and turn it into a sailing vessel. This man was clearly born to turn every woman in his path into an instrument of pleasure. This was not Esme's malleable little neighborhood masseur, the cater waiter, or the wet-behind-the-ears MBA with mother's milk on his breath. This was a seducer, a Napoleon conquering hearts across a wide swath of territory. The great capitals of the world were littered with the spent bodies of his victims. All the elegant divorcées on five continents had tried to win him. Four women had wed him and been left wealthy but bereft. Now, he was hers to conquer. The only question remaining in her mind was whether to bed him tonight or delay their gratification a bit more so that she could have him completely in her thrall. For all his vaunted power, he was like any other man. If you made him wait long enough, eventually he was yours.

"Have you skied Klosters?" he asked.

"Not since I was sixteen. With my parents," she answered.

"Best heli-skiing in Europe. Five thousand meters up, snow so pure and unbroken. To be the first one to set foot on it. That's pleasure. Of course, there's always the risk of an avalanche. But you don't strike me as a girl who lives in fear of anything."

*No, not even master seducers like you,* Esme thought, taking another sip from the Margaux and another bite of succulent veal.

"Come," Michael commanded, rising from his Empire chair with swans' necks for arms. He walked to her side of the table and pulled out her seat. She rose, as if drawn by a magnet or by Dr. Mesmer himself. It was a pleasure to be led, instead of forever leading the seduction dance.

"Where are we going?" Esme asked, entranced.

"I want to show you something while dessert is prepared. Soufflé takes a moment in any case." He proffered a strong forearm, sheathed in a cashmere and wool sports coat that suggested the perfect lines of his athletic build without vulgarly giving them away. Standing inches away from him, she inhaled the sandalwood of his cologne that mingled with the scent of his skin and evoked nights of toe-curling pleasure. Savoring the scent, she envisioned the wonders that lay beneath the bespoke gates of heaven. She imagined him sprawled across the expanse of his Léron linen–clad bed, and her own body draped over his, in postcoital languor, her head buried in the delicious crevice between his pectorals.

"Follow me," Michael entreated as he led her down a corridor with walls lined in coral stone. This was the first disconcerting touch in his otherwise perfect home. She had only seen such stone paneling in homes in the tropics, where their oppressiveness was offset by sun, sea, and sand. In a New York apartment, the stone blocks suggested nothing so much as a tomb. "Are you frightened, my dear? You're quaking," Michael asked.

"Afraid? Me? Don't be ridiculous!" Esme scoffed, feeling suddenly vulnerable that he could read her so easily. They emerged from the darkness of the corridor into an enormous drawing room. Each wall boasted a still life illuminated from above, as in a museum.

"The French and the Italian have their glories, but for my money, you can't beat the Dutch. I started with portraits, but one doesn't want to live surrounded by dozens of staring eyes, so I sold the lot of them. I keep my Frans Hals in the country. Here I've settled on the Ruisdaels and the Van Goyens. Soothing, aren't they?" Michael asked in his basso profundo voice.

*To a sadist, maybe,* Esme thought to herself as she stood before a lifelike rendering of a recently shot hare dripping blood on a wooden table below it, right next to a hunter's flask. Like the coral stone, the picture unsettled her.

"That's the prize of the collection," Michael stated, standing directly behind her. She felt his breath on the back of her neck as he inhaled and exhaled. Once more, she reveled in the scent of his cologne wafting hypnotically toward her. One more moment and she might have leaned back into his chest and let him wrap his arms around her. It was all the more tempting because not once all night had he laid a finger on her.

*He knows how to make his prey come to him,* Esme thought. Looking at the dead hare reminded her of all the women he'd devastated. *I will be different,* she reassured herself. He had finally met his match.

She turned to face him, tossing her hair back. She looked him directly in the eye. He stared back. Each waited for the other to blink first. Neither wavered. Finally, in a tactical move, Esme decided to look away.

"What's over here?" she asked as she walked along the wall. She felt Michael's hand grab hers and whip her around. He pulled her into his arms, then held still for a few thrilling moments. Slowly he lowered his mouth onto hers and Esme's body melted into his. Finally, a man who understood that a kiss was like a play in four acts, a microcosm of the sexual act itself. Michael's kiss began with foreplay as he let their breaths commingle. Then he introduced just the tip of his tongue, and it played at the perimeter of her mouth before penetrating completely. Slowly their mouths joined and parted until after several luscious minutes, he withdrew. Just as his tongue receded to the opening of her mouth, he gave her lips a small but sharp bite. The gesture startled her. She touched her lip to make certain it wasn't bleeding.

Disregarding her slight displeasure, he led her toward a coffered door. He opened it to reveal a dark paneled elevator. He motioned to her to step in. She followed, and they descended two flights at an even pace. Exiting the elevator, they walked down another long corridor, lined in the stifling coral stone. Esme hovered between delight and trepidation. She was still in her "tonight or not tonight" quandary but realized Michael was leading her to the point of no G-string and no return. He opened a heavy walnut door and indicated to her she should pass through it.

"Make yourself comfortable, I shall be down directly," he explained as he shut the door behind him.

Esme found herself alone in a room with walls covered in tapestries, and she soon noted, not a single window. Surely this wasn't the master bedroom. No one with such an apartment would have forgone the view of Fifth Avenue and the park below. On the California king–sized bed lay a black chiffon negligee perfectly arranged. Esme picked it up and noticed a price tag still hung from it. She and Michael planned this dinner on the fly. How could he have been "lingerie ready"? Who laid this peignoir out so carefully? The mute footman? The thought so disgusted Esme she tossed the garment back on the bed. On the bedside table sat a beautiful sixteenth-century tortoiseshell chest. She opened it and found condoms in a variety of textures and flavors: ribbed, ringed, passion fruit, and peppermint. It reminded her of her brothers' descriptions of brothels in Amsterdam. She noticed a wall of closets and threw their doors open. There she found three racks of peignoirs and teddies in varying styles from the elegant to the downright hookeresque. She even found a full array of leather and latex ensembles with their matching whips and chains.

She stepped back, horrified. This wasn't the room of a lover of women; it was a stop on a love machine's assembly line. And she was lover number 1,392. God knew who preceded her here, very likely women who advertised their "massage" services in the back pages of *New York* magazine and on websites for the hot and the horny. Esme had gone from wanting to take it all off to wanting to get the hell out. She picked up the negligee from the bed and raced out of this chamber of erotic horrors. It took her a moment to find her way back upstairs in the maze of corridors. Finally, she located the staircase and ran to the foyer. She grabbed her mink from the coat closet and threw it over her shoulders. With enormous gusto, she ripped the peignoir in half and tossed it down on the marble floor.

"Is black not your color?" Michael asked. Esme looked up to see him standing at the head of the staircase. She seethed as he casually strolled down the long flight of stairs. His arrogance, so appealing only moments ago, now completely repulsed her. He planted himself directly in front of her.

"What do you think I am?" she spat.

"My dear, we both know what you are. We are merely haggling over the wardrobe," he answered very pleased with his paraphrasing of Shaw. His words instantly obliterated the effect of four glasses of wine. Esme saw the steely coldness in his eyes. Her hand flew through the air and she smacked Michael's left cheek with such force he faltered.

"That's who I am!" she said acidly, then turned to run as fast as she could out the door. She raced down the corridor, stopped in front of the elevator doors, and frantically pressed the button. Unwilling to wait another moment in the vicinity of Michael's lair, she headed for a door marked "Exit." Her feet flew down the stairs, and she leapt onto each landing as if fleeing a fire. In minutes she reached the ground floor, and, much to the doorman's consternation, sped through the elegant lobby and out into the street.

Once she found herself outside, she headed down Fifth Avenue at a clip. She had one goal in mind: to get as far away as she could, as fast as she could. She was furious at Michael for his disdainful treatment, and even more so at herself for overestimating the power of her charms. She had really believed she had reeled him in, just as she had countless men before him. Far from becoming her father, she'd just been treated like one of his mistresses, not even a "functional," but a "disposable," to be had and discarded with the condom. She was no match for someone as coldblooded and ruthless as Michael. For the first time in ten years of marriage, she longed to return to the humdrum safety of her Connecticut home and to the arms of her husband, a man who would never have made her feel cheap. Perhaps it was time she stopped playing with fire. And Tim deserved better than she'd given. Vowing in her head to stop her games, at least for a while, she hailed a taxi. If she hurried, she'd catch the 9:06 train to Greenwich.

## chapter forty-five

India rushed out of the taxi and onto West Sixty-seventh Street. Through the leaded glass windows of the Café des Artistes, over the leaves of potted plants, she spotted the top of her mother's head silhouetted against the murals of nude, early-twentieth-century beauties. India was almost an hour late for their dinner date and very tempted to jump back in the taxi and skip it altogether. Her already flagging spirits didn't need this final tug into the abyss. A sense of filial duty or masochism—in the case of her family they were one and the same—propelled her through the glass double doors. As if sensing her presence, Elizabeth looked up from her wineglass, brightening at the sight of her pride, joy, and lifelong emotional crutch.

"There you are! 'She walks in beauty, like the night / Of cloudless climes and starry skies / And all that's best'!" her mother declaimed across the room as several fellow diners turned to stare. India hastened over lest her mother recite the entire poem as she had on more than one occasion at this restaurant. She took the seat facing Elizabeth and braced herself for a "guilting" over her tardy arrival.

"I'm sorry, Mum. I got stuck at the office, then couldn't get a cab. Didn't they give you my messages?"

"Yes, I've had my watercress salad and half my entrée. Do try the lamb. It's divine tonight."

"I'm not hungry."

"Ah, *l'amour*. It does quell the appetite. Never mind diet and exercise, find an object of affection and your thighs melt like icicles in the tropics! How is Julien?"

"He's fine," India fibbed, not daring to look her mother in the eye. She had not told her about the airport debacle. It was difficult enough to face her failure without having to share the news.

"Let's hit these lines, Mother, because I still may have to go back to the office," India insisted brightly, by way of circumventing further discussion of her pathetic love life.

"How inhuman! You're not their indentured servant. You should leave those exploiters!" Elizabeth commanded grandly. India stared at her, nonplussed. Her mother had been prone to spouting socialist platitudes ever since she played Emma Goldman in a biopic for the BBC.

"And go where, Mum?" India asked in a monotone.

"Anywhere! You're brilliant. You can do anything!"

*Except keep a relationship going,* India thought to herself.

"If I leave Hallingby, who will write your divorce summons every year?" India reminded Elizabeth.

"How true," her mother answered thoughtfully. "Well, onward." She dumped the dog-eared script in front of India. "I'm having trouble with the address to the women of Corinth. I keep skipping passages," she said, as she took a swig of her wine, clearly baffled at her sudden loss of memory.

"Do you think maybe the alcohol might be hampering you, Mum?" India suggested, weary of her mother's apparent lack of even a scintilla of self-awareness.

"The alcohol? No! What a ridiculous idea. I've been drinking and working for years! Just as the British Navy would never survive without buggery, where would the British theater be without Scotch? Now, cue me!"

"Am I the nurse?" India inquired flatly.

"Yes, but she doesn't say anything. It's the soliloquy: 'Of all creatures that have breath' et cetera . . . 'we women are the most unfortunate . . .' You've got that right, Euripides."

"'First, at an exorbitant price—'" India read.

Her mother reeled off the rest, projecting through the restaurant, "'At an exorbitant price we must buy a husband and take a master for our bodies,'" she recited, clawing her breasts.

Having heard these words hundreds of times, India allowed her mind to wander back to Julien, standing devastated in the middle of the Air France terminal. She had revisited the scene in her head many times in the last few days, to castigate herself and remind herself that Keith's betrayal was her punishment for cheating. Through this self-mortification, she hoped to atone for the hurt she caused. Her mother continued her recitation.

"'For this is what makes one misfortune even more galling than another, to suffer loss and be insulted to boot. The outcome of our life's striving hangs on this, whether we take a good or bad husband. For divorce—'"

As her mother rambled, India pondered the fact that at thirty-seven, she was still where she was at seven: sitting in this restaurant running lines with Medea, aka Mom. Nearly half of her life had passed and she'd made no progress whatsoever, other than in her career. Was she doomed to spend her remaining years writing her mother's divorce summonses and helping her prepare for the same three tragic roles? The prospect overwhelmed her, and she started to sob quietly. Noticing her tears at last, her mother ceased in midspeech.

"Darling?" she said. India looked up at her. The obvious pain in her mother's face reassured her that, somehow, she'd read her thoughts and understood. Elizabeth took her hand, and India gratefully extended the other. Caressing India's head, Elizabeth asked, "Am I that dreadful? The critics liked me." India instantly withdrew her hand.

"Everything is not about you, Mum!" she protested.

"Did I ever say it was?" Elizabeth asked, all innocence. India looked up at her imploringly. She tried always to exercise patience with her mother, because she knew how much she loved her. Every once in a while though, she longed to be a daughter, instead of the perpetual audience for the one-woman show that was Elizabeth Blakely's life. "My darling, you're in pain," Elizabeth said earnestly.

"I've been in pain for a long time, Mum."

"You need some port and so do I. You there!" Elizabeth bellowed to a passing waiter. "Two glasses of Taylor Fladgate tawny. Ten-year." At this, India sobbed afresh.

"Twenty-year?" her mother asked, baffled. India shook her head.

"Mum, I've made a big mess."

"Don't be so hard on yourself. Tell Mummy what happened. We can run lines later," she said, shutting the script with a flourish. Certain that her mother had finally called an intermission and was prepared to listen, India decided to tell all.

"I went to Paris with Keith and Julien found out," she admitted. Her mother stiffened, arching her back like a cat about to pounce.

"I see," she said grandly.

"I know it was wrong, but I had to go," India insisted.

"Why? So you could find out just how much of a bastard shit that Keith Wentworth is?" Elizabeth asked, bitterness dripping from every word.

"He's not a shit! He loves me. At least he said he did, and I believed him," India admitted.

"He doesn't deserve you! He never did, and all he'll ever do is hurt you. He cheated on you in front of everyone with a cheap trollop!" Elizabeth yelled, furious.

"Once! It was once!" India defended. *And who taught me that such behavior from a man was acceptable?* she wanted to add but refrained. It was too cruel, and her mother refused to face the reality of her own situation. She lived her life like it was a movie script set to music, *Wuthering Heights* on the Upper West Side.

"And he'd do it again. I'll wager he already has! Everything he admires about you he also wants to control, stifle, and destroy. You are magnificent, and magnificence like yours should not be contained!" Elizabeth shrieked.

Her words resonated more than India cared to admit. Keith had said it himself, "What am I going to do with you?" He wanted someone who would bend to his will. But what did she want?

"If he loves you so, why aren't you in his bed tonight instead of sitting here doing *Medea* with me?" Elizabeth added.

Just as India contemplated tossing the content of her port glass in her mother's face, she looked up and spotted Richard, her stepfather, entering the restaurant. To India's horror, he escorted a gaunt young woman with flowing black locks and pale skin. She bore a striking resemblance to the naked Howard Christy wood nymphs in the murals adorning the walls. Like an aging cock of the walk who had snagged a pert little chick, Richard proudly paraded the young woman as she ran a long bony finger down his sagging cheek. She wore the making-do wardrobe of the graduate student in literature: a velveteen jacket with sleeves an inch too short for her arms and a fluid flower print skirt. She fit the mold of Richard's mistresses of choice: the adoring PhD candidate. India's fury at her mother for speaking the truth turned to panic. She had to get Elizabeth out of there before she saw her husband.

"Oh, that's my iPhone," India lied, wiping her tears.

"What is? I didn't hear a thing. And you know I can't bear technology at the table. One might as well masturbate in public!" Elizabeth declared.

India looked down at her iPhone. "Oh, no!" India exclaimed, "Mum, I'm so sorry, but I have to get back to the office. What a pain. Waiter, check please!"

"Check? We are not leaving here until you have come to your senses," Elizabeth objected.

"I have, Mum, I promise. I heard you about Julien. Loud and clear. I'm saved," India answered, all the time watching Richard and his damsel.

"Don't lie to me, young lady," Elizabeth scolded. India breathed a little easier as the maître d', who'd known India's parents for three decades, led Richard and his acolyte to the restaurant's upper level. The maître d' nodded at India and gave her the "all clear" sign, their special signal meaning "I hid them in the corner." India and he had been in this predicament before with a variety of women from old to barely legal, educated to charging by the hour. When the check arrived, India hurriedly scribbled her name on the credit card receipt and rose.

"Come on, Mum. I really need to go." Elizabeth gathered her belongings with deliberate lack of speed.

"I feel as though I'm being rushed off an overcrowded omnibus. Nonetheless, I'm ready, Miss Haste," she announced. She led the way and, as she passed the headwaiter, graciously bowed her head.

"See you soon, Tony," she purred.

"Yes, Miss Blakely," he answered, inclining his torso. He and India nodded to each other, relieved to have averted a head-on collision yet again.

Once out in the street, Elizabeth turned to India. "You must go to Julien and beg his forgiveness," she advised.

"Why would he forgive me?" India asked sadly.

"Because he loves you. And you deserve to be forgiven." India absorbed her mother's words. It was a relief to know someone she loved thought her worthy of pardon.

"But what if he's not the one, and I hurt him again?"

"A man who loves you unconditionally, as you are, is the one. Julien will never wound you. Living with a cheater eats you alive," she added as an afterthought, staring off into the night. That part of India that still wanted to believe that by some miracle she would end up with Keith, and that he would make her happy winced at this truth. Why did passion have to come at so high a price?

As a cab rounded the corner, Elizabeth tossed a double-jointed arm in the air and it screeched to a halt. After she opened the door, she looked back at India, putting a hand on India's arm.

"I saw him, darling. Next time, just let me finish my port." With that she slid into the backseat and slammed the door shut, leaving India dumbfounded.

## chapter forty-six

India fingered the ticket to Paris she held in her right hand. *Yes, this is the right thing to do,* she told herself as the Lincoln Town Car sped along the Brooklyn-Queens Expressway to Kennedy Airport. For once in her life she was going to follow an impulse, and that impulse was to confront Julien face to face, tell him she was sorry for her transgressions, and beg him to give her a second chance. Of course, her work responsibilities allowed only forty-eight hours for such a mission of atonement. As she wheeled the tiniest suitcase she'd ever packed up the ramp toward the terminal, she silenced all the "What ifs" that trespassed upon her sense of hope. What if he wouldn't take her calls? What if he was so hurt he sent her and her stewardess-sized bag packing? Then at least she'd know. And if she did end up alone, raising a dozen cats, it wouldn't have been for lack of effort or taking risks. Besides, Julien had never canceled her ticket. Surely that was a sign he had intended her to follow him at some point.

She strode up to the Espaces Affaires counter, ticket in hand. Once again, she was greeted by the indiscreet man from Martinique, the unintentional agent of all her woes.

"*Vous revoilà.* Alone this time," he commented.

*How impertinent of him,* she thought, but decided to rise above his sniping commentary. After all, she was about to embark on perhaps the most fateful voyage of her life. She was not about to let a ticketing agent rain on her parade.

"Anything to check?"

"No," she announced triumphantly. It was liberating taking to the open road of life with just the Chanel on your back. So what if she ended up without enough to wear? With any luck, where she was going, she wouldn't need clothes. Once ensconced in the business class lounge, she poured herself a large glass of Bordeaux. Bravo to the French, stocking great wines in an airport waiting room. How could one not love them? She checked her emails, deleting three from Keith without even reading them. Her sense of power was boundless. She felt as though the gods of love were smiling upon her quest. Certainly the encouraging glances from the handsome Julien look-alike seated across the lounge served to confirm and justify her confidence. Her phone buzzed, signaling the arrival of an email. She opened it and read:

Miss Thing,

I need your help. Hector wants me to loan him the money to buy a car. I can't do it without Wayne getting suspicious. Can you advance me ten to fifteen in cash? I'll repay you. You know I'm good for it. I just have to help my baby.

Monique.

India shuddered at the thought that Monique, tough-talking, tell-it-like-it-is Monique, had succumbed to lust to this degree. It was pitiful. And yet, to her horror, she realized such weakness lay in all women with libidos. She shot off a text message in response, hoping that the speed would save Monique from making a tragic mistake.

Dawkins. Snap out of it! A man who demands car payments does not love you.

She hesitated at the cruelty of that remark but felt she must be blunt to pierce the fog enveloping Monique's sense of judgment.

Don't give him the money and call this thing off!

She pressed the send button. She waited a few moments, watching her iPhone screen. Sure enough, a response appeared almost immediately.

You're wrong. Hector is so tender and loving. He just needs some help. If you can't give me the money, I have no one else to ask. Please.

This answer only strengthened India's determination to make Monique see the light. She was on the path to doing the right thing, and she wanted her friends to follow suit.

You're like a junkie trying to borrow money for her next fix. I will not help you destroy yourself, and your marriage.

She sent the message. Then Monique answered.

At least I know what I want. Can you say the same?

India shut off the phone, but the question haunted her. She had convinced herself that indeed she did have the answer to her personal dilemma, but Monique's challenge reawakened her nagging doubts. Perhaps utter certainty about a lover or spouse was too much to ask of herself, of anyone over the age of seventeen. She forced herself to stop her "analysis paralysis." She sipped her wine and perused the copy of *Vogue* she had packed. The magazine opened on an ad for a Vera Wang wedding gown: strapless duchess satin, not the usual neovirginal meringue offered by every other wedding gown designer. This utterly modern creation would appeal to Julien with his love of the deconstructed look. He would also love the fact that it would accentuate her every curve. India tore out the ad and tucked it into her purse. She might need it in the not too distant future. And it would bring her good luck on the journey.

The doors of the lounge burst open and a male voice loudly asked, "Has Miss India Chumley checked in yet?"

"Monsieur, we cannot give that information," the matron guarding the entrance to the airline sanctuary insisted. India turned and saw Keith, looking wildly about. Her first impulse was to rush toward him, but she forced herself to remain seated. He spotted her and strode resolutely in her direction.

"What are you doing here?" she asked, completely shocked.

"I didn't come after you six years ago. That was the biggest mistake of my life. I'm not making it again." India absorbed the meaning of this gesture. As she always warned her clients, "Don't listen to what men say. Watch what they do." She had to admit, Keith was doing a lot.

"How did you even know I was here? And how did you get through security?"

"I bought a ticket. When you didn't return my phone calls or my emails, I figured you might be going back to Frenchie. I got your assistant to tell me where you were. It wasn't easy. When I want something, India, I know how to get it."

His words thrilled her. He was saying everything she had ever wanted to hear. Still, she tried not to let her excitement get the best of her.

"So what is it you want?" she asked cautiously.

"You." India longed to believe him but didn't yet dare. Keith sensed her lack of trust and jumped into the breach.

"Right now you're wondering if you should still get on that plane because Julien's such a good guy. You can't. He's wrong for you. You need a challenge. I mean, what are you going to do, talk truffles with him for the rest of your life?"

"Don't talk about him," India warned.

"You know I'm right. He'll bore the wine out of you. I know you. I know how you think and what you think. We're two sides of the same coin."

"We're not. I can't trust you," India said, as much to remind herself as to put him off.

"So you trust him? He doesn't even know what it means to be

American, let alone black. How are you going to raise children with someone like that?"

The question had plagued India since Julien's naïve outburst at Monique's dinner party. When she had experienced racial slights at the office, she had never bothered to share them with Julien, knowing he would have given his pat response: "They are stupid and you are beautiful." These were nice words, to be sure, but they didn't help her fight the battles. Keith always had a strategy, a plan of attack for such moments. Children raised by him would have been brilliant warriors able to survive anywhere, not peace wimps lamely singing "We Are the World" in a society riven by tribalism.

"You know I'm right, India," Keith pressed. To India's complete astonishment, he got down on one knee, right there in the middle of the lounge. "Marry me!" It was not a question, it was an order. By now, several passengers in the lounge indiscreetly craned their necks to listen. India blushed. The last time he had proposed, six years before, it was in the privacy of a suite at the Plaza Hotel. So great was Keith's pride then that he couldn't bear any witnesses to his declaration. Now he projected his intentions for all to hear.

*He has changed,* India told herself.

"I've got the car downstairs. We can drive to Connecticut where they don't require a blood test or a waiting period. If we leave now, we'll reach the justice of the peace's by ten PM. And I picked up some rings on the way over here," he insisted. He fished two gold bands out of his pocket and placed them in the palm of India's hand. She could barely believe her eyes. The proposal was not a spur-of-the-moment upping of the ante. He had come to the airport with intent.

"Not the finest, I know, but we'll replace them later. And you'll have the biggest, most beautiful engagement ring the world has ever seen," he added, looking up at her like a hopeful adolescent pinning his girlfriend for the first time.

India's heart was in her throat, just as it was when Keith proposed over dinner in their suite overlooking Central Park. That part of the hotel no longer existed, having been converted to condos for the obscenely wealthy. India's excitement at this proposal was tempered with the gnawing sense that a golden era was past and could not be re-created. And yet part of her still hoped that with a simple yes, she could resurrect the dream love of her youth. She could wake up every morning to Keith's exquisite face. Her days could be filled with heated debates with him over politics, economics, and the solutions to the world's problems. She could have his babies and one day tell her brilliant grandchildren, "Your grandfather proposed to me in the airport lounge." She wanted to yell "Yes!" but somehow she couldn't utter the word.

"Please, don't leave me hanging," Keith begged sotto voce, taking her hands in his. She tenderly caressed his hair. She closed her eyes and inhaled the smell of him. It was delicious. All she wanted to do was follow him out of the lounge and into his car, but her reason forced her to remain realistic.

After a few moments of sitting, unable to move, she asked, "What did you tell Serena?"

Keith looked away. India's high hopes came crashing to the ground. With an aching heart she faced the truth: the leopard had not miraculously changed his spots.

"You didn't tell her anything, did you?" she pursued.

"I'll tell her later."

"That's a pretty phone call. 'Hi, Serena, how was your night? By the way, I'm married!'"

"What do you care?"

"Because that could be me someday," India answered. Keith looked at her pained. He knew he couldn't refute the possibility. Still, he decided to go on the offensive.

"So, what do you want, a guarantee? A lifetime warranty? Nobody can give you that—nobody! And if they do, they're lying!"

"You're still hedging. And you always will be." India pulled her hands away from his.

"I just asked you to be my wife," he said pleadingly. India nodded. It was her highest hope to marry him, the man she loved, this extraordinary fighter, intellectual, and lover. But it would have proved her greatest misfortune down the line. Each time he walked out of the door of their home she would have found herself wondering, *Where is he going and with whom?* Keith took her hands in his again. She put her arms around him. It felt so right to have his chest against hers, to feel his heart beating, to hear his breath so close. Letting go was like amputating a limb, and yet at times, that was what it took to survive. She held on a little while longer, knowing this was the last time she'd ever have him so near. He barely moved and didn't say a word or dare to look at her. Finally, India forced herself to pull her arms from around his shoulders and sit up straight.

"You should go back to Serena," she said quietly. Keith looked at her, incredulous. He waited for her to retract the comment, but India was resolute. "Go back to Serena," she repeated more forcefully, knowing she needed to get rid of him before her willpower faltered.

Keith started to speak, but stopped himself. India wondered what thought he had wanted to share. Some small part of her hoped against hope it might have been the magic words that would allay all her fears. She mentally chastised herself for such foolishness. She'd lived long enough to know people did not change. Keith rose silently from his kneeling position and, without even saying good-bye, started to walk away. Suddenly, he stopped and turned back.

"If you let me walk out that door, I'm never coming back," he warned. India knew he meant what he said. He had too much pride to ever prostrate himself before her again. With one word, she could have kept him in her life forever.

"Good-bye, Keith," India summoned the courage to say.

He took a last look at her, then turned and strode out the door. India watched him leave, wondering what she had just done. She became aware of the stares of the other passengers in the lounge. An older woman looked at her with an expression that seemed to say,

"How could you let him go, honey? Are you crazy?" Indeed, had she gone mad? Would it have been so bad to be married to a man that compelling who occasionally cheated, as Monique had suggested? What was it she was planning to do with her life that was so important that it required such vestal-like dedication? It was not like she was Condoleezza Rice or Mother Teresa, after all. Would she look back when she was old and gray and regret not saying yes? Yet, along with the sinking feeling that she was now one step closer to being the cat lady, there came a sense of relief: *"This chapter was definitely closed."*

# chapter forty-seven

Brash fluorescent lights illuminated the empty cubicles in the skyscraper across the street. *It's fitting that I should look out at such a punishing view,* India thought to herself, *after the way I've bungled my personal life.* What right had she to win Julien's heart and then break it? She imagined Julien alone in his tiny Paris flat and began to write furiously. The words flowed freely from her pen. She marveled at how easy it was to express oneself when telling the truth.

Dear Julien,

Tonight I nearly boarded a plane to Paris to come and find you. But then, I decided to save us both. As you may have gathered over the last year and half, I am a confused and, for a lack of a more elegant way to put it, utterly fucked-up person. I come by my emotional chaos honestly. Six years of therapy have done little to erase the possibly irreparable damage caused by growing up around the mentally ill and witnessing my mother's constant pain. I don't know how to trust a man. I don't know how to trust myself. I have little to offer anyone. None of this excuses the pain I caused you. Of all the stupid, clumsy, pathetic missteps I've made in my life—and there have been many—I most regret what I did to you. I'm sorry I couldn't accept the magnificent gift you offered: your untarnished soul. I hope and pray that you find a woman who is less of a mess and utterly worthy of your love. Please know that if I could take back what I did, if I could erase your pain, I would. As it is, please accept an apology that comes from the very bottom of my heart. I am truly sorry.

India

She began to reread herself, but fearing that she would lose the courage to do what she knew to be right, she placed the letter in an envelope, sealed, stamped, and addressed it. She walked out to place it in Una's outgoing mail basket and was stunned to see Manni Sobel, opposing counsel on the Diamond case, making his way toward her through the maze of desks. He was not his usual perfectly groomed, metrosexual self. His shining black hair was wind tossed, his Ferragamo tie hung loosely around his neck, and his suit coat was a rumpled mess. He looked like the scruffy victim of an all-nighter.

"How did you get in here? This building's got tighter security than the Pentagon," India said.

"Not if you show the guard a business card and slip him a bottle of tequila." Manni headed back toward India's office. She followed him.

"Looks like you've been hitting the Cuervo Gold yourself."

Manni plopped himself on top of her desk as if he didn't have the physical or emotional energy to take another step. Sensing his *désarroi*, India placed herself beside him. She smiled at him warmly. She'd never seen him anything less than "on." He was the perpetual deal maker, constantly in fighting mode. It was disconcerting to see him so subdued. Perhaps she was not the only person having a really bad night.

"My wife left me," Manni admitted at last. India placed a sympathetic hand on his shoulder. Manni had been an operator for as long as she had known him, but his love for his wife was sincere. She was his "one true thing," his emotional core beneath all the gamesmanship.

"Can you believe it?" Manni continued, incredulous. "Just when things were really getting good." Either because of her recent emotional debacles, or because of the length of their association, his pain resonated vividly. Manni and his wife had been together since high school, save a few brief hiatuses, during one of which India and he had their table incident.

"I'm so sorry," India said softly.

"Fifteen years married, twenty-three years together," Manni wistfully recalled. Seeing him without his mask of invincibility emboldened India to level with him.

"Was it because you cheated?" she asked.

"Absolutely not!" Manni answered, insulted.

"Sorry, I just thought . . ." India started to explain but trailed off.

"You thought wrong. I love her. Her problem is that I'm too obsessed with my work. Do you believe it?"

India was supremely amused by his utter bafflement. How little people saw themselves. He probably thought of himself as a doting spouse in spite of the fact he was known to bring his legal briefs to the gym in order not to waste a moment and had been caught holding cell phone conversations with clients at the urinal.

"I'm sure you're very attentive," India lied to comfort him.

"I am. I called her every day at noon, no matter what. Can't believe she would do this."

India wondered if Keith was thinking the same thing about her refusal to marry him. Was he sitting up in his bed, in his apartment high above Central Park West wondering how she could turn him down? Was he depressed or cursing her name? She reminded herself that her days of worrying about Keith Wentworth's feelings, however real, were over. She had made her choice and she needed to live with it. It would have been easier if there were nothing redeeming about him. If he were just a cold-blooded killer. It was his complexity that always held her in thrall, the glimmer of hope that he could overcome his selfishness and become a decent husband. But one could not build a life on a glimmer. Perhaps that was what Manni's wife had decided, all these years and two children later. India tore her thoughts away from Keith and focused on her "one true thing": her work. She had Manni right beside her. They had a case pending. Knowing him, he probably hadn't come just to unburden his soul. She decided to strike before he did.

"What are we going to do about Diamond?" she asked, ashamed to be employing Manni's technique of negotiating when your opponent was at his weakest, and yet unable to resist the opportunity.

"Just take twenty grand less," Manni responded, glassy-eyed.

"What will that mean to your client? He's worth millions," India answered.

"He just wants to feel he won something."

"Fine, it's a deal."

"Great!" Manni said, suddenly revived and giving her a hearty handshake.

"Did your wife really leave you?" India asked, now suspicious of the whole scenario. It was not unlike Manni to play for sympathy. They hadn't called him the Abominable Snow Job Man for nothing. India wanted to kick herself for falling for his ploy.

"She did, I swear. Would I walk around looking like this if she hadn't?" he said, indicating his wrinkled jacket.

"How did you even know you'd find me here?"

"You call me from the office all the time after nine. And I'm usually at mine. Maybe my wife's right."

India sympathetically placed a hand on his thigh. His muscles flinched and tensed in response. They were as taut as they had been in law school. They were strong soccer player, "I'll bounce you up and down during sex" thighs. He wore her favorite men's cologne, Antaeus, a heady blend of amber and fern. Its traces remained on his shirt and suit. As she inhaled his scent and considered his sexy construction-worker hands, India found her nipples hardening with arousal in spite of her strong objections to his undeniable sleaziness.

"You're beautiful, you know," Manni's husky voice whispered in her ear as his nose grazed her earlobe. India closed her eyes and absorbed the compliment. She needed it after tonight, when she had landed squarely on emotional rock bottom. He began to massage her neck with his warm hands as she sat on her desk with her legs dangling over the side. She let his fingers release the pain of the last three weeks. Each press caused a slight pinch and then relief, as he kneaded her rhythmically. He glided a hand down her spine and she felt herself grow moist, swelling with desire. She leaned back into his hand. Their mouths met, and Manni pushed her down on the desktop and climbed on top of her. It would have been so nice to give in, to savor what she'd wondered about for fifteen years. She let him unzip her pants. She ran her hands through his hair. Even in its messy state, it was like silk through her fingers. His bulge was rock hard as it pressed through his trousers onto her pelvis. The motion heightened her excitement. Their hips gently rocked against each other. *But he's still married,* she reminded herself. Instantly, she pushed him off of her and he landed on the floor with a thud.

"What the hell was that?" he asked, stunned.

"We can't do this," she answered, sitting up and zipping her pants.

"Why not? I want to, you want to."

"Yes, I do," she said without shame. "I want to fuck your brains out on this desktop all night."

"Then let's go," he said, preparing to climb back on top of her.

"'I want to' is not a good enough reason," she said, holding him back.

"Jesus, Chumley, if you keep living your life this way, you're gonna end up a dried-up sexually frustrated prune. Either that or you'll be humping any man in a walker at the nursing home."

"Thank you for that image. I'm not the little uptight priss I was in law school. I've let myself go. And I made a mess of everything," she admitted, the pain of the evening finally catching up with her. Manni shook his head sympathetically. He rubbed her back gently, not as a come-on, but out of compassion.

"I never understood why you had so much trouble with men," Manni commented.

"It's a long story. But as Katharine Hepburn said, 'Before thirty, it's your parents' fault; after thirty, it's your fault,'" India responded. "Go home to your wife," India said. "Promise her you won't bring your BlackBerry to bed anymore."

"How did you know about that?" Manni asked.

"I don't know myself too well, but I do know other people. Go home," she insisted. Manni slowly rose and made his way to the door. As he reached it, he turned back.

"One day, Chumley, it's IUD and me." With that elegant promise, he walked out. India couldn't help but chuckle at his smugness.

As she looked at the empty offices across the street, she wondered how or when she would ever forge a normal relationship. And yet perhaps adulthood and fidelity entailed leaving some questions unanswered, like how good Manni was in bed. But one of the main questions of her adult life had been answered once and for all. In terms of both Keith and Julien, she needed never utter the words "It might have been." That was more than many people could say, and for that she reminded herself to be grateful.

# chapter forty-eight

Monique's brand-new five-hundred-dollar demi-platform pumps clicked against the hospital corridor's linoleum floors, loudly proclaiming her every stride. Monique had no fear of being heard or seen. After ten years in this hospital, she practically owned the place. As she walked toward the head of obstetrics' office, she knew her already bright future was about to get a further burnishing. Dr. Somerville had asked to see her personally. He'd always admired her hard-nosed, "I'm a worker, not a whimperer" approach to her career. As she entered his office with its glass walls looking out on Central Park below, a view that had been the gift of very wealthy benefactors whose relatives died in the old, unrenovated concrete dungeon, she found Somerville behind his desk.

"Dawkins-Dubois, come in. So glad to see you."

"Not as happy as I am to be here," Monique answered, grinning from ear to ear. Somerville flashed a somewhat halfhearted smile.

"Have a seat," he answered, indicating one of the chairs before him. Monique ran her hands down the front of her lab coat, smoothing it before gracefully perching herself at the edge of the ergonomic chair facing the doctor's enormous metal desk. She folded her hands comfortably on top of it and leaned in, the A student never afraid to meet with the professor. She looked at him with the delighted expectation of a child about to be served an enormous ice cream sundae. After the meeting, she might have celebrated by going out to have one, in fact.

"How is everything with you, Dr. Dawkins?" Dr. Somerville began pleasantly, in his cordial New England Yankee manner. With his cobalt-blue eyes and abiding love of skiing, he reminded Monique of many of her professors at Cornell Medical School: Caucasian men in their fifties and sixties with faces weather-beaten by hours of outdoor sport and full heads of salt-and-pepper hair they had never really bothered to groom.

"Wonderful," Monique answered.

"Your girls are what age now?" Dr. Somerville inquired.

"Eight, going on nine, or thirty-nine some days," Monique responded, wondering where this line of questioning was leading.

"They're at Chapin?"

"Sibley. Getting A's," she answered, humoring him.

"Well, with a mother like you. And your husband?"

"Doing great, kicking a—" she stopped herself.

"I've heard the word before. And as a doctor, I've seen my fair share," Dr. Somerville reassured her.

"You get the idea," Monique answered with a chuckle.

"So overall, things are going well in your life?" Dr. Somerville rose from his chair.

"Yes." Monique was growing impatient with the pleasant little chit-chat. It was fine once a year at the hospital fund-raiser, feigning interest in each other's personal lives and having idle conversation about favorite ski resorts to prove one wasn't totally uncivilized. But now she was ready for him to get to the point.

"Do you know an employee by the name of Hector Quinones?" Dr. Somerville asked evenly.

"Yes, he drives an ambulance," Monique answered, unfazed by the mention of Hector's name yet surprised that it would have surfaced in a discussion of her career at the hospital.

"What's your opinion of him?" Somerville continued. Monique shrugged.

"Don't really have one. I don't know him that well." She smiled inwardly at how masterfully she told that lie. She learned her poker-face manners playing pinochle with her uncles. She could bullshit the best. It was why Wayne never questioned her absences. If you were going to play the field, you had to know how to spread the fertilizer.

"Well, and it pains me to say this, Mr. Quinones has a different view of matters. He's brought charges against you of sexual harassment."

Monique's jaw dropped. She couldn't believe she'd heard correctly. "Excuse me?" she asked.

"Mr. Quinones has lodged a formal complaint against you with human resources."

"That's what I thought you said," Monique responded. She could see herself floating above her own body and Dr. Somerville's like a patient who had temporarily died on the operating table. *This isn't happening, it can't be,* she thought.

"Would you like me to read this complaint to you?" Somerville asked gently.

"Yes, please," she answered, her mind spinning.

" 'Plaintiff, Hector Quinones, alleges that Dr. Monique Dawkins-Dubois, obstetrician, continually pursued him for a period beginning in September and lasting eight months, cornering him in utility closets, particularly on the fourth floor for purpose of demanding sexual favors. Particularly,' " Dr. Somerville cleared his throat, " 'oral sex. On several occasions, plaintiff claims, Dr. Dawkins tried to remove plaintiff's pants and force herself upon him. In plaintiff's words, 'She tried to ride me like a superfreak.' Plaintiff's repeated requests to be left alone were met with derision by Dr. Dawkins. At Christmas, the doctor presented plaintiff with a gold watch valued at fourteen thousand dollars to purchase his silence.' I think you get the gist," Dr. Somerville concluded.

Monique sat frozen. She remembered with mortification the many afternoons she and Hector had ducked into the utility closet for a quickie. It was he who had dragged her in there, he who had admired the gold watch in the window of Tourneau. How could she have let him play her? She had fallen for all his lines. She thought their unoriginality resulted from his lack of education. In fact, they sounded trite because he was nothing more than a gigolo. She knew she had to say something and soon, before Dr. Somerville started to believe the claims.

"Doctor, I don't know what to say. This is—"

"I know, Monique." The doctor placed a reassuring hand on her shoulder. "Human resources were going to call you in. Legally, you are still required to meet with them, but I thought I'd give you a heads-up. It's the least I can do given your distinguished record of service at the hospital." Monique cringed at the last phrase. It was the sort of phrase used to describe doctors who were being fired or who had died, the last verbal laurel leaf tossed on the coffins of their careers. "Distinguished record of service." Translation: the door would smack your ass on the way out, and it was heavy. Inwardly, she started to seethe. That oily little shit thought he could bring down everything she'd built, and all because she wouldn't buy him a car. If only she'd been able to get him that damn car she wouldn't have been in this mess. And she had slept with him just two days earlier. He had been planning this and still had the nerve to ride her "like a superfreak."

"I don't need to tell you that this is a serious matter. By law, the hospital must explore all such claims, however far-fetched they may seem. I shouldn't comment, but I must say the idea of you in a utility closet trying to exact sexual favors is patently ridiculous."

"Yes, ridiculous," she laughed a bit too loudly.

"Every effort will be made to see the truth comes out."

"The truth will set us free," Monique commented wistfully.

"Well, human resources will be contacting you. In the meantime . . ." He trailed off as he searched for the right words, then clumsily offered, "Carry on!"

"Thank you, Dr. Somerville," Monique said, looking him square in the eye as she shook his hand.

"We'll get this cleared up," he reassured her.

"Yes, we will," she said with forced confidence. She walked out of his office, head held high. Her first instinct was to head straight down to the EMT lounge and beat that son of a bitch down with her bare hands and the five-pound heels of her shoes. Instead, she forced herself to remain calm.

"Payback not murder, payback not murder," she repeated to herself. She would not lose everything over an orgasm. Even those as good as the ones he had given her. She forced herself into the elevator. Maybe if she threw herself into her rounds, she wouldn't end up on the front page of the *Post* for stabbing Hector with the heel of her brand-new platforms. He wasn't worth ruining the shoes.

## chapter forty-nine

Esme and Tim tumbled through their front door. As Tim struggled to extract the key, Esme wrapped her arms around his waist.

"How'm I supposed to do this? I can't get it out," Tim laughed.

"Since when is that problem? Most men are trying to get it in," Esme taunted. Tim laughed and leaned in to kiss her. This was the way she liked him: in an upbeat mood, attentive and playful but not dead at her feet like a slave. Suddenly, he pushed her away. That only made her lunge for him more forcefully. He pointed toward the living room.

"The children are still up."

"So? It's good for them to see their parents being affectionate," she rebutted, taking aim at his neck with her lips. The tingling sensation melted Tim's proper Presbyterian resolve, and he relished the sensation. Little Esme ran past, chased by Julio.

"To the left, to the left," she chanted. "Everything you own in a box to the left!" she sang as she danced a circle around her parents. Esme noticed a bracelet sparkling on her arm, a cascade of flowers of white, pink, and green stones.

"*Buenas noches,* Señores Talbot," Zulma said with a slight bow as she shuffled in from the living room.

"What's that on her arm?" Tim asked.

Esme shrugged. "Probably something from the Disney store."

"*No, señora, llego una caja* [no, ma'am, a box arrived]," Zulma corrected.

"*A ver?*" Esme asked with furrowed brow. Zulma retrieved the box from the top of the credenza. It was a gray leather jewelry box and bore the stamp Van Cleef & Arpels in elegant gold leaf.

"It was addressed to Esme Sarmiento-Talbot. I thought it was for you, Señora, but Little Esme wanted to open it."

"Who is this from?" Tim asked, grabbing the package. Esme's eyes zeroed in on the bracelet. She'd seen enough good jewelry to know the authentic article. Her daughter was sporting at least $100,000 worth of diamonds around her eight-year-old wrist.

"There is a note," Zulma stupidly volunteered. At this very moment, Esme wanted to have her deported by the INS. Where on earth was the woman's common sense? No one so stupid should have been allowed to stay in the United States, let alone in her house. Esme intercepted the note as Zulma was about to hand it to Tim. Sure enough, it boasted Michael's initials in burgundy: MA.

"I can get another you in a minute," Little Esme continued to sing as she gyrated around the foyer, a diminutive video vixen.

"Esme! Esme!" Tim shouted. Little Esme stopped in midtwirl, bewildered by her father's sudden anger. "Give me the bracelet, sweetheart."

"No," Little Esme said, thrusting out her pouty lower lip.

"Give it to me, now!" he insisted. Little Esme knew not to disobey that tone. She pulled in her lip and slipped the jewels off her arm. Tim examined the bracelet and felt its substantial weight in his right hand. Esme put the note behind her back. Maybe she could drop it in the fireplace before anyone was the wiser.

"Let me see the note," Tim demanded, extending a hand without looking at his wife. Esme stalled for a moment. A dash for the front door or the compost heap would only have been glaring admissions of guilt. But there was no guilt—in this case. She kissed Michael once. That hardly constituted infidelity. She boldly thrust the note in Tim's hand. What could it possibly say? Tim quickly scanned the ten-ply engraved card, his jaws flexing in anger as his eyes darted across the words. He tossed the card to the ground and turned to Zulma.

"Zulma, take the children upstairs and put them to bed, please."

Esme didn't dare pick the card up off the floor, but she glanced down. She could make out the words:

Give a reprobate a second chance. Let pleasure bloom again. MA.

There was nothing so incriminating in that and, fortunately, no admission of identity. She squared her shoulders. She could get out of this one. Zulma led the protesting children out of the room.

"Who's MA?" Tim asked, his voice colder than an arctic wind.

"*Mi amor,* this is so stupid," Esme purred. She started to put her arms around Tim's neck, but he grabbed her wrists before she could make contact with his sensitive flesh.

"Who is he?" he asked again.

"How do you know it's a he?" she taunted.

"So you're sleeping with women now?"

"How dare you!" Esme yelled, full of unrighteous indignation.

"Stop bullshitting me!" Tim yelled. His tone took Esme aback. All this time she had thought he suspected nothing. She underestimated him, and suddenly she felt ashamed, though she'd do everything in her power to hide it. "Who is this guy you're fucking?" Tim demanded to know.

"It's Michael Alders, and I never fucked him!" *Though God knows I wanted to,* she thought to herself, *and I should have for this headache.* "He offered me a job at his vulture fund and I turned him down."

"So you could fuck him!" Tim accused.

"Are you deaf? I told you, I never slept with him."

"So strange men send you diamonds for turning down their jobs."

"That's the way you men are. The more we say no, the harder you try."

"Stop with your theories about men. You hate men." Once again, she had to admit to herself he was right. She hated what men did to women and swore to herself as a child that she would never be a victim. And she wasn't. The surest way to lose the match was to share all this, so she had to change the subject.

"I swear, I haven't done anything with Michael. I've done everything to discourage him."

"Can you honestly tell me there's been no one else, Esme?" Tim looked up at her. In his eyes she saw despair and a faint glimmer of hope. She would play on the hope, throw him a lifeline and this episode would be behind them.

"Yes!" she cried emphatically, a Joan of Arc prepared to burn at the altar of truth. Tim studied her a moment, standing there before him with her round breasts thrust forward, daring him to doubt her.

"You're lying," he said with dead calm, calling her bluff, then turned to go up the stairs. She ran ahead of him and cut him off in front of the staircase.

"How dare you call the mother of your children a liar!" she yelled. "Apologize!"

"Get out of my way, Esme," he said with chilling equanimity.

"No!" She crossed her arms in front of her and stuck out her lip much like her daughter had moments before.

"Esme, this game is over." He pushed her out of his way.

"Where are you going?" she called after him, panic setting in. He'd never taken it this far. She had never thought he would.

"Away. Just away from you," Tim said, his back still turned.

"What do I tell our children?" she called out in a desperate last ditch.

"Anything you want. They know I love them," he answered as he walked wearily up the stairs. Esme knew not to follow him. She heard a door slam shut and shuddered. No one had prepared her for this move in the game.

# *chapter fifty*

Monique swerved her pearl gray BMW onto Hamilton Terrace. Its hill loomed before her, bordered on both sides by immaculately maintained brownstones and gingko trees in emerald bloom. The streetlamps glowed in the dusk, wrought-iron sentinels guarding this sliver of peace and prosperity in the midst of Harlem's socioeconomic jumble. Monique glided her gleaming vehicle into a parking spot right in front of her limestone mini-manse. Her eyes traveled from the polished copper roof guards to the bas-reliefs of rose garlands that crowned the fifth floor like decorative icing on a tiered wedding cake. Monique could calculate the cost of each flower in hours spent at the office and in medical school. She and Wayne had combed the Yellow Pages and the World Wide Web in their quest for a craftsman worthy of restoring their family home. And now she had singlehandedly brought the entire edifice of their dreams to the brink of destruction.

Digging her nails into the leather-bound steering wheel, she renounced every single orgasm Hector ever gave her. Damn him! If only someone had warned her that the price of infinite pleasure was infinite regret. She shut off the ignition and thumbed her blue-and-white enameled Bavarian Motor Works key chain. Soon, no doubt, this precious talisman of upward mobility would be replaced by a pleather circle bearing the stamp of some tin can factory in the Korean hinterlands. And for her stupidity alone she deserved to be brought low in the automotive world. She should have known a young peacock like Hector was after only one thing: her money. Yet she had allowed herself to believe that she had turned his pretty-boy head.

As she unlocked her carved mahogany front door, she heard the tumbrel roll of feet scrambling down a staircase.

"Mommy! You're here!" Madison and Tiffany squealed in unison as they threw their arms around her hips. Monique caressed their bony backs and kissed the tops of their heads, grateful for the love they offered so blindly. Wayne stood behind them, beaming. Where usually she could tick off his physical "imperfections" by rote, tonight he appeared utterly lovable to Monique. Her first impulse was to throw herself at his feet, like Mary Magdalene seeking mercy from sweet Jesus. She refrained.

"We've got a surprise for you!" the girls screeched, dragging her toward the kitchen.

"What is it?" Monique asked, braced for yet another blast from the winds of ill fortune.

"We made dinner for you!" the girls yelped, indicating a three-course spread elegantly laid out on the center island.

"Pasta, salad." Madison pointed to each dish like a game show hostess.

"And cake," Tiffany concluded. "But we cheated. We bought that," she added sheepishly. If only they realized how unworthy she was of such attentions. She was the cheater and the fool.

"What's the occasion?" Monique managed to ask.

"It's all for our working mother of the year." Wayne beamed as he uncorked a bottle of Dom Pérignon.

"Put that champagne away!" Monique snapped. "I'm no one's anything of the year," she added more gently.

"Oh, yes, you are, and we've been waiting—" Wayne started to say.

"Forever and ever," the girls whined.

"For you to get here so we could tell you."

"Tell me what?" Monique inquired, apprehensive.

"Sibley called. You've been voted both the Working Mother and the Sibley Alumna of the Year. You're the first woman—I don't mean the first black woman—I mean the first woman ever in Sibley history to win both." Wayne raised a champagne flute to her.

Monique's heart sank. Now on top of being a cheater and a fool, she was a fraud. When Sibley discovered she had a sexual harassment charge pending against her, would they ask her to publicly surrender her award plaques? Would she be the Marion Jones of New York private schools, embarrassing herself and the race?

"And they want you to speak at assembly," Madison added breathlessly.

"In front of the whole school," Tiffany added.

The sisters clasped hands and danced in circles around their mother chanting, "Mom is the bomb! Mom is the bomb!" Her husband's sincere pride and her children's wild joy over her undeserved honor dealt the deathblow to Monique's self-possession. She convulsed into sobs. Wayne rushed over to put his arms around her. The girls froze in stunned terror. They'd never ever seen their mother cry. Madison clutched her little sister's hand.

"Hey, hey. What's wrong?" Wayne asked gently.

Her words sputtered out in the unintelligible staccato of the distressed. "No-thing, love . . . you . . . girls . . . want . . . lose you."

"You won't lose me. Unless you mess up my shirt with your mascara and that nastiness dripping out of your nose. Come on, baby, this is a Turnbull and Asser," he chided, placing a protective hand on his shoulder. His comment halted her sobs. She suddenly burst into maniacal laughter. The girls stared as if she'd lost her mind. Monique knelt before them and extended her arms. They approached tentatively. Monique grabbed them and buried her head in the midst of theirs.

"I love you, I love you, I love you," she repeated, savoring true ecstasy: the splendid normalcy of the life and home she and Wayne had built. She hoped against all hope that her actions had not doomed this perfect happiness to destruction.

## chapter fifty-one

Though Esme had never cared for the brick Colonial she lived in, she had made the greenhouse her tropical refuge. She'd filled it with orchids, and a macaw from her native Colombia perched above it all, repeating "I hate New England" at ten-minute intervals. Esme always found ways to take revenge. She lounged Camille-like in a huge brown wicker chaise while Abby filled her glass from a tall pitcher of Long Island iced tea. In the matching chaise, Monique nursed her third libation and scooped Cape Cod potato chips by the heaping handful from a gargantuan silver bowl on the table beside her. India sat upright in a chair, sipping sparkling mineral water and biting her straw to suppress the temptation to dive headlong into the chip bowl. Now that she'd eliminated not just one but two potential husbands, she could not afford to get thick and blowsy.

"I cannot believe he could do this to me. Leave me with two young children. At the end of the day, men are all pigs," Esme lamented.

"He might come back. Especially if you apologize," Abby suggested.

"Why should I apologize for sleeping with someone I didn't even sleep with?"

"Because you've slept with everybody else," India deadpanned, trying to drag Esme out of the melodramatic movie she was starring in and back to reality.

"He doesn't know that!" Esme protested.

"They always know," Abby contradicted. "Especially when they're in love with you. They can feel the changes." The reminder of the depth of Tim's feelings for her silenced Esme and struck the chord of sadness she spent her life tap dancing to avoid. In Tim, she had found someone who loved her unconditionally, something she had never known in her own emotionally stunted family. She had married him because of that love, and she had always believed he would put up with anything, that he would never leave her. Now she faced the prospect of his never returning. The thought unmoored her. She refilled her glass.

"We need to brighten up, ladies," she insisted, resorting to her classic survival mechanism: avoidance at all cost. "Let's do something constructive. Go shopping at the mall or have a pedicure."

"At least you still have a job," Monique lamented. "If this case blows up, I'll be lucky to be allowed to deliver coyote puppies in Tijuana. Wayne will divorce me and take my girls. Some hoochie with a big weave and a headrest booty will snap him up. I'll see my girls again when they get married. And I'll show up in an old jalopy and a dress from JCPenney, while the bitch who raised them is in my Oscar de la Renta, and her daughter, Brittany, has squeezed her fat ass into an Yves Saint Laurent her mama bought her in Paris."

"Who's Brittany?" Abby asked, utterly confused.

"Isn't that what they always name their children by the second wife?" Monique responded. India rose and removed Monique's glass from her hand.

"You've had enough of these," she insisted. "You've got to snap out of it and get in the fight. If Oprah could defeat the beef lobby, you can defeat some slimy high school equivalency diploma holder without a legal leg to stand on."

"What's my defense, Counselor? The old 'It wasn't sexual harassment, it was consensual' excuse? 'He wanted to sample my sushi in the utility closet?'"

"There is a way out of this," India insisted. "I just haven't found it yet."

"I fucked up. For a little bit of fucking. Well, a lot of fucking, but it wasn't worth it."

"Cheating is only fun if there's someone to cheat on," Esme added solemnly.

"That's profound." India instantly regretted the comment when she saw tears in Esme's eyes. She crossed to hug her friend, but Esme pushed her away, ever the proud, unbreakable woman.

"I'm fine," Esme insisted. "I'm not crying. Men don't make me cry. Ever!" The tears streamed down her face.

"It's just us," Abby reassured her. "You don't have to be the iron lady."

At that comment, Esme buried her head on Abby's shoulder and allowed the sobs to come in earnest, loud, and guttural. India watched the happy-go-lucky Carmen dissolve into a frightened child. She didn't dare tell Esme it would all work out; she feared Tim might indeed have had his fill of the games. Tim was the sort of stoic who bore all until one day he snapped.

Little Esme ran through the room wearing the infamous bracelet and belting out "I can find another you in a minute!" At the sound of her child's voice, Esme sat up, wiped her eyes, and smiled. In spite of her attempt at covering up, Little Esme noticed the change in her mother's demeanor. She stopped singing and approached.

"*Qué pasa*, Mommy? Why are you crying?" Little Esme asked. Esme knew firsthand what the sight of a crying mother did to a child, how helpless it made her feel. Perhaps she had destroyed her marriage, but she would not rain misery upon her daughter.

"I'm not crying," she protested boisterously. "Mommy *tiene* hay fever today." Little Esme eyed her warily, not quite buying the story. Esme smiled more brightly. "Show your tías how you dance. Come on, sing," she insisted. Little Esme obliged, reluctantly at first, but as India, Monique, and Abby cheered her on, she belted out her song with gusto. "I can find another you in a minute, matter of fact he'll be here in a minute," she crooned, shaking her narrow eight-year-old hips and

tossing her arm in the air. Esme noticed the Van Cleef & Arpels bracelet dangling from her daughter's diminutive wrist. A happy thought
occurred to her, in the midst of this dreary afternoon.

"Just a minute, ladies," she announced. "We can make *el taquito* go
away. Courtesy of Michael Alders and a very expensive bracelet." She
smiled and raised her glass. For the first time all afternoon, Monique
smiled, too, understanding Esme's train of thought.

"You'd do that for me?" Monique asked, genuinely touched.

"Cheaters have to stick together," Esme whispered. Monique and
Esme clinked tumblers, sealing the bargain.

"Wish I could help you out with Tim," Monique offered sotto voce.

"It's my own fault. I messed up my bed, now I have to remake it,
if I can," Esme answered, resigned. India looked at her stunned. She'd
never seen her take responsibility for any of her actions.

"It's actually, 'I made my bed, now I have to lie in it,'" India pointed
out.

"Okay, fine, Miss Correction. You get the idea." India did and made
a mental note to herself that should she ever get married and feel
tempted to cheat, she would remember Esme's regret, to say nothing
of her own.

## chapter fifty-two

Abby entered her apartment, carrying a plastic bag from Shun Lee West. It was her first Saturday night as an officially separated woman. She paused in the entryway to absorb the stillness. The quiet was underscored by the coat pegs bereft of even a single child's jacket. The children were with Nathaniel in the temporary apartment he'd rented downtown. Abby wondered what they were eating, probably pasta. And would the shiksa call during dinner? Whom would Nathaniel say he was speaking to when Noah asked? Abby switched off the thoughts. She had a full order of crispy and tender scallion pancakes with plum sauce to keep her warm.

She entered her kitchen and was startled to find her mother sitting at the center island reading the latest issue of *The New Republic.*

"Mom, what are you doing here?"

"I let myself in. You know I don't usually intrude, but I thought you could use some company, and I knew if I called and offered, you wouldn't want me to leave Papa."

"I could have come over to see you guys," Abby said.

"Your father wouldn't have been able to resist giving you the litany of Nathaniel's shortcomings. You didn't need to hear that. Not tonight."

"He's not the only one with shortcomings." She didn't regret the separation but wasn't proud of her own dalliance. She would have felt better if she had remained the blameless goose as opposed to following in the footsteps of the wandering gander. Yet, she had to admit, the moments with Sage were among the happiest of her recent life, of her entire life in fact. Ah, well. Now it was solace in Chinese food.

"What are we having?" Her mother poked her nose in the bag.

"The usual!" Abby gave her a wink. Eleanor rubbed her hands together.

"Brown rice or white?"

"Both," Abby said.

"Fabulous!" Her mother began to set the table. Abby divvied up the golden-brown pancakes and spooned out the thick plum sauce. She and her mother sank their teeth into the pancakes in unison.

"Mmmm. What did we do before these?" her mother asked, chewing slowly.

"We went to that awful place on Ninety-third Street and Broadway with the greasy egg rolls," Abby answered remembering.

"Don't knock those. They got us through many a Sunday night after driving in from Fire Island."

"Now there is a Body Shop there," Abby commented sadly.

"Time changes everything. We can't cling to the past," her mother reminded her, placing another pancake on Abby's plate.

"Mom, did you know Nathaniel was wrong for me?" Abby ventured. Even in the days when she was head over heels for Nathaniel, she sensed her father's misgivings. Her mother had always greeted him with open arms and acceptance, as one would one's own son. Her mother took a moment before answering.

"Yes," she said.

"Why didn't you stop me?"

"Your papa wanted to. He wanted to object at the wedding. I wouldn't let him. We all have to live our lives. And just because a relationship ends or changes doesn't mean it wasn't meant to be. You have three gorgeous children to prove you and Nathaniel were meant to be. Whatever else he is or isn't, he's a good papa. He managed to change that in his life when his turn came. That's not easy. Don't judge people against some ideal standard. Give them credit for how far they've come from where they started."

*By that measure,* Abby reflected, *Nathaniel has done a decent job.*

"He was really determined from the time Benjamin was born to be there for him. He used to beg me to let him do the two AM feedings," Abby said, smiling at the memory. "And remember the wooden toys he would carve for them every Christmas? Anything they requested. One year, Rachel asked for a narwhal. Nathaniel made one, horn and all. It's still up in her room."

"You know, baby, it doesn't suit you."

"What?" Abby said looking down at the peasant blouse and skirt her mother had seen her in several dozen times.

"I mean the guilt."

"Mom."

"Sage has been asking for you in music class. And looking miserable. I think you two should resume whatever it was you were doing."

Abby was stunned. Though she had usually told her mother everything, she'd never divulged this affair. She was too ashamed. There was relief in discovering her mother knew and didn't seem to disapprove. If her mother forgave her, perhaps it was time she forgave herself.

"How did you know? How long have you known?"

"Since before you two consummated. It was just going to happen, that was obvious."

"But it's over. It has to be."

"Why?"

"Because I'm not even divorced yet."

"So? You're supposed to sit here and knit an afghan until papers come through?"

"It's just not right."

"It's not like Nathaniel was sitting around letting the grass grow under his feet."

"That doesn't justify my behavior."

"We are a people of guilt but not sexual guilt."

"Mom, you never had an affair."

"No. I was tempted, but it wasn't worth it. I don't think that's the case with you."

"I think I'd rather be having dinner with Dad and hear him rag on Nathaniel," Abby said, uncomfortable at the allusion to Sage. She had not allowed herself to think about how very much she missed him.

"Okay, well, just know that as of this week, I am no longer available to take Noah to Free to Be a Prodigy."

"Mom!" Abby protested.

"And since only relatives can bring him, and your papa's not available, that leaves you. Unless of course you want to send Nathaniel," her mother informed her. Abby sank her teeth into another scallion pancake as she considered seeing beautiful Sage again. Her heart filled with sheer joy at the prospect. He was too young, she was too old. India would probably disapprove, for practical reasons. But Abby had never been practical.

# chapter fifty-three

Khadija Udoje sat across the desk from India, smiling broadly as the latter explained the terms of her divorce settlement.

"So, I'm going to have enough money to go to school?" Khadija exclaimed, ecstatic.

"Yes, what would you like to study?" India asked, genuinely curious.

"Accounting. I was very good at maths at school," Khadija replied, using the African colonial term for "math."

"If you could make it to this country and raise three children while holding down two jobs, I believe you can do anything," India reassured her. "Many of the women I deal with don't know how they can go on living now that they have to downgrade to four-star hotels. That's not you," she added.

"He wanted me to stay, you know," Khadija informed her in a tone of confidence. "But a man who would do that to me does not love me. In his way he loves, but it's not the way I want to be loved," Khadija explained. India agreed wholeheartedly. Sharing was not an option, however many PhDs advocated it as a solution to the shortage of marriageable black men.

"Most important, you can get out of the shelter," India reassured her.

"It wasn't so bad. They were nice. And one night, a man brought us food, fancy pastries. Nice man. French. Nice-looking. My ghells thought he was Santa Claus."

India smiled to herself remembering Julien's meringue gazelles. They had almost convinced her she should marry him. Anyone that kind deserved consideration. She was saddened at the thought that he had not responded to her note. India didn't blame him. She deserved his silence but would remain grateful for the experience of his boundless kindness. She only wished he could say the same of her. With regret, she admitted to herself that was far from the case.

"Thank you, for everything. Next time, I bring my ghells," Khadija declared brightly as she rose to leave. India had the satisfaction of knowing at least one of her clients would take divorce as the beginning of a new way of living.

"I have a feeling you won't ever need my professional services again." She led Khadija outside. As they passed Una's desk, the latter jumped up to stop India.

"Ms. Armstrong wants to see you to congratulate you on your success in the Winston case," Una explained. India started to walk quickly in the direction of Constance's office, then stopped and turned back. She knew she had done well and didn't need a pat on the head from the headmistress to justify her existence.

"Please tell Constance that's lovely of her, but I have work to finish. I'll see her in a few hours," India answered.

"Okay, boss," Una responded.

"Also, Lucinda Diamond called. She's buying several tables to that Bonnets of Beautification luncheon at the park, and wants to know if you'll join her and bring some friends," Una added.

"Sure, put it on my calendar, please." India made a bet with herself about how long Mrs. Diamond's fifty million would last at this rate.

As she walked down the corridor, she heard an unpleasantly familiar voice call, "Chumley!" She turned to see Eddie O'Donnell, tomato red from a week's vacation in the Cayman Islands.

"Heard you pulled Robert Winston's chestnuts out of the fire," he said gruffly.

"Worked out pretty nicely. He's getting a third of the fortune and, most important, the children," India answered nonchalantly.

"That's good. How'd you do it?" Eddie asked, incredulous that India was able to pull it off. India considered telling him about the tactics she had employed, then realized there was little point; it would only depress him. Instead, she decided to spare his fragile ego. She leaned in conspiratorially, as if divulging a secret and said:

"The judge was black, a lesbian," she paused for dramatic effect before adding, "with a white mom." She pointed to herself as if to say, "How could she resist me?" O'Donnell nodded, relieved. Now it all made sense: the sisterhood of multiculti mongrels.

"Thanks, I wondered. Well, congrats," he said, and walked away, standing a little taller. India had the satisfaction of knowing that though she had stolen his fee, she'd restored his sense of dignity.

# chapter fifty-four

India headed down the corridor to conference room F, the room of discretion. She opened the door to find Monique already waiting for her. Monique nervously tapped the table with her manicured fingers. If she were a smoker, she would have been halfway through a pack.

"You okay?" India asked, concerned.

"I just want to get this over with." Monique set her upper lip.

"Did they offer you anything to drink?"

"Not anything worth drinking," Monique quipped. India placed a reassuring hand on hers. She may have had no life, but she had a reasonable chance of helping Monique save hers.

The door opened and Una announced, "Mr. Quinones," then whispered to India, "He asked me to do that," as she rolled her eyes and exited.

Hector strutted in wearing his Sunday best: a wide-lapeled pinstripe suit with an orange tie and black-and-white patent leather shoes. His bodybuilder's frame was very evident through the polyblend fabric. Monique closed her eyes to suppress the memories of pleasure. She would definitely miss those ten-minute orgasms.

"Thank you for coming in today, Mr. Quinones," India said with great dignity, though the irony was not lost upon her that her apartment served as the trysting place for this pair. She was as much a pimp as he appeared to be in his zoot suit. If nothing else, representing Monique would help her atone for that "sin."

"So, you have a proposition for me. Let's hear it," Hector announced, slouching into a chair opposite them, spreading his legs, and unbuttoning his jacket to reveal the powerful bulge in his pants. India couldn't help but take notice of his endowment. She forced herself to focus on his face. He chewed on a toothpick, rolling it around his mouth as though sucking on something delicious. Even in his crassness, he oozed sex. India looked at Monique with deep understanding of her "fall." If India worked at the hospital, she'd probably have played Lady Chatterley to his lover.

"You have leveled false charges against my client," India said, her arch tone masking her state of arousal.

"That's for her to prove." Hector smacked his gum and noisily popped a bubble.

"Precisely. And doing so would bring to light the consensual affair the two of you had, which runs counter to hospital employee policy. You would both lose your jobs, in all probability." Hector shifted uncomfortably and threw one side of his jacket over his crotch, as if to protect his now threatened crown jewels. India was relieved, since he did have enough down there to wreck her concentration on the issues at hand.

"That's only if they believe her," he protested.

"Which, given your prior record, I think they will," India countered.

"Hey, I never spent any time in the joint!" he said with indignation.

"I'm referring to your record of employment. You were fired from your last job for cause, and I have here the names of three women, coworkers, with whom you had consensual sex, and from whom you tried to extort money. Should this case go to trial, I will subpoena all of them," India elaborated.

"So what are you saying, lady?" Hector asked, now leaning in menacingly.

"I'm saying it would be better for all concerned to go a different way. This all began, I believe, because you wanted my client to purchase a car for you and she wouldn't."

"I couldn't," Monique protested. India stared her into silence. She couldn't believe Monique still wanted to justify her actions to this walking snake oil dispenser. Once again, she was reminded that good sex with the wrong partner was as dangerous for women as crack: it robbed them of all common sense.

"We are prepared to give you an amount that will enable you to make said purchase, in exchange for your signing a quitclaim dropping and recanting all charges."

"How much?" Hector squared his jaw.

"Twenty-five thousand dollars," India stated.

"Are you shitting me? What am I supposed to get with that, a Yugo?"

"On a payment plan, you can do better than that. It's this, or court and the unemployment line. I think my client will find a job much sooner than you will, given her credentials."

Hector pondered the offer. Monique did not take her eyes off of him, trying to read his body language. His slouch indicated to India that she hadn't scared him enough.

"You need to make a decision quickly, Mr. Quinones. If you don't, I'm also prepared to file a countersuit of extortion, using your former victims—Valerie Trumbull, Susan Jones, Jessica Wong—as my witnesses," she said with a grin. Hector sat back again, still gnawing at the toothpick as he looked India in the eye and considered. India maintained a resolute expression though inwardly she worried he'd walk out the door. Monique sat panicked, looking from one to the other.

"Thirty and you have a deal," Hector said at last.

"Done." India handed him the quitclaim and the pen. He signed.

"When do I get my check?"

"My assistant has it for you."

"I should have asked for thirty-five!"

"Your bad," India volleyed, thrilled her gamble had paid off.

"Thanks for the memories," Hector said with a wink to Monique as he rose from his chair and strutted out of the room. Monique let out a deep breath.

"I thought you were going to offer him at least fifty," Monique objected.

"I had a suspicion we could get him for less."

"What if he hadn't taken it?"

"Sometimes, you have to be willing to gamble," India told her.

"With my life, thank you very much, Miss Thing."

"We risked and we won," India reminded her.

"I guess you're right. I have my job, my girls, and my husband," Monique said with bittersweetness. "Thank you," she added.

"What have we learned?" India asked.

"That cheating doesn't pay." Monique thought a moment, then added, "It feels good, but it doesn't pay."

As India watched her friend walk out the door, she took pride in having restored her to the family she loved. She rolled the mental videotape on her own past lovers. Was there anyone other than Keith who had rocked her world to the edge of reason, to the point of selling everything and everyone else down river? No, Keith was it. Maybe, in time, she would find someone who brought her a different kind of happiness. In the meantime, work would be its own reward.

# chapter fifty-five

Abby walked up the last flight of the six it took to reach Noah's music classroom. She wanted to slow down, calm down, and delay the delicious moment of seeing Sage again. She was also slightly apprehensive he'd moved on, to someone age appropriate, with no stretch marks.

"Why didn't we take the elevator, Mommy?" Noah whined.

"Elevators are for wimps," Abby answered, hoping the arduous climb had added color to her cheeks and tone to her behind.

As they entered the classroom, the cluster of alpha moms fell silent. They all stared at Abby.

"She's back," one whispered audibly to the others. *Do they know?* Abby wondered. Had she become fodder for the Mommy-and-Me gossip grapevine? It didn't matter. She wasn't anxious to join their cappuccino coven. She looked up and saw Sage beaming at her. There was no mistaking it: he was thrilled she'd returned. For the first time in a long time, Abby knew she was exactly where she belonged.

"Welcome back, Ms. Rosenfeld," Sage said with a bow of his head. "We've missed you."

"Thank you, it's good to be here."

"Let the class begin," Sage announced. He and Abby smiled at each other with the promise of happiness to come as the children sawed away on a half dozen tiny violins.

# chapter fifty-six

As India stood on the steps leading to the secret garden in Central Park where the annual Bonnets for Beautification luncheon was held, she surveyed the sea of pastel straw hats in search of a recognizable pate. She smiled at the sight of New York society women in their glory, showing off their new spring suits and chapeaux they would then consign to the back of the closet, unless they were crossing the ocean to attend Ascot. New York was not a hat town, except on this particular day, on this particular patch of lawn in Manhattan, when ladies shelled out five hundred dollars a head to see, be seen, and keep the park beautiful. India had chosen to eschew tradition. Her hat was her own crowning glory, not pressed, not blown out, but full and frizzy, a barometer measuring the precise degree of humidity in the air. Her mane drew stares, some of approval, others of horror, but it didn't matter anymore. India had come to have fun.

As she entered the tent the size of a football field, she was hit by a thousand feminine voices all chattering and screeching at once. She made her way unimpeded to Table 125, edging past clusters of women air kissing each other as though they hadn't been together in years, when in fact they were probably at the same black-tie benefit the night before. To her delight, Abby and Monique were already seated. Both wore hats, and Abby's hair was bone straight.

"Wait a minute," India teased. "What's going on with you?"

"Please, it's a hairdo, not a reflection of deep inner states. So let's not put me on the couch over a blowout," Abby insisted.

"You, on the other hand, what are you trying to prove? This is not the place to go native. You're embarrassing the race," Monique admonished, only half-joking.

"Disown me then," India said, taking a sip from a glass of white wine with her name on it.

"Did you see the paper on Sunday?" Monique asked tentatively.

"I was too busy. I only got through the front section," India answered, taking a bite of cheese biscuit.

"So you missed this," Monique said gently, pulling a copy of the "Vows" section from her oversize purse and handing it to India. It read:

### May 4th, Serena Charles and Keith Wentworth II

Serena Jane Charles and Keith Wentworth II were married yesterday at the National Cathedral in Washington DC. The Reverend Joseph Bliden presided. Mrs. Wentworth, 26, graduated magna cum laude from Wellesley and received her MFA from NYU. She is assistant curator for contemporary painting at the New York Museum of Contemporary Art. Ronald Charles retired as General Manager of Texas Electronics and her mother, Wanda, is a homemaker. The groom is CFO of Wentworth Foods, a company founded by his father, Elihu Wentworth. The first marriage for both . . .

India stopped reading and absorbed the information. So it ended, not with a bang but with a *New York Times* announcement. In spite of her preparedness, she was struck by a sense of loss. It was the bereavement one experiences when a door shuts forever. Her pain was succeeded by relief at knowing the choice no longer existed to torment her thoughts. Keith belonged to someone else until death or a cheap blonde did them part. Abby looked at her apprehensively.

"I hadn't seen it," India admitted. "I knew it was coming. So here it is. He didn't waste much time."

"That's men, fine men like him. One down, on to the next. They're nothing but hos. I'm sorry, I didn't mean to rain on your parade," Monique explained, softening. "I just wanted to make sure you knew." India wondered how soon Keith had given his mother the go-ahead. On the drive home from the airport after being rejected by her? He was proud, impetuous, and vengeful enough. She could picture Livia, four-star general in party planning, snapping into action, deploying her army of florists, caterers, and tent builders to transform their ample backyard into Shangri-La while she barked orders from her veranda. She regularly hosted sit-down dinners for seventy at home. If anyone could pull off a lavish "insta-wedding" it was Dragon Lady Wentworth.

"Did you go?" India asked, half hoping she did so she could hear the details.

"No, I sent Wayne. I had a 'hospital emergency.' I didn't want to sit through that. This should be you, not her."

"No, she's Serena Wentworth. I'm India Chumley. I'm not changing my name and my identity for anybody. The right man will understand that," India declared. One's pride and self-respect were not the worst consolation prizes in the world.

"You're right. He will. But I won't," Monique insisted. "Whose slamming house on Martha's Vineyard am I going to stay in now?" They laughed. India envisioned the Wentworths' white-gabled manse surrounded by its endless lawn. It had been the scene of a very uncomfortable weekend when Keith first introduced her to his parents. For the first time in her life, people of color were treating India like a creature that had crawled out of the nearest swamp. Keith's mother made it clear to her that everything about her was wrong: her coloring (darker than theirs), her hair (a stranger to relaxer), and most especially her white *actress* mother. India chuckled to herself as she remembered Livia's sneering questions. "How long has she been in that profession?" she'd asked as if referring to prostitution. In Livia's presence, Keith went from cocky alpha male to doting mama's boy. India had not allowed herself to dwell on this unpleasant memory. As it rushed back to her, it obliterated any lingering regret over her decision at the airport.

Esme arrived at the table dressed in a wasp-waisted red suit that made her stand out like an addictive poppy in a field of faded daffodils.

"Let the fun begin! Where's my wine?" she demanded. A handsome waiter appeared brandishing a bottle. He smiled at Esme as he poured. She offered a very formal "Thank you" and turned to the girls. They were astonished at her nonflirtatious response.

"What did you do, go to 'Seducers Anonymous'?" India asked.

"Yes, since when do you pass up the chance to bat your eyes at a cute guy?" Abby asked, incredulous.

"Ladies, the time for games is over. I have a date," Esme said solemnly.

"Oh, okay. Who this time? Michael? Is he out of the doghouse?" Abby asked.

"Never. With Timothy Talbot."

"He agreed to see you?" India asked, amazed.

"I wrote him a long letter. Of apology." All three women gasped. Apology had never been part of Esme's vocabulary. "And we've been speaking on the phone. He agreed to meet so we can talk things out," Esme explained without any of her usual "I don't give a flying Fendi" bravado. "I miss sleeping in his arms at night and finding him in the morning, eating breakfast with the children. When you almost lose something, you realize you should take better care of it," Esme continued. "But I will get him back," she said with forced conviction. "I've never lost a man before. I won't lose my husband. He's the only man I've ever loved," Esme added, her voice breaking. She gripped Abby's hand. She refused to have another sob. She had to forge ahead, no matter what.

"I'll drink a toast to that," Abby proposed, raising her glass. The others joined her.

"To Esme and Tim," they chanted in unison.

"When are you seeing him?" Monique asked.

"This afternoon," Esme answered a bit more calmly.

"Is that the right outfit to send him the message you've changed and you're willing to work on it?" India asked.

"Yeah, that suit has unrepentant hoochie written all over it. It's Cavalli, isn't it?" Monique guessed.

"It says, 'I've changed, but I still know how to show you a good time,'" Esme explained with a twinkle in her eye. India was pleased to see her fighting spirit was undiminished. She prayed for Esme's sake that it would lead her to triumph: reconciliation with her loving husband.

"I'll drink to that!" Monique declared, raising her glass.

"To good times!" India cheered.

"I like the untamed hair, India," Esme commented of India's bush, changing the subject.

"So did the lady with the Carmen Miranda fruit basket on her head. I think she's the only one in the place who lives below Sixty-first Street," India joked.

"How long does this shindig last? I have to pick my girls up at figure skating," Monique said.

"It's quick and dirty," India assured her. "They'll stand up and give a speech no one will listen to. The women will make a mad dash for the gift bags, and those that don't have cars will enter the stiletto foot race to find a taxi."

"Good. I don't want to miss the end of their lesson. The skating instructor is fine!"

"Oh, no, please. Not again. I'm not sure I can get you out of another jam," India groaned.

"You won't have to. I've learned my lesson. Don't dip your pen in the company ink. But you've still gotta live." Seeing India's horrified expression she added, "Relax, I'm kidding." India was not convinced her contrition was real. She hoped for Monique's sake that it was. Years of working as a divorce lawyer had taught her that most people did make the same mistake twice. Her own behavior had taught her that when a woman wanted to cheat, no lecture from a loving friend or warnings of consequences would stop her.

"By the way, Esme, here's a check for part of the thirty I owe you. I can't give it all to you at once without my husband finding out, so if it's okay with you, we'll have an installment plan," Monique said, pulling an envelope out of her purse.

"You don't owe me anything. That bracelet didn't belong to me. In fact, I'm going to invest the rest of the money for all of us. In case we ever need it, for anything, shoes, another love nest apartment." India looked at her, shocked. She was about to lambaste her when, reading her thoughts, Esme added, "I'm not serious. But life is a long proposition." She looked off into the distance with an expression of melancholy.

"Yes, it is," India assented as she watched Lucinda Diamond passing by on the arm of a young beefcake who looked slightly uncomfortable in a boater, a crisply starched shirt, and linen sport coat. India recognized him from the private detective photos as Antonio, the infamous dog walker who almost cost Lucinda her children and her settlement. Now Lucinda was parading him for all of New York society to see. If one garnered a large enough settlement, all was forgiven, even of an adulterous woman. As Lucinda waved at her, India wondered how long the fifty million would last. That was no longer her problem. She could help, but she could not rescue.

"India," Abby called. "What are you looking at?"

"The past," India answered.

"Well, we want to make a toast to your future. May it be full of love!"

India accepted the toast with a gracious smile, but she was not certain it was founded on anything more than pipe dreams, the wishful thinking of good friends. She smiled, reckoning she was well on her way to becoming the fascinating spinster aunt with the intriguing career but little more than her prized collection of handbags and shoes to keep her company on a cold winter's night.

# chapter fifty-seven

India had hoped to share a quiet coffee with Abby after the luncheon, but she had to run off to pick up the children at school. Everyone seemed to be rushing home to real lives, with families and loved ones. Even the strangers at the luncheon cast nervous glances at their watches and anxiously hailed taxis, not wanting to be late. India didn't need to be on time for anyone on the splendid May afternoon, not even a client at the office. She decided to catch an American Ballet Theatre matinee. Her cab pulled up to Lincoln Center and she ran across the plaza just as the gongs rang. She managed to purchase a standing room ticket. She slipped into her space at the back of the orchestra section as the majestic bars of the overture of *Onegin* began to play.

The ballet, based on the Pushkin verse novel of the same name, was one of her all-time favorites. The ballet tells the story of a young, innocent woman who falls madly in love with a brooding dandy. He abandons her and years later, once she had married a thoroughly decent prince who worshipped her, tries to reclaim her. While tempted, she stands firm in her commitment to her husband and renounces the passionate love of her life once and for all. *How apt this piece is in the wake of Keith's marriage,* India thought.

A handsome man in his forties slipped into the spot beside India's. He smiled at her. She reflexively smiled back, liking what she saw, but then forced herself to look away. *A grown man at the ballet in the middle of the afternoon can only be unemployed or worse yet, an actor,* she told herself. She'd been down that dead-end road and was not going back anytime soon, thank you very much. Such detours were appropriate for the early postcollege career years. They were unseemly in a woman nearing the years of permanent hair color. Still, something about the stranger's presence made the experience all the more pleasant . . . a little pick-me-up on a somewhat melancholy afternoon.

"It's hard to believe those two will never dance together again," the stranger said of the two principal dancers at intermission. India was pleasantly surprised he was so up-to-date.

"You follow the ballet?" she asked.

"Can't get enough of it. And I've been a fan of Alessandra Ferri's since I first saw her dance Juliet twenty years ago. It won't be the same with her retiring."

India should have seen it coming. He was gay, gay, gay. She didn't mean to stereotype, but that was one that held true. Straight men might eat quiche, but by and large, they didn't passionately follow the careers of ballerinas.

"Will you excuse me? I'm going to brave the ladies' room line," India said, giving this handsome stranger the brush-off. She could talk ballet with Abby or her mother for that matter. She didn't need some good-looking new gay friend to wax rhapsodic over Ángel Corella's tours jetés. She really did need to find deep within the bowels of her being some scintilla of interest in sports and sports matches. Otherwise she was doomed to encounters like this one: a flicker with no chance of ever bursting into flame unless she underwent a sex-change operation.

As they stood through the final act, India became aware of the stranger's stare. She turned and sure enough, he was looking over every inch of her being. The attention threw her. *Then again,* she reminded herself, *I am rather well put together today and beautifully accessorized.* The man was probably an aspiring designer. He was examining her ensemble head to toe so he could knock it off. India clutched her beige crocodile handbag close to her chest. Life for a single woman truly was a minefield of experiences requiring self-protection.

As the curtain fell on Tatiana tearing herself away from Onegin and casting him out of her boudoir once and for all, India blurted, "Why is it like this? We strive all our lives for an ideal of love that doesn't exist, and we end up either destroying ourselves for passion or wasting away in sterile marriages of convenience."

"Maybe there's a happy medium," the stranger gently suggested. India noticed for the first time the depth and smoothness of his voice, the perfection of his ebony skin.

"And what might that be?" she asked, a little too snippily.

"True, mature love." He stated it with such assurance that India felt certain he knew of what he spoke.

"By the way, I'm Lucius Boateng," he said, cordially extending a hand.

"India . . ." She hesitated to give her real name but relented. "Chumley."

"What a beautiful and original name. Sounds West Indian, by way of a white mother," he teased, hitting the ethnic nail on the head, much to India's surprise.

"How did you know?"

"I've been around. I have a few relatives who look like you."

"I'm guessing you are Ghanaian, by way of . . . Connecticut," she countered. He smiled, delighted.

"Most people think my name is Chinese. Especially over the phone. They faint when I show up."

"I know what you mean," India concurred, pleased to find someone who knew the feeling of being an alien, of having to explain himself everywhere he went. It was quite a shame he played for the other team.

"Well, India Chumley, may I take you out for a drink?" Lucius offered.

All of India's assumptions had just been thrown overboard. This was not the approach of a man who wanted to copy her outfit. She was ashamed of her own narrow-mindedness. If only to atone for that she said, "I'd like that."

She instantly regretted accepting. There was a quarter pound of dark chocolate truffles with her name on it at La Maison du Chocolat. This was a much wiser move than going off to imbibe liquor with a perfect stranger. *How do I extract myself now?* she wondered.

As they joined the throng exiting the theater, she spotted Julien speaking animatedly with a slender, dark-haired woman. She had the wiry physique and distinctive first-position duck waddle of a ballerina. She knew she'd run into him eventually. But did it have to be today, here? To India's terror, her column of exiters would soon merge with Julien's. An encounter was inevitable. Julien looked up and saw her; the smile vanished from his face.

He seemed to steel himself, then said, "*Allô*, India." Her name obviously registered with the young woman. She turned to look at Julien, concerned, then gave India the "female rival once-over." India was very grateful she was wearing her control-top panty hose.

"Hi, Julien. Hello," India said graciously to the young woman. "Have no fear. I'm not going after him. Been there, done that," she wanted to add, but refrained.

"This is Claire Rickdale," Julien explained.

"Claire, nice to meet you," India said, offering her hand.

"Nice to meet you, too," Claire answered, sizing her up from head to Giuseppe Zanotti–clad toe.

"Oh, this is—"

"Lucius Boateng," Lucius said, warmly extending a hand.

"This is Julien," India stated, forgetting to add his last name, as though Lucius knew this was "the Julien."

After an awkward silence during which Claire coiled herself more tightly around Julien, Lucius asked, "Wasn't that a great performance?" Everyone agreed it was, a bit too enthusiastically.

"Thank you for the letter." Julien's tone betrayed no emotion. India wished she could ask if it helped ease the pain or if he had found it useless. There was so much she would have liked to say but obviously couldn't, not there, not then.

"No, thank *you*," she said hoping her eyes conveyed all she wanted to share in the moment and could not out of courtesy to the doting Claire.

"We're going this way, backstage. Claire has friends in the company," Julien explained politely. "See you," he added with a wave then turned and walked away with Claire.

India stood watching them go, happy that Julien had moved on, yet guilt ridden at the wounds she had inflicted. She almost wanted to run after him and explain, "This isn't what it seems. I just met this man, and he may be gay for all I know. I'm still doing penance, really."

"You know, you should forgive yourself, because he has," Lucius's soothing voice assured her. India turned to look at him shocked.

"You think so?" she asked, genuinely interested in the answer.

"I know so. We're guys, we just don't say much. But he wouldn't have spoken to you at all if he hated you."

"Thank you." India was relieved at the insight. Indeed, Lucius was probably right. Julien could simply have pretended he didn't see her and avoided speaking to her altogether. But he didn't. Somehow, he did understand it had all turned out for the best. Even if at this juncture they both felt uncomfortable.

"Now, the first thing we need to discuss is this completely depressing view you have of love and relationships," Lucius said. Again, his perceptiveness startled India and made her long to hear more of his thoughts. He was right. And there was no time like the present. "Ideals are for gods and saints. Things don't have to be perfect to be absolutely wonderful," he elaborated.

"So you're of the 'It is better to have loved and lost than never to have loved at all' school of thought?"

"Hell, yes!" Okay, definitely not gay. Gay men did not curse in the presence of women, at least not the gay men she knew.

"When did you ever lose?" India challenged. In her experience, men who looked like Lucius—particularly black men with an education—rarely found themselves on the receiving end of a dumping.

"Four years ago. My wife, to cancer."

India, apoplectic with embarrassment, spouted a torrent of apologies.

"How stupid of me. I'm so so so sorry, I—"

"Relax," Lucius reassured her. "You didn't know. It's okay to make a mistake."

The last sentence was the absolution India had refused herself her entire perfectionist life. Indeed, the world did not come to an end, nor even fall off its rotational axis because she, India Chumley, made a misstep. She did not know who this man was or what he wanted. She didn't know if he was the man of her dreams or a kind passing stranger sent by God to deliver the simple message that "it's okay to make a mistake." She only knew for certain that to spend an hour with him would enrich her life far more than another quarter pound of even the world's most delectable chocolate. And on this perfect May evening in New York, that was quite enough to free her for once from questioning and analyzing and second-guessing. For that day, that hour, that moment, India Chumley knew in her heart she was exactly where she was supposed to be: on the verge of a joyous adventure.

# Acknowledgments

Let us "begin the beguine" at the beginning, with Tom Dyja, brilliant novelist who encouraged me to have fun rather than write something wrenching. Hopefully I've written something fun, but on the way, Tom, it was wrenching. I offer my heartfelt thanks to the "midwives" of this book: my agent, Suzanne Gluck; the magical Adriana Trigiani; my lifelong muse, Glenn Berenbeim; gifted pre-editors Julia Hays and the lovely Lavelles; and of course my incisive, thoughtful, and ever encouraging editor, Greer Hendricks. Greer, you have taken me "from shadow into sunlight." Bless you for finding the right title, a greater feat than writing a book. An enormous thank-you to Judith Curr and the entire team at Atria Books.

And now, an Oscar-length list of thanks not necessarily in order of importance: Toni Trigiani (without you, I'd be buried under a pile of newspapers and magazines from the turn of the last century); comrade in arms Charles Randolph-Wright; the "pookessa," Carol Sidlow; my other brother, Peter Bacanovic; Rusty O'Kelley; my emotional anchors: my sister, Nanon De Gaspé Beaubien, Nannette De Gaspé Beaubien, Nan-B De Gaspé Beaubien, Neena Beber, Jennifer Beber, Robbin Mitchell, the fabulous Gayle Perkins Atkins, Catie Marron, Rima Vargas-Vetters, Anne Simmons, Sarah Heming, Alex "It takes money, honey, but that ain't all" Hitz, Sharon Handler, Amy Fine Collins, Alison Taylor, James Marion, Josh Berger, Sarah Evans, Margaret Evans Langhorst, Lucy Evans, Priscilla Fales, Frederika Stevenson,

Jean-François Boissier and Antonella Rossanigo, Suzanne Patricia Ottilie Kay Bamford, Deanne Lay, Debbie Allen, Jeanne Moutoussamy-Ashe, Lynn Whitfield, Christina Robert, Grace Gibson; my godson, Aidan Mattrick, and my "niece," Tatianna Mattrick, and my "other daughter," Misty Copeland. To my other mothers: Korby Britton and Judith Mallon.

To the fierce and fabulous who always inspire: Robin Smith, Alessandra Ferri, Sloan Lindemann Barnett, Phylicia Rashad, Pamela Fiori, Iman, Veronica Webb, Thelma Golden, Lowery Stokes Sims, Alfre Woodard, Kitt Shapiro, Caroline Weber, Jenny Lumet, Teresita Alvarez-Bjelland, and Roberta Flack.

To the Hottie Crew: John Markus, Peter Lyden, Juan Paysse, Brad Black, Eric Masella, and Dimitri. You all combine chivalry, humor, smarts, and what Cole Porter called "that thing!" Keep making women smile.

To all my Veritas "brothers," you know who you are and you are "simply the best." Thank you for always looking out for me and constantly teaching me that life is long and vast. "In a very unusual way, you've made me whole."

To Pamela Reynolds, Jennifer Lanier, and Soraya Herrera, who have been with my child in the hours I had to miss and helped to shape her into the extraordinary human being she is.

To everyone at American Ballet Theatre, especially the dancers.

To the board of directors and the entire staff of the New York Public Library (Lincoln Center and Forty-second Street branches), my sanctuary and a gift to the people of this city and the world.

Amelie Somer at the George V, and George Gharbi at the Ritz, à bientôt j'espère.

To my psychiatrist, obviously I need one, Dr. David McDowell. To James Horvath, the ultimate healer, and Raymond Sandler, all that a doctor should be.

Special recognition of whoever invented the chocolate truffle, an excellent alternative to adultery.

Last, and certainly not least, my eternal love, my apologies, and my thanks to my endlessly patient husband (you are the father every girl should have and a great partner) and our miraculous daughter (I must have done something awfully good in a past life to deserve you, my beloved J. B.). Forgive me for missing so many Saturdays. Here's to many more.